Dalkeith leaned forward. 'Cameron, I can't help fe...
that we could begin to do business if you were to drop t...
pretence and stop acting like a nun who has just been
propositioned. I wish to avail myself of your services.
Let's not pussyfoot around.'

There was an uncomfortable silence for several seconds
as Dalkeith found himself subjected to intense scrutiny. He
knew he was being assessed as friend or foe. He waited.

'All right, Mister Hobson. You tell me what the contract is and I'll tell you if I can provide.' Cameron eased
back in his chair.

Inwardly, Dalkeith breathed a sigh of relief. He had
cleared the first hurdle . . .

D1175509

By the same author

Crow's War

JAMES McGEE

Trigger Men

GRAFTON BOOKS

A Division of the Collins Publishing Group

LONDON GLASGOW
TORONTO SYDNEY AUCKLAND

Grafton Books
A Division of the Collins Publishing Group
8 Grafton Street, London W1X 3LA

Published by Panther Books 1985
Reprinted 1989

ISBN 0-586-06439-7

Printed and bound in Great Britain by
Collins, Glasgow

Set in Bembo

1

One hour before midnight.

They watched the bungalow through the windows of the stationary Peugeot 504; a silent and malevolent presence.

There were no street lights. The suburb, situated north of the capital, lay in darkness. There were no pedestrians either. No late night revellers returning home nor lovers strolling arm in arm. Nobody walking the dog. Nobody to interfere.

The watchers had been in position for almost an hour for it had been a minute after ten o'clock when the car had cruised slowly into the street and glided gently up to the kerb. There had been a moon then but it was now hidden behind cloud.

During the wait the three men had smoked their way through a packet of cigarettes. The floor of the car bore the evidence; a scattering of dog ends and deposits of grey ash. Not the cheap local brand either but English Players, brought in on the last airlift from Stansted along with the crates of Black and White whisky, Phillips tape recorders and the new red Mercedes 300 SEL ordered by Major Juma, head of State Security.

The driver withdrew the big Browning automatic pistol from his waist band, opened the car door and eased his bulk onto the street. His companions joined him. They were dressed casually, as if on their way to a party, in gaudy open necked cotton shirts and dark, flared slacks.

They stood by the car for several seconds and glanced up and down the street, taking stock of their surroundings and objective. A few lighted windows indicated that not all the residents had retired to bed. That didn't worry them.

The bungalow, white washed under a red corrugated roof, was framed by oleander trees and dense hibiscus bushes. A narrow earthen path had been worn across the front lawn and joined the veranda to the street. The lawn was little more than a dry, dusty square of sharp brown stubble. It had not rained in Lugamba for two months. In the half light the coarse surface looked grey, like a thread-bare blanket that needed darning.

Halfway along the path they paused. By this time all three men carried weapons. Two had Brownings while the third hefted a Russian-made Tokarev. One man broke away and traversed the lawn to disappear around the corner of the house. The others watched him go, waiting for him to melt into the shadows before proceeding.

They stalked onto the veranda. Two doors barred their entry into the bungalow; an outer mosquito screen – thin mesh on a wooden frame – and the wooden front door. The driver pressed the bell set into the wall. Hands holding the guns behind their backs, they waited.

David Holt preferred to work at night. It was cooler for one thing and there was less chance of interruption. He was seated at the desk in his study at the rear of the house. When he heard the bell he raised his head in surprise and placed the fountain pen on the blotting pad next to the sheets of writing paper.

Holt was sixty one years old. He was a slim man, fair haired and balding, with a pale face and thin lips. His slight figure had never looked in the best of health. He glanced at his watch and frowned. Five minutes after eleven and he wasn't expecting visitors at this late hour.

The bell rang again. He pushed back his chair impatiently and walked out of the room and down the passage to the front door. At the third ring Holt switched on the veranda light and drew the bolts on the door. As the door swung open the two figures on the veranda sprang into focus and Holt felt the first stab of apprehension in his stomach when he saw that they were blacks.

He stared at them through the mosquito screen, noting with quiet relief that the bolt on the inside of the door was pushed home. Unsmiling, the two men returned his stare. Something gnawed uncomfortably at Holt's sixth sense.

'Well?' His question was aggressive. 'What is it? What do you want?'

One of them reached for the handle on the screen and was plainly annoyed at not being able to open the outer door. He increased the pressure and the screen groaned against the hinges as it resisted his efforts.

'Stop that!' Holt flared. 'Who the hell are you?'

The black with his hand on the door spoke. His English was atrocious and little more than a snarl. His intention, however, was crystal clear; he wanted Holt to let them in. Holt was no spring chicken and the blacks looked young and fit. Holt wasn't stupid either. He stayed where he was.

'I think you had better leave,' Holt advised. 'Before I send for the police.'

The other man spoke this time. His English was a definite improvement.

'Let us in, Mister Holt.'

They brought their weapons out from behind their backs and pointed them through the screen.

'We are from the Department of State Security, Mister Holt. Open the door.'

Holt's face turned the colour of death.

The sudden crash of breaking glass at the rear of the bungalow made him swing around in panic. As he did so, one of the men placed a foot against the screen and kicked it inwards. The frame splintered and as the door slammed back on its hinges, the two men thrust their way into the

7

passage, sweeping Holt off his feet, driving him backwards into the lounge. Instinctively he fought their grip but it was like swimming against a rip tide.

They threw him onto the sofa. He sprawled there, winded, as the third member of the trio arrived, gun in hand. Holt felt the rush of fear course through his veins. The three men found his discomfort amusing, judging by their laughter and chatter. Like apes, Holt thought.

The driver stood over him as the others ransacked the room. They rolled back the rugs on the floor, upturned tables and chairs and ripped the doors on the stereo cabinet off their hinges. They twisted paintings off the hooks in the walls and dragged Holt away from the sofa so that they could turn over the cushions. Holt watched them in silent, seething anger.

The Department of State Security was staffed by Southern Sudanese, Nubians and members of the Makesi tribe whose homeland lay to the north near the Sudanese border. Looking at the men, Holt thought that the one who had spoken the better English was probably a Makesi. The scars on his cheek implied as much. Three vertical slashes – tribal markings that gave the young men the nick name 'One Elevens' in British Army slang. The others were undoubtedly Sudanese. The latter were recruited from the north west. Holt knew that truckloads of Sudanese, previously trained by DOSS, were driven through the bush at dusk across the undemarcated border. Once across, the men were dropped in their home territories where they offered their friends work, promising high rewards. The next day the new recruits were brought over the border to commence their training in the compounds outside the capital, Kendura.

The Makesi was standing by the sofa, grim faced. Mutilated cushions, broken records and glass splinters littered the floor at his feet. From the other rooms the

8

sound of violent breakage told Holt that the rest of the house was being ransacked. They were searching for something. Holt knew what it was.

The man loomed over him and tapped his cheek with the gun barrel. Holt flinched.

'Where have you hidden the papers?' the Makesi snapped. The man looked evil, as though he was on the verge of a fit. The triple scars on his cheek stood out as the muscles in his face contorted with rage.

Holt looked blank. 'What papers?' He was dreadfully aware of the break in his voice.

The Makesi screamed: 'Do not play games! We know all about you and about the lies you have written!'

Holt's lips trembled. 'I have no idea what you are talking about!' He spluttered: 'My God! You force your way into my home, assault me, wreck my furniture and smash my property to pieces! You have no right! The High Commissioner will be informed of this outrage, you can be sure of that! Now get out!'

The Makesi drew his arm back and scythed a blow at Holt's head. The latter tried to turn his face away but the Makesi's fist caught his cheek. For a brief second the room went dark and he felt the tears welling up. Indignation at being struck had him struggling to his feet to face his assailant on even terms.

'You bastards!' he cried.

Another blow forced him down. He put a hand to his mouth and felt the loose teeth and the blood from his split lip trickle onto his chin.

'Shut your mouth!' the Makesi yelled. 'Your government will be told that you have been involved in subversive activities. You are an enemy of the state, Mister Holt. The penalty will be severe. Your Commissioner cannot help you now.'

Holt fought back the sudden urge to vomit. His gaze

was transfixed on one of the Sudanese who had reappeared carrying a cardboard box under his arm. At a sign from the Makesi the contents of the box were emptied onto the floor. Holt stared down with the awful realization that his troubles were only just beginning. Then he threw up.

The manuscript – two hundred typewritten pages of foolscap secured in a ring binder – lay on top of an out of date desk diary and an assortment of bills, letters and receipts. The Makesi knelt and picked it up. He flicked through the pages. The third man had appeared. He stood nonchalantly by the door, holding the Tokarev in one hand as he reached into his trousers with the other to scratch idly at his crotch. His face was like a stone mask, quite devoid of any expression.

With a grunt of satisfaction the Makesi jerked his head and his companions hauled Holt to his feet where he swayed unsteadily like a sailor trying to find his land legs. His face was chalk white and his shirt was stained with the result of his retching.

He was moaning as they marched him roughly through the house and down the path to the car. As they bundled him unceremoniously into the back of the Peugeot, Holt was struck with the absurd thought that he had not finished writing the letter to his daughter. Half finished, it was, no doubt, somewhere in the ruin that had once been his study.

Anthony Warren-Chase, Her Majesty's Acting High Commissioner in Lugamba, walked slowly into his office and collapsed into the seat behind his desk. He was a tall, well groomed man with a narrow face topped by sparse strands of grey hair with which he attempted, without much success, to conceal his creeping baldness. Despite this, he was considered to be good looking in a gaunt sort of way. Added to which, he carried himself well and was an elegant dresser, able to wear fashionable clothes generally seen on men fifteen or twenty years his junior. He was fifty seven years old. This morning he felt every year of his age and his Cecil Gee ensemble didn't make him feel any better.

He opened his calf leather briefcase and took out the bottle of Disprin. Gulping a brace of pills he screwed up his face in distaste as they began to dissolve at the back of his throat. Closing his eyes he began to massage his throbbing temples, willing the headache to subside.

The door opened and Henderson poked his earnest face into the room. 'Morning, sir.'

Warren–Chase grunted in return and Henderson tiptoed tentatively into the office. James Henderson was thirty years old, bespectacled, clean shaven and conservatively dressed. He looked every inch the competent secretary, which he was.

Through half closed eyes Warren–Chase studied the curious gait of his aide. Henderson was treading as softly as though he was walking on egg shells and Warren–Chase had the distinct impression that this was not solely out of deference to his current ailment. He became uncomfortably aware that the expression on young Henderson's face was one of trepidation. Henderson reached the desk and hovered. Warren–Chase regarded his aide's woeful features. They resembled those of a faithful though crestfallen gun dog that had been dispatched after a wood pigeon and failed to retrieve.

'Out with it, James,' Warren–Chase said heavily. 'I don't think I can stand the suspense any longer.'

Henderson stared woodenly over his superior's shoulders at the portrait of the Monarch, as if seeking guidance. Her Majesty was not much help. She smiled benignly. Henderson took a deep breath.

'It's Holt, sir. Something's come up.'

'Oh, God,' Warren-Chase said. 'What's the silly old sod done now?'

The Acting High Commissioner certainly had a delicate turn of phrase at times, generally reserved for moments of acute stress. Henderson presumed that the migraine attack would not be conducive to benevolence. He cleared his throat.

'He's been arrested, sir.' There, he'd said it. He was instantly conscious of the dreadful expression that was creeping over the other's face like a returning tide. Henderson began to wish he was somewhere else.

'What did you say?' It might have been the headache, but Warren-Chase had paled visibly.

'David Holt has been arrested, sir. He was picked up by the President's goon squad last night at his bungalow. About eleven o'clock.'

Warren-Chase's forehead was now positively vibrating with pain. He groaned inwardly.

Henderson said: 'I've only just been informed. Their Foreign Minister phoned a couple of minutes before you arrived.'

Warren-Chase sighed. A low moan escaped his lips, and he clasped his hands together as though about to pray. 'I think you had better tell me all about it, Henderson. Now, what the hell has happened?'

The story did not take long in the telling.

To have said that Warren-Chase was perturbed at the news imparted by his secretary would have been a gross understatement.

Warren-Chase knew all about David Holt.

Out of the seven hundred souls that made up the British community in Lugamba, Warren-Chase had met only a small number. He counted a dozen or so among his friends. The majority were merely acquaintances, people he had bumped into at forgettable social gatherings either by accident or through well meant introductions by mutual friends. Not much of a selection. Businessmen mostly; front men for British firms. And their numbers were declining rapidly, had been in fact for the past few years. The political climate had created an economic wasteland that could no longer support the business companies or their representatives.

Warren-Chase had met Holt before. It had been an interesting though brief confrontation; the result of rumours circulating among the British that Holt was hard at work on a book, the contents of which would do little to improve the already strained relations between Lugamba and the United Kingdom.

Warren-Chase, as Acting High Commissioner and therefore stuck with the unenviable role of whipping boy, had felt obliged to sound out Holt with a view to finding out just how inflammatory the book was likely to be. He had called on Holt to discuss the matter.

Prior to the meeting Warren-Chase had gleaned what information he could about David Holt, to find out what made him tick.

David Holt was sixty one years old. He had been educated at Manchester Grammar School and Trinity, Cambridge. He had chosen journalism as a career and to that end he had travelled extensively, particularly in Central Europe. During the Second World War, as a captain, he served in the Middle East as liaison officer with the Polish forces due to his ability to speak the language. After the war he returned to journalism and teaching. He spent a number of the post war years in Turkey and wrote a book about his travels there. In 1950 he married a German girl, Marie Konrad, a daughter of an upper class lawyer from Mannheim. Their only child, a girl, was born in 1952. He first arrived in Lugamba in 1964 and taught English at Manziri University and later at the

National Teachers Training College at Lekasu. Holt liked the country and the people and was unhappy at the thought that one day he might have to return and live in Britain. This view was not shared by his wife who divorced him in 1967 and returned to England taking their daughter, Joanna, with her. Holt remained in Lugamba. In 1972 he made a brief visit to London for an operation on an abdominal cancer. On his return to Lugamba he found that his job had been filled and to occupy himself started to write another book. It was to be part autobiographical and part travel stories. Naturally much of it dealt with his life in Lugamba. Holt made no secret of the fact that it was critical of the present Lugamba regime that had come to power in 1971 after the coup; for in the years following the takeover Holt had seen the decline of the things he cherished in the country, in particular the way of life of the Lugamban people.

He could see it daily and if he couldn't see it he could sense it. In their bodies as they shuffled along the streets; in their faces – blank expressions. And always the eyes told the story. The oppression and stark fear. As though the dead had got up and walked.

Warren-Chase was in a difficult position, for what should the diplomatic representative of a country do when one of its subjects is clearly endangering himself and other members of his community through his open criticism? Already the relationship between Lugamba and the United Kingdom was far from harmonious, especially since the expulsion of the British High Commissioner, when Warren-Chase had been appointed to cope as best he could. For the latter it was rather like starting the Grand National on a choleric nag that had only three legs. In short he didn't stand much chance of keeping ahead of the game.

So, Warren-Chase had called on Holt. He was unprepared for the outcome. Try as he might, Warren-Chase could make no headway. Holt had been coldly polite and surprised at the interest shown by Her Majesty's representative. Curiosity had turned to resentment when Warren-Chase hardened his tone on passing the warning to Holt that the British position was tenuous enough without him adding fuel to the fire. Holt's reaction had been far from diplomatic. He had sent Warren-Chase away with a flea in both ears. To put it bluntly; the Acting High Commissioner could mind his own business.

Now, events had come to a head, though Warren-Chase was hardly in a position to say I told you so.

Warren-Chase waited for Henderson to finish before exploding.

'God Almighty! Why the bloody hell couldn't he keep his mouth shut! He's been on about that damned book for the past year. Quite frankly I'm amazed that they haven't taken him sooner. Christ! I know my chat, if you could call it that, was tantamount to pissing against the wind but you'd have thought he would at least have taken the hint. I mean he could have kept quiet about the whole thing, sent it to a publisher in the UK and no one would have been any the wiser. We're sitting on a knife edge here. One slip on our part – that's all Mabato needs.'

'Yes, sir,' Henderson said, polishing his spectacles with a snow white handkerchief.

'Did you ever see Holt at work? My God, you only had to pass his house to hear him pounding away at his Olivetti. When I went to see him he was on his veranda, togged up like Sanders of the bloody river and pecking the keys like an arthritic Hemingway. Looked like something out of an Ealing comedy.'

Warren-Chase rested his chin on his hands. 'You know, James, I should have gone back to the UK when I had the chance. They did offer me that job in Whitehall, you recall?'

Henderson nodded. 'Yes, sir, but think of the intrigue and back stabbing.'

Warren-Chase eyed his aide speculatively, not sure if the latter was being sarcastic. He could never tell with Henderson. He said: 'Quite so, but at least the back stabbing would have been metaphorical. Over here it's for real. Which brings us back to the matter in hand. I suppose I can expect a summons from you know who? The last time he sent for me he was still babbling on about that development loan that failed to materialize and the spare parts for those armoured cars we were stupid enough to sell him. And he hasn't paid for them yet. Mind you, not that I'd dare to mention the fact. He is like a ten year old with a new set of Dinky toys. If a wheel comes off he pounds the table until mummy rushes in to to fix it. Anyway, you had better get in touch with Nkuto at their Ministry. Usual stuff, outraged indignation, demand an explanation, don't take no for an answer. You know the ritual. We might as well go through the motions and put up some pretence.'

Henderson said uncomfortably: 'I don't think that will go down too well, sir.'

'How's that?'

'You've already been summoned. As I said they telephoned before you arrived.'

Warren-Chase shrugged. 'Oh, well, you'd better get the car ready. When and where?'

'Ten o'clock at the Command Post.'

Warren-Chase looked up sharply. 'Command Post? I thought you said the call came from their Ministry.'

'I did, sir, but they were relaying a direct order from the President. He wants to see you himself.' Henderson sounded apologetic as though it was his fault. 'There was one thing,' he continued somewhat hesitantly.

Warren-Chase pursed his lips. 'Go on.'

16

'They said not to be late.' Even second hand the words had a chilling echo.

Warren-Chase ran a finger across his brow. His headache had intensified.

By eleven o'clock Warren-Chase was back in his office. He was as white as a sheet. Ignoring his aide's raised eyebrows and unspoken questions, he walked purposefully to the cabinet behind his desk and reached unerringly for the bottle of Johnnie Walker. The hand that lifted the glass to his lips had begun to shake noticeably.

Henderson had never seen him in this state before so it was with a terrible sense of foreboding that he asked Warren-Chase what had transpired during the visit to the Command Post.

It took Warren-Chase several tense moments and another drink to reply.

'We have rather a problem,' he said slowly. His voice was a whisper as he sat down abruptly.

Henderson approached cautiously. 'Well, what did he say? The President backed down of course.'

Warren-Chase appeared to be staring down through his desk to the carpet underneath as though he had x-ray vision. He said huskily: 'The President did not back down. It is even worse than we imagined.'

'Sir?'

Warren-Chase gazed forlornly into Henderson's face. He seemed to have aged ten years and even before he spoke again his secretary knew it was going to be bad news.

'They're going to shoot him,' Warren-Chase said. 'They're actually going to shoot David Holt.'

The words struck Henderson with the force of a sledge hammer. He groped his way to a vacant chair. 'They can't mean it! They're insane!'

'Oh, they mean it.' Warren-Chase sighed heavily. 'President Mabato convinced me of that in no uncertain terms. I have no doubt whatsoever that sentence will be carried out unless, that is, HMG agrees to certain conditions.'

'Conditions? What bloody conditions?'

'He will make them known to us shortly.'

This is madness, Henderson thought to himself. Aloud, he said: 'How on earth can Mabato even contemplate such action? He's barmy!'

'That psychopath's state of mind has never been in question,' Warren-Chase snapped. He frowned suddenly and went on: 'Look, James, we'll have to get the bloody ball rolling. Let's try and do something to retrieve the situation. Shoot a cable off to London immediately.' He shuddered. 'God knows what they'll make of this in the corridors of power! We'll just have to keep whittling away at Mabato in the hope that he gets to see sense though something tells me this is going to be a lulu!'

2

It never ceased to amaze David Wood that no matter what time of day he arrived at Number Ten there was always a sea of expectant faces waiting to see who would emerge from the limousine. Day or night, rain or shine, they were there; ready with a wave or a less polite gesture, depending on their political bias.

It was ten-thirty in the morning and raining. In the grey precincts of St James faceless civil servants glared wetly at each other from under soggy bowlers and along the lofty and grimy sills of Whitehall pigeons huddled and fluttered together in misery. The city was damp, dismal and disconsolate. It was sulking.

As Foreign Secretary, David Wood had been informed of the developments in Lugamba as soon as the news reached the Ministry less than an hour before by cable from Warren-Chase, relayed via the High Commission in Nairobi. Wood, staggered by the enormity of the problem, had wasted no time in contacting the Prime Minister, Arthur Lennox.

Lennox had been about to meet with a delegation from the National Union of Mineworkers when the call came. The delegation had been far from happy at the sudden postponement and Lennox's apology hurriedly relayed through a minion but by the time the members of the NUM had collected their thoughts into one voice of dismay the PM was already en route to Downing Street.

The gawpers outside Number Ten that morning had a field day. Despite the weather, about fifty or so brave souls were clustered together hoping for a sighting, like monster seekers on the banks of Loch Ness. They were not disappointed. Not only the Prime Minister but also the Foreign Secretary! Too good to be true.

Lennox arrived first. The constable on duty saluted briskly as the stocky, sandy haired figure left the shelter of the Daimler and ducked under the umbrella held by his aide. Despite the inclement weather and the desire to gain the warmth of the house Lennox found time to turn and wave to the crowd, a smile fixed on his face like the advanced stages of rigor mortis.

They actually cheered Wood when he arrived. He was that popular. Tall, handsome, debonair and at forty three the youngest member of the Cabinet. A bit of a whizz kid it was felt. Good at his job of course. That was the main thing. A nod and a wave and he too vanished into the sanctum. The crowd, unable to believe its luck, settled down to await the next visitation.

The Prime Minister greeted Wood warmly. Lennox was sixty years old and a product of Leeds Grammar and Oxford. He liked to think of himself as a rough diamond. A Prime Minister with the touch of the common man. He had a tendency to slip into his native northern accent when excited, though he sometimes actually practised this affectation, especially prior to party political broadcasts and radio and television interviews. The voters, he felt, should always look upon their leader as someone they could relate to.

Lennox took Wood along the corridor to the Cabinet Room at the rear of the building while directing a secretary to provide fresh coffee. 'We'll talk in here, David,' he said, opening the door. 'Sit yourself down.'

Lennox lit his first pipe of the day, sucked loudly at the stem and said: 'Right, David, suppose you start from the beginning.'

Wood began with the cable from Lugamba. The facts

were plain. A British subject was being held by the Lugamban authorities, under sentence of death – unless certain demands were met.

A dense cloud of Clan tobacco smoke drifted across the long table. Wood's eyes began to smart.

'Give me a run-down on Holt,' Lennox said.

Wood gave Lennox a brief biography.

When he'd finished, Lennox grunted: 'You mentioned a wife and daughter. Where are they now?'

'His ex-wife's dead. A car crash two years ago. His daughter married a Canadian, a civil engineer, I believe. They live in Calgary.'

Lennox accepted the information and studied the bowl of his briar. He swore suddenly. 'The man's a bloody lunatic!'

'You mean Mabato?' Wood raised an eyebrow.

'Him as well but I was referring to Holt. You're telling me that he'd already been warned about the consequences of writing this book?'

'That's right, according to Warren-Chase. Mind you, had the manuscript contained, shall we say, less derogatory statements about Mabato, I shouldn't think we'd be sitting here now.'

'Refresh my memory. What did Holt call him?'

'A mindless dictator, among other things.'

Lennox closed his eyes in silent anguish. He opened them as if in great pain. 'What about this chap Warren-Chase? Not prone to exaggeration by any chance?'

'By no means.' Wood shook his head decisively.

'As I recall, he was one of the legacies we inherited from our friends in the Opposition.' Lennox pondered the fact.

There was a knock on the door. The secretary entered, bearing a tray with coffee, cream and sugar.

'Thank you, Simon.' Lennox smiled. 'I'll ring if I need you. Oh, and if the media call you know what to do. Let the Press Officer earn his keep.'

The debonair man nodded and left the room.

Wood poured himself a cup of coffee. 'Warren-Chase was the best man for a particularly unenviable job,' he said, reaching for the sugar. 'There was no need to replace him, though as a mark of thanks he was offered a post here at home. Anyway it's common knowledge that he turned the offer down in order to remain in Lugamba to protect his business interests, though Christ knows what state they must be in these days. I think we are fortunate to have a man of his calibre over there. Hell, when Mabato announced his intention of expelling the Asians, Warren-Chase was the first to tell him he was making a big mistake.'

'It's a pity the stupid sod didn't listen to him,' grated Lennox. He gazed through the tall windows at the rain beating against the panes. 'Let's run through those demands again,' he sighed.

Wood extracted a manilla file from his attaché case and laid it on the table. 'I've a copy of the telegram and I've extracted the salient points. They are as follows:

'Britain must stop all malicious propaganda against the President, the Government and the people of Lugamba mounted in Britain and the international news media.

'Britain must expel all Lugamban exiles who are spreading unfounded rumours against Lugamba.

'Britain must stop fruitless attempts to persuade other countries not to give technical, financial or material assistance to Lugamba, while at the same time trying to persuade potential tourists not to come.

'Britain should also desist from making baseless reports that Lugamba is in a state of chaos.

'The British Government must sell Lugamba all the spare parts required for military equipment bought in Britain.

'Arthur Lennox or the Queen must give President Mabato written acceptance of the ultimatum within ten days, otherwise David Holt will be shot.'

22

Wood looked up. 'Well, that's it.'

'Doesn't want much, does he?' Lennox said bitterly. He stood up and clasped his hands behind his back. 'I suppose he means it?'

Wood pursed his lips. 'It could be that, taking the ultimatum into consideration, Mabato wants to wring as much as he can out of our predicament and has no intention of killing Holt. So there may well be room for negotiation. However, one has to take a look at Mabato's track record. Let's not forget that only a year ago the International Commission of Jurists reported that Mabato had ushered in a reign of terror worse than anything in recent African history. The Commission thought that between one hundred and two hundred thousand people died in the ten years following Mabato's seizure of power. Good Christ, the man is as unpredictable as warm gelignite! He's capable of anything and that includes killing Holt!'

'I was afraid you'd say that.' Lennox stole a glance at his watch. 'I've asked George Dalkeith to join us by the way. Maybe the three of us can come up with a solution. Quite frankly, I'd like to have some answers ready for the House this afternoon. My bones tell me that today's session is going to be a bugger.'

'What time is Dalkeith due?'

'Eleven and if I know George, he'll be here on the dot.'

As if on cue the door to the Cabinet Room opened and Paul Hamilton, the Prime Minister's Principal Private Secretary announced the arrival of Dalkeith. Wood rose to his feet in anticipation.

Sir George Dalkeith was Director of Operations SIS. He was a tall distinguished man with a military haircut and a pencil slim moustache. He was immaculately dressed in a navy blue pinstripe three piece with a cream shirt, maroon tie and matching handkerchief in his top pocket. He walked erect, like a Guards officer, on dress parade.

'Good morning, Prime Minister, Foreign Secretary.' The voice was refined and almost a drawl.

Lennox and Woods shook hands with Dalkeith who took a seat at the table.

'Right,' Lennox said. 'Let's get down to business. George, you'll take coffee?'

'Thank you, yes.' Dalkeith helped himself to a cup.

Lennox said: 'This Lugamba mess. What I need are workable ideas on how to get ourselves out of it. It would seem, however unpalatable, that Mabato has us by the proverbials. For George's benefit, David, I suggest you run through the points in that ultimatum again.'

Wood did so and Dalkeith listened without interrupting, his face betraying no emotion. When Wood finished his synopsis Lennox asked the SIS man for suggestions.

'Well, firstly, we must assume that Mabato means what he says.'

'We had established that fact,' Wood agreed.

'Just so long as we know where we stand,' Dalkeith said.

Wood said: 'Of course, we don't give in to him.'

'So, we let them execute Holt?' Dalkeith's voice had a distinct bite.

'I didn't say that.'

'Well, look,' Dalkeith said. 'We've agreed the threat is genuine. What do you propose? That we sit here and mull the situation over until Holt is shot? The ostrich syndrome; bury our heads in the sand and hope that if we ignore the problem it will go away.'

'I didn't mean that either,' Wood said tartly.

'Christ!' Lennox broke in. 'Don't tell us what you didn't mean, David. Tell us what you do mean. We're not bloody mind readers!'

Wood said: 'Why don't I fly out there and . . .'

'Like hell!' Lennox exploded. 'If you think this government intends to bargain with that maniac you can collect

24

your cards right now! We are not going to give in to this blackmail.'

'Even if it means saving a British subject's life?' Wood asked.

Lennox glared at the Foreign Secretary. 'If you were to fly to Lugamba and the visit resulted in Holt being spared the way is open for Mabato to use any one of the seven hundred people British people still in the country as hostages for further demands. God! It would set a terrible precedent. You are not going and that's final.'

'So, stalemate.' Wood sighed. 'What next?'

'Let us go through the alternatives,' suggested Lennox. 'As I see it, there are three fronts on which we can act. Military, economic and diplomatic. Let's take them one at a time. Ignoring gunboat diplomacy for the two simple reasons I'm not Palmerston and Lugamba is land locked.'

Dalkeith and Wood remained silent, content to listen to Lennox, who then said: 'We could fly in troops.'

'Not feasible,' Dalkeith cut in almost immediately.

'Details, George?'

'The nearest bases we could use would be Gan, in the Indian Ocean, and Cyprus. They are almost two and a half thousand miles from Kendura for a start. Gan can be ruled out as there are no troops there and the airfield was run down when we reduced our Indian Ocean commitment.' Here, Dalkeith paused for effect. Lennox and Wood digested the point but said nothing.

Dalkeith continued, undismayed. 'Cyprus is more likely but not much use as the most direct route would probably result in our aircraft getting shot down over Egypt. Transport Command would have to ask for overfly rights over Israel and then fly down the Gulf of Aqaba. That's provided, of course, that Transport Command's VC 10s can be placed in operational condition and an air refuelling operation could be implemented. Let's assume we have a

"Go" situation. We could then have some two thousand men in Lugamban air space with no fighter cover because Lugamba is out of range of any of our fighters. Mabato has a squadron of MiG 15s.

'A land operation is unthinkable. Mabato has Scorpion armoured cars, Ferret scout cars, and tanks, most of which are courtesy of Her Majesty's Government. He also has over twenty thousand men in his army, which is probably the only efficient institution left in the whole country. We wouldn't stand a chance and the cost would be astronomical.' He shrugged. 'That's about it.'

Lennox said: 'David, what about economic sanctions?'

'I don't think they'll help us either,' answered Wood heavily.

'Explain.'

'Coffee is our best weapon. We could stop importing from Lugamba. The country is our biggest supplier of coffee beans; about sixteen million pounds' worth last year. That's twice as much as Brazil and three times as much as Kenya. Even so, our share is only seventeen per cent of Lugamba's total crop. Mabato would have little difficulty finding an alternative buyer. Hell, we account for only about twenty per cent of Lugamba's foreign trade. That's hardly a basis for a stranglehold and don't forget that Mabato's a Muslim and therefore gets a lot of help from the Middle East; in particular Libya, Iraq, Saudi Arabia and Kuwait. The only way I see that the country could be isolated would be for Kenya to close Lugamba's rail and road outlets to the sea, through Mombasa. We cut off foreign aid in 1972, when he expelled the Asians. He still owes us twenty five million for those armoured cars.'

'Which brings us to our third alternative,' Lennox said. 'Diplomacy.'

'I thought we had discounted that. You said that you didn't want me to fly out.'

26

'I don't want anyone to fly out. At least not on the terms he dictated to us.'

'What about someone else to intervene on our behalf?'

'I'd thought of that,' said Lennox. 'Don't forget that there is a summit conference of the Organization of African Unity due to take place in Kendura. The delegates are hardly likely to look favourably on someone who has sentenced a man to death for writing a book. There have been reports that Mabato is canvassing for support to be elected the next Chairman. I don't think this will help his chances.'

'Big deal,' Wood said icily. 'I'm sure Holt is counting on that as a reprieve.'

'Nevertheless, world opinion has surely got to have some effect, I would have thought.'

Wood declined to comment. He turned to Dalkeith. 'What about your lads in SIS, George? Could we send someone in to get him out? One of the Sandbaggers?'

Dalkeith shook his head. 'The chance of a lone agent succeeding in a rescue would be virtually non existent. My men aren't superhuman. We would need a small team and I don't have that number of experienced men to hand. I know what you're thinking now. We could use the SAS but if we sent in a squad covertly and they were rumbled, Mabato would have a field day. Notwithstanding the embarrassment of being found out, we have another seven hundred souls over there. My God, we could initiate a massacre. Is it worth the risk?'

'Dammit, it's a British life we are talking about here!' The Prime Minister looked despairingly at Wood for support.

Wood looked thoughtful. 'There might be another way.'

Dalkeith and Lennox stared expectantly at the youthful Foreign Secretary.

'Go on,' Lennox prompted.

'We could sub–contract.'

Dalkeith sucked in his breath.

'I'm not with you,' Lennox said, perplexed.

'Look,' Wood answered. 'Let's backtrack a little. As of now we are agreed that we do not give in to blackmail and I'm not going to Lugamba to negotiate terms for the man's release. We can't send in troops and economic sanctions would have no effect. Correct?'

Lennox nodded and studied the bowl of his pipe. 'So, get to the point, David.'

'A cloak and dagger operation launched by us could put even more lives at risk. Added to which, in the event of a failed rescue attempt, we would be forced, almost certainly, to give in to Mabato's demands. Hell, public opinion would see to that. We'd never live it down. We need to cover both avenues here. In other words if a rescue attempt did fail we would be required to deny all knowledge of such a foolhardy venture, enabling us to continue negotiations on a diplomatic level with the possibility of breaking Mabato down bit by bit until he capitulates. On the other hand if a rescue mission was successful, well, problem solved.' Wood spread his hands.

'So?' Lennox said again.

'So, we need someone to take the risk for us. Someone to take action independently so that we could condemn it if things went wrong.'

'Which means?'

'We hire someone to do the job for us surreptitiously.'

The Prime Minister's eyebrows rose. 'Don't tell me you believe in Wonder Woman and the Secret Seven?'

'Let me put it this way,' Wood countered. 'There must be somebody who would consider taking on the job and the attendant risks – for a price.'

Lennox nearly choked on his pipe.

'Jesus Christ Almighty! You have got to be out of your bloody mind! Of all the hare-brained, imbecilic schemes I have heard during all my years in politics, that has got to be the most lunatic. Have you any idea what you are proposing, man? Good God! Mercenaries!'

'I'm putting forward a suggestion,' Wood said calmly.

'That's all? I can't believe I'm actually hearing this!'

Wood simply shrugged. 'It worked in the Congo.'

'Bloody Nora!' Lennox was appalled. He glanced at Dalkeith. 'You haven't said much.'

'I'm speechless,' Dalkeith said and looked it.

'Fine,' Wood said. 'Forget it. It was a dumb idea.'

'That is the most sensible thing you have said this morning.'

Lennox couldn't grasp the fact that the conversation had taken this sort of turn. He gathered his dazed wits together into a vague semblance of order and managed to say in a voice that was none too steady: 'I've arranged a Cabinet Meeting for this afternoon, after Question Time. I suggest we have a rethink to see if we can come up with a solution to the problem. A sensible solution, David. Also we'll have to draft a reply to Mabato I suppose. I'll leave that to you too, David. Have something ready by three will you?'

'As you wish, Prime Minister.'

'Very good. Oh, and one thing, David.'

'Yes?'

'I would keep some of your ideas to yourself this afternoon. You never know, someone might get the wrong end of the stick.'

Later that afternoon Lennox and Wood were together again in Downing Street. This time they were in the Prime Minister's first floor study. Lennox sat behind his desk. Wood occupied one of the armchairs.

'Well, that was a bloody disaster and a half!' Lennox said explosively.

The two politicians had been discussing the Cabinet Meeting that had followed their return from the House of Commons where Lennox had been bombarded mercilessly by a barrage of questions from the Opposition and his own back-benchers. The questions were, needless to say, variations on a theme. What were his plans to secure the release of David Holt?

Lennox, to his chagrin, had been unable to supply answers that pacified save for stressing mechanically that Her Majesty's Government would never give in to blackmail. All very laudable but of no immediate comfort to David Holt who was three thousand miles away with the threat of a bullet in his brain – or worse.

Lennox had left the floor, chastened.

'I wouldn't like to go through that again,' he said, knowing full well he would have to.

The Cabinet Meeting hadn't provided him with any ammunition either. In fact he felt that the meeting had been a complete waste of time and said as much as the meeting adjourned, to the vexation of his ministers.

'God, I could do with a drink!' Lennox moved to the cabinet in the corner of the room, 'David, you'll join me?'

Wood shook his head and watched as Lennox poured himself a Haig. The Prime Minister walked back to his desk, sat down and stared fixedly at the glass in his hands. After several seconds he looked up, his expression severe. With great deliberation he said quietly: 'David, what I am about to say is absolutely for your ears alone. If one word of our conversation was to leak out of this office the consequences could be – in fact would be – disastrous. Not just as far as our political futures were concerned but disastrous for the Party. It would suffer a blow so damaging that it would never regain credibility. Do I make myself clear?'

Wood felt his stomach muscles tighten with expectation. 'Of course, Prime Minister.'

'Very well. After that debacle in the House and that apology for a Cabinet Meeting this afternoon I have, despite my initial reaction, given a great deal of thought to your suggestion. You know to what I am referring, of course?'

Wood held his breath and nodded, his mind racing.

'Let us suppose, just suppose mind you, that such a plan was feasible . . .'

'But . . .'

'Let me finish, David. I want you to institute discreet inquiries. Find out what the prime considerations would be and give me something by this time tomorrow. We can stall Lugamba until then. Can you do it?'

'Christ!' Wood said. 'I'll see what I can find out. What about Dalkeith?'

Lennox shook his head vehemently. 'At this time, I want this only between you and me.'

'I think I'm going to be hard pressed on my own. Besides, he'll have contacts; names I can go on. He will be useful. Damn it all, I don't honestly think we can go ahead without him.'

'I didn't say we would go ahead. All I want at the moment is information. However, I concede the point. Use Dalkeith.' Lennox paused. 'One last thing.'

'Which is?'

'This must never be traced back to this office. You understand what I'm saying?'

'Of course.' He must think I was born yesterday! Wood thought.

'All tracks must be covered. There will be no loose ends. My God! If the Opposition or the press ever got wind of this, especially after the Angolan fiasco!'

Lennox was referring to the recruitment of a British

mercenary force by the FNLA – the National Front for the Liberation of Angola – to fight in Angola against the Marxist faction led by Agostinho Neto. What had started as a clandestine recruitment drive had developed rapidly, due to adverse publicity in the British press, into something closely resembling a Sunday school outing for soldiers of fortune. To make matters worse the action was a failure with fifty British mercenaries killed, two executed, the rest imprisoned. Despite the latter's subsequent release after long incarceration in Sao Paulo gaol, memory of the affair was still fresh. If word ever leaked out that HMG had even considered hiring such men the consequences didn't bear thinking about.

Wood was tense and thoughtful as he made his way back to his office. As he closed the door behind him he realized with distaste that his palms were damp with sweat. He reached his desk and sat down, hazy, half formed ideas running through his mind like termites in a nest. He pressed a button on his intercom and when the voice of his secretary answered he told her to hold all calls for the next two hours.

So, where to begin?

First requirement: Men who, for a price, would be prepared to risk their lives in order to enter hostile country and snatch a man from gaol. How many men? Where would he find them? How much would it cost?

This is absurd, he thought. The whole idiotic scheme was totally beyond his comprehension. Whatever had possessed him to contemplate such a ridiculous venture? He would have to call George Dalkeith, and God only knew what he would think of the idea.

'Well, if you ask me,' Dalkeith drawled, 'I think the idea is insane and you, if you'll pardon my directness, are out of your skull to have thought of the damned fool idea in the first place.'

'Quite,' Wood said. 'If you recall, similar sentiments were expressed earlier today, in no uncertain terms.'

'You could have taken the hint.'

Wood winced. He had asked for that. 'Nevertheless, I have been asked to look into the possibility of such a scheme. As you must appreciate my contacts in this field are somewhat limited, which is why I called you in.'

'In other words, you want me to recruit for you.'

'I want you to get me information. I know I suggested the idea but . . .'

'You don't want to get your hands dirty.'

'That's not it at all,' Wood said vehemently, aware that Dalkeith could read him like a book.

'Very well. What do you want me to do exactly?'

'Find out if anyone is available and how much it will cost. I want details by tomorrow morning.'

Dalkeith's eyebrows rose. 'You're not serious?'

'Totally.'

'I don't suppose you'd like me to throw in a solution to the Ulster crisis for good measure?'

Wood permitted himself a smile. 'One thing at a time, George. Let's not get carried away.'

'Christ!' Dalkeith said.

'And, George . . .'

Dalkeith held up his hand. 'Let me guess. The buck stops with me, correct?'

'You know how it is, George,' Wood said amiably.

Dalkeith rose to his feet. 'Don't I just.' He marched out of the room before Wood could think of a suitable reply. The Foreign Secretary watched Dalkeith depart before flicking the intercom switch. 'All right, Joan,' he sighed. 'I am again available to my public.' And God help them, he thought.

* * *

Registry was housed in a dry windowless basement behind steel grilles and a taciturn duty officer, an ex-marine sergeant called Willowburn.

Willowburn was impressed and not a little surprised to see Dalkeith. This was tantamount to a visitation from the gods. As a formality he acknowledged Dalkeith's identity card before releasing the lock mechanism to allow the intelligence chief into the vault.

'I'll call if I need you,' Dalkeith said, forestalling any offer of help that might have been forthcoming.

'Very good, sir.' Willowburn secured the door, locking them both in the basement and returned to his desk and paperback.

The vault was lined with rows of gunmetal filing cabinets, corridors of them. When you walked along the line it was like inspecting the troops. There was a comprehensive index system and it took Dalkeith only a matter of minutes to find the file he wanted. The contents covered events in Angola from the time of the left wing military coup in April 1974 to date.

Now, he had to find a name.

Circumstances dictated that Dalkeith had to study the file on site. He couldn't risk signing the documents out of the records vault and drawing attention to his interest in them. Willowburn still had his head buried in the book. Dalkeith studied the file.

The SIS man concerned himself with the details surrounding the recruitment of mercenaries by representatives of the FNLA acting under the direction of Holden Roberto.

Dalkeith had to admit that the affair had been a sordid and bloody fiasco from the outset but he wasn't concerned with the ethics, only the men involved. The recruitment had been undertaken by an assortment of individuals with, it appeared to Dalkeith, one overriding consideration – to make as much money as possible.

The recruits had been promised £150 a week during the term of their contract. The recruiting officers were to receive a £200 bounty for every man they recruited. Needless to say, with that sort of inducement the recruiters were not particularly interested in the morals of the men they were hiring. Although, ideally, men with army backgrounds were preferred, men with more nefarious skills were not turned away.

The police and the security service had been aware of the machinations of the mercenary recruitment agencies such as the International Security Organization and the Camberley based outfit, Security Advisory Services, and were naturally interested to learn that the final recruitment drive and briefing would be held at the Tower Hotel in London. Dalkeith's department had dispatched men to the hotel to cover the meetings.

The mercenaries had been registered at the hotel as members of the Manchester Sporting Club and the briefing had been held in room 324. Dalkeith's agents, in a brief liaison with Special Branch, had bugged the room.

A transcript of the briefing was included in the file now being read by Dalkeith. The meeting had opened with Holden Roberto's representative, Nick Hall, giving a run-down of the mission followed by questions from the men. The briefing seemed to be progressing smoothly until an argument erupted between the two main recruiters, Hall and John Banks, ostensibly over who was to accompany the men to Angola. However, it was, in effect, a struggle for possession of the purse strings of the recruitment funds.

This sort of argument in full view of the assembled recruits did little to boost morale. It resulted in some men leaving the room. If the debacle of the briefing was any indication the mission would be a disaster. Dalkeith studied the file carefully. He was interested in the characters of the men who had sensed disaster.

Two of the men had subsequently turned up again in the dossier, having changed their minds, and had travelled to Angola with another group some months later. Dalkeith wasn't interested in them. He wanted the third man. The surveillance at the Tower Hotel had yielded a list of names. He found the one he wanted.

Iain Cameron.

There was an appendix to the Angolan file in the form of dossiers on all the men involved in the briefing. Cameron warranted two pages of typescript and a photograph taken in the hotel lobby. Dalkeith scanned the details.

Iain Cameron was ex-SAS and was not the sort of man Dalkeith would have chosen to meet down a dark alley, or anywhere else for that matter. However, the man's record was impressive and Dalkeith, reading the dossier, knew he had an ideal candidate for the job he had in mind.

As a member of the Special Air Service Cameron had been part of an elite force, the hard men of the British army, well versed in clandestine operations. He was highly trained. A specialist in, as the army's LOM – Land Operations Manual – put it, 'Intelligence gathering; the ambush and harassment of insurgents; infiltration of sabotage, assassination and demolition parties into insurgent held areas; border surveillance and the training and control of friendly guerilla forces operating against the common enemy.'

Cameron had left the army after a Dhofari rebel's knife had removed his left eye in a hand to hand battle following an SAS reconnaissance mission in the mountains of Oman.

Having been trained and honed into a ruthless killing machine capable of parachuting, blowing bridges, shooting the eye of a sparrow at a thousand yards and killing with his bare hands he found it irksome trying to fit into a mundane nine to five civilian role. After a variety of jobs including commercial salesman, travel courier, insurance assessor and even garage mechanic he had decided to put his SAS skills and contacts to some use. He had become a freelance mercenary. One of his contacts had been the founder of the SAS, Colonel David Stirling. Stirling had run an organization called 'Watchguard' that provided bodyguards for Middle Eastern, Far Eastern and African heads of states who considered themselves prime targets for assassination. He also provided mercenaries – former SAS and Para Regiment officers – for overseas contracts.

The contracts that Cameron accepted took him to a number of countries. In May 1971 he was in Vietnam as part of a small army of British mercenaries. They were organized into killer groups assigned to infiltrate communist territory and harrass the enemy in rapid strike sorties. Their objectives were demolition and assassination.

1972 saw Cameron in Kurdistan fighting on the side of the Kurd separatists against Iraqi government troops. It was a hard, gruelling campaign and Cameron returned to England after four months. His experience as a mercenary made him aware that there was a market for highly trained ex-soldiers and he felt that his experience and contacts could prove invaluable.

Cameron set himself up as a mercenary recruiter. To establish exactly how many men he would have available he placed an advert in the classified columns of the *Daily Telegraph* and the *Daily Mail*. The ads read simply: 'Ex commandos, paratroopers, SAS troopers wanted for interesting work abroad.' He enclosed his telephone number.

There was an immediate response and within a week he had the staggering total of fifteen hundred applicants. As well as British ex-paratroopers and SAS the list included a variety of nationalities – Germans, Belgians, South Africans, Italians, Rhodesians and French – as well as ex-Foreign Legionnaires and Vietnam veterans.

It was plain that Cameron sorted the wheat from the chaff. He wasn't interested in thugs and bully boys. He wanted intelligent men able to plan strategy and assess tactics as well as fight. He was left with a card index containing the personal and service record of eight hundred men. An elite mercenary job centre.

Cameron did not dispatch operatives for the sole purpose of gaining a hefty recruitment fee like a Roman lanista who sent gladiators into the arena for the glory of the games. Cameron concerned himself with the morality and feasibility of the contracts before he undertook recruitment. The men he used relied on him to sieve the facts, knowing he had their interests at heart. It was hardly surprising, therefore, that Cameron, having attended the Angola briefing, had walked out, refusing to be associated with such a badly organized venture.

Dalkeith's mind was made up. He decided not to waste any more time. Cameron Security Consultants boasted an office in Sloane Street. Very up market. The address was in the dossier. Armed with the information he had come for, Dalkeith called for Willowburn to let him out of the vault.

Iain Cameron was a broad shouldered man of medium height. He was very tanned with strong chiselled features and black hair cut short. The black leather patch that covered his left eye gave him a piratical look that most women found attractive and Cameron used that fact to his considerable advantage.

His good eye viewed the visitor with interest.

Dalkeith, very presentable in natty bowler, camel hair overcoat and English brogues. A city gent through and through.

'Good evening, Mister Cameron. Or is it still Major? I do apologize for calling on you so late in the day.' He smiled.

A bit smarmy, Cameron thought. In fact more than a bit. 'I'm a civilian now,' he said. 'And you are?'

'Hobson,' Dalkeith said slowly. 'Gerald Hobson.' He took off the bowler and looked for somewhere to put it.

Cameron came to his rescue, pointing to the visitor's chair on the other side of his desk. 'Take a seat, Mister Hobson. Tell me how I can help you.'

'I need men.' Dalkeith sat down and rested his bowler on his knees.

'Oh, yes,' Cameron said cautiously. 'For what exactly? Bodyguards?'

Dalkeith shook his head. 'I have read your sales brochure, as it were. The task I have in mind is covered in the section dealing with military style operations.'

'The brochure, as you call it, isn't available in W.H. Smith's,' Cameron said. 'May I ask how you got hold of it?'

'An acquaintance,' Dalkeith said.

After the Angola affair Dalkeith had assigned an agent to break into Cameron's office. The agent had come away with a list of clients and information which outlined the impressive array of talent that Cameron had at his disposal. The agent had left no trace of his entry.

'So, you've read the blurb. What part of the contents are you interested in?'

'The uplifting of individuals from hostile territory or captivity,' Dalkeith quoted.

'I see.' Cameron pursed his lips.

Dalkeith leaned forward. 'Cameron, I can't help feeling that we could begin to do business if you were to drop the pretence and stop acting like a nun who has just been propositioned. The fact is that your organization recruits mercenaries. I wish to avail myself of your services. Let's not pussyfoot around.'

There was an uncomfortable silence for several seconds

as Dalkeith found himself subjected to intense scrutiny. He knew he was being assessed as friend or foe. He waited.

'All right, Mister Hobson. You tell me what the contract is and I'll tell you if I can provide.' Cameron eased back in his chair.

Inwardly, Dalkeith breathed a sigh of relief. He had cleared the first hurdle. 'I'd like assurance first,' he said.

'What?'

'Your sales brochure's impressive but provides only the gloss. I'd like to know the quality of the undercoat. The men you recruit; what calibre are they?'

'All combat experienced. They've seen action in virtually every theatre of war or insurgence. Vietnam, Malaya, Borneo, Cyprus, Nigeria, Rhodesia, Central and South America, Ulster. You name it, they've been there.'

Dalkeith nodded. 'Angola?'

Cameron's expression hardened. 'That was a long time ago. Some of them may well have gone but not through my efforts. I'm concerned about the men I employ and their welfare. I have turned work down. Angola was a prime example. I've lost a lot of friends in the business. I try to minimize risk as much as possible. Sending men to Angola was a futile enterprise. They were ill equipped in arms and transport with no effective organization or discipline except for the pathological tendencies of that bastard Georgiou. How he lasted as long as he did amazes me. You can't lead men by fear. You have to command their respect. If I'd been there I'd have shot the son of a bitch myself. He deserved to die if anyone did. If the recruiters had been more concerned with the welfare of the men than with the bounties perhaps fewer men would have died. It was chaos, total fucking chaos.'

'What about money?' Dalkeith asked.

'I thought we'd get to that. It depends entirely on the job. If I send men into a war zone on an unlimited contract they'd get a weekly amount, usually £200 to £300 a week. For a one-off mission a lump sum would be paid.' Cameron paused. 'Which brings us to your proposition, I'm thinking.'

'I rather think it does,' agreed Dalkeith.

'So?'

'So, I want a small group of men willing to undertake a rescue mission. A snatch and run job.'

'Where?'

'East Africa. To be specific, Lugamba.'

'Christ!' Cameron said. 'You're talking about Holt aren't you? I read about it in tonight's *Standard*.'

A nod from Dalkeith. 'Can you do it?'

Cameron shook his head. 'That's one hell of a contract, man.'

'You're saying no?'

'I'm saying I'll think about it.'

'I need an answer,' Dalkeith said.

'Don't pressure me, Hobson. That ploy won't work. Anyway, what's your interest in the man? Whom or what do you represent?'

Dalkeith had prepared himself for such a question. 'I'm here on behalf of a group of people who find it appalling that an ignorant black dictator should hold the British Government to ransom.'

Dalkeith hoped he had injected the correct amount of pomposity into his voice. Shades of Colonel Blimp.

Cameron nodded silently. 'It will be expensive. Can your group afford it, I wonder?'

'We are not without substantial reserves,' Dalkeith said with what he prayed sounded like supreme confidence. 'What sort of sum are we talking about?'

'In the region of £25,000 per man and I'm thinking in terms of a four to six man team.'

Maybe they could raid the tea fund, Dalkeith thought

wildly and said: 'Very well, I will relay the information to my associates. When can you give me a definite answer?'

Cameron shrugged. 'Why don't we say this time tomorrow. How will I get in touch with you?'

'You won't,' replied Dalkeith. 'I'll contact you. At six.' He rose. 'This has been most interesting, Cameron.'

Cameron permitted himself a thin smile. 'It certainly has, Mister Hobson. I'll speak with you tomorrow.'

David Wood, clutching a tumbler of Bell's and ice, picked up the telephone in his study. It had been ringing for several seconds.

'Yes?' His voice was curt. It was an indication of his displeasure at being dragged away from the Mozart concert on the radio. He didn't get many opportunities to relax in the comfort of his study. His wife was visiting a friend and he had the Chelsea town house to himself.

'We could be in business,' Dalkeith said. He sounded as though he was in the next room.

'You've made contact?' Wood tensed.

'An approach has been initiated.' Dalkeith sounded subdued. 'I will have a decision regarding acceptance at this time tomorrow.'

'Very well,' Wood answered. 'I take it the individual involved had no idea who you represented? A stupid question, I know.'

'Yes,' Dalkeith said.

'Yes, what?' Wood felt his stomach muscles contract.

'Yes, it was a stupid question.'

Wood opened his mouth to redeem himself but Dalkeith had already hung up.

David Holt viewed the mess on the tin plate with acute disgust. Cold rice and stringy chicken. At least it might have been chicken, he wasn't certain because he hadn't

42

plucked up enough courage to taste it. He had sipped some water from the mug. It had tasted brackish.

The cell was a rancid box, ten by ten, with a door opening into a dry dusty corridor. Three stout metal bars at the tiny window interrupted the view out on to the exercise yard of the Lubiri detention centre.

This was Holt's second night in confinement and from the way things looked it would match his first in discomfort.

After being pushed into the Peugeot Holt had been driven straight to the detention centre. Every attempt to reason with his three abductors had met with a scream of abuse. Holt had given up. With luck he would be able to see someone with authority who could arrange his release. That thought turned to stone when he realized his destination.

The high mesh fence of Lubiri met his gaze and he sat in fear as the car swept through the gates into the compound. Holt allowed himself to be escorted into the reception block. To have resisted would have been futile. His escort left him with two unsmiling warders.

Major Farouk Juma, head of the Department of State Security, regarded the Englishman with contempt. He rose from his desk and stood before Holt, his eyes, brown lifeless pools, on a level with Holt's chin. His thin face was heavily pockmarked – the legacy of a childhood infection. A pencil moustache traced the outline of his fleshy, effeminate upper lip. His black greasy hair was cut very short. With his slightly protruding teeth he resembled a bush rat on the verge of hysterics. Holt thought the little Nubian was the most evil looking human being he had ever encountered.

Major Juma was dressed in an open neck khaki shirt and slacks. The shirt was a size too large. The epaulettes overlapped his narrow shoulders and his thin brown arms hung like twigs from uniformed sleeves rolled above his elbows. A bank of medal ribbons provided three rows of colour above his breast pocket. He carried a malacca swagger stick in his right hand.

He smiled malevolently at Holt and the latter recoiled from the foetid breath. He tapped Holt on the hip with his cane. The Englishman looked nonplussed, not understanding the intent. Juma's smile faded and without warning he thrashed Holt's right hip, the malacca cane flicking through the air like a whip. Holt yelled and tried to dodge. His arms were grabbed from behind in two vicelike grips. Like a rabbit transfixed by a stoat he watched with chilling fascination as the tip of the cane touched the inside of his thigh and traced a line to his groin. He was aware of Juma nodding to the two goons over his shoulder and flinched from the expected blow. Instead Kuma sidestepped and Holt was pushed forward over the desk. He felt hands fumbling at his pockets, hauling out his meagre possessions. They made a pitiful pile on the desk top. A bunch of keys, small change, a pair of nail clippers and a grubby handkerchief. He was dragged upright.

The tears began. 'Please,' he mumbled. 'What are you going to do with me?'

Juma smiled again and Holt's stomach crawled.

'We shoot you, mister.'

'But you can't!' Holt whispered, his mind reeling. 'I demand to see the High Commissioner.'

'You see no one,' Juma said harshly.

'You can't keep me here!' Holt grew bolder.

'We keep you here,' Juma answered. 'Then we shoot you.'

'God Almighty!' cried Holt. 'You wouldn't dare! Even if you're going to keep me here, you won't just shoot me. There will be a trial.'

Juma looked blank. 'Trial?' Then he laughed, a wild

44

inane cackle that was taken up by the goons. The awful sound echoed around the room. 'No trial, old man! We bloody shoot you!'

He jerked his weasel head and Holt was frogmarched out of the room and down the passage. He was struck with the realization that, apart from the sound of his own progress, the centre was totally silent. One would have expected to hear the night sounds of people confined; snoring, coughing, talking in their sleep, sobbing even. Nothing. It was like being in a tomb.

They stopped outside an open door. By the dim light in the passage Holt could see that the cell was empty. He was thrust through the entrance and as he tripped to his knees the door slammed behind him.

He had been left alone the next day. The dawn light that crept slowly over the compound wall filtered through the bars on his window and found him huddled under a filthy threadbare blanket on a bug infested mattress that he had found propped against the wall of his cell. The mattress stank of vomit, urine and other deposits too appalling to contemplate but it was better than sleeping on the floor.

At first he had attempted to attract the attention of the guards by hammering on the door. This action had met with total indifference. He had given up.

Sometime during the day – noon if the position of the sun was anything to go by – Holt's attention had been attracted by sounds in the next cell. The sound of the door opening and something falling to the floor followed by someone – he presumed a guard – shouting at the top of his voice. Then came the scream; a single cry that stopped as abruptly as it had begun.

It rose again; a racking sob that grew into a wail that slowly increased in volume to reach a shriek of such ferocious intensity that Holt had to cover his ears. He would never have believed that a human was capable of making such a dreadful sound. It was like a pig being butchered. The sound that had Holt retching was the last grotesque gargle from the victim as his agony was cut short by a noise that resembled a ripe pumpkin being struck by a shovel.

Holt remained huddled on the mattress until the evening, when the tin plate was pushed through the gap at the foot of the cell door. He hadn't eaten for twenty four hours. He picked at the gruesome contents on the platter, wrinkling his nose as the smell assailed his nostrils. Someone had to turn up soon, he reflected. What the hell was the Acting High Bloody Commissioner doing, for Christ's sake?

Warren-Chase lay in bed and stared morosely at the ceiling. The reply from London in response to his cable informing them of Holt's predicament had hardly inspired confidence. It had been at the worst inadequate, at the best diplomatic. In other words: sit tight, we're working on it. Not very reassuring.

His tossing and turning served only to wake his wife who wasn't pleased at having her slumbers disturbed by her insomniac husband. Despite her imploring, Warren-Chase couldn't drop off. They lay beneath the single sheet like twin bolsters. It was too hot to do anything else.

3

Seven thirty in the morning. Cameron walked through the sliding doors into Heathrow's Terminal One and approached the British Airways desk.

'My name is Cameron. I've a reservation on your flight 406.'

The girl checked her computer screen. 'Yes, sir. How do you wish to pay?'

Cameron handed over his American Express card. Just like the adverts, he thought.

She handed the blue card back with the receipt and ticket, trying to avoid staring at Cameron's eye patch. He really was quite attractive, she mused. 'Your flight is checking in now.' She smiled readily.

Cameron collected his boarding card at the check-in desk and walked through the departure control to the gate. He was dressed in fawn slacks and an open neck shirt under a light tan leather windcheater. He'd one item of hand luggage; a black leather briefcase.

As the Trident pushed back from the blocks, Cameron settled into his seat. He would be in Amsterdam in a little over an hour.

'So,' Lennox said. 'Dalkeith has made some progress.'

'He phoned me last night. I'd have let you know earlier but you were at that reception.'

'Bloody waste of time that was!' grated Lennox. 'We had lobster. Bloody stuff never agrees with me.' He massaged his stomach.

'You should have told them,' Wood said.

'I should have left,' Lennox muttered. 'Now, you've got something else for me?'

'Another cable from Lugamba. Apparently Mabato won't let Warren-Chase see Holt. They're keeping him in the city detention centre. It's a cross between Broadmoor and Catterick barracks. Not exactly *Homes and Gardens*.'

'That's to be expected. Anything else?'

'Another demand from Mabato.'

Lennox looked aghast. 'Christ! What's he want now?'

'He wants me to deliver written acceptance of his demands. That's the one signed by yourself and Her Majesty.'

Lennox appeared pensive. 'I don't suppose he'd be satisfied with some coloured beads, mirrors and a bolt of cloth?'

'Hardly,' Wood said patiently. He assumed the PM was being facetious, he couldn't always tell. 'There's another development.'

'You're doing this on purpose.' Lennox sounded peeved.

'I think this might be to our advantage.'

'How's that?'

'My office had a call from Sir Garrick Kirby.'

'Who the hell's he when he's at home?' Lennox gawped.

'He was Mabato's commanding officer in the 4th King's African Rifles.'

Lennox perked visibly. 'Was he now? What did he want?'

'To offer his services in any way we might require. He read the news in the *Standard* and took it upon himself to contact us.'

'Very enterprising,' agreed Lennox. 'Any suggestions then?'

'How about getting the letter written and signed and have Garrick Kirby deliver it?'

'That's tantamount to accepting the ultimatum.'

'I didn't mean that. The letter can simply be a plea for clemency from the Palace and yourself, delivered by Garrick Kirby who could add a few sentiments of his own. It seems that Mabato had a tremendous affection for the general. Looked upon him as a father figure.'

'Brings tears to my eyes,' said Lennox. 'Still it might do the trick. Would Garrick Kirby be prepared to go to Lugamba?'

'He offered his services in any capacity. His very words.'

'But postman? It'll be singing telegrams next.'

'We stand more chance this way than with the GPO.'

'Oh, very droll. However, I've informed Her Majesty of the situation so I'll broach the subject of the letter. I can't see any problems. Get hold of this character and tell him we may well take him up on his offer. He can put his money where his mouth is. Now, what about Dalkeith?'

'He said he'd made contact. He's going to let me know this evening if the contract would be accepted. I presume we may still go through with it?'

'Let's say we keep our options open,' Lennox replied. 'You never know, this Garrick Kirby fellow could save the day.' He grinned. 'Like the cavalry riding to the rescue.'

'Quite,' Wood said. 'But remember what happened to Custer.'

Thomas Keel fastened the button on his shirt cuff and reached for his jacket that was draped over the back of the chair in the surgery.

'Well, Willy, what's the verdict?' he asked.

'As ever, Thomas, considering your age, you are in remarkable shape.'

Keel frowned. 'What the hell is that supposed to mean? I may be the wrong side of forty but I'm hardly in my dotage f'r Christ's sake!'

'Perhaps I should have rephrased that,' the doctor said,

smiling at Keel's expression. 'I meant that it is remarkable that you have in fact reached your present age.' Doctor Wilhelm Vanderhuik gazed at his patient with some fondness. Keel was a long time friend.

Keel shrugged himself into his jacket. The doctor had been correct in his observation. Keel was a tall man. Six feet of hard muscle packed into a big frame. His even tan was natural and only a shade or two lighter than mahogany. He was clean shaven with short steel grey hair and clear ice blue eyes that looked as if they had seen more trouble than they cared to remember.

Keel showed his even teeth in a twinkling grin as he addressed the doctor. 'I'm not sure if that was an insult or a compliment. Maybe I should just cart my hypochondria elsewhere. Then where would you be?'

'Probably examining patients more worthy of my skill and devotion. Head hunters in the Amazon Basin for example,' replied the doctor, his roly poly body shaking as he chuckled. He stroked his goatee beard and winked broadly.

Keel laughed. 'You're a rotten liar, Willy. You appreciate the good life too much and don't deny it!'

Vanderhuik wagged a finger like a housemaster ticking off an erring pupil. 'Sometimes, Thomas Keel, you go too far!'

'Come off it, you old quack! Admit it. My visits are the highlights of your year. How many times have you told me that you wished more people would have regular check ups. And that's in spite of the appalling fees you'd charge them!'

'Indeed. But only those involved in similar high risk careers.'

'*Touché!*' Keel said dryly. For a brief second the light in his eyes dimmed.

Vanderhuik caught the change of mood. 'When was your last contract?'

'Nine months ago,' Keel answered, recalling the job; escorting a Middle Eastern potentate on an arms buying spree around the munitions markets of Western Europe – West Germany, Sweden, France and Great Britain. Not very exciting but lucrative. His Highness had been more than generous but when one had spent seventy million dollars on military hardware one could hardly begrudge paying the hired help an extra few thousand. The contract lasted four weeks. The prince had returned to his desert and Keel to his bar on the Zeedijk. At least he had that to fall back on. Unlike most soldiers of fortune who, between contracts, were forced to exist solely on their bounties, haunting the mercenary recruiting stations like moths around a flame. Brussels, Lisbon, Marseilles, Milan and Athens. Different countries, different cities. But they were all the same when you didn't know where the next meal was coming from. Or the next job.

'The trouble with you, Thomas Keel,' Willy Vanderhuik said sternly, 'is that you are bored.'

'What do you suggest? Stamp collecting?'

The doctor shrugged. 'It was a diagnosis based on obvious symptoms. I cannot guarantee a cure.'

'Because the illness is terminal?' Keel asked.

Vanderhuik shook his head in sympathy. 'Only you can answer that, my friend.' He clapped his hands suddenly. 'Now, Thomas, forgive me but I have other patients to attend.'

Keel nodded. 'Sure thing, Willy. I'll leave you to it. I'll be in touch.'

The little doctor smiled. 'Good day, Thomas. Take care.'

'You too, Willy.'

Keel strode through the waiting room and out of the building. He walked down the steps on to the street. Willy Vanderhuik watched him depart before calling forward his next patient.

51

Keel turned right on to the Spui Straat and walked towards the Dam Square. It was mid morning and the city of Amsterdam was bathed in hazy sunshine. The tourists were already up and about. In the square the Minolta set mixed with the combat jacket brigade, clustered around the Dam like unwashed sheep.

Avoiding the milling cyclists he cut across Warmoes Straat and headed towards the canal. Along its banks the morning sunlight filtered through the trees casting silver reflections on the calm brown surface of the waterway. Houseboats and brightly painted barges hugged the edge of the canal and a loaded tourist launch skimmed along like a large Pyrex water beetle.

Keel was entering the Red Light district. Narrow cobbled streets where sexual favours of every kind could be purchased. The girls sat in armchairs behind large windows, an open advertisement for carnal pleasures. A welcoming smile, pink tongue flicking over coral lips, fingers tracing stockinged thigh and taut panties and the window shopper was hooked. The girl would leave her seat to state the price and entice the client inside and a curtain would be drawn across the window like a cab driver engaging his 'For Hire' sign. Twenty minutes later the client would emerge to button his overcoat and the girl would open the curtain and resume her pose.

The girls were as different as chalk and cheese. Sultry titian haired beauties, more suited to gracing the centrefold of *Playboy*, would solicit beside ravaged fifteen stone Amazons and leather clad peroxides. All tastes catered for.

Keel knew a number of girls by name and usually acknowledged their friendly heckles. So far he had resisted their ribald advances but he was sure the ladies of the Zeedijk had a book going to see who would bed him first. One day he would put them out of their misery. Who would he choose? Helga probably. The face of a goddess with silky auburn hair and a figure to cause traffic jams. Her room was next door to Keel's bar and flanked on the other side by a porno theatre; a poky fifty seater owned and run by two homosexual brothers, Rennie and Johnny Braake. The place specialized in live acts as well as movies.

The theatre was open for business and in her doorway Helga was chatting to one of the brothers. She caught Keel's eye, grinned and winked suggestively over Rennie's shoulder. Keel returned the grin as he walked past.

The interior of the Pelican was cool and wrapped in a low hum of discreet conversation. The bar was low lit and the atmosphere was comfortable and intimate. A counter of polished oak ran along the right hand wall. The main floor area was partitioned into waist-height three sided booths that ensured a degree of privacy for the occupants.

Keel employed a staff of four. One barman, an ex-strip club bouncer called Peter Van Dijk, and three friendly waitresses; Agnes, Brigitta and Marie-Anne. The girls were the reason, Keel was convinced, that he had so many male customers, though Van Dijk's dark Latin features had many admirers, not least among the hookers on the street. They only admired him from afar. Van Dijk was heavily involved with a petite KLM stewardess.

The bar boasted a mixed clientele. Customers included business men, elderly matrons, husband and wives, husbands and mistresses, ardent bachelors and ladies of the night. The latter regarded the Pelican as a kind of refuge from, as Helga put it, their daily grind. Keel had strict house rules. No soliciting by the girls. Approaches by prospective clients were difficult to control but the girls were quick to bring it to the attention of the bar staff if they felt they were being pestered. Van Dijk was always there to provide assistance in the form of a hand on the back of the offender's neck and any customer who had to be ejected was not readmitted.

A dozen or so customers were present. Most of them were businessmen enjoying a quiet cigar and coffee over the morning paper, taking time off to glance admiringly at the girls' tight jeans as they served at the tables. The majority were regulars and nodded happily to Keel as he strode in. Peter Van Dijk was behind the counter cleaning glasses. As Keel approached, the barman moved his eyes in the direction of a corner booth.

Keel walked to the table where a dark haired man leant back in his seat and returned his gaze over an empty coffee cup.

'Hello, Thomas,' Iain Cameron said.

'I wondered when you'd show,' Keel said. He smiled and held out his hand. 'I hope you haven't been waiting long, Iain. Good trip?'

Cameron shook hands. 'Turbulence approaching Schiphol but not too uncomfortable. I've been here about fifteen minutes.' His good eye followed Keel as the latter sat down opposite.

'A drink?' Keel asked. 'Something to eat?'

'Just another coffee.'

Keel caught Brigitta's eye. She took his order for two coffees and smiled openly at Cameron before moving over to the hot plate at the end of the bar. Cameron watched her go. 'Wow!' he said.

Keel grinned. He was used to the effect the girls had on his customers.

Cameron averted his gaze reluctantly and smiled. 'You're looking well, Thomas.'

'For my age?' replied Keel automatically.

'Sorry?'

'Skip it. I was thinking aloud.' Keel paused then said: 'I

was surprised to get your call last night. It's been quite a time, Iain.'

It had been nine months since the time of Keel's last contract. The sheik's arms buying spree.

Iain Cameron had given a great deal of thought to the contract offered by the man he knew as Gerald Hobson. The job would be extremely hazardous and he would need men with extraordinary cunning and exceptional skills. Cameron realized the mission was virtually suicidal but the predicament of the lone Englishman held prisoner by a monstrous regime over three thousand miles away grabbed him in a way he found difficult to explain and he knew instinctively that, providing he found the right team, the contract would be undertaken.

Cameron decided to go for a four man team. His time with the SAS provided the reason for this. As a member of the Regiment's active service units he had seen the practicality of small killer squads and had used the same format to deadly effect in Vietnam. For the Lugamba contract he had such a team in mind and one of the men he wanted was Thomas Keel.

Keel had begun his warfaring with D Company, the 'Pathfinder' unit of the 2nd Battalion of the Parachute Regiment. Keel spent three years with D Company before transferring to the Battalion's Special Patrol Company, a unit specializing in deep penetration sorties into enemy held territory. After seeing action in Aden, Borneo, Cyprus and Malaya, it was a natural progression for him to join the Special Air Service and it was in the Oman, while serving with the Regiment, that he met Iain Cameron.

They were both on attachment to the Sultanate, assisting the undermanned and poorly armed Omani forces in their fight against the Chinese trained Dhofar Liberation Front led by an ex-lorry mechanic called Musallim bin Nuffl. The Marxist guerillas waged a hit and run war from their strongholds within the Republic of South Yemen, the land once known as Aden.

The ageing Sultan of Oman relied heavily on professional mercenaries from Britain, white South Africa and Pakistan to bolster his army and under an agreement with the British Government, British Army officers could volunteer for attachment to the Oman on two year contracts. The Sultan benefited from the expertise and Britain benefited by being able to use the Omani airfield on the Plain of Salalah as a staging post in its Indian Ocean commitment.

Together, Keel and Cameron trained and led squads of Omani troops and Baluchi mercenaries in strikes against the Marxist rebels in the Qara mountains. When not leading raids they acted as bodyguards for oil company executives.

It was towards the end of their nine months tour in the southern region that Cameron sustained his injury and Keel accompanied him in the Beaver that flew him north to the medical centre at Bayt al Falaj. Cameron returned to England. Keel remained in Oman.

At the end of his two year contract Keel found himself in something of a quandary. His stint in the Oman ran parallel with Britain's growing inclination to withdraw from bases east of Suez. Keel had no immediate desire to return to the UK but could see no alternative scope for his talents other than extending his contract with the Omani Sultanate and by this time he was looking for a change of scenery. He resigned his commission and went freelance.

The Biafran campaign was eighteen months old by the time Keel arrived to join the Federal forces of Major-General Yakubu Gowan. Keel joined the Third Commando Division under Colonel Benjamin Adenkunle and led raiding parties over the Cross River to strike at the heart of the rebel forces led by Colonel Ojukwu. The war was bloody, the rebels determined and relentless and in some cases better equipped than the Federal side.

Keel survived the duration of his contract and was one of a squad of officers who escorted Ojukwu on his flight to Lagos to surrender to General Gowan on the 10th of January 1970.

His next contract involved the smuggling of gold bars from Dubai across the Arabian Sea to India and Pakistan. His partner, a Persian exile called Idrisi, set up the contacts on the Indian mainland and Keel provided the muscle. He made more in ten months than he had in the previous three years and soon he had accumulated enough in his bank account to purchase the bar in Amsterdam.

Then he met Cameron again, who by now was in the same line of business.

They were nine months in Vietnam attached to the American Special Forces then, when Cameron moved on to Kurdistan, Keel found himself in Rhodesia as a member of the elite Selous Scouts organizing cross border raids to flush out Zambian guerillas.

And so it went on; moving from one contract to another like a wild west bounty hunter. Chad, Venezuela, Uruguay, Assam, Thailand; the list was awesome. Yet always returning to his bar in Amsterdam during the slack times which tended to grow more frequent as he got older.

Until Cameron, who by now was acting as his broker, made contact again.

Like now.

'So,' Keel said. 'You've got a job lined up.'

Cameron shrugged. 'A possibility. I'll pitch it to you and you can tell me what you think. For obvious reasons I didn't want to go into details over the phone. By the way, how's Sekka?'

'He's well. He's out to lunch with our accountant.'

'Good. I hope I'll get a chance to see him before I leave. I'm booked on the KLM flight at four this afternoon.'

'What's the contract, Iain?'

The coffee arrived. Cameron took his black and unsweetened.

'Someone wants us to get David Holt out of Lugamba.'

'Christ!' Keel breathed softly.

'You've read about him, I take it?'

'The press over here gave him a few paragraphs and there was a report on the radio this morning.'

Cameron reached for his briefcase and extracted copies of the *Daily Telegraph* and *The Times*. He passed them over. 'I picked up this morning's editions at Heathrow.'

Keel said: 'He was only taken the day before yesterday. Your client moved bloody fast. Who is he?'

'His name's Hobson and he's spokesman for a group that finds it despicable that a semi-literate black should be holding Her Majesty's Government over a barrel. He struck me as a cross between Colonel Blimp and Sir John Mills. All camel hair overcoat and regimental tie. Shades of the Raj, old boy. Don'tya know, what?'

'Is he genuine?' asked Keel.

'I would say yes. He didn't flinch at the fee I proposed.'

'Maybe he was speechless with shock.'

'I quoted the going rate.'

'Which is?'

'£25,000 per man.'

'Good enough. Tell me though, why me?'

'I knew you were available,' Cameron said. 'This could be a rush job. By all accounts Holt has precious little time left.'

'I think I'm flattered,' Keel said.

Cameron said sharply: 'Look, Thomas. You know how I work. I could have saved the cost of the air fare and for the cost of a train ticket to Aldershot I could have popped into the bar of the Queen's Hotel and picked up the first ex-SAS thugs I bumped into. I don't want thugs, man. I want professionals, in every sense of the word. That's why I came to Amsterdam.' His eye flashed angrily.

Keel held up a hand. 'Okay, I take your point. Anyway, dammit, I'm getting stale. My last job was nine months ago. I'm beginning to stagnate.'

'But this place keeps you busy surely?'

Keel shrugged. 'Hell, Iain, the place runs without me. I have a good staff. When Joseph and I are away Peter and the girls manage the bar. I'm like the hookers that come in. This place is a refuge. I retire here to lick my wounds and gain my strength. It's my safety valve if you like.'

'And Sekka?'

'No need to ask,' Keel said. 'He'll come with me. All I have to do is say where and when.'

'Like a gun dog,' Cameron said, regretting the words instantly.

Keel's eyes were like chips of ice as he said: 'Joseph Sekka is his own man, Cameron. He's the best back up man I've ever had and one of the bravest men I've ever known. We're a team. He's saved my life more times than I care to remember. He might be my business partner as well but that does not mean he's taken for granted. When I said he would come I was stating a fact not a directive.'

'I know, Thomas. I spoke out of turn.'

Keel said: 'I'll need more information if I'm to take the job. You know that.'

'I've a few things here that should help.' Cameron reached for his case again.

'A year ago,' he explained, 'I was approached by a man who claimed to be a supporter of Hamilton Kemba. He offered me £50,000 to set up the assassination of Solomon Mabato. He had it all planned. He even provided me with this dossier on Mabato and his henchmen. It contains

59

photographs, maps and character sketches. Some of the background stuff I added myself.' He passed Keel a buff coloured folder.

'How come you didn't accept the contract?'

'Because I don't run Murder Incorporated, Thomas. I sent him away with a flea in his ear. He damned near got my boot up his arse as well.'

'You kept the dossier?'

'I'm not stupid, Thomas. I figured it would come in useful one day.' Cameron smiled.

'How up to date is the information?'

'It was current two months ago. I kept on updating some of the stuff. For information on Holt, you'll have to read the newspapers.'

Keel nodded. 'Fair enough. You understand that my taking this folder doesn't constitute acceptance of the contract. I'll read and assess the information and let you know.'

'That's all I would expect,' Cameron said. 'But bear in mind that my client will want an answer soon. I promised him one by this evening.'

'He'll have to wait. I won't be rushed. In any case I'll have to discuss it with Joseph and if I accept I'll need to get a team together; men I've worked with before.'

'Like Harry Roan and Paul Schiller?' Cameron said.

Keel started. 'I don't think they're available. Paul is in Mexico and Harry is in Mozambique hunting gooks. At least that's where they were three months ago.'

'They moved,' Cameron said. 'I knew if you took the job you wouldn't want to work with anyone else so I made a few phone calls. They are in the Gulf on a bodyguard contract.' He glanced at his watch. 'At least they were last night. By now they should be halfway to London, courtesy of Gulf Air. If they are lucky they'll be in Amsterdam this evening.' He grinned at Keel's expression.

'You bastard!' Keel hissed. 'You're so bloody cock sure!'

'Of course. I've even booked two rooms at the Okura.'

'For whom?' asked a voice at Cameron's shoulder.

Cameron looked up into a face that might have been carved in ebony. The tall, slim negro was one of the most striking men Cameron had ever seen. Joseph Sekka stood an inch over six feet and, although he was not as broad as Keel, his athletic physique exuded an aura of controlled power. A power that could be unleashed with frightening speed. Cameron sensed this as he took in the immaculate three piece suit, silk shirt and hand stitched Gucci loafers. Sekka carried a combination locked, burgundy briefcase in his hand. He grinned at his seated partner as Cameron stood up to shake hands.

'How are you, Iain?' Sekka's grip was firm and dry.

'I'm fine, Joseph. You're looking fit.'

Sekka smiled. 'I keep myself in trim. I still have regular sessions with Tekuji.'

'Tekuji?' Cameron asked.

'Japanese karate master,' Keel explained. 'They knock the stuffing out of each other.'

Cameron noticed the ridge of hard muscle along the heel of Sekka's hands.

Sekka said: 'I still can't match you, Thomas. Tekuji insists you're one of the best European fighters he has faced.'

'He's being polite,' Keel said. 'How was the meeting with the accountant? I thought it was going to be an extended lunch?'

'Just brunch, as our American friends would say. We had a useful discussion. We aren't as broke as we thought we were.'

'And the loan?'

'Should be no problem.'

Cameron's ears pricked up. 'Loan?'

Sekka sat down next to Keel and waited for his partner to explain.

'Joseph and I are thinking of opening a restaurant,' Keel said. 'The Pelican has been doing very well and we decided it was time to expand. Premises have become available on the Keizersgracht so we've been hustling a little. Hence Joseph's meeting with our accountant. And yes, before you say it, Iain, the fee from the contract would come in very handy.'

'Ah, yes,' Sekka said. 'Suppose you fill me in.' His face, cast in jet, remained bland but Cameron detected a strange light in the negro's eyes. The light of battle, he mused. Was that it?

Keel said: 'How'd you like a couple of days in Lugamba, Joseph?'

Sekka's reaction was to roll his eyes and mutter: 'Oh Lordy!' He looked like a slim Rochester, minus fur coat. 'I doan like de sound o' dat, Massa Keel.'

Keel glanced at a bemused Cameron and then inclined his head towards Sekka. 'Don't take any notice of the house boy, Iain.'

Sekka chuckled. 'All right, what's the job?'

'We lift David Holt,' Keel said.

'Piece of cake,' said Sekka and rolled his eyes again.

'We'll read your dossier, Iain,' Keel said. 'I want Harry and Paul in on it before I give you a yes or no. Pass that on to your Mister Hobson.'

'Fair enough.' Cameron nodded acceptance of the terms. 'I will contact you tomorrow for your decision.' He looked at his watch. 'I might even make an earlier flight.'

'Not until we've taken you to lunch,' Keel said. 'Then I'll run you to the airport.' He called over to the barman: 'Peter, ring De Gouden Eeuw and book a table for three. We'll be there in thirty minutes.'

As Van Dijk picked up the telephone Keel turned back

to Cameron. 'We'll show you our new site while you're here. I think you'll be impressed. Mind you, De Gouden Eeuw might not take too kindly to the competition.' He picked up the dossier and the two newspapers. 'These go into the safe until we get back.'

After the meal Sekka returned to the Pelican and Keel drove Cameron to Schiphol, pushing the metallic blue Saab through the afternoon traffic with consummate ease. The tannoys were announcing Cameron's flight as they walked into the terminal.

Cameron held out his hand. 'I'll be in touch, Thomas.'

'Have a safe flight, Iain,' Keel said. He turned abruptly and strode away.

For a second Cameron looked thoughtfully after him before making his way to the KLM desk and the flight to London.

By the time Keel returned to the bar Joseph Sekka had retrieved the Lugamba dossier from the safe and was studying it, stretched out on the low sofa in the flat they maintained above the Pelican. Each man had his own apartment in Amsterdam but they found it convenient to have accommodation on top of the business.

'You haven't wasted any time,' Keel said as he walked into the room.

Sekka had removed his jacket and loosened his tie. He looked as relaxed as a big cat after a kill.

Keel pulled up a chair. 'Okay, Joseph, what do we have?'

'Well, it isn't going to be easy, Thomas.'

'Get away,' Keel said. 'You do surprise me.'

Wordlessly, Sekka passed over the first section of the dossier.

It was a summary of Mabato's rise to power. Some of the details were familiar to Keel but even so, reading them again, he knew that if they accepted the job, Mabato would be a lethal adversary.

Born into the Makesi tribe, Solomon Mabato had tended goats in his youth, in the dry and arid scrubland that composed the West Nile region of Lugamba. In 1946, aged twenty one, he enlisted in the 4th Battalion of the King's African Rifles, as a cook. He could manage a few words of English and was a keen athlete and a popular recruit. One of his British officers summed him up as a tremendous chap to have around and such was their enthusiasm that they turned a blind eye to his inability to speak much English. Mabato began his rise through the ranks.

True, he experienced some difficulty in passing the English examination between the ranks of corporal and sergeant and scraped through by the skin of his teeth. From then on his superiors tended to overlook his short-comings in the academic field; as he was such a fine soldier it seemed a pity to hold him back.

He still excelled at sport, in particular rugby and boxing, and became the Lugamban heavyweight champion; a title he never lost. He ran out of challengers.

Ironically, the British could be held ultimately responsible for his rise to power. By 1961 Mabato was a sergeant major and Lugamba was driving towards independence. It was felt that as the first step towards Africanizing the regiment a small number of Africans should receive a commission. Mabato was among those chosen from the 4th Battalion.

By 1963 Lugamba had achieved its goal and six months after independence had been granted Mabato was promoted yet again, this time to major, and became Deputy Commander of the Lugamban Army under a man he detested, Morris Lule. Lule had been commissioned at the same time as Mabato and he was directly responsible to the new president, Hamilton Kemba.

Having gained this lofty position, Mabato's true character began to emerge. His ruthlessness became apparent. In 1965 Mabato informed Kemba that he had uncovered a plot by Lule to overthrow the presidency and assume control of the country. Such were Mabato's powers of persuasion that Kemba fell for it and gave the Deputy Commander full power to act as he thought fit. Lule and what supporters he had were arrested and shot before they could begin to protest their innocence. Mabato was now in complete control of the Lugamban Army.

He seemed to be unswervingly loyal to Kemba but the latter was beginning to have doubts. He was aware that Mabato was promoting the Northerners in the army, men from his own district, and rumours were trickling through to the President that his Army Commander was not the most honest of men, with emphasis on details of Mabato's personal wealth.

During this period the Belgian Congo was in the throes of civil war and it was well known that Hamilton Kemba was sympathetic to the rebels fighting the newly formed government run by Moise Tshombe and his Chief of Staff, Mobuto Sese Seko. Kemba wished to aid the rebels and provide them with arms and transport. He used Mabato as his link with the dawa crazed rebels under their leader, Mulele.

The rebels, however, had no cash with which to purchase arms but they did have truckloads of gold and ivory, seized as they retreated from towns they had controlled. Mabato's job, as Mulele's contact man, was to sell the gold and ivory and use the profits to buy arms for Mulele and his followers.

In these dealings no records were kept and Mabato did not have to account for what he sold. He began to bank the money for himself and news of his sudden wealth filtered through to the ears of the Lugamban President. Parliament demanded an inquiry.

There was no inquiry, due chiefly to the fact that four of the ministers who had supported the charges against Mabato disappeared into thin air. There were vague reports of decomposing bodies and graves in the forest but nothing was ever found. It was thought that maybe the Nile crocodiles knew the answer to the riddle but nobody plucked up the courage to ask them why they were smiling, So, the charges against Solomon Mabato were dropped through lack of evidence. Hamilton Kemba began to wonder just how powerful his Army Commander was.

Then came the attempt on Kemba's life.

On December 19th 1969 the President attended an evening meeting of the Lugamban People's Congress. After the meeting Kemba and some of his ministers left the conference hall and waited outside in the cool night air for their cars to arrive.

A shot rang out. Pandemonium ensued. Kemba and company flung themselves to the ground, scrambling for cover. Even as they dropped in panic a grenade was lobbed towards them. Miraculously it failed to explode but the marksman fired again. This time Kemba was hit. The bullet tore through his lip, demolished two teeth in his lower jaw, emerged from his open mouth and nicked his private secretary in the neck. Incredibly, Kemba was not seriously hurt. Although he was rushed to hospital he returned to his office within a week.

The would-be assassin was shot as he fled from the scene. He was identified as a Makesi, a member of Mabato's own tribe. Because Mabato had not been present at the meeting that evening he was suspected by many people of being involved in the attempt on Kemba's life. Again there was a distinct lack of evidence but by now the seeds of doubt had been well and truly sown in Kemba's mind. He would have to watch every step he took.

Six weeks later, during a meeting of senior army

officers, Mabato's second in command, Brigadier Henry Orayo, quarrelled with Mabato over the subject of army discipline and Mabato's methods of promotion. Orayo was not a member of the Makesi. Three days after the heated argument the bodies of the brigadier and his wife were discovered in a waterlogged ditch on the outskirts of their home village. The corpses were soaked in blood and riddled with bullets. The brigadier's head had been almost severed from his body by a machete blow. His wife's breasts were criss-crossed with knife cuts.

Mabato covered his tracks well. He thwarted all attempts to investigate the crime. Police inquiries usually pointed towards people in the army so Mabato was able to block all avenues of investigation. Those men who were about to be questioned were suddenly transferred to remote units or were given leave in order that they would be out of the country at the right time. In the event no one was ever convicted.

June 1970 saw the second attempt on Hamilton Kemba's life; a machine gun attack on an official entourage on the road leading to the capital, Kendura. Kemba was on his way to an early morning Cabinet meeting, seated in the rear of his limousine. The car was preceded by a police escort with lights flashing to warn other traffic. As the convoy passed the Three Moons Hotel on the last leg of the journey to the parliament building there was a sudden ear shattering burst of machine gun fire. Bullets thudded into the bodywork of Kemba's Mercedes. The windscreen imploded and the chauffeur's head blew apart in a crimson cloud of blood and bone fragments. As Kemba threw himself across the back seat bullets smashed the side windows and tore into the upholstery, missing their target by millimetres. By the time the escort car had reversed between Kemba's car and the source of the attack the gunman had disappeared and Kemba was hauling himself unceremoniously out of the ruin of his car on his hands and knees like a Muslim bowing towards Mecca, a badly shaken man.

After that incident he appeared less often in public and directed his secret police to round up suspects, which they did with enthusiasm. The people began to doubt Kemba's ability to govern and Kemba doubted his subjects' loyalty. The overriding question of course was whether Mabato had been responsible for the attack.

In September 1970 Mabato accepted a longstanding invitation to visit Egypt. Kemba saw this as a prime opportunity to conduct investigations into some of Mabato's activities and to make new army appointments from men other than Mabato's supporters. Mabato, however, with a fat finger in every pie, had more than a few contacts within Kemba's security service who warned him of the President's intentions. He returned to Lugamba unexpectedly, much to the discomfort of Hamilton Kemba, needless to say.

Strangely, over the next few months, a kind of impasse existed and Kemba, lulled into a false sense of security, announced his desire to attend the forthcoming Commonwealth Conference in Singapore.

On the 25th of January 1971 Hamilton Kemba was relaxing in the first class section of a Boeing 707, heading home after attending that conference. The aircraft was two hours out of Bombay, en route to Nairobi, when the news came through.

Mabato had struck with a vengeance.

George Nsheka, Kemba's private secretary, was on the flight deck, chatting to the crew and monitoring the radio when he picked up the report on the BBC World Service. The BBC quoted a Lugamba Radio announcement that had stated briefly that army officers, under the command of Major General Solomon Mabato, head of the Lugamban armed forces, had seized power. Nsheka was not slow in reporting the matter to Kemba and when the aircraft landed at Nairobi the news was confirmed.

Wisely, Kemba had no intention of continuing to Lugamba. Instead he and his party boarded an East African Airways DC-9 and flew to Dar-es-Salaam in Tanzania. Julius Nyerere, President of Tanzania, welcomed them and offered the hospitality of his country. Kemba's term of exile had begun.

In Lugamba Kemba was not missed. It was good riddance as far as the majority of his subjects were concerned. The devious machinations of Kemba's secret police were reasons enough for those sentiments.

The people dubbed Mabato 'The Liberator'.

Until they realized their mistake and by then it was too late. From the outset Mabato announced that this would be only a caretaker administration. Free elections were promised in a matter of months. A civilian cabinet was appointed, including some ministers who had served under Kemba. The future looked rosy.

Then the slaughter began.

Starting with the Army. Anyone who was a member of Kemba's tribe, the Basengi, was detained and placed in Maboru prison, as well as all the officers who had survived Mabato's initial purge. Mabato did not bother with the tiresome rigmarole of a trial. The men were hacked to death and their remains were buried in pits in the bush. Mabato replaced them with members of his own tribe, the Makesi. Now the Army was totally loyal to the Liberator.

Two months after the coup Mabato issued his Armed Forces Decree which gave the armed forces the powers of search and seizure, placing them above the law. His Detention Decree granted the power of imprisonment without trial and the Robbery Suspects Decree gave his men the power to shoot on sight anyone acting suspiciously.

In other words carte blanche in respect of anything done or omitted to have been done for the purpose of maintaining public order or public security in any part of Lugamba.

Ten thousand were butchered in the first four months.

And the world stood by and watched.

Britain was among the first to recognize officially the new regime. Kemba had always been an outspoken critic of British arms sales to South Africa and Her Majesty's Government hoped that Mabato would be more sympathetic. Such was the British Government's initial enthusiasm that it promised a ten million pound development loan.

The murders continued. Mabato's men were now killing by the hundreds and it was becoming impossible to dispose of the bodies in graves. Truckloads of rotting dead were driven to the banks of the Nile where they were thrown over the Kiggala Falls.

The falls were almost two hundred feet high. Not much was left of a body after it had been smashed, mauled and sliced by the rocks and tumbling water. Whatever was left was disposed of by the huge Nile crocodiles. At first anyway.

As the number of dead increased disposal became more difficult so that decomposing corpses found their way on to the banks of the river where they lay stranded for days while the vultures and crocs ate their fill at leisure.

The reports were horrifying. The entire population – men, women and children – of Kemba's home village was eliminated in one night, or so it was said. None investigated the matter too deeply. None dared.

Also Mabato was annoyed at the fact that the ten millions promised by Britain had failed to materialize. His reaction was drastic.

Most of Lugamba's trade, factories, plantations and

stores were controlled by Asians, many holding British passports. They were the managers, accountants, doctors, lawyers and technicians. Mabato called them the Jews of East Africa.

He gave the Asian community, sixty thousand souls, ninety days to leave Lugamba. Any that remained after the deadline would be placed in detention camps. Forty five thousand were airlifted out in six weeks. Some went to Canada, some to India and Pakistan. Britain took twenty five thousand. The rest were put into the camps; dry, dust ridden compounds erected in the remote north eastern region of Lugamba, only fifty miles south of the Sudanese border. In one insane move Mabato had deprived Lugamba of the very people who made the country's economy function. The refugees had been allowed a one hundred dollar personal allowance. A stop was put on their bank accounts. Their property – houses, stores and cars – was distributed among members of the forces, without whose support Mabato could not maintain his position of power.

Mabato had taken the country on its first steps down the road to economic ruin.

Over the next few years the purges continued, by which time Mabato had replaced his civilian cabinet with military men. Those ministers who escaped death did so by fleeing into Tanzania and Kenya, usually clad only in the clothes they stood in. It was estimated that one hundred thousand people had been killed since the coup.

Then Hamilton Kemba attempted a comeback.

In September 1977 one thousand guerillas, supporters of the exiled President, invaded Lugamba from Tanzania. It was a farce. The men were badly trained and ill equipped and didn't stand the ghost of a chance. They had meant to attack during the early hours of the morning but were delayed crossing the border. By the time they had sorted

71

themselves into some semblance of order they had lost the element of surprise. It was a massacre. Those that did not die during the first assault were hounded into the bush and killed. More bodies were dumped into the Nile.

In a fit of temper, Mabato accused Britain and Israel of helping to finance the raid. All Israeli personnel and the British envoy were ordered out of the country and, as a direct affront to both countries, Mabato set about wooing the support of the Arab States and Russia and he duly sent men to the Soviet Union and Libya for military training.

Mabato's rule of terror was enforced by two factions: the Department of State Security and the Search and Seizure Unit, known as SASU. Both outfits were staffed mainly with members of Mabato's own tribe with a sprinkling of Nubians and Sudanese.

The Department of State Security had been set up by Mabato after the coup, ostensibly as a military intelligence unit but it was, in effect, an extension of his unit of bodyguards. The department was under the command of a slim, tight lipped Nubian, Major Farouk Juma, who was answerable only to Mabato himself.

SASU was an arm of the civil police, formed to deal with armed robbery that had been rife after Mabato's takeover. Led by another Nubian, Hassan Boma, the members of the unit carried sub-machine guns and were allowed to shoot robbery suspects on sight.

Under the decrees issued by Mabato both terror units were given complete freedom of action and between them had been responsible for all the murders that had been committed under the Mabato regime. They had the world's highest per capita homicide rate.

Amazingly there were still Britons in the country. They numbered about seven hundred and were composed mostly of doctors, teachers, engineers, and missionaries working in some of the isolated villages in the bush.

Despite numerous attempts by the British Government to get them to leave Lugamba, they and their families were content to remain. After all for most of them it was the only home they had. It would have been unthinkable for them to pack their bags and take off.

Since the expulsion of the British envoy in 1977 they had none to look after their interests other than the hard pressed Warren-Chase who had been cajoled into the role by the High Commissioner in Kenya. The British Government, however, ensured the safety and well being of its subjects in a curious way.

Twice a week a Lugambian Airlines' 707 freighter arrived at Stansted Airport in Essex. These trips were known as the Whisky Runs. On arrival at Stansted the aircraft, usually piloted by American ex-servicemen, veterans of the Vietnam War, were loaded up with every sort of luxury goods, ranging from crates of whisky and cartons of cigarettes to transistor radios and new limousines. The goods were for the officers and men of the twenty thousand strong army; the men who kept Mabato in power. Britain was paying Mabato protection; if not in cash then at least in kind.

There had been assassination attempts but the man appeared indestructible. Standing six and a half feet tall and weighing two hundred and fifty pounds, President Solomon Mabato towered above his countrymen. His very size enhanced his awesome reputation. The man's reign seemed impregnable.

Keel pursed his lips and laid the papers to one side. Sekka was studying photographs. Colour as well as black and white prints of individuals and landmarks, with titles on the reverse side.

Head and shoulder shots of Mabato, Major Juma – head of the Department of State Security, Boma – head of

SASU, minor government ministers and officials in Mabato's corrupt Cabinet. Also army officers; many, like Mabato, sporting the Makesi tribal scars on their cheeks.

There were photographs of Mabato's official residence in Kendura, which sat a few yards away from the DOSS headquarters, and views of the army barracks, hospital, railway station, parliamentary buildings and airport. There were even some aerial shots of Mabato's hideaway; a villa in the northern territory, overlooking the village of his birth. Also maps of Kendura and the main highways and railway lines of Lugamba. It was an impressive dossier.

'We can use this stuff without any doubt,' Keel said.

Sekka glanced at his partner. 'We're going in, Thomas?'

'I didn't say that,' countered Keel.

Sekka chuckled softly. 'Come off it, Thomas. I can read you like a book. You'll accept the contract. I never doubted that for a minute.'

'Why are you so damned sure?'

'Because you are bored.'

'You mean I'm not doing it for the money?'

'Oh, there's that aspect of course but that isn't the reason. Ever since that nursemaid job with the sheik you've been craving for a chance like this. You want to get back into the action. Over these past months you've been like an addict in need of a fix. Cold turkey, my friend. Pure and simple.'

'Oh, so we're a bloody psychoanalyst now!' Keel rasped. 'I don't need you to diagnose my afflictions. I had enough of that this morning!'

'And that's the other thing,' Sekka went on, like a dog worrying a turnup. 'Why a check now? Some coincidence the morning after you get a call from a recruiter.'

'You're clutching at straws,' Keel said.

'Tell me I'm wrong.' Sekka raised his eyebrows questioningly.

Keel stared at the carpet between his feet. 'Dammit! You

know you're not wrong! I am bored. Bored out of my skull if you must know! I suppose that gives you a fair old margin of plum satisfaction?'

'Actually I'm relieved if anything,' replied Sekka.

'What?'

Sekka raised himself in a fluid movement to a sitting position. 'Relieved, Thomas, to find that your symptoms and diagnosis match mine entirely.'

'You son of a bitch!' Keel laughed. He laid a hand on Sekka's arm. 'We've come a long way together since Uzuakoli, Joseph.'

Uzuakoli was a Methodist leper settlement. It lay south of the town of Okigwa and west of the main railway line that joined Port Harcourt on the southern coast to the northern capital of Enugu. The troops of the 1st Federal Division were pushing south against the rebel positions, heading for Bende, Ojukwu's headquarters in his fight for an independent Biafra. Keel was leading forays north in an attempt to forge a link between the 1st Division and Adenkunle's commandos.

As Ojukwu's rebels pulled back from the Federal advances they did so with vigour, plundering villages and towns for food and other provisions.

Joseph Sekka's family were Hausas from the north. Sekka's father was a doctor at the leper colony. The family was wealthy and had been able to send Sekka to school and on to university. Sekka had left his roots to study in England and had taken a law degree at Cambridge. His family was immensely proud and looked forward to his visits home. He was able to see his parents two or three times each year. His father was a dedicated man and the rebellion had not made a jot of difference to his work with the lepers. Sekka often assisted him when he was home on leave from his studies.

On this particular occasion Sekka's father was visiting an

outlying community within the settlement when he was stopped by a rebel unit. The rebels stole his medical supplies and then castrated him, leaving his mutilated corpse for the buzzards, before escaping south. The remains of his body were found by an advance unit of the 3rd Commando and returned to the hospital. One hour after Joseph Sekka saw his father's corpse he made his way into the bush to the Commando Brigade's headquarters and joined up. Three days later he was acting as guide to Keel's reconnaissance group.

Keel had honed and shaped Sekka into an integral part of his squad and Sekka, fired by hate and a desire for revenge, became a natural killing machine. Keel came to rely on the man more and more and a unique and deadly partnership developed. In the months leading up to Ojukwu's surrender Sekka acquitted himself against the rebel forces with a ferocity unmatched in Keel's experience. To Keel it was as if Sekka was regressing to the basic instincts of his tribal ancestors, the warriors of the Hausa.

After the surrender in January and Keel's exit from the war, Sekka moved north to his family home. They lost touch, until Keel arrived in Rhodesia and joined the Selous Scouts and found out that it was Sekka who was leading them through the bush to pinpoint the Zambian guerilla bases. Keel had Sekka attached to his own squad on a regular basis and the old team was reactivated. When Keel left for his next contract Sekka went with him.

When Cameron came calling now, the recruiter had the expertise of a lethal team to rely on.

'Anyway, Thomas,' Sekka said, 'that's two out of four. All we have to do now is convince Harry and Paul.'

'And something tells me that we won't have to try too hard,' Keel replied.

* * *

76

Cameron had reached London and was in his office when the telephone rang.

The refined voice said: 'This is Hobson. Do you have an answer for me yet?'

'Yes and no,' Cameron answered. By the silence on the other end of the phone he had the sudden thought that he might be addressing an empty line.

'Explain.' The voice carried a distinct chill.

Cameron said carefully: 'I have outlined our requirements to my associates who have the necessary qualifications and they will give me their answer by noon tomorrow.'

'I wanted an answer now.'

'You'll have to wait. They were not prepared to be rushed into a hasty decision.'

'I could go elsewhere.'

'No you couldn't because you still wouldn't get an answer any earlier. You'll just have to be patient.'

A pause. 'Very well. I will contact you tomorrow.' The tone dropped. 'I don't suppose you could give me any indication as to what the decision might be, based on your previous dealings with these people.'

'That,' Cameron said, 'is the original sixty four thousand dollar question.'

'Well?'

'Well,' Cameron replied. 'I think you had better prepare for a raid on your piggy bank.'

Wood lifted the receiver in his home at the second ring.

'I'm experiencing a slight delay,' Dalkeith informed him. 'We'll have an answer by noon tomorrow. However, my contact did hint that there is every indication that the contract will be accepted. I suggest you pass that information to He Who Must Be Obeyed and pencil me in your appointments diary for one o'clock. We could have a spot of lunch.'

'I'll pass it on,' Wood said. He replaced the receiver. His hand, he realized, was shaking violently.

Madness, Wood thought to himself. One reckless suggestion and an idea was hatched; to recruit a mercenary force for the sole purpose of rescuing one old man from the clutches of a power crazed dictator. One old man who should have known better. Total bloody madness born out of a moment's aberration and his career was on the line.

A promising career too. Or at least it had been. Sifted from obscurity on the back benches thanks to the patronage of Arthur Lennox who had seen potential in the young David Wood. A sharp rise through the ranks of junior ministers and already a seat in the Cabinet with at least a fifteen year start on his nearest rival. Not bad for the son of a draughtsman was the thought that flitted often through Wood's mind.

Home life rewarding also; Dorothy and the boys. A family man; loving husband with devoted wife; doting parent, very much the proud father.

And still on the up and up. Patience, Dorothy frequently advised. Lennox wouldn't always be the kingpin. Wood had been groomed for stardom. He had the support of the leader and the party. He was unstoppable.

Unless he did something really stupid.

Even as George Dalkeith was relaying the news, at Schiphol KLM were announcing the arrival of their flight 124 from London. Thirty minutes later two men threaded their way through the passport controls. Each carried a canvas holdall and a leather shoulder bag. They were both very tanned and wore lightweight slacks and jackets over cool cotton open neck shirts. One was blond and very slim. His companion was stocky with thinning black hair and a heavy black moustache speckled with grey.

Leaving the terminal they approached the taxi rank

where the slim man asked in fluent Dutch for them to be taken to the Okura Hotel on Ferd Bolstraat.

The Pelican was filling up. Business was brisk and Peter Van Dijk and the three girls were doing their best to serve everyone with minimum fuss and maximum courtesy. Joseph Sekka and Keel were circulating, exchanging pleasantries with their regular customers. Keel was chatting to a plump architect and his red haired mistress when Van Dijk approached.

'A call for you, Meinheer Keel.'

Keel excused himself and walked to the bar where he picked up the telephone. 'Keel,' he said sharply.

He was rewarded with a chuckle at the end of the line.

'Your telephone manner always was abrupt, Thomas.'

Keel relaxed.

'We have arrived,' Paul Schiller said. 'See you in one hour.'

Keel caught Sekka's eye as he replaced the instrument. He could not disguise the pleasure in his voice as he said: 'They're here, Joseph.'

4

Earlier in the day David Holt, weary and grubby and fearful, had been transferred from his cell in Lubiri.

At ten o'clock that morning he had been escorted down the unlit passage to the reception block where he had been handcuffed before being taken outside to a black Range Rover. From Lubiri he was driven to Mengo District Court and left in the cells beneath the building. The cells were full to overflowing with the dregs of humanity. Drunks rubbed shoulders with pickpockets, pimps, whores and murderers. The whores were waif like and soiled and a far cry from the oiled, fleshy girls who used to haunt the lobby of the Three Moons Hotel.

Holt was the only European in custody. As he sat manacled to a sweating guard his ears were assaulted by the wails and screams of the other prisoners. A harsh cry caused him to stare to his left where a burly hard faced police sergeant was beating a cowering man across the shoulders with a thin bamboo cane. Blood was running from the victim's nose. Holt flinched at each blow and looked quickly away.

The trial was a travesty. Gaunt Nubians in casual dress listened in silence as the charge of treason was read out and the manuscript — or at least a copy — was waved in the air. Holt was given no opportunity to speak in his own defence and no counsel was provided. Neither was there a representative from the High Commissioner. Perhaps, Holt thought, they had not been told the trial was taking place.

Holt heard the verdict in silence. Guilty of course.

He was hustled back down to the cells to the taunts of

the blacks and taken to the Range Rover parked in the dust outside.

When the vehicle passed the turning to Lubiri Holt, peering through the windows, experienced a massive jolt of fear. If he had been standing his legs would surely have collapsed. He turned frantically to the guard who was picking his nose and staring over the driver's shoulder.

'Why have we turned off? Where are we going? Where are you taking me?' His voice had dropped to a tremulous whisper. 'Please.'

The guard grinned, showing ravaged gums and stubby yellow teeth. 'Maboru!' he hissed.

It had been said that the Department of State Security had taken over Maboru because of its distance from the capital. Stuck as it was on a promontory jutting like a thumb into Lake Victoria, three miles from Kendura, the prison was isolated. President Mabato would not have to suffer the screams of the inmates disturbing his sleep. It was a formidable structure, bounded on three sides by steep, rocky slopes reaching down to the lake. The main entrance was approached by a dusty road that ran at a right angle to the main highway that skirted the northern shore of Lake Victoria, linking Kendura to Nairobi and the port of Mombasa.

Half a dozen guards in army fatigues took Holt to his cell. They removed the handcuffs and his belt. As he gathered his scattered wits the tramp of his escort's boots receded down the corridor. Holt was left alone with his thoughts.

An hour later he heard voices approaching. He was on his feet, a pathetic figure clutching shirt tails and waistband while trying to maintain some semblance of dignity in the face of his captors.

Perhaps it was someone from the High Commissioner. Pray to God it was. The door swung open and a man stepped into the cell.

His excellency Al Haji Field Marshal Dr Solomon Mabato, VC, DSO, MC, President-for-Life had come to visit.

Mabato towered over Holt. Over six and a half feet tall and a hulking two hundred and fifty pounds, Solomon Mabato presented an awesome figure. Grossly bloated with a head the size of a large black melon, his piggy eyes glared at Holt for several seconds. The tribal scars stood out on his cheek like vivid tram lines. He was in uniform. Medal ribbons traced across his chest in splendid array. He held a fly switch in one hand and swatted abstractedly around his head as he studied the wretched man before him. Then he smiled. Holt felt his stomach curdle.

Holt, still clutching his waistband in clammy hands, watched mesmerized as Mabato tapped his clenched knuckles with the fly switch.

'Drop the trousers,' Mabato said.

Holt responded by clutching his waistband even tighter. This was not the reply Mabato desired. He tapped Holt Holt again.

'Drop the trousers.' Sharper this time.

Holt, despite himself, felt his lower lip quiver. Again a tap on his hand with the cane. Slowly Holt let the material slip through his tingling fingers. He was aware of his trousers sliding over his bony hips and down his thighs to collect in a huddle at his feet. Mabato looked on as though bored with the procedure. Holt, although wearing under-pants, cupped his hands together to protect his groin.

Almost inevitably Mabato tapped his hands again.

'Now these,' he said.

'Please . . .' Holt pleaded.

'Now!' hissed Mabato.

Holt tucked shaking fingers into the top of his under-pants and rolled them down to join his slacks around his ankles. The tears began to trickle down his cheeks.

The switch flicked down to his genitals. Using the end of the cane Mabato touched the tip of Holt's member. Holt's body jerked at the feel. The cane lifted Holt's penis.

Mabato said: 'You are afraid, my friend. That is good. If you told me that you were not afraid then you would be a liar. Do you know how I deal with liars, Mister Holt? I will tell you. When I was fighting the Mau Mau with the King's African Rifles my officers were very impressed with my skill at making prisoners reveal where they had hidden their weapons. I would put a long table in the middle of the room. When the prisoners were brought before me I would order each man to place his manhood on the table. I would say to them "Where are your spears?" They would always answer "We have no spears."' Mabato smiled grotesquely. 'But my panga was very sharp, Mister Holt. I would hold it high and ask them again and then of course they would tell me. Sometimes I would use the first man in line as an example, you understand?'

The fly switch let Holt's penis drop. Mabato said: 'Now, Mister Holt, never lie to me.'

Mabato turned on his heel and ducked through the doorway. Holt was alone again.

With his trousers and underpants still around his feet David Holt sank back on his haunches and folded his arms about his knees. Tears flowed down his cheeks as he rocked himself backwards and forwards like a small child alone in his nursery after a scolding from his nanny.

Paul Schiller and Harry Roan looked stunned. The Lugamba dossier was on the table before them. They were in the apartment above the Pelican.

'That's one heck of a job, Thomas,' Roan said, stroking his moustache thoughtfully. Only the slightest trace of a drawl betrayed his Memphis origins and a boyhood spent largely on his grandfather's knee, listening with rapt attention to the old man's tales of the con men and gamblers, heroes and villains who plied their trade on the broad decks and in the plush saloons of the big Dixie paddle steamers that threshed their way up and down the Mississippi River.

Roan was to recall often the old man's words as he plied his own deadly trade along the creeks and sandbanks of another great river half a world away; the Mekong. When he'd been part of a DELTA recon team, Roan and his unit had used hovercraft to patrol the river and its tributaries.

Roan had met Keel when the latter, along with Iain Cameron, had been involved in the operations of the Special Forces Search and Destroy teams in the jungles of Cambodia and Laos. They operated out of Bien Hoa, the United States tactical air base a grenade lob north of Saigon.

They called it the Parrot's Beak; a twenty-five by thirty mile rectangle of Cambodian territory extending into South Vietnam to the west of Saigon. An area of rough country, dirt roads, ragged hamlets, bisected by the main highway linking Saigon to the Cambodian capital, Phnom Penh. Here, around the border region and along the banks of the Mekong, were located Viet Cong sanctuaries, long considered inviolate to US forces. Officially.

It was in this type of country that Roan and Keel and men of the Special Forces units, assisted by Montagnard tribesmen, fought a guerilla campaign against the NVA. It was brutal and bloody with no quarter given or expected. Any thought of conventional warfare was ignored in the struggle. Roan's side took the war to the enemy, becoming like the VC; engaging in terror tactics, hit and run strikes, always on the move, living rough off the land, surviving like animals.

Their missions across the border were classified as 'sterile'. The men were instilled with total light and noise discipline – all moving parts of their rifles taped down and trigger guards removed for ease of firing. Unit members wore manufactured replicas of North Vietnamese uniforms with captured gear and weapons. All of them were without identification. Sometimes they carried cards stating that they were working for military intelligence but on certain forays even these flimsy means of ID were abandoned. If they were killed or captured in compromising localities the US disavowed all knowledge of their actions, sometimes even of their existence. They were maverick units. On their own. Isolated.

Vietnam, someone once said, was a brutal Neverneverland where boys didn't have to grow up. They just grew old before their time. Roan had seen many of his buddies grow up rapidly. He had also seen many of them die. By the end of the war, looking back on it all, he considered that maybe the most worthwhile part of the experience was the fact that he had lived through it. That and the fact that the skills he had acquired had no place in civilian life. And it was by virtue of the type of service Roan had seen that made it impossible for him to accept the discipline required in peacetime soldiering. There was only one solution. Freelance.

He and Keel were ideally matched. Roan's inherent good nature and his homely accent belied his impressive record in combat. He was an intelligent, quick thinking operative and the bond of friendship had been cemented early.

Paul Schiller studied the maps and photographs and narrowed his eyes as smoke from his thin cheroot rose before his youthful face like mystical vapours.

Schiller had been a member of the West German GSG-9 anti-terrorist squad formed under Ulrich Wegener shortly after the Black September attack on the Israeli athletes at the Munich Olympics. He had been among the team that had stormed the Lufthansa 737 at Mogadishu and so was experienced in operating within the confines of a small unit. He had put his skill to good effect when, following his resignation from GSG-9, he had become a mercenary and joined the Rhodesian Light Infantry. He had met up with Keel and Sekka during raids into Mozambique. When Harry Roan joined with them in the summer of 1978 the team was complete. Now, whenever possible, on a contract requiring an active service unit, the four of them worked together, with Iain Cameron as broker.

'What interests me more than anything, Thomas, is the person putting up the money,' Sekka said.

'Cameron figured on a business cartel with this man Hobson acting as go-between.' Keel reached for the half empty bottle of 'Johnnie Walker Black Label that stood on the table by his elbow and poured himself two fingers. 'Iain Cameron's a shrewd operator and I'm inclined to rely on his intuition on this one. Whoever they are, they have funds behind them. Let's face it, we don't come cheap.'

'What's the rate for this one, Thomas?' asked Schiller.

'Twenty five thousand sterling per man plus expenses. Including Cameron's cut that would total one hundred and thirty thousand – give or take.'

'I'd be less than honest if I didn't say that I think the contract is a bitch,' Harry Roan said candidly.

Keel addressed Schiller. 'What about you, Paul?'

Schiller shrugged. 'We've had difficult contracts before. The Sorgensen job for one. Now, that one was a bitch.'

Schiller was referring to the time, two years before, when they had been hired to find and free a Swedish businessman being held by Tupamaros guerillas in Salto, Uruguay. The job had been tricky and they had been lucky to bring it off.

'Yeah and I've still got the scars to prove it,' Roan grimaced. He massaged his left arm abstractedly. A livid puckered weal ran from wrist to elbow. It showed whitely against his tan.

'I thought you got that running for a bus,' Sekka said.

'Smartass!' Roan laughed.

'So?' Keel looked at each of them in turn. 'We've read Cameron's dossier. He wants an answer. What'll it be?'

Not that there was ever any doubt in his mind.

'Dalkeith has done very well, David,' Arthur Lennox said. 'Better than I expected in the time available.' He studied the bowl of his pipe intently and then sucked violently on the stem. 'The problem of course is the fee.'

'The amount?'

'I was thinking about the source. Where's it going to come from?'

They were in the Commons, in the Prime Minister's room behind the Speaker's chair.

'I've been considering that,' Wood answered. 'I might have found a solution.'

Lennox narrowed his eyes. 'Go on, David.'

'I was chatting to Callum St Clair, one of the secretaries at the Treasury, two days ago and just in passing he mentioned the Merrison Report.'

What that had to do with a mercenary contract fee, Lennox couldn't begin to guess. The report was the result of a government enquiry into mental health facilities.

'I'm not with you. The report was published ages ago and the committee disbanded. I don't see the connection.'

'Let me finish. St Clair was saying that although the Merrison Committee was disbanded after the enquiry, the central fund, due to a bureaucratic balls-up, was not liquidated.' Wood paused and studied the expression on Lennox's craggy face. 'I can see you're way ahead of me.'

'How much?' Lennox said slowly.

'A shade over two hundred thousand,' Wood replied. 'Sitting there doing nothing except gathering mildew.'

'Christ!' Lennox looked hard at the Foreign Secretary. 'How are we going to deal with it?'

'I believe the word we are looking for is launder. This has got to be a job for Dalkeith. He could use SIS fronts. A transfer here, a transfer there . . .'

'I hope this isn't going to get out of hand.'

'You want to abort?'

Lennox shook his head. 'No. We need irons in the fire.'

'Well, one iron's ready,' said Wood.

'Oh?'

'I had another call from Garrick Kirby this morning. He's very keen to help out.'

'Fine,' Lennox said. 'Well, this is his big chance then.' He reached over his desk and picked up a buff quarto sized envelope. 'I have here one letter signed by Herself and yours truly, delivered by winged messenger this very day. Tell Garrick Kirby to pack his jammies. I want him on the next plane to Lugamba. This will tell us how keen he is to play diplomat.'

'I'll get on to it right away. By the way, there will be two of them.'

'Good God! He's not taking his bloody wife!' Lennox nearly dropped his pipe. 'This isn't a holiday!'

'His aide. A Major Garside. Garrick Kirby asked if it would be in order. Garside is also acquainted with Mabato. A twin barrel-led attack might be more effective.'

'Very well,' Lennox sighed. 'But that's it, David. He's not taking any camp followers. Just the two of them.'

'There's a flight out this afternoon. Sabena to Brussels and then a connection to Kendura via Nairobi. They'll be there first thing tomorrow morning, barring fog at Heathrow or a hi-jacking.' Wood kept a straight face as he spoke.

'Don't tempt fate,' Lennox said curtly. 'Things are bad enough without that. Keep me posted and no word to the press just yet.'

'Naturally,' Wood nodded. He paused at the door. 'Let's hope we won't have to rely on plan B, Prime Minister.'

'Amen to that,' said Lennox.

Dalkeith was perturbed and said as much to Wood over lunch. By this time he had been in touch with Cameron and had passed on to the Foreign Secretary the decision to accept the contract.

'What's your problem?' Wood asked brusquely. He concentrated on squeezing lemon juice over his Dover Sole.

'The problem,' Dalkeith said icily, 'is that the contract has been accepted and now you tell me that you're sending two envoys out to Lugamba to mediate. What the hell am I supposed to tell my link man now? Forget it? Go home?'

'Look George, if this mission succeeds we won't need to use these . . . individuals. I'd rather avoid that if possible.'

'These men won't wait indefinitely for Christ's sake. If they are to be effective in any way they are going to have to move soon. Surely you can see that? How long before we know if we'll need them?'

'I think we'll know twenty four hours after the envoys get to Kendura.'

'I think we'll lose valuable time if we wait much longer,' Dalkeith said. 'I suggest we give the team the go ahead.'

'Not while Garrick Kirby is in Lugamba for Christ's sake!' The Dover Sole remained untasted. 'Use your head, man!'

Dalkeith seethed at the rebuke. 'So what do you suggest?'

'I suggest you contact your man and come up with a game plan. Something feasible based on the outcome of

Garrick Kirby's plea for clemency. If the envoys fail we send the men in.'

Dalkeith admitted to himself that it made sense to place the team on standby. There was, after all, a remote possibility that Garrick Kirby's trip might pay off.

'Very well,' Dalkeith said. 'I'll pass it on and let you know.'

'That's right, George.' Wood speared a sliver of fish. 'You do that.' He dabbed his lips with his napkin and eyed Dalkeith warily. 'About the Merrison fund, George. Any progress?'

'What Merrison fund?' Dalkeith's face was a picture of innocent inquiry. 'That's been liquidated. For quite some time I believe.'

Wood, very wisely, took the hint and decided not to pursue the matter. What he didn't know wouldn't hurt him. At least that's what he thought.

Dalkeith arranged the meeting with the recruiter.

Cameron rested his elbows on the parapet and gazed out over the Serpentine. The water was calm except for the erratic splashing of the rowers in the blue and yellow rowboats. There was a flash of oar as an orange kayak jinked out of the path of one of the rowers, its occupant looking like a hunchback in his bright life jacket. On the bank, weeping willows drooped sad fronds into the water's edge and ducks waddled backwards and forwards in formation, like ratings on parade. Behind him, au pairs trundled their squalling charges over the bridge in prams, like district nurses at the wheels of their Morris Minors.

He pushed his hands into the deep pockets of his burberry and from the corner of his eye studied Dalkeith's approach along the path. The latter was wearing a dark trenchcoat and bowler and carried a black brief case. He walked to the parapet and joined Cameron.

'So much more pleasant than your office, don't you agree?' Dalkeith said. He looked down to the water and watched a laughing youth attempting to retrieve an oar that had dropped over the side of his boat. The lad's girlfriend was giggling helplessly and splashing him with water as he balanced precariously over the gunwale.

Cameron agreed to the tentative game plan.

The team would fly out to Nairobi and wait for word from Cameron as to whether they should proceed with the rescue. He asked Dalkeith how long they might have to wait.

'Forty-eight hours max.'

Cameron nodded. 'That'll give my men time to equip and get into position.' He added: 'And the contract will cost you one hundred and thirty thousand. Half up front and the remainder if and when Holt is in Nairobi.'

'Agreed.'

Cameron stood with his back to the lake as he watched Dalkeith walk away towards Hyde Park Corner. He also spotted the lone figure in a leather jacket and faded jeans detaching itself from one of the park benches and following Dalkeith along the path. Iain Cameron grunted in satisfaction and strolled across Rotten Row in the direction of Sloane Street and his office. He wanted to get back there in order to take the telephone call.

But one detail nagged at Cameron. The man he knew as Hobson had hinted that a diplomatic mission was in progress. Two envoys would be leaving for Lugamba to try and secure Holt's release. Cameron's involvement would hinge on the results of the mission. Interesting that Hobson knew about that when neither the lunchtime editions nor the radio news bulletins had carried so much as a hint of the story. So, how did he know? Unless he had friends in high places. Or something . . .

In his office, Cameron ignored the first buzz of the telephone.

'Thought I might have missed you.' The hushed voice carried the rasp of damaged vocal cords.

'You didn't,' Cameron replied. 'What have you got for me, Frank?'

A chuckle at the end of the line. 'That had to be one of the easiest jobs you ever gave me, Mister Cameron. He hadn't a clue he was being tagged.' There was a brief pause. Cameron heard the click of a lighter and the sound of a man drawing on a cigarette.

'So?' Cameron prompted. 'What else?'

'I followed him to a car park. The big underground one.'

'And?'

'He got into his car and buggered off. I couldn't follow him. I'd no wheels of my own.' The hoarse voice sounded disgruntled.

'No matter.' Cameron reached for a pad and pen. 'Make and registration?'

'Rover. Dark blue. Two years old.'

'Number?'

Cameron wrote down the registration as it was relayed.

The line crackled. The noise was followed by a sudden bout of coughing. Cameron jerked the receiver away from his ear. Frank found his voice. 'You there, Mister Cameron?'

'Still hanging on, Frank. Good work. I appreciate it.'

'Anytime, Mister Cameron. You know where to find me.'

'You bet. Take care, Frank. Oh, and one other thing.'

'Mister Cameron?'

'Not a word to anyone. Stumm on this one. Got it?'

A sigh. 'Do me a favour, Mister Cameron!'

Cameron grinned. 'I know, Frank. Cheerio. Be good.'

The switchboard operator at New Scotland Yard sounded bored when she asked Cameron which extension he required.

'CID, love. Detective Sergeant Macraig.'

'Hold the line.'

Cameron tapped his fingers on his desk and stared thoughtfully at the number he had jotted down.

'Macraig.' The voice was nasal, carrying the hint of a Scottish burr that had been tempered by years in the south and dealings with a wide cross section of the capital's murky underworld.

'Alec? It's Iain Cameron. Fancy a jar?'

'Iain! Ah, music to my ears but I've an in-tray that looks like the side of Ben Nevis.'

'I need a favour, Alec. What time can you get away?'

'About a week on Tuesday, but as a special dispensation I can fit you in about eight thirty tonight. Make it the Pheasant and mine is a pint of Special and a whisky chaser. What's it about then?'

'Not over the phone.'

'Okay. In that case I'll see you later. Set 'em up.'

'Done,' Cameron said.

In the VIP lounge in Terminal Two a small group of men waited patiently for the departure of the Sabena flight to Brussels. The group comprised the Sabena passenger services manager and the terminal security officer as well as Lt General Richard Garrick Kirby, Major Robert Garside and Gavin Niall from the Foreign Office.

Garrick Kirby was a tall man with a receding grey hairline, a weathered face with calm brown eyes and a humorous curve to his lips. Garside was dark and saturnine. They were both dressed in conservative light-

93

weight suits. Garside carried a brown, leather attaché case.

Niall looked at his watch. 'Not long now, gentlemen.' He glanced at the Sabena manager. 'Your staff have been briefed of course?'

Niall was in his early thirties. His blond hair was parted in the centre and combed back over his ears and collar. He wore a pair of large tortoiseshell framed spectacles and looked ever so slightly like a condescending owl.

The Sabena man – Rawlings, efficient and dapper – smiled with enthusiasm. 'Yes indeed, we're all set. We'll board you shortly, General. Before the other passengers of course.'

Garrick Kirby nodded, anxious to be off.

Niall said: 'The Sabena people will ensure a smooth connection, sir. You'll have about a fifty minute transit but should there be a delay blocking at Brussels, the on-going flight will be held.'

Rawlings confirmed Niall's prediction and catching the eye of the gaunt security officer, he announced it was time for the envoys to board the aircraft.

Niall extended his hand. 'Well, this is it. Have a safe trip, sir, and good luck to you both. We'll be keeping our fingers crossed over here.'

They shook hands and the general and his aide turned to leave. Niall hesitated.

'One last thing, sir – '

Garrick Kirby raised an eyebrow and Garside looked on expectantly. Niall's face remained passive.

'For Christ's sake,' he said. 'Don't lose the bloody letter!'

There was the briefest of pauses. Garrick Kirby smiled.

'Don't you worry, my boy. Major Garside has it safe and sound.' He glanced at Garside. 'Right Bob?'

Garside's face dropped. 'Er – actually, sir, I thought I gave it to you.'

Niall's insides did a double flip. A brief vision of himself sifting through a billion motor tax application forms in darkest Swansea flashed through his mind. He was aware of Garside grinning at his discomfort, and he flushed in response and swung away angrily. He had the distinct impression that he could still hear Garrick Kirby chuckling as he walked back through the terminal towards the spot where Hanson, the ministry chauffeur, had parked the limousine.

Niall hoped the airline wouldn't screw things up. They had used Sabena because the British Airways cabin crews were on strike and Sabena, in any case, was one of only two airlines – neither of them British – that operated scheduled services to Kendura out of European capitals.

Hanson dropped the *Daily Mirror* as Niall emerged from the terminal and opened his door.

Niall waved him back. 'It's okay, John, I've got it.'

He opened the rear door and slid into the Jaguar. Hanson took them down the ramp and into the tunnel, en route to the M4.

By nine o'clock the Pheasant was filling up and there was still no sign of Macraig. Cameron was sitting in the corner nursing a screwdriver with Macraig's order on the table in front of him. He tried to avoid the barmaid's eye as she sought to attract his attention by thrusting her chest across the bar.

Most of the early evening punters had pushed off home to their congealed Bisto and the last five minutes of *Dallas* and the second string were beginning to saunter in for their tipples; husbands escaping from wives and drunks from reality.

Macraig arrived three minutes past the hour looking harassed but not apologetic. 'Got held up' were his only words. It seemed the inspector was having one of his purges.

He was a big man with a florid complexion and a bald head, high domed and freckled like a song thrush's breast. His hands were huge and heavily mottled and covered with fine red hair. The forefinger and middle finger of his right hand were stained with nicotine and as he sat down he flicked a cigarette from a packet of Stuyvesant with practised ease. He sank half the pint and the Scotch before asking Cameron the reason for the meeting.

Cameron flicked a page from a notebook across the table, avoiding the puddles of beer, in which the coasters sat like stepping stones.

'I'd like you to run a check on this number, Alec. Find out who owns the car.'

Macraig blew a cloud of cigarette smoke into the air. 'You've got a bloody nerve.' He picked up the piece of paper. 'Got me here under false pretences.'

'I didn't get you here under any pretence. I told you I had a favour to ask. This is it.'

'Aye, so you did.' Macraig looked less than impressed. 'I don't suppose you'd like to enlighten me at all? I mean this is a real no-no, Iain. You realize that?' He peered at the registration number. A corner of the paper grazed a puddle of lager and the ink was beginning to run. He blew on it and said: 'I suppose if I told you to get stuffed you'd only remind me that I owe you one.'

Cameron's good eye glittered. 'You've got it. You got your stripes because of the tip-off I gave you.'

'As you never cease to remind me,' Macraig said heavily.

Macraig was referring to the murder of an underworld gang boss. The contract, carried out on behalf of a rival crime lord, had been the work of two sometime mercenaries who had needed ready money. Cameron, through contacts in the mercenary hierarchy, had passed the names of the two killers to an ex-army colleague turned police-man – Alec Macraig. The two men had been cornered in a tiny flat in Bayswater. Like rats in a trap the killers had turned and fought, attempting to shoot their way out. Two policemen were wounded before Macraig battered his way in. One of the mercenaries died with a bullet in the throat and the other, confronted with the huge figure of Macraig brandishing his revolver with all the panache of Wyatt Earp at the OK Corral, surrendered with alacrity. Macraig had inevitably received commendations and sub-sequent promotion.

Cameron smiled. 'Thanks, Alec. I knew I could depend on you.'

'Yeah, like a fucking crutch,' Macraig said. He drained the rest of his beer. 'Seeing as I'm here, I suppose you'd like another dram?'

'I wouldn't want to put you to any trouble,' Cameron said.

There was quite a crowd in the pub now. Macraig got to his feet and shouldered his way through the scrum towards the bar. Cameron noticed that not many people obstructed the big man's passage. Macraig returned to the table with his hands full and a thumb in his chaser.

He sat down, flicked another Stuyvesant into his mouth and lit up. He narrowed his eyes and picked a shred of tobacco from his lower lip. 'Got something on then, have you, Iain? A contract is it?'

'Nothing definite,' Cameron answered guardedly. 'Just irons in the fire at the moment.'

'I see and how much difference will it make, knowing who owns the motor?'

'I can't answer that, Alec,' Cameron replied truthfully.

'Aye, well I'll see what I can find out anyway.'

They stayed in the pub until closing time. By then the bar was virtually empty and Cameron was feeling quite mellow. Alec Macraig pushed a cigarette stub into a beer puddled and watched it sizzle.

'I don't know about you, man, but I could murder a curry. The Star of Bengal's just around the corner. What d'you say?'

'Why not?' Cameron finished his drink in one swallow and followed Macraig out of the pub.

Paul Schiller had phoned Air France and made reservations on the flight to Paris and the connection to Kendura via Athens and Nairobi. There was no direct flight from Amsterdam and the flight from Brussels to Nairobi was full.

Roan had been wondering where they would pick up their equipment; in particular firearms as there wasn't a snowball's chance in hell that they could carry weapons with them.

Keel told them that they would obtain everything they needed from Mendoza in Nairobi. The Portuguese could provide anything – if the price was right.

'They wouldn't let me see him,' James Henderson said angrily, polishing his spectacles feverishly. He replaced them on his nose and stared at Warren-Chase speculatively. 'They wouldn't even let me into the bloody gaol.'

'Bastards!' Warren-Chase muttered. He looked dishevelled, like a man who had gone without sleep for some time. 'What time are the dynamic duo arriving?'

'Nine forty, sir.'

'What's the betting their bloody bags end up in Hong Kong,' Warren-Chase growled. 'I take it His Excellency has been informed of their arrival in the morning? Bearing tidings from the Great White Queen from over the water.'

'He knows,' Henderson said.

'Of course, James, it's not that I doubt your competence. I'm under a great deal of strain, you understand.'

'We all are, sir.'

Warren-Chase grimaced. 'All right, James. I asked for that. Point taken. Things could be worse. I could be David Holt.'

5

Engines screaming like a dying hyena, the Sabena 707 rolled to a halt and a handful of passengers vacated their seats and reached into the overhead lockers for their belongings.

In the first class section, Garside, who had the window seat, remarked: 'I don't see any welcoming committee.'

Garrick Kirby straightened his tie and smoothed his hair. 'No sign of Himself?'

'Not yet.'

A stewardess with splendid legs and a fixed smile approached down the aisle. 'You may disembark, gentlemen.'

'Thank you, my dear.' Garrick Kirby glanced at Garside. 'Well, Bob. This is it.'

They walked to the open door of the aircraft and looked out over the steps. Half a dozen passengers were walking slowly across the tarmac to the grubby terminal building.

Most of the airport facilities had been built by the Israelis but since their expulsion had been ill maintained. Half a mile away three MiG 15 fighters stood like metal ants against a boundary fence; an open indication of Lugamba's political ties. Fire tenders and fuel tankers were parked haphazardly about. There seemed to be scant evidence of order or discipline. The whole area looked unkempt and run down.

The sky was a cloudless light blue. There was no breeze and the air was heavy with kerosene fumes. Garrick Kirby, standing at the top of the boarding steps in full dress uniform, could feel the sweat trickling down from his armpits that were already beginning to itch abominably. He felt sure he cut a ludicrous figure and cursed at what appeared to be Mabato's weak sense of humour at demanding that the envoys should arrive in Lugamba in such flamboyant attire.

'Hell!' Garside muttered, as he emerged into the sunshine. 'And it's only mid morning!'

Garrick Kirby was aware of a small huddle of men waiting at the foot of the steps. No sign of the President though. He felt a stab of concern at this.

One of the group broke away and moved forward as Garrick Kirby's foot hit the tarmac.

'Good morning. I'm Anthony Warren-Chase,' announced the tall balding man quickly. 'I have the misfortune to be the Acting High Commissioner. I don't have to ask who you are.' He smiled readily, aware of Garrick Kirby's discomfort in the constricting uniform. They shook hands and Garside was introduced. The two envoys viewed Warren-Chase's lightweight white suit with envy.

Warren-Chase lowered his voice conspiratorially. 'Er – as you may have gathered, His Exellency is not here. Naturally, he sends his er – regrets and trusts you will accept his apology. He has seen fit to delegate Brigadier Epunau to receive you and escort you during the inspection.'

Warren-Chase ushered the envoys towards the waiting group. Brigadier Lucius Epunau was a short unintelligent looking individual with a double chin and a blank gaze that suggested he was unused to such ceremony, however superficial. His handshake was a limp gesture. Warren-Chase also introduced Joshua Nkuto, the Foreign Minister; a grave man dressed in a grey pinstripe suit. He also sported an Eton tie which, Garrick Kirby felt, must surely have been purchased second hand. He wore heavy framed sun glasses. Garrick Kirby glimpsed himself in the reflection. It was like being introduced to a zombie; the walking dead.

'Good grief!' Garside couldn't help himself.

Garrick Kirby swung around. To his amazement he too found himself staring at a phalanx of men standing rigidly to attention some yards away from the aircraft, like toy soldiers. Mabato had provided a guard of honour.

And a band.

Trumpets, trombones, tubas sparkling and glinting in the sunshine. The bandmaster, baton raised expectantly, stared back at the two British Army officers.

'Great Scot!' Garrick Kirby exclaimed. 'They're wearing kilts!' He seemed totally nonplussed, faced with the bizarre spectacle of thirty or so negro musicians togged up in what looked suspiciously like Black Watch tartan.

Garrick Kirby closed his eyes and reopened them slowly. Maybe it was some strange mirage.

No such luck. They were still there; instruments poised.

Warren-Chase said throatily: 'I take it you are ready to inspect the guard of honour?'

Garrick Kirby nodded wearily and turned to look for the brigadier. He surprised the latter idly scratching his crotch and looked to Warren-Chase frantically for some semblance of normality. Garside looked equally stunned but he managed to drag Warren-Chase to one side.

'What the hell is this? The Old Man's ready to tear somebody's head off!' He indicated Epunau. 'If that guy's the brigadier, the pope's Jewish!'

'Recently promoted,' Warren-Chase said.

'From what? Corporal?'

'Close,' Warren-Chase said. 'He was Mabato's driver two weeks ago.'

'Jesus effing Christ!' Garside looked horrified as Epunau jammed a finger in his left ear and wiggled it around experimentally.

'He doesn't speak English either, by way of an encore.'

'You do surprise me!'

Garrick Kirby looked around for his aide. 'Get us out of this pantomime.'

'Er . . . the inspection,' Warren-Chase stuttered. The brigadier was now exploring his other ear.

Joshua Nkuto stepped forward and said in faultless English: 'Perhaps you would care to follow me, General?'

Garrick Kirby composed his features into a mask. 'Of course.'

Such an Alice in Wonderland situation. Lt General Garrick Kirby, accompanied by an unsmiling government minister and a half witted brigadier, approached the guard of honour and the band struck up the tune 'Tea for Two'.

Maybe it's all a terrible dream, Garside tried to persuade himself, and he'd wake up on the parade ground at Aldershot.

Unfortunately it wasn't a dream. Both Garside and Garrick Kirby finished the inspection in a daze. The brigadier, all pretence at sophistication cast aside like an old coat, stomped off to the terminal building followed by Nkuto.

'We're being dangled like puppets on a bloody string,' said Garside angrily.

'Why, of course.' Warren-Chase was surprised that the major had even seen fit to voice such an obvious fact. 'Mabato's simply laying down the ground rules. He has us exactly where he wants us, like a cat playing with a sparrow.'

'So, what do we do now?' Garside asked. 'Twiddle our thumbs?'

'All right, Bob. Simmer down. Getting steamed up won't help matters. Especially in this damned heat. God! I'd forgotten how hot it could be out here.' Garrick Kirby wiped his brow with his handkerchief and then he wiped the headband of his cap. 'You're the expert, Warren-Chase. What do you suggest?'

'Play it cool. No pun intended. There isn't much else you can do. I don't have to explain to you the delicacy of the situation.'

'Quite,' Garside said icily. 'Do you think we could get out of the sun. My scalp's beginning to grill.'

'My God, yes!' Warren-Chase said apologetically. 'The car's waiting. We'll see to your bags of course.' He pointed to Garside's attaché case. 'I presume the Word is in that?'

'On tablets of clay,' Garside said. He'd forgotten he'd been holding the document. The case had become part of him during the trip, he'd grown so used to carrying it.

They walked towards the terminal.

'I suppose Mabato will summon us when he's ready,' Garrick Kirby said to the Acting High Commissioner as he matched him step for step across the tarmac.

'Oh, don't you worry about that,' Warren-Chase answered. 'It'll be soon enough. By the way, you'll both be staying at my place for the duration of your trip, I had the idea it might be convenient.'

'I'm sure we will be very comfortable,' Garrick Kirby said.

'Excellent,' Warren-Chase continued. 'Now let's get you out of the midday sun. I'm convinced Coward had this place in mind when he composed the song, despite what everyone else says. Anyway, I should think you'd like to rest up after your flight?'

'Yes indeed. We didn't get much sleep on the way down but then I've always found it difficult to nod off on an aircraft.'

'I know the feeling, General. Let's go. If anything breaks, I'll let you know. Until then there isn't a lot we can do except await Mabato's pleasure.'

'Oh wonderful,' said Garside.

Alec Macraig looked distinctly worried. Cameron waited for him to speak. It was lunchtime and they were back in the Pheasant. The customers were mostly business men and there was no sign of the overendowed barmaid, Cameron was happy to note.

'I'm not sure . . .' Macraig began.

'Well?'

'Either you gave me the wrong number . . .'

'No chance.'

'Or . . . you're in trouble. I hope it's the first alternative.'

Cameron felt the first twinges of apprehension. There was no mistaking the concern in Macraig's voice.

'The registration was correct,' he said.

Macraig pursed his lips. 'What are you up to, Iain?'

'Don't hedge, Alec. What's the matter?'

'You're the one who is hedging, mate. I asked you a question.'

'Look, all I've done is ask you to run a registration check for me. Why the third degree? You aren't normally this inquisitive.'

'This one is different.' Macraig lit a Stuyvesant.

'How?'

Macraig sighed. 'The number you gave me is rather special. The car is a pool vehicle. It doesn't belong to an individual.'

'So what's the name of the firm?'

'It isn't a firm.'

'I'm not with you. You just said – '

'I don't know what game you're playing, Iain, but – '

'For fuck's sake, Alec!'

'The car is one of a pool of vehicles used by senior executive officers at the Ministry of Defence. Christ, they'd have my balls if they knew I was telling you this.'

'What department?' asked Cameron.

'I don't know.'

'Like hell!'

'But I can make a guess. I used a contact in Special Branch and I had the impression I was being blocked. And that frightens me.'

'How did you cover anyway?'

'I hinted that the car had been spotted in a tow away zone and told them that next time they'd have to pay to get it out. I was told to shove it. It wasn't a hint so much as a warning. You know what I mean?'

'So what do you think?'

'I think,' Macraig said slowly, 'that your chap is attached to the funny men.'

'Intelligence!'

Macraig shrugged noncommittally. 'It's only an opinion.'

'Policeman's hunch?'

Macraig allowed himself the briefest of smiles. 'If you like.'

Cameron was silent. His mind was racing. This was not what he had expected. How was he going to deal with it? He said carefully: 'Alec, if I asked you to try and find out who used the car on a certain date, could you find out?'

'You're bloody joking! I've been warned off once. These blokes don't frig around. They play tough, dirty games. I don't intend to become a punchbag on your behalf. Not for all the Scotch in Ardnamurchan!'

Cameron was surprised at Macraig's vehemence.

The policeman's eyes narrowed. 'Iain, what the hell is going on?'

'I don't know yet.' Cameron stood up. 'Don't let it worry you, Alec. I appreciate your help. I'll be in touch.'

'You mean that's it?'

'Oh, no,' Cameron said. 'That's not it. Not by a long chalk.'

'So?'

'So thanks for the drink, Alec.'

Macraig watched, stupefied, as Cameron walked out of the pub. The big man waited ten minutes before making his exit. And just what was Iain Cameron up to? The question nagged him as he walked down the street towards an in-tray that still looked like Ben Nevis.

'What sort of photographs, Mister Cameron?' Cigarette smoke curled up before Frank's narrowed eyes. 'Birds?'

'I'm afraid not, old son. We'll leave that to David Bailey.'

'So, who do I take pictures of?'

'Me,' Cameron said.

'Eh?' Frank's jaw dropped.

'Well, me and someone else actually.'

'Porn? You and a bird? I don't know about that, Mister Cameron.' Frank started to shake his head.

'Easy, Frank. You're letting your imagination run riot.'

'Thank God for that. I wouldn't have been able to hold the bloody camera still anyway.'

They were seated at a formica topped table in a tiny and moderately unhygienic establishment off Leicester Square. A bottle of HP sauce, a sugar dispenser and a red plastic tomato stood between them along with two chipped cups containing scummy tea. Cameron, in donkey jacket, and Frank in his windcheater and jeans were the most respect-able looking customers. For the most part the tables were occupied by grubby little men in gaberdine raincoats. Bank messengers or strip club touts taking a lunch hour.

Frank Ketch was a leg-man and sometime-minder. His patch was strictly up market; Soho and the West End clubs. He was in his early thirties, not tall but well built with hair almost as dark as Iain Cameron's. He had an olive – almost Latin – complexion which he used to great advantage around the clubs. He was rarely short of female companionship.

His mutilated larynx was the result of a club brawl in which Ketch, in his role of minder cum bouncer, had had a difference of opinion with a brace of football supporters. In the melee a broken chair leg had smashed against his throat. The soccer thugs, however, had been taken away in an ambulance. They had been discharged from the hospital after a week and Ketch figured they had got off lightly. Ketch was an ex-marine.

He performed odd jobs for a lot of people. Cameron was one of them.

'Let me explain,' Cameron went on. The tea looked rancid. He pushed the cup away with a grimace. 'I'm going to meet someone and all you have to do is take a few shots of us. Preferably without the other person knowing anything about it.'

'So much for the commissions from *Mayfair* and *Penthouse*,' Ketch said. 'Just my bleeding luck!'

'Maybe next time.' Cameron grinned.

'What about a camera? I don't even have an instamatic.'

'No problem. I'll supply that. It'll have a good lens too so you won't have to poke it up our noses. All you'll have to do is point it and press the tit, without being bloody obvious about it. Capiche?'

'Capiche, Mister Cameron.'

Thomas Keel, Harry Roan and Paul Schiller had arrived in Nairobi, where they had booked themselves into the Intercontinental on the Uhuru Highway and City Hall Way.

Joseph Sekka had travelled on the same Air France flight

but as the aircraft continued on to Kendura he had remained on board. This had been decided before leaving Amsterdam. Sekka would be able to move around more freely than the others – for obvious reasons – and reconnoitre.

It was pointless for all of them to proceed before it was confirmed that the mission was on. Keel, Roan and Schiller would remain in Nairobi and await word from Iain Cameron via cable from London. If the snatch was on they would fly in and team up with Sekka. The latter would wait four days. If the others hadn't sent word in that time he would board a plane and fly back to Kenya, the mission aborted.

While in Nairobi Keel would have the opportunity and time to obtain the equipment they would need. It was the best plan they could come up with in the time allowed.

Joseph Sekka, in sports shirt and grey slacks, gazed thoughtfully out of the rear windows of the battered Mercedes as he was transported noisily from Kendura airport to the International Hotel in the centre of the city. The driver changed gear erratically and more than once Sekka had to grab the well used strap above the window to avoid bouncing over the neck of the driver.

Although there had only been a dozen or so passengers entering the country, the immigration procedure had been slow and the customs officials pedantic to the point of insolence. Not wishing to draw attention to himself, Sekka had endured the protracted examination of his documents. On being asked the reason for his visit, Sekka divulged that he was a freelance journalist doing an article for the Nigeria *Star* on the preparation for the imminent OAU conference.

Sekka had spotted the security men the second he entered the customs hall. Two of them; standing either side of the double exit doors. Floral shirts, black flared slacks, reflective sun glasses, Kalashnikovs over their shoulders, studying the arriving travellers. Sekka felt the stirring of alarm in his belly as he walked towards the doors, suitcase in his hand; but the duo, bored with duty, did not even spare him a second glance as he strode through the exit and into the sunshine beyond.

The taxis were all of the same decrepit appearance. Sekka chose the first one in the rank, out of convenience rather than for its aesthetic quality. A mile from the airport he was beginning to think it had been a bad move.

The highway ran north from the airport through flat countryside; scrubland that occasionally gave way to an acre or so of arid cultivation, shallow furrows of sun bleached rock hard soil that boasted isolated shrivelled brown shoots, victims of the merciless sun.

The outskirts of Kendura were little more than slum areas; huddles of corrugated iron and wooden boxes, erected over inadequate drainage ditches that were euphemisms for open plan latrines. Miserable cardboard- like ghettos, one storey high. A warren of stinking alleyways inhabited by the untouchables; rotting heaps of garbage, flea infested dogs, urinating children in ragged hand-me-downs.

These hovels gave way to the workers' flats. At one time this had been the Asian belt; the homes of the prosperous Indian community that had run Lugamba's shops and industries. The flats had, before the purge, presented a well kept face to the visitor. Now, with the Asians expelled, the itinerants had moved in. The evidence was a web of broken window panes, cracked paving stones and paint daubed walls. They were now nothing more than high rise slums and served only to complement the shanty town that sprawled in their shadow.

Beyond the blocks of flats the land sloped up to a bushy

110

skyline, broken by the eggshell cracked walls of the old colonial style villas that would, in earlier years, have housed embassies and consulates. Now they were occupied by Mabato's officers and henchmen. The diplomats – those that remained – had moved into squat, drab cubes hidden behind high walls and railings as protection against riot and demonstration.

The Kendura International Hotel broke into view around a bend in the street and the taxi turned into the forecourt. Once a fine old edifice, it reminded Sekka of the Raffles in Singapore during its heyday but now sadly run to seed. Even in the bright sunshine it looked unkempt, jaded, trying to maintain a semblance of dignity like a fading dowager. There was no commissioner on duty.

Sekka eased himself out of the car and searched his pockets for the fare. He hadn't had time to change money so he offered American dollars. They disappeared into a pocket in the driver's shirt with a flourish. Sekka eyed the man speculatively.

'There might be more where that came from,' he said.

Blank look.

Sekka shuffled some notes. The man's face lit up and then his expresion turned to one of suspicion.

Sekka smiled. 'I'd like someone to drive me around. Show me the sights. A couple of hours maybe.'

This time his offer was rewarded with a smile. 'Ah, special tour? Sure, my friend. You gotta deal. I drive you around the city. Tourist eh?'

'Almost,' Sekka said.

The driver grinned, showing a gap in his front teeth. 'Okay, I wait. You check in and leave bags.'

Sekka shook his head. 'Not now, later.' He looked at his watch. 'I need a couple of hours' sleep. You be here at six this evening.'

The driver looked more than a little hesitant. Sekka

guessed that this was due to the man not wishing to drive around the city after dusk. He allayed the driver's fears by handing over a substantial tip and the deal was struck.

Two fans in the ceiling of the lobby revolved reluctantly in a valiant effort to alleviate the sticky heat. Sekka had to ring the bell on the reception counter three times to get attention. Eventually a short, sweaty negro waddled into view, looking faintly surprised that the hotel had a prospective guest.

To the right, in the lounge area, a group of Libyans were gazing vacantly through the large windows on to a sun parched strip of stubble that had once been a neat garden. Now it was merely an apology.

Only a few years ago the lobby would have been filled with guests milling about; signing in, ordering valet service, booking cars and airline tickets or organizing trips to the northern game parks. The manager then had been Austrian; Kurt Hildebrandt. A splendid individual; courteous, efficient and generous in dealing with the whims of each guest. Even he had conceded defeat and returned to his home city of Graz, a refugee from the oppressive rule of Mabato, leaving his hotel in the hands of Mabato's lackeys who had let the proud and comfortable haven crumble into forlorn decay. Without Hildebrandt's extrovert personality the clientele stayed away.

The reception handed over a key. Sekka smiled, picked up his bag and walked to the lift.

The sign above the shop read: Mendoza: – Imports and Exports. Keel opened the door and walked into the cool interior. Above his head, twin blades revolved slowly, the noise of their turning almost masking the sound of the traffic in the street outside.

Bright native rugs and animal skins adorned the walls of the emporium along with the heads of gazelle, rhino, dik

dik, buffalo and zebra; glass eyes gazing vacantly into space. Open fronted cabinets contained tribal masks, carved dolls, ivory and jade statues and onyx chess sets and Keel could detect the fragrance of incense as he walked between the tiers of Chinese and Persian rugs and intricately carved tables and screens. Another rack of shelves held crocodile skin handbags and snakeskin belts coiled like the reptiles they had once been.

A bead curtain at the rear of the shop parted and a smiling Indian stepped out to greet him.

'A pleasure to see you, sir. What can I do for you. You are looking for something in particular? Jade? Ivory? We have Masai jewellery – '

'I'd like to see Mendoza,' said Keel.

'I am sorry, sir. The proprietor is away on business. However, I am sure I can be of assistance. We have many fine rugs as you can see. Perhaps a chess set?' The Indian moved towards one of the open cabinets.

'What I want,' Keel said, 'is Mendoza.'

The Indian's gaze flickered almost imperceptibly towards the bead curtain but his movement had not gone unnoticed.

'Nice try,' Keel continued. 'Tell him Major Keel is here.'

The Indian hesitated.

'Now,' Keel said.

The Indian disappeared and was replaced two minutes later by the Portuguese.

Carlos Mendoza was fifty years of age with an olive complexion and black hair combed back from a widow's peak. He had a heavy moustache and a gold tooth glinted in his mouth. He had well manicured hands that were held outstretched to greet Thomas Keel.

'Well, well, Major. It has indeed been a long time.'

'Nearly eighteen months,' Keel said.

'Ah yes,' Mendoza said. 'That business in Namibia I recall. It went well?'

'Well enough.'

Mendoza digested the noncommittal answer then said: 'You caused my assistant some concern, Major.'

'Sorry about that,' Keel said. 'But he was being somewhat unhelpful.'

'He was merely protecting my interests, Major.' Mendoza smiled, showing a lot of teeth and a speck of gold.

'Well, you can't be too careful I suppose. Especially in your line of work.'

A light flashed in the brown eyes. 'I presume this visit has some significance, Major Keel. I am a very busy man. Let us not prevaricate.'

'In private,' Keel said.

'As you wish.'

Mendoza led the way into the back of the shop to a small office that held a desk and two chairs and the Indian assistant. Mendoza dismissed the latter and closed the door.

'I'm on a contract,' Keel said. 'A team of four. I need equipment and that includes transport.'

'I see,' Mendoza replied. 'What makes you think I am still involved in that sideline? I have a very profitable enterprise here, Major. I am a respectable businessman.'

'Because I would have heard if you'd retired. Your name is still in most of the mercenary recruiters' address books. Six months ago you were acting as arms broker for the FAN rebels in Chad. You also supplied a consignment of Russian grenade launchers, automatic rifles and anti-personnel mines to the Tanzanian Freedom Front via your agent in Dar es Salaam. And I presume you are still selling arms to the Mozambique guerillas through the import-export agency in Sofala.'

Keel knew that the arms arrived in Dar es Salaam on

board Russian freighters from where they were transported by air to Mendoza's agents.

'Anything else you want to know, Carlos?'

The tubby Portuguese was silent for several seconds then he said: 'I see you are as well informed as ever, Major.'

'In my line of work it pays to be.'

'So, what do you require?'

'Machine pistols, hand guns, spare ammunition, pangas and plastique with timers and detonators. I'll need packs and shoulder holsters for the hand guns. I want man stoppers. Brownings. Also combat clothing.'

'Very well. You mentioned transport.'

'I require a light aircraft with pilot, big enough to carry five passengers.'

Mendoza raised an eyebrow. 'When do you want all this?'

'Within twenty four hours. Thirty six at the outside.'

'That might not be easy. You have not given me much time. The weapons present no problem but the aircraft may take a little longer to arrange.'

'We don't have the time,' Keel said. 'Who's in town?'

A shrug. 'Rolf Steyn left for Maputo yesterday. John Lafitte is on charter service in the copper belt in Zambia.'

'No one else?'

Mendoza paused. 'There is Lassiter.'

'Lassiter? I thought Lassiter was airlifting supplies to the FNLA?'

Mendoza shook his head. 'Lassiter is in Nairobi though I have had no contact. That one always was a loner.'

'Maybe I can do some digging,' Keel said. 'In any case, see if you can get hold of Steyn just in case. Tell him there'll be a large bonus.'

'As you wish. You have not told me where you wish to be taken.'

115

'I was saving that until last. We will want dropping at the mission station at Masambabule.'

Mendoza jumped as if he had been shot. 'But that is in Lugamba!'

'Right first time.'

'I see,' Mendoza replied thoughtfully.

'No you don't but don't lose any sleep over it. Get the stuff ready and I'll let you know if I get hold of our friend Lassiter. We'll take it from there.'

'Where can I reach you?'

'The Intercontinental.'

Mendoza nodded. 'I will send word, Major.'

'I'll count on it.'

The Portuguese blinked. 'There is one other thing. I recall hearing that Lassiter was seen at Jack Case's establishment a few nights ago.'

'The gaming club?' Keel looked surprised.

Mendoza said unhappily: 'I heard there was a scene. Your friend got into a big game and lost some money.'

'So, maybe some cash would come in useful. See if you can find out where Lassiter's staying.'

'I will do what I can.'

Back at the hotel, Keel checked with the reception desk to see if any messages had been left though he thought it unlikely that Cameron would have got in touch so soon. They had been in Nairobi less than a day. There was no message.

He took his room key. Since arriving that morning he had not rested. As a seasoned air traveller he had managed to catnap on the plane. He felt hot and sticky and in need of a shower and a beer.

He was emerging from the shower, reaching for a towel when he heard the knock on the door. He tensed immediately.

'Who is it?'

116

The voice was indistinct but he caught the word 'telegram' and the hair on his nape tingled. Word from Cameron, sooner than expected. He wrapped the towel around his waist.

He opened the door and the gun was jammed against his stomach, forcing him back into the room. Two negros. Tall, well built. One in a cream suit, the other in a light tan jacket and brown slacks. Fit, confident, dangerous. The muzzle of the automatic moved up through his chest hairs. Keel held his arms away from his body. The weapon was held by Cream Suit. The other visitor closed the door.

'No fuss, Major Keel.' The gunman stepped away, keeping the weapon trained on Keel's belly. 'Get dressed.'

Keel eyed them carefully. 'Give me a clue,' he said. 'What happened to the telegram?'

'Merely a ruse, Major.' Cream Suit sat on the bed. His silent companion stood by the door, hands loose at his sides.

Not robbery or mugging. They'd used his old rank. So who were they?

Standing in the middle of the room wrapped in two square yards of damp towelling wasn't going to get him any answers. Where the hell were Roan and Schiller? Sleeping at a guess. No bail out there and he couldn't take two of them. Not in a bloody towel toga he couldn't.

'I told you to get dressed,' Cream Suit said. His voice was educated, indicating public school and morning prayers. These were not your ordinary heavies.

Keel pulled a shirt from the hanger in the wardrobe and underwear from his holdall. During his dressing Cream Suit's gaze and the mouth of the gun barrel never wavered.

Keel stood dressed and waiting. Now he felt slightly less vulnerable but they still had the upper hand. For the time being.

Advantage visiting side.

'We will leave quietly, Major. Do not attempt anything. You will not be harmed if you obey my instructions. When we reach the lobby simply hand in your key. Walk out of the hotel and get into a white Mercedes that will be parked outside.'

It sounded easy, straightforward. Maybe they'd be lulled. Maybe he could take them in the corridor or the lift. And maybe he wouldn't because he was curious, wanting to know what they wanted and, more important, who they were working for.

The automatic remained hidden during the trip in the lift and the walk through the lobby to the street where the 450SEL waited patiently at the kerb. A negro sat in the driving seat and turned lazy eyes towards the three men as they left the hotel.

Cream Suit sat in the back with Keel. Tan Jacket joined the driver.

They drove north through the suburbs to where the road curved in a steady gradient through the private estates. Then they turned off.

Tall iron gates blocked their path. On either side, a high white brick wall retreated into the foliage. The driver pressed the horn and two men appeared from a gate box. They studied the car through the bars of the gate. Over the driver's shoulder Keel saw that they cradled Stechin machine pistols.

The gates swung open and the Mercedes slid by. Keel swivelled and watched the gates close.

The house lay a mile or so along the track. It was a two storied villa, framed by bright oleanders and scarlet flamboya trees. They were met by a stocky negro in the uniform of a retainer: white jacket and black trousers. He led the way into the house, Cream Suit and Tan Jacket flanking Keel.

The interior was light and cool with rush matting on the

118

floor and cane furniture dotted around the hall. Keel was escorted to the rear of the house into a large comfortable drawing room with French windows opening on to a veranda from which steps led down to a paved terrace and swimming pool. Beyond the pool a vast lawn stretched to where the white boundary wall weaved through the edge of the bush. One hundred yards away, to the left, a man was patrolling the perimeter, a sleek Dobermann at his heels, machine pistol over his shoulder.

The villa was a fortress.

They went down to the terrace. White stucco tables and chairs sat under sun umbrellas. Sun loungers faced the pool. There was a portable bar and a telephone stood on one of the tables.

A man was sitting under one of the umbrellas. He was dressed in a dark blue shirt and matching slacks. The clothes were cut very formally and looked almost like a uniform. A cane handled fly whisk lay on the table within easy reach. The man's face broke into a smile of welcome as he rose to his feet.

'Major Keel, my dear fellow. Welcome, welcome. It is a pleasure to see you again.'

Standing, the negro was of medium height with deep set eyes under a high forehead, giving an intelligent cast to his features. A small goatee beard enhanced the effect so that the overall description might have fitted a university professor. He was about fifty five years of age.

'Good afternoon, Mister President,' replied Keel, shaking hands. 'I wondered what had become of you.'

For a man living in political exile, Hamilton Kemba appeared to be coping with the ignominy remarkably well. Keel said so.

Kemba shrugged and waved an arm to encompass his surroundings.

'Trappings, Major. A facade if you like. The very fact

119

that I have a roof over my head is due entirely to the benevolence of the President of Kenya and I would venture to suggest that his generosity is bounded only by political expediency. In other words, Major, my presence is politely tolerated. However, I admit the roof is a comfortable one.'

'I understood you were living in Tanzania,' Keel said.

'For a while,' Kemba said. 'However, poor Julius. Certain pressures were brought to bear. He became embarrassed. He made approaches to the Kenyan Government on my behalf. I shall be eternally grateful of course. President Nai took me under his wing and you find me thus. But I am forgetting my manners. Allow me to offer you some refreshment.' He snapped a finger and Tan Jacket moved to the bar like a trained hound.

'Vodka with fresh lime juice,' Keel directed. 'Lots of ice.'

He looked westward. The sun was low over the horizon and sinking like a golden orb. The sky was the colour of burnished copper, breathtaking in its magnificence.

'Let us walk, Major.' Hamilton Kemba took his arm. 'Let us view my domain and discuss matters.'

They walked along the edge of the pool; still water, midnight blue flecked with silver.

Keel watched the far-off guard and Dobermann disappear around the bottom end of the lawn past the edge of the house.

'You seem well protected, sir.'

'Adequate, I would say. Enough to deter enthusiastic amateurs but hardly a threat to a determined group.'

'Is that likely?'

'Anything is possible, Major. There are those who would like to see me dead.'

'Like Solomon Mabato, for instance?'

Kemba smiled. 'But of course. He above all others.'

'Which presupposes that he considers you a threat. Are you?'

'Major, I am an exile from my own country. I want Lugamba back. I want to wrest it from the hands of that madman. Mabato has murdered over a quarter of a million of my countrymen. He has taken Lugamba to the edge of the abyss. He must be stopped!'

'And you are the man to do it? You have tried once before and failed.'

'You are referring to the 1977 invasion? Not the most professional enterprise, I will admit.'

'You can say that again. It was a disaster. Your men were badly trained and poorly led. They never stood a chance.'

'They would have succeeded if you had accepted the contract I offered,' Kemba pointed out.

'No they wouldn't. They were the wrong calibre. Totally inept and ill equipped. All the training in the world wouldn't have forged them into the crack fighting unit that was required. I wouldn't have accepted the contract if you'd trebled the bounty. I remember that I told you that at the time.'

'And I appreciated your candour, as I recall.'

'A pity you didn't act on it.'

Kemba flared. 'Major, it is enough that I have the deaths of a thousand men on my conscience without you having to remind me of the fact!'

They had reached the perimeter track and had turned to follow the curve of the boundary wall. Back at the pool, Kemba's bodyguards watched their progress through narrowed and suspicious eyes.

'Why don't you get to the point,' Keel said. 'You didn't get your goons to drag me here to talk over old times.'

'Of course not. Though in speaking of old times, since I last saw you I have been following your career with some interest.'

'I think I'm flattered.' He remembered he'd said that to Cameron in Amsterdam.

Kemba seemed unconcerned at the slight. 'Your contracts as a mercenary have been varied, Major. You have remarkable powers of survival.'

'Let's not discount luck,' Keel said.

A stillness lay in the air. From over the wall creatures of the night twittered, croaked and rustled.

'You are going into Lugamba, Major. I would like to know the reason.'

So there it was.

'You've talked with Mendoza.'

An inclination of the head.

Mendoza has a big mouth, thought Keel. Aloud, he said: 'No deal.'

'Major, Lugamba is my country. I am entitled – '

'You're entitled to damn all. Your claim on Lugamba was severed when you were ousted in '71. Mabato, maniac though he may be, now controls Lugamba. Like it or not, that is fact.'

They were now close enough to the terrace for Keel's raised voice to have carried to the ears of Kemba's men. They tensed but relaxed at a signal from the deposed ruler.

'Have you accepted a contract, Major? Is that it?'

'Didn't Mendoza tell you?'

'He admitted he was supplying you with equipment.'

'This is something between the client and myself.'

'Major, I will be frank with you. I have already stated that I want Lugamba back. If I can gain an advantage through someone else's efforts I fully intend to do so. Tell me your contract.'

Keel regarded Kemba calmly. They were by the pool once more.

'I intend to try and rescue David Holt.'

122

'That is all?' Kemba looked surprised.

'Isn't it enough?'

'It is not what I expected.'

'You thought I might be leading another invasion force?'

'Something like that,' admitted Kemba. He looked bemused.

'I'm sorry to disappoint you, sir.'

Tan Jacket approached with Keel's vodka. Kemba accepted iced tonic water.

Hamilton Kemba stared down at the water in the pool. His eyes seemed to plumb its depths. 'I have a proposition for you.'

'I don't think I'm going to like it much.'

'Humour me, Major Keel.'

It was now dark. Without warning the lawn was bathed in light as a time switch activated the security screen in the grounds. Keel realized that anyone in the house would have a clear field of fire right up to the perimeter wall.

Kemba said: 'Major, I will pay you fifty thousand American dollars or the equivalent in any currency you care to name if you undertake to assassinate Solomon Mabato.'

Keel put his glass on the table. 'No.'

'Why not?'

'I'm a soldier, not a professional assassin.'

'If it is money, I – '

'The money has nothing to do with it. The offer is very generous.'

'Then why?'

'I've told you. Furthermore, I've already accepted one contract; to lift David Holt. That is my sole aim. I will not accept another that may jeopardize the success of the prime objective; the rescue mission. My client expects one hundred per cent dedication and he will get it.'

'It appears that once again I must accept your candour,

123

Major Keel. I thank you at least for listening. I had hoped we might come to some agreement.'

Keel said: 'I'm sorry, sir.'

Kemba smiled ruefully. 'Who knows? Perhaps next time?'

'Perhaps,' Keel agreed.

Kemba held out his hand suddenly. 'I wish you luck in your venture. My men will see you return safely to your hotel.'

They shook hands and Keel turned abruptly towards the house, escorted by Kemba's bodyguards. Kemba watched him depart, a half smile on his lips as though he harboured a secret. He took a quiet sip of tonic and waited.

The man moved in silence through the big windows, across the veranda and down the steps to the terrace. A sixth sense made Kemba swing around and he stared at the figure that blocked the light from the drawing room.

'You move like a leopard in the night, Qetuka,' Kemba breathed in admiration.

The man moved closer. 'Who was he?'

'A soldier of fortune. A gun for hire. He was under the mistaken impression that I could offer him employment.' In a sharper tone, Kemba said: 'He did not see you?'

The man shook his head.

Hamilton Kemba studied the man before him.

Tall and well built, the Negro's head was shaven and his clear brown eyes regarded Kemba with something close to arrogance, the look of a man supremely confident in his own ability. Qetuka was a Zulu. He was also thirty four years of age and an assassin.

Qetuka's great grandfather had been an inDuna with the iSangqu regiment and had fought with the impis at Isandhlwana and Rorke's Drift. The blood of the warrior flowed through his veins.

'Sit down, Qetuka.' Kemba indicated a seat.

The Zulu sat facing the open windows.

'You know why you are here,' Kemba said.

'I received word that you had a contract for me.'

'Yes and it is rather special.'

'All my contracts are special,' Qetuka said. 'Whom do you wish me to kill?'

'Solomon Mabato.'

There was no change of expression as the Zulu said: 'Very well. My fee will be one hundred thousand American dollars.'

Kemba pursed his lips. 'A substantial amount.'

'It is my usual fee. I do not give discounts to deposed heads of state nor do I haggle like a vendor in a market place.'

'I will pay the amount you ask for. Cash?'

'Naturally.'

Kemba chuckled. It sounded like small bones cracking. 'I need not have asked. Half now, half when the job is completed. Agreed?'

'Agreed.'

'Excellent, excellent. Tell me, how do you propose to carry out the assassination?'

The Zulu rose to his feet, the unwinding smooth and unhurried, like a serpent uncoiling. 'You are paying me a great deal of money for my services. I am an expert in my trade. Have no fear that the contract will be accomplished. Solomon Mabato will be dead within the week.'

Kemba disguised his impatience. 'So be it. You must forgive my exuberance. I have waited so long. The first instalment will await your collection in the morning. You will also be given the name of someone who is close to Mabato. Someone whose help could be of use to you.'

'Very well,' Qetuka replied, his voice neutral. 'If there is nothing further . . . ?'

* * *

Kemba was alone in the room. He stood by the open windows. A soft evening breeze carried the scent of jasmine along the veranda.

He was thinking about his conversation with Keel. His ploy of trying to undercut Qetuka's fee by using the mercenary had failed. A pity. The assassination would still cost him one hundred thousand. But Kemba had lost nothing in making the approach. Keel might well have accepted the secondary contract. Kemba, however, hadn't allowed for the mercenary having his own particular code of ethics.

Footsteps on the terrace. The guard with the black and tan Dobermann on a leash. The guard carried the Stechin like a baby. The dog eyed Kemba through bright alert eyes, muzzle twitching as it caught his scent.

The man acknowledged Kemba's greeting with a brief nod and pulled the dog to heel before disappearing into the shadows. Kemba was struck with the observation that the Dobermann's unblinking gaze reminded him of the stone cold features of Qetuka and, despite the warm breeze against his cheek, he felt a chill between his shoulder blades. Involuntarily he shivered and retreated into the villa.

6

The receptionist handed Keel his key and a message. It was from Mendoza. He had traced Lassiter.

Harry Roan opened his door at Keel's first knock. The American's hair was wet, evidence that he had been under the shower.

'Jesus! Where the hell have you been? Paul and I were going to call out the troops. The guy at reception said you'd left with a couple of guys. What gives?' He virtually hauled Keel into the room.

Schiller lay on the bed, hands behind his head, a cheroot stuck in his mouth. When Keel entered the German swung his feet to the floor and removed the cheroot. 'You had us worried, Thomas.'

'I wasn't too thrilled myself,' Keel said.

'So, where have you been for the last two goddamned hours?'

'Harry, do I detect a note of concern in your tone?'

'Call it bare assed curiosity, Major Keel.'

'I went to see Mendoza. We need weapons and an airlift.'

'Right. So you saw Mendoza and everything is hunky dory. So, who were the goons who picked you up when you got back?' Roan searched Keel's face closely. 'Thomas?'

'Mendoza passed word to Hamilton Kemba that I wanted dropping into Lugamba. Kemba had two of his boys escort me to his redoubt. He had a proposition for me. A profitable supplement to our contract, so to speak.'

'Kemba! That bastard, Mendoza! I knew he was a liability. What did Kemba want?' Roan towelled his hair furiously.

'He wants Mabato dead. He offered me fifty thousand dollars to hit the fat slob.'

Roan stopped towelling. Schiller drew on his cheroot slowly.

'I turned him down before you ask.'

'You should have raised the ante.' Roan saw the look on Keel's face. 'Okay, Thomas. Just a joke. We've done enough jobs together for me to know that we never take on secondary contracts. Y'know, what bugs me is that Mendoza might just have spread the word a wee bit further afield. I'd trust that son of a bitch as far as I could spit!'

Keel said: 'I don't think so. The Portuguese is the main broker for weapons and mercenary recruitment in East Africa. Kemba wants Lugamba back and anyone in his position would keep someone like Mendoza on a retainer. He'd be interested in any contract that would pose a threat to Mabato and give him a toe hold again. And don't forget that Kemba knows me. It was through Mendoza that he offered me that job in '77.'

'Yeah,' Roan answered, 'and turning him down was the wisest thing you've ever done. If you hadn't, your bones would be fertilizer in a Lugamban cane field by now.'

'I know it.' Keel frowned.

'Something on your mind, Thomas?' Paul Schiller asked.

'He didn't try hard enough,' Keel said, brushing a hand over his cropped hair. 'I wonder why?'

'Say again?' Roan cadged a cheroot from Schiller, throwing his towel aside.

'Nothing I can put my finger on but he didn't push it when I said no. It was almost as if he expected me to refuse but he tried anyway. Hell, maybe I'm imagining it.'

Schiller cut into his thoughts. 'What about Mendoza? Can he supply what we need?'

'No problem. He was stuck for a pilot as Steyn and Lafitte are out of town but he's come up with an old friend of mine.'

'Who's that?' Schiller asked.

'Lassiter.'

'Oh boy!' Roan said.

'I heard Lassiter was in Angola.' Paul Schiller's brow furrowed. 'Airlifting medical supplies to the FNLA.'

'I heard the same story.' Keel nodded.

'The two of you go back aways, Thomas,' Harry Roan remarked.

'Biafra. Lassiter took casualties from the front line to the field hospitals.'

'So, looks like we've got ourselves a pilot,' Roan announced happily.

'Maybe. Mendoza didn't make a deal. He's left that to me. All he's done is tell me where Lassiter is. That drink will have to wait. I'm off to the airfield now. I'll catch you later.'

'You want to watch it, Thomas. For a man of your age, all this gadding about is likely to lead to a coronary.'

'I love you too, Gramps.'

'Wise-ass!' Roan grinned.

'Don't wait up,' Keel said. 'This may take a while.'

The lights were on in the maintenance hangar. The white and red Piper Chieftain crouched in the glare like an anaesthetized patient in an operating theatre, awaiting the arrival of the surgeon. The double doors of the hangar stood ajar, casting a thick beam of light on to the dark tarmac outside.

In the lee of the building, like lighters around an ocean

liner, sat a selection of aircraft: Cessnas, Beavers, Commanders and a brace of sleek Lear Jets, property of the Intercorp Oil Company.

Inside, a few feet away from the fin of the Chieftain, Lassiter was bent over a tool cluttered work bench, jaw clamped in concentration. The ruptured fuel line lay on the bench like a dead snake.

Lassiter was naked under a one piece overall that had, eons ago, been snow white. Now, it bore the smears and stains of years of do-it-yourself aircraft maintenance, the arms and legs frayed like a cowpoke's waistcoat. The pilot's feet were encased in a scruffy pair of Dunlop Green Flash that looked as though they had splashed through a million puddles.

Lassiter didn't hear the stealthy footsteps on the tarmac or the soft tread of rubber soled shoes on the floor of the hangar as the two men slipped through the open doors.

The first the pilot knew about their presence was when Ferris said casually: 'Well, well. And aren't we the complete mechanic.'

Lassiter whipped around, elbow dislodging a heavy spanner. It clattered noisily to the floor, the sound echoing up into the high dark corners of the hangar.

Ferris: the European, tall and thin, almost gangling in his movements. A young thin face topped by a tumble of blond curls breaking into a smile of delight at the surprised expression on Lassiter's face. The black's name was John John. He was a good foot shorter than Ferris. Broad, bull necked, standing square on his feet like an ebony statue. He eyed the pilot like an expectant gun-dog awaiting his master's command to retrieve. His master would be Ferris.

'What do you scum want?' Lassiter addressed Ferris.

John John regarded the pilot through narrowed brown eyes.

130

Ferris grinned. 'Mister Case sent us. He wants the money you owe him.'

'Mister Case is going to have to bloody well wait. I told him that three days ago.'

'Well, that's the problem you see, because Mister Case wants his money now.'

'Are you hard of hearing, Ferris? I've just told you that he'll have to wait. I don't carry that sort of cash on me for God's sake! Not six thousand dollars!'

'Seven thousand,' Ferris said. He smiled pleasantly. 'Don't forget the interest.'

'One thousand dollars in three days! What sort of rate is that, Ferris?'

'Quite reasonable if you ask me,' Ferris replied evenly. 'I mean, Mister Case did take you at your word when you left the club the other evening. You said you'd have the money in three days. Now, Mister Case, it seems to me, was more than generous in allowing you to leave his gaming establishment owing him six thousand dollars in the first place. The point being that it is now a few hours away from midnight of the third day and you still have not settled your account, so to speak. Mister Case, as you can imagine, is none too happy with this state of affairs.'

'So, he sent you and King Kong there to persuade me to settle up.'

A sound that closely resembled the throaty growl of a large mastiff came from John John's mouth. He waddled forward like a squat robot. Ferris held out his arm like a policeman on point duty and John John shambled to a halt.

'I bet he can roll over and fetch sticks,' Lassiter said, eyeing the negro speculatively.

'He's very obedient,' Ferris agreed. 'I only have to snap my fingers and he'll move in.'

131

Lassiter sighed. A resigned look. 'Ferris, I don't have the money here. Be sensible. I wired my bank for the cash the morning after I left the club, but for some reason it hasn't arrived. That's hardly my fault. Blame the bank. They cocked up the transfer, not me.'

Ferris shook his head sadly. 'Sorry, old thing, but Mister Case doesn't see it quite like that. He feels he's given you more than ample time to pay up.'

Lassiter held out a hand in a plea. 'Look, Ferris, couldn't you have a word with him. Put in a good word for me. Couldn't you do that, Ferris?'

An unhappy regretful shake of the blond curls. ''Fraid not, old thing. That'd be more than my life's worth.'

'Well, sod you, Ferris!'

John John gobbled at the raised voice.

'I'm having difficulty restraining him,' Ferris said.

'So, what are you going to do, you preening bastard? Break my legs?'

'Good heavens, no. If I do that, old thing, you won't be able to toddle off to the bank to collect Mister Case's money now, will you?'

'What then?'

'Mister Case suggested that I might take something as surety until you paid him back.'

'Oh, really? And what had he in mind? My left arm?'

'Only as a last resort,' Ferris said. 'He was thinking more along the lines of that.' Ferris pointed a finger at the Chieftain.

'Not bloody likely, Ferris! That aeroplane is worth a hell of a lot more than a piddling six thousand dollars!'

'Seven thousand,' Ferris said. 'You've forgotten the interest again.'

'Screw the interest you son of a bitch! You'll take that plane over my dead body.'

'That,' Ferris said calmly, 'can be arranged. Don't tempt me.'

'For Christ's sake, Ferris! The money will be in the bank tomorrow. Can't you see that?'

Ferris shook his head. 'It's not me, old thing. It's Mister Case. Come on, be reasonable. All we do is take the keys, registration papers, log book and certificates. We hang on to those and hand them back when you hand over the seven thousand dollars. In fact, looking at my watch I see that it is even closer to midnight, and you know what that means, old thing, don't you?'

'You turn into a pumpkin, Ferris?'

'Wrong. The seven thousand dollars turns into eight thousand dollars. On account of another day's interest, you see.' A gurgle of glee at this.

'You're off your trolley, Ferris.'

'Oh, I forgot one other thing,' Ferris went on. 'If you haven't paid the money in seven days, we keep the aircraft – for good. And don't say over your dead body because that is also part of the arrangement. Now, keys and documents, old thing, if you please or I shall be forced to unleash my accomplice.'

Lassiter swung to the work bench and grabbed the first heavy tool that came to hand; a foot long monkey wrench. The pilot held the wrench double handed and dropped to a crouch.

'Take one move towards me or my aircraft, you pouf, Ferris, and I'll lay you out.'

Ferris looked pained. 'Now, there's no need to resort to personal abuse.'

'Let me tell you that if that dwarf takes another step I'll personally abuse him with this wrench.'

John John, hands hanging by his sides, shuffled crablike to his left. The black was grunting to himself. Ferris nonchalantly moved to the right. Lassiter, back to the bench, gripping the wrench in sweaty palms, eyed them warily.

John John, inevitably, was the first to make a move. He uttered a ferocious squeal of rage and darted in at bewildering speed. Lassiter, although tensed and half expecting it, was almost caught napping. Twisting frantically, the pilot scythed the wrench towards John John's melon shaped skull. If the blow had connected, John John's head would have caved in like an egg shell. As it was, caught off balance at the last moment, Lassiter's swing missed its mark. The wrench glanced off the black's shoulder. Even so, it was enough to draw a roar of anger from the squat attacker.

Ferris chuckled. 'He nearly had you that time. My, now you've really annoyed him.'

'Sod off, Ferris!'

'Why don't you take the easy way out, old thing?' Ferris cajoled. 'Just hand over the keys. That way, nobody will get hurt.' He approached Lassiter, arms spread, beseeching. His hands were a blur as he aimed a blow to Lassiter's head. The wrench curved to connect again and John John, seeing a gap in the defences, sprang forward. One ham sized fist grabbed Lassiter's wrist and the other clamped around the back of the pilot's neck. Ferris followed through. Ramming his knee between Lassiter's legs, he reached for the struggling pilot's other arm and twisted. The wrench bounced off Ferris's leg and dropped to the floor. Ferris cursed and slammed the back of his free hand against Lassiter's cheek.

The pilot's head jerked away. John John, hand gripping like a vice, forced Lassiter down until the pilot was kneeling on the cement floor of the hangar. Ferris, confident in John John's hold, released his grip and stepped away. He smoothed a hand through his blond hair. He looked more than a little flustered.

Despite the ungainly position, Lassiter, in a last ditch effort, thumped a fist towards Ferris's stomach. The latter sidestepped and then swung his arm back for the strike.

'NO!'

The voice cut through the air like a whip.

Ferris spun like a top in the direction of the sound.

Keel stood feet apart, left foot slightly forward, hands clenched into fists held at waist level.

John John was shaking Lassiter like a kitten.

'Tell him to let go.' Keel's demand was pitched low.

'Whoever you are, old thing,' Ferris said, 'I suggest you take off. Otherwise you might get hurt.'

'I don't think so,' Keel said. 'Now, I've told you once. Tell your man to let go.'

Keel was two yards from Ferris. Ferris, smiling, said: 'Oh dear, don't say I didn't warn you,' and moved towards the intruder.

Keel took half a pace forward. He seemed to sway momentarily and then he pivoted. Ferris didn't think it possible that anyone could move that fast. He was still thinking that when Keel's boot struck him an inch under his ribcage, thumping him backwards in a tottering stagger, breath whooshing out like gas from a cylinder. By the time his backside hit the floor, Keel was facing John John. He wasn't even breathing hard. He stood relaxed . . . waiting.

The negro looked puzzled but he hung on to Lassiter. The pilot was still struggling and for John John it was like grasping a handful of minnows. Muttering a snarl of annoyance, he thought that of the two, Keel undoubtedly held the most threat. He flung the pilot aside and lumbered towards Keel. Lassiter, released from the vice, fell against

135

the leg of the work bench, forehead taking a glancing blow. A trickle of blood emerged from the cut.

Keel waited for the attack.

Which was when Lassiter smashed the wrench down on to John John's foot. It was almost comic the way the black hopped around. Lassiter hadn't finished. The wrench swung again and John John, clutching his genitals, hit the ground in a bubbling, whimpering heap.

Lassiter sat back against the work bench. Keel stepped up and retrieved the tool. He threw it on to the bench and grasped Lassiter's shoulders. Behind him, Ferris was rising groggily to his feet, his face ashen.

Keel jerked his head at the twitching John John. 'Get him out of here. Now.'

Ferris, one hand clutching his stomach, caught John John under one arm and tried to haul him to his feet. John John retched noisily.

Lassiter was touching the head cut with tentative fingers.

Ferris had resorted to half dragging half carrying John John across the floor to the open doors. Keel watched them struggle away. He crouched over the pilot. 'Lassiter, for Christ's sake, are you all right?'

The pilot's eyes were glazed. Someone was rasping out questions. Through the blur a face shimmered into view. Stern features, tanned, steel grey hair, ice blue eyes. Now, identification.

The dazed pilot blinked and stared. Keel grinned. 'I was getting worried about you.'

Focused fully.

'Oh hell!' Kate Lassiter said. 'It's Keel. That's all I bloody need!'

'Damn it, Keel, you bastard! That stings!'

They were in the Chieftain. Keel was administering

136

iodine from the aircraft's first aid box to the cut on Kate Lassiter's forehead. He was dabbing the antiseptic on with a ball of cotton wool.

'Keep still!' Keel ordered.

Kate Lassiter's green eyes regarded Keel with wry amusement. 'Has anyone ever told you that you've a lousy bedside manner?'

He grinned. 'You never complained before.'

Her eyes flashed. 'That was when I was young and foolish.'

He was silent for a few moments as he applied a strip of band aid to cover the cut. 'I think you'll live. I'd better take a look at the bench while I'm here. You gave it a nasty knock.'

'Oh, droll, Keel. Very droll.'

'That's me, Kate. Always able to manage a chuckle in the face of adversity. That's what has kept me sane all these years.' Keel replaced the first aid kit in its locker and gazed intently at her.

Kate Lassiter was beautiful. Of that there was no doubt. Keel saw her as the most stunning woman he had ever encountered. She was tall and statuesque with firm full breasts – even now straining against the top of those greasy overalls – narrow waist and legs that went on for ever. Her face was striking. Flawless skin, high Slavonic cheekbones, straight nose and a generous mouth. Her eyes, set under fine brows, were of emerald intensity. Thick raven hair that usually framed her face in an unruly tumble, was drawn back and held at the nape of her neck and served only to emphasize her classic features. She was thirty eight years old.

Kate carried her beauty with a nonchalance that bordered on contempt. She neither exaggerated nor underestimated her sexuality. She accepted it.

Despite her obvious attractions, few men had penetrated her outer defences. Many of them, if truth be told, were overawed by her looks as well as her intelligence and fierce independence. There had been relationships, usually just physical and a means of assuaging a need, but with two men it had been different. Thomas Keel and her late husband.

Sam Lassiter had been Chief Warden in the big National Game Reserve in Tanzania. Kate was twenty when she met Lassiter, a rock of a man with a heart as big as the country he controlled. They had known each other only ten days and yet Kate was sure this was the man she wanted to spend the rest of her life with. Sam Lassiter was twelve years older than his bride to be. They were married in a registry office in Mombasa and their honeymoon was a month long trip around the reserve. From Sam, Kate contracted the disease: a deep love of Africa; the country, the people and the wild animals. She also discovered another love: flying.

Two years later Sam Lassiter was killed and Kate's life was shattered.

Lassiter had been after the band of ivory poachers for months. They had been decimating the herds. Word came that a gang of half a dozen men had been spotted carving up an old tusker in an isolated corner of the reserve. Maintaining radio contact with his native rangers on the ground, Lassiter had flown to the area in his Auster, planning to direct the rangers to the scene to grab the poachers red-handed with their haul of ivory.

Sam Lassiter had been too busy concentrating on his search of the terrain below his wings to see the big Martial eagle as it spiralled up towards him on a thermal. The eagle hadn't known too much about the collision either. The huge bird slammed into the propeller with the force of an exploding grenade, splattering the windshield with blood and feathers. The single Lycoming, choked with the mangled remains of the eagle, seized and the plane slammed into the side of a djonga, exploding on impact. Lassiter never stood a chance.

When news of the crash reached Kate it took no time at all for her to commandeer one of the reserve's other aircraft and fly north to continue the hunt for the poachers.

The rangers on the ground had been drawn to the poachers' camp by the sight of Kate Lassiter's plane dive-bombing the gang like a Stuka. The gang had virtually run into the waiting arms of the rangers for safety; anything to get away from the maniac above them.

Kate was offered repatriation to England, She refused.

With the insurance money she invested in a second hand Beaver and chartered herself out. It was while she was in Blantyre, awaiting a consignment of medical supplies destined for the mission hospital at Lake Chiuta, that she met Thomas Keel.

Keel, on leave from the fighting in Biafra, had spent a fortnight with Kate Lassiter. It had been a wild, unrelenting affair, both needing the other's companionship and love with an urgency neither of them had expected. It had been a time for Keel to cleanse himself of the horrors of the war and the first chance Kate Lassiter had of finding the outlet for her pent up emotions and stress caused by Sam's death.

Keel had returned to complete his contract, never expecting to see Kate again. It had been a brief interlude, nothing more. Until Kate and her aircraft had turned up at the airfield at Uli with drugs, blankets and six cases of Black and White. Kate was no camp follower, Keel knew that. The job had brought her to the front line, not her longing for the grey mercenary. At least that's what Kate tried to tell herself. Inevitably, they snatched moments together, brief encounters in between Keel's hit-and-run missions behind the rebel lines and Kate's mercy flights, ferrying drugs and wounded back and forth from base hospital to field medical units. She was the only woman pilot in the Federal forces and the men treated her as an equal. They also viewed her as Keel's woman, and therefore untouchable.

Following the surrender of Ojukwa and prior to his gold running activities, Keel returned to Europe. He made no attempt to persuade Kate to go with him. He knew she wouldn't leave Africa. In a way Keel felt certain she had been grateful that he hadn't asked and thus hadn't needed to make a decision.

Keel's contracts had taken him to many places since then. He had returned to Africa on several occasions – the jobs in Rhodesia, Chad and Namibia as well as the contract offered by Hamilton Kemba to lead a task force into Lugamba. On every contract he had spent time with Kate. She hadn't changed. Still totally self reliant, cool, sophisticated, even more beautiful and eminently desirable.

A month prior to his bodyguard contract with the arms buying sheik, he'd heard that Lassiter had been involved in the ongoing Angolan conflict, flying out stretcher cases from Sao Salvador to Kinshasa in a Fokker Friendship.

'Earth calling Keel,' Kate Lassiter said.

He jerked his thoughts back to the present. 'I was miles away.'

'I could see that.' She smiled.

He frowned. 'So what did Goldilocks and Man Friday want?'

Kate loosened her hair and combed a slender hand through the dark waves. Keel found the gesture faintly sensual. She didn't notice.

'I owe Jack Case money. A gaming debt.'

'How much?'

She told him and Keel winced. 'You're in deep, kiddo.'

'Hell, Thomas, I can pay it back. I've wired my bank for the dough but the stupid bastards haven't sent it through.'

'I didn't know you gambled.'

She grinned wryly. 'I don't . . . normally. But I've just finished a bitch of a job and decided, unwisely as it turned out, to let my hair down. Unfortunately I chose Jack Case's club to do it in. I should have known better, damn it!'

'Case is a roach,' Keel said. 'Always has been, always will be. From the days he used to hawk the three card trick round the Mombasa waterfront he hasn't missed an opportunity to screw something out of someone.'

'He might be a grade A one flim flam man but his club is legitimate. Private and very selective. His patrons include government ministers and the Police Commissioner. Needless to say, the authorities turn a blind eye to any indiscretions. He's almost a pillar of society, for God's sake.'

'Stroll on!'

Kate Lassiter frowned then. 'Come on, Thomas Keel. I know that look. You're plotting something. I can tell. Which brings me neatly to my next question. What the hell are you doing here? I haven't seen you for eighteen months and you pop up from nowhere doing St George impersonations and I can't recall rubbing my magic lamp, come to think of it.'

She rested her palm on his cheek, emerald eyes gazing softly into his. 'Not that I'm not pleased to see you, you understand?'

Keel returned her look. 'I came with a job offer, Kate. I need a pilot.'

141

'And here was I hoping it might have been for my beauty.' The flippant remark didn't disguise the edge to her voice.

'Low blow, Lassiter.'

Kate smiled. She arose, stroked his shoulder briefly as she moved to the rear of the cabin. A casual gesture but Keel knew it was her way of letting him know she was pleased to see him.

'I've a bottle of Black Label here somewhere.' There was a break in her voice. So low, Keel almost missed it. She had her back to him, crouched in front of one of the aft lockers. He moved towards her so silently that she was unaware of his closeness until she turned with the half empty bottle and found herself against him. Keel held her shoulders. He could feel her body shaking. Her face lifted to his. The green eyes were moist.

'Damn you, Thomas Keel! You always did have the infuriating knack of making me feel inadequate.'

A tear glistened and trickled slowly down her smooth cheek.

'I've missed you, you bastard!'

And her mouth sought his, hungrily.

God! Sekka thought, as he walked from the hotel. He actually looks pleased to see me!

It was dusk and in the half light the Mercedes looked even more forlorn and dilapidated. The driver was waiting by the car with a hesitant smile on his face and a gap between his front teeth. His name was Philimon Mkekwe. A name to conjure with.

Sekka got in the back seat. 'All right, Philimon. Drive on.'

The taxi moved out of the forecourt. 'Where to, sir?'

'Just drive me around. I want to see the city.'

It was a curious sensation. The streets appeared to be deserted except for army personnel who carried machine pistols and long riot batons. Occasionally, the car passed a group of youths congregating around some dimly lit doorway, their posture insolent and aggressive.

Most of the store fronts, Sekka noticed, were protected behind wire mesh frames. There were no window displays of the kind seen in European cities, no bright neon lights or pouting mannequins. Just a uniform starkness. Facades of dirty panes, peeling paintwork, faded posters, creaking signs hanging in the dark shadows. It presented a depressing picture.

'Where are all the people?' Sekka asked. 'All I see are soldiers and layabouts.'

The driver shrugged. 'They stay inside. It is safer.' He seemed reluctant to talk. Sekka pressed for more information.

'We have a saying in Lugamba,' Philimon said. 'We call it "to put someone in the boot".' He could see in the rear view mirror that Sekka's face registered a blank. 'It means to arrest someone. Notice the other cars in the streets: Datsuns, Peugeots, Toyotas. Most of them belong to the SASU. The men from SASU put their victims into the boots of their cars when they arrest them. They arrest a great many. Usually for no other reason than because it gives them pleasure. They enjoy seeing the terror on the faces of the people when their Datsun pulls in to the kerb. This is why the people stay indoors. They are afraid.'

They passed a row of squalid shops, windows gaping like caves.

'What do you live on?' Sekka was curious.

'Our wits.' Philimon answered without a pause. 'What else?'

'What do the people eat?'

143

'Rice mostly. Some mutton and chicken. Lugamba has very thin chickens.' Philimon almost permitted himself a smile.

Sekka believed him. The hotel fare had certainly left a lot to be desired: curried chicken cooked without salt. Also, there had been no soap in his room or, for that matter, hot water.

They turned a bend in the road and Sekka saw the soldiers immediately. They were lounging around a jeep parked against the railings of a high fence. Sekka felt the driver stiffen.

'What is it?'

'The Command Post,' Philimon said. 'President Mabato's city residence.'

Instinctively, Sekka drew back from the window.

At one time Mabato's Command Post had been a fine colonial mansion. It sat at the end of a wide gravel drive that stretched away from the huge wrought iron gates. Two pill-boxes flanked the entrance and they were both buttressed by a wall of sandbags. The defences were hardly subtle. The camouflaged fatigues of the sullen troops matched the shading of the jeep. A soviet Pulemet SGM machine gun was mounted in the rear of the vehicle, its grooved barrel pointing at the road. The soldiers looked bored. They were smoking cigarettes, cupping them in their hands like loafers the world over. They paid the Mercedes only a fleeting glance as it rolled past.

'The Liberator is not at home,' Philimon said.

'How do you know?'

'If he was, you can be sure they would not be lounging at his gate. We would have been stopped and searched.'

'And arrested?'

'Perhaps,' Philimon admitted uncomfortably.

They drove on, Philimon pointing out the various

144

landmarks. They went past the university, Magula Hospital, the law courts, the police barracks, newspaper offices and the Parliament Buildings. One building stood out above the rest, literally.

The International Conference Centre rose above the road like the side of an ocean liner made of glass. It had been built with Libyan money and Yugoslav labour and it was almost complete. The opening day would coincide with the OAU Conference due to take place in Lugamba in six days' time. It was well known that Solomon Mabato was campaigning to be elected Chairman for the coming year. The Conference Centre had been built specially and at great expense.

Another building had a more menacing aura. It was the headquarters of the Department of State Security. The three storied block, also built by Yugoslav labour, was a brooding ogre standing behind a brick wall. It sat one hundred yards away from The Lodge, Mabato's other haunt. There were unconfirmed reports that a tunnel linked the two buildings, providing Mabato with an escape route if The Lodge was ever attacked. On the other side was the building that had previously housed the Israeli Embassy. It was now used by the PLO.

Sekka looked at his watch. They had been out for nearly an hour and he sensed that the driver was growing nervous. 'One last thing,' he said. 'I want to see Maboru.'

The car swerved towards the side of the road and pulled up short. Philimon Mkekwe looked like a man whose bones had frozen.

Maboru! His passenger was mad! Philimon told him so. Nevertheless.

1840 and the Sultan of Muscat, from his stronghold on the island of Zanzibar, dispatched the Berber ivory hunter and slave trader, Hajji Sahain, into the interior to bring back what treasures he could find.

Sahain, warrior and explorer, crossed Lake Victoria by dhow and established his encampment on the north western shore. From this place, raiding parties scoured the country for game and ivory and slaves.

So, Sahain's men returned with their booty, both animal and human. The slaves – Black Ivory – were interned in the camp before being transported across the lake and then across what is now known as the Serengeti Plain and the Masai Steppe to the coast and the markets of the Sultan.

As his raiding parties criss-crossed the land, always returning with greater bounties, so the settlement grew. Sahain supervised the building of a watchtower and stockade on the promontory overlooking the shore of Lake Victoria and the surrounding delta marshes.

Now and again the local tribes would muster and attack the stockade in vain attempts to free their brothers and sisters and drive the raiders back across the Great Water. Sahain strengthened his defences and the stockade grew into a fortress with walls eight feet thick.

Hajji Sahain met his end under the thundering feet of a huge bull elephant that had been protecting its cows and calves from Sahain's ivory hunters. What remained of Sahain's body after the enraged tusker had jammed it into the branches of a baobab tree, had been carried back to the watchtower by his weeping men.

As a dreadful mark of respect for their dead leader, the hunters butchered the inmates of the compound – one hundred and sixty men, women and children. The Arabs departed, transporting Sahain's body back across Lake Victoria, to Zanzibar, leaving the watchtower as a memorial. To the tribes in the local villages that had been decimated by Sahain's raiders, the place became known as The Hill of the Dead.

Then came the Europeans – Speke and Grant and the

Bakers – and in their wake, the God Botherers, who converted the watchtower into a mission from where they dispensed religion and crude medicines in equal quantities.

Prior to the Great War, fearing the colonial expansion of a warmongering Germany, the British Army commandeered the mission and converted the building into barracks for the Askaris and their white officers. It was a natural progression for the barracks to then become a prison compound once again, though of a sturdier design than the slave enclosure of Sahain.

As the town of Kendura developed into a city, the prison overlooking Lake Victoria took on an awesome presence. Under the rule of Solomon Mabato, the prison came to epitomize the depths of human suffering. It became a place to avoid. Parents, in the way that parents have, used it as a threat to their children. If they were naughty they would be taken to the evil place. The people of Kendura had their own gruesome nickname. They called it Maboru, the Makesi word meaning 'The Sentinel' – custodian of life and death.

Sekka watched the prison and felt the skin along his spine tingle. They had driven north from Kendura, along the highway, and then taken a right turn towards the lake. The track led without deviation to the main gates. The moon was full and, when not hidden behind cloud, cast its eye over the high grey walls and the northern shore of the lake that lay beyond.

He was on his own. Philimon had driven less than a mile down the track before his nerve broke. If Philimon Mkekwe was going anywhere that night it was home to his overweight wife and his underfed offspring. Sekka, sensing the man's fear, made no attempt to dissuade him. The driver's teeth were chattering with terror. Sekka pressed notes into the shaking hands and slid out of the

147

taxi. He had barely shut the door before the vehicle had slithered in a wide turn and bumped away down the track towards the highway.

The trail was bordered by dense bush. Sekka stepped sideways into the enveloping blackness and waited to see if the Merc's engine had attracted unwanted attention. Around him, the forest was still. Unusually so. It was as if Maboru had cast its shadow over the land, stunning the bush into silence. It was uncanny.

One hundred yards away from the gates he sank to his haunches and studied the place from the cover of a stand of thorn scrub.

The outer walls were about thirty feet high with a guard tower at each corner. Entrance to the prison was through an archway in the east wall. The heavy wooden doors were set under the arch and the sentries above the entrance had an uninterrupted view of the approach road. There was a glow at the top of each tower – illumination for the guards – and Sekka knew that the towers were equipped with search lights to cover the compound.

The outer walls had no windows and the only way in was via the main gates. Sekka felt his heart sink. The project looked pretty much impossible.

And staring at it wouldn't help matters. He'd seen enough.

He retraced his steps through the undergrowth and reached the junction with the highway. It was a two mile walk back to Kendura and the hotel.

By keeping off the main thoroughfares, Sekka's trek into the capital went unnoticed by the SASU and DOSS patrols, though more than once he had to duck back into the shadows as a vehicle approached.

He was only a block away from the hotel and he knew he was being followed. He had known for some time, at

148

least a few minutes, but he took no evasive action. He wanted to know who was trailing him and why. He was aware of the small sounds behind him; the scuff of footsteps and a brief exhalation of breath that was so slight he almost missed it. And he realized there had to be more than one person and in all probability someone would be waiting for him around the next corner. One to confront, the other to block his retreat.

As it happened, there were three of them.

Young men, in cast-off clothes that spoke of poverty, with a hungry look that reflected feral cunning and street wise ambience that could be found in a thousand ghettos from Harlem to Hanoi. Two of them stepped out from the alley ahead of him, moving apart into a pincer formation. They held weapons, heavy staves that Sekka recognized as pick handles. He knew the third man was close for he could hear him coming up behind, closing in.

Sekka gauged the distance quickly and spun his back to the wall. He didn't want to give them any more room than he had to. He wanted them where he could see them.

The possibility that they were a scouting party for a larger group passed through his mind but he dismissed the idea. A big gang would surely attract the attention of a security unit. It was more likely that they were self contained, a three man team on the lookout for easy pickings, roaming the streets and alleyways like jackals picking off strays from the herd. For the moment they were viewing Sekka with interest, no doubt noting the cut of his clothes and wondering perhaps if he was a member of one of Mabato's goon squads. Sekka returned their gaze evenly. They probably wanted money or his watch, though if they thought he was either a SASU or DOSS man this was an excellent opportunity for them to vent their feelings. In which case the sheer pleasure of killing him and leaving him dead would be reward enough. Either way they weren't just going to let him walk away.

The one who had been following Sekka was holding a thin bladed knife in his right hand, his thumb resting against the blade.

Sekka saw the attack coming. It was telegraphed light years in advance.

With his back to the wall, Sekka had already adopted a defensive posture; the Sanchin stance, with both legs slightly bent, the knees pulled in towards each other and hips rotated forward and upward. Sekka held his arms to the front, elbows pulled in tight. His fists were clenched, the thumbs uppermost. In this position, Sekka would be as solid as a rock and able to absorb blows and attacks from almost any angle.

The knife came in low and very fast. Sekka's left forearm rotated downwards to block the strike, turning the man's hand away and opening his body to present a target. Sekka's right hand punched hard, delivering the blow in a screwing motion, accelerating the impact force of the fist with the first two knuckles extended, against his attacker's ribs. The man reeled back and collapsed, the knife slipping from inert fingers.

Sekka resumed his stance and regarded the other two with something close to pity. He waited.

They moved in together, clubs swinging. They expected him to back away. Instead Sekka attacked. His knee lifted and his foot crashed into the man on his left, heel smashing against the kneecap, dislocating the bone and ripping cartilage. The youth shrieked and dropped the pick handle. The third mugger's momentum carried him forward, the club whipping past Sekka's head and slamming into the wall. Off balance, the man was immediately vulnerable and Sekka caught him with an elbow strike in the stomach. Sekka straightened and exhaled slowly, relaxing. He viewed the cripples with distaste. They really hadn't stood a chance and yet they had been lucky. Sekka could have killed them.

Now they would crawl away to some dark place and nurse their wounds and maybe it would be a long time before they ventured out again in search of easy prey.

Sekka stole away, still sticking to the shadows. The whole affair had taken place in a timespan that could be measured in minutes but the last thing he wanted was to draw attention to himself. His three victims were unlikely to broadcast their defeat, however. Nevertheless, Sekka was mildly annoyed that his position could have been severely compromised. A security patrol could have chanced upon the fracas and that would have been disastrous. Above all, he had to keep a low profile. First rule: never draw attention to yourself.

Back at the hotel, Sekka headed for the bar. The place had all the cosy intimacy of a British Rail buffet. The prices were exorbitant and there was no ice as the hotel's refrigeration unit was out of order – again.

After two lukewarm beers Sekka was quite thankful to gain the isolation of his room.

The stomach pains started that evening.

At first, Holt thought it was indigestion but the pain persisted and common sense told him otherwise, particularly when he was kneeling, head hanging over the bucket in the corner of the cell, retching violently, watched by a totally unsympathetic guard who was standing over him with a rifle cradled in the crook of his arm.

The stench in the cell was appalling. Holt closed his eyes in agony as his stomach muscles, already strained to the

151

point of rupture, twisted with the effort of puking the remains of his meal. With his hands clasping the rim of the bucket like a baby clinging to its mother, Holt was in no fit state to reflect on the position he was in. He was completely drained and began to sweat freely within the cloying, foetid confines of the tiny room.

After what seemed like an eternity Holt forced himself to his feet. He acknowledged that that in itself was a major achievement. An acute case of food poisoning was the last thing he needed in his present predicament. He couldn't maintain the posture, however, and he fell forward on to the single ragged blanket that covered his rock hard bunk. The pain in his belly and groin had dulled to an ache. Holt slipped into unconsciousness. He was unaware of the tread of boots in the passage or the fumbling of hands that lifted his limp, unresisting form off the bunk and carried him out of the cell.

7

The helicopter was a yellow and black striped Bell Jet Ranger and they boarded it in the western corner of the airport.

It was barely dawn but very warm. Both Garrick Kirby and Garside were in dress uniform again and they were feeling hot and sticky and half asleep. They had been roused at what seemed to have been the dead of night to be told that Mabato had summoned them.

To Jimbu.

Garrick Kirby dredged his memory. It was Mabato's home village. One hundred and fifty odd miles away. Oh, God.

Their pilot, a tall rangy individual, regarded the envoys with cautious interest. He waited until the passengers were strapped in the rear seats before he addressed them.

'Make yourselves comfortable, gentlemen. Sit back and enjoy the view.' The nasal voice was pure Strine. More Alice Springs and Hall's Creek than the African bush. 'I'm Clem Wallace and this walking pustule is Corporal Tembu.'

The pilot jerked his thumb at a squat African in army fatigues who was about to climb into the other crew seat. Tembu was adorned with weapons. He had a hip holster containing a heavy automatic, a sheathed panga at his waist and in his podgy hands he clutched a Kalashnikov automatic rifle. The banana shaped magazine was quite unmistakable.

'He's here to protect you,' Wallace went on. 'Though

153

from what I can't imagine. Besides, it'd take him half a bloody hour to find the safety catch. Wouldn't it, you syphilitic little fart?' He grinned and nodded to Tembu who grinned back like a monkey. 'As you may have gathered, his command of English ain't so hot.'

Garrick Kirby and Garside exchanged glances. Wallace merely chuckled as he showed them their headsets and started the rotors. The Jet Ranger vibrated and rose from the tarmac like an angry wasp. The Australian angled the stick and the Bell dipped and slid around before gaining height over the maintenance sheds and side slipping over the field. With a few curt words to the tower, the aircraft whisked its way into the sky and turned north.

'Easy,' Wallace told them a while later, 'I do it for the money.' He had answered Garside's obvious question.

They were flying at a height of two thousand feet, having traced the river north for some time before altering on to a course that took them over a harsh expanse of brown plain dotted with thorn trees and criss crossed by what looked to be dozens of dried river beds. An uninviting land that was, despite its stark features, hauntingly beautiful in the early light of dawn. The sky to the east was streaked blood red.

'Heck,' Wallace explained. 'They're paying me six thousand bucks a month. Where else could I earn that sort of money? It ain't illegal and it sure as hell beats crop spraying and there's a lot of ex-service blokes who've been reduced to doing that for a living. Me? I'm single, over twenty one and no responsibilities. They've even thrown in free board. I think my place used to belong to the Minister of Culture before Mabato threw him out.' He glanced sideways at the corporal who was busy studying the geography. 'Mind you, I'm not saying that I like the people I work for. Mabato's a bloody barbarian. I'm not stupid. I know what goes on here. Most of us Vets know but we're banking the cash and just waiting for the day when we've put enough by to be able to get the hell out. And I'll tell you something. When I go this little bird goes with me.'

Wallace patted the controls of the chopper affectionately.

'If you think I'd leave her in the hands of those ignorant bastards, you've another think coming. Ain't that a fact, Tembu my old mate?'

The corporal, hearing his name, grinned good naturedly before resuming his examination of the terrain, the Kalashnikov cradled across his stubby knees.

'Stupid little prick,' Wallace said. He gazed ahead through the morning haze. 'Almost there, folks. Extinguish all smokes, fasten safety belts, usual crap.'

Garside looked over his shoulder, through the screen. They had lost height and were buzzing along the floor of a dry valley. Ahead, two hills rose like breasts from the plain. In the cleft between them, Garside could make out a collection of huts and thorn fenced livestock pens. As they dropped closer, the people emerged to stand in small groups to observe the landing.

The helicopter settled, the spinning rotors flicking dust and stones into the faces of the villagers.

Wallace removed his head mike and thrust a hand through his tousled fair hair. 'This is it, mates. If the world had piles, it'd have 'em here.'

The heat was solid, like a wall. Garrick Kirby and Garside, heads thrumming, clambered from the chopper and waited.

'Stone me!' Wallace breathed. 'What a bloody dump!'

There was a commotion among a group of villagers. They broke apart and from their midst strode a short skinny figure in an ill-fitting uniform.

155

Major Farouk Juma marched to within a yard of the expectant envoys, threw up a travesty of a salute and through rotting teeth said: 'Good morning, General. I will take you to His Excellency.'

Juma about turned, giving them no chance to reply. They followed at a brisk pace and hadn't gone ten yards before they were both soaked in perspiration.

Clem Wallace watched them go then he climbed into the rear of the helicopter. From a locker he removed a portable ice box and lifted from it a blue and silver can of Fosters. He stared at the backs of the two Englishmen as they were swallowed up by a curious throng of natives in various stages of undress and emaciation.

Wallace raised the can to his lips. 'Good luck, mates. Don't forget to keep that upper lip stiff,' he muttered. He took a gulp of lager and looked around for the corporal. He was probably having it off with one of the women. The man had the morals of a goat.

'Corporal Tembu!' Wallace yelled. 'I hope you get the clap, you little turd!'

The villagers were a sorry looking lot; men sullen, women subdued, children patently undernourished. A few mangy dogs ran and tumbled in the dust around the huts and scrawny bush fowl pecked unenthusiastically at a pitiful scattering of corn husks. With downcast eyes, the natives followed the path of the envoys as they walked across the beaten ground to one hut that was slightly larger than the rest. It appeared to be constructed with a framework of staves and a tatty covering of haphazardly strewn hides. The entrance was low. Following Juma's directions, Garrick Kirby and his aide had to stoop almost double in order to enter.

Hampered as he was by his dress sword, Garrick Kirby had some difficulty maintaining his balance as he entered the hut and he stumbled forward almost on to his knees. The interior was dark and smelled of unwashed bodies and goats. Garside, bringing up the rear, collided with Garrick Kirby's backside and cursed violently, all pretence at dignity now destroyed.

At first, Garrick Kirby thought it was a trick of the light or maybe the effect of the heat. He blinked in the gloom and digested the sight that met his astonished gaze. Garside groped his way forward and pulled up with a jolt.

Arrows of sunlight were piercing the ragged walls of the hut and now that the entrance was unblocked it was becoming easier to see.

Solomon Mabato sat on a low kaross covered stool in the centre of the hut. He appeared totally unperturbed at the reaction of the two envoys. Mabato's head-dress was made from the finest ostrich feathers. A lion's tooth necklace hung around his thick neck, its lower loop lost in the folds of his vast belly. The maned pelt of a magnificent lion lay across his broad back, the front paws reaching over his shoulders and entwining on his chest. His bulbous calves were gartered with mane. In his hands he held an oval hide shield and a knobkerrie. Like a resurrected Dingane, he surveyed his audience.

Behind his back stood two of his Nubian bodyguards in army fatigues, festooned with weapons, including the inevitable Kalashnikovs. They regarded the awestruck envoys with undisguised suspicion.

Juma pushed his way to Mabato's side. The President beamed. 'My dear friends! Welcome! How good it is to see you after all these years.'

'It is a great honour, Excellency.' Garrick Kirby managed the words with some effort. He wondered if he was expected to bow and then thought to hell with it.

Mabato said: 'I regret I was unable to meet you on your

157

arrival but affairs of state, you know.' He waved his hand vaguely. 'You have been looked after well?'

Garrick Kirby had a brief vision of Brigadier Epunau excavating his ear and said: 'Everyone has been very considerate.'

Garside took the opportunity to clear his throat. He was still trying to come to terms with the sight of Mabato clad in a loin cloth and not much else. But at least the fat slob was cool. He could feel sweat running from his armpits like rivers.

Garrick Kirby said formally: 'We both know, Excellency, why Major Garside and I are here. Perhaps we could get to the matter in hand? I have the letter – '

'You will be silent!' Mabato's voice was like a rumble of thunder. 'I did not give you permission to speak! Garrick Kirby, you are no longer my commanding officer. Or had you forgotten? You are here at my will. You would do well to remember that!'

Garrick Kirby went rigid with indignation. Garside stiffened. The ball had been played. What the hell was the Old Man going to do now?

Incredibly, Mabato was smiling again. 'You must be in need of refreshment after your journey from Kendura. What did you think of my helicopter, General? Is it not a fine machine? It was donated by my good friend Colonel Gadaffi. A generous ruler and a truly great Muslim. He has been a major source of inspiration to me since I adopted the true faith.'

'I'm sure he has,' Garrick Kirby said.

'Come, gentlemen, be seated. Let us not stand on formality. We are old comrades. Sit down, sit down.'

Mabato flapped his hands expansively. It took a second for them to realize that they were being offered the comfort of the bare mud floor of the hut. Mabato watched

158

them impassively as they sank down uncomfortably, constricted by their uniforms.

Mabato laid the shield and knobkerrie aside and clapped his hands together imperiously. Incredibly, there sounded the distinct rattle of teacups and the entrance was again blocked as a thin figure entered the hut with a tray balanced precariously in his hands. The tray contained a china teapot, three cups and saucers, sugar basin, milk jug, teaspoons and a pair of silver tongs.

The tray bearer negotiated his way gingerly around the squatting envoys and stood, head bowed, awaiting Mabato's orders. Garside followed the servant's progress, senses reeling. As the face of the man came out of the shadows, Garside heard the hiss of astonishment escape Garrick Kirby's lips. Mabato watched their dumbstruck expressions with acute enjoyment.

David Holt, head bowed, hands shaking visibly, was having a job to stop the tray and its contents from rattling. Clad in a freshly pressed khaki shirt and matching shorts, with sandals on his feet, he looked like a man teetering on the verge of collapse.

God in Heaven! Garrick Kirby swung at Mabato. 'What is the meaning of this?'

'My new house-boy,' Mabato said casually. 'He is still learning but I will soon . . . how do you say it, General? Ah, yes. Lick him into shape. I remember those words when I was a recruit in the 4th Battalion. Now, shall I be mother?' He chuckled. In the strained atmosphere, the sound was chillingly grotesque.

Garrick Kirby struggled to his feet, his expression carved in flint. 'This is monstrous! An outrage! As a representative of Her Majesty's Government, I protest most vigorously at this . . . this inhuman display!'

'Yes,' Mabato said. 'Do you take sugar, General?'

Christ! Garside thought Garrick Kirby was going to strike out. The hand holding the hilt of his sword was white. Holt's expression hadn't altered. It was vacant as though he was on drugs. Maybe he was, Garside pondered. Or maybe it was just fear.

Garside leaned forward and touched Garrick Kirby's sleeve. 'Perhaps, sir, we should wait and see what His Excellency has to say. We are here as his guests after all.'

Garrick Kirby's look was venomous. His eyes flamed for a brief second then he nodded slowly and cleared his throat.

'Yes. Quite right, quite right. We must respect His Excellency's hospitality. Forgive me, sir. That outburst was quite uncalled for.'

Mabato nodded slowly, his brutal face blank as he gazed at Garrick Kirby. The latter felt tendrils of apprehension crawl along his spine.

Mabato snapped his fingers and Holt shuffled forward. Mabato, ostrich feathers dipping as he performed the task, poured three cups of tea and handed two to the envoys. Garrick Kirby, totally frustrated, accepted his and sat down again.

'As you can see, General, Mister Holt is in excellent health,' Mabato said. 'In Lugamba we do not mistreat our prisoners. All are well cared for. Good food, clean cells, clean clothes. All the things that the British Press say about conditions in Lugamba are lies.' He pointed at Holt. 'Ask him if he is treated badly.'

Garrick Kirby looked at David Holt who in turn looked as though he wanted to be anywhere but where he was.

'Mister Holt?' Garrick Kirby addressed the subdued figure. 'Do you know why we are here?' He indicated Garside as he spoke.

No reply.

160

Garrick Kirby frowned. This was not what he had expected. He tried again. 'Mister Holt, I am General Garrick Kirby and this is Major Garside. We are here to help you. I want to know if you are all right.'

Holt stirred and gazed at Garrick Kirby through vacant eyes. Or was there a glimmer of mute appeal? Garside felt uneasy.

'They are treating me very well.' The voice was low, barely audible. 'My cell is clean and the food is quite adequate.' He paused as though uncertain. 'I am very sorry for all the trouble I have caused.'

'You see,' Mabato cut in. 'Was I not right?'

Garrick Kirby said: 'I would like to speak to Mister Holt alone.'

'I regret that is not possible, General.'

'Why not?'

'Because I said so.'

Garrick Kirby, with a great deal of self control, held himself in check. Don't push it.

With a dismissive flick of his wrist, Mabato indicated that Holt's presence was no longer required. The cowed and pale hostage left the tray at Mabato's feet and backed out of the hut.

'There, General. It is as I said.' Mabato smiled.

Garrick Kirby shook his head. 'Despite your assurances, sir, I am not convinced that Mister Holt is a healthy man. He looked weak and disorientated.'

The President shrugged. 'He has been in prison, not a rest home. We have been very lenient with him.'

'Nevertheless you intend to execute him?' countered Garrick Kirby harshly.

'Of course.' A smile played along the full lips. Mabato looked almost benevolent. Garside felt his stomach curdle.

'You know, General,' Mabato said conversationally, 'I

161

was very sorry to have missed the royal wedding but I did of course send a greeting to my great friend Queen Elizabeth.'

'Er – ' Garrick Kirby's eyebrows lifted and he looked at his aide for assistance.

'I'm sure Her Majesty understood,' Garside answered gravely. From what he remembered of the event, there had been consternation that Mabato would invite himself to the ceremony after having been deleted from the list of desirables some considerable time before.

The same degree of unease had been voiced during the weeks prior to the last Commonwealth Conference in London. Mabato had announced regally that he would be flying to Heathrow in his own 707, complete with personal aides and two hundred members of the State Dance Troupe. The corridors of power had positively vibrated at that one. In the event, to Whitehall's relief, Mabato had decided to stay in Lugamba. This had not prevented him from expounding his views to the other Commonwealth leaders from afar. Or for that matter any other world leaders. He touched on a variety of subjects, ranging from admiration of Hitler's Final Solution and his intention of erecting a statue of Der Fuhrer in the heart of Kendura to wishing Nixon a speedy recovery from Watergate.

'When this Holt affair is over,' Mabato continued, 'I will make a State Visit to Great Britain and ride through London with the Queen and we will talk of many things.'

Garside could see that Garrick Kirby was beginning to flounder at this turn of events. He said hurriedly: 'We have a letter for you from the Queen. Perhaps she mentions a visit?'

God forbid.

Garrick Kirby, with the look of a drowning man clutching at a straw, saw his chance and accepted the envelope from his aide. He handed it to Mabato.

'Ah, yes,' Mabato said. 'The letter which begs for the Englishman's life.'

The reading took a few moments, Mabato's broad brow furrowing as he concentrated on the text. At least he's got the bloody thing the right way up, Garside thought.

Mabato looked up. 'So.'

The envoys waited expectantly.

'The letter talks of the respect that the people of Lugamba and Great Britain have for one another. This is a very fine sentiment.'

The President held the paper in his fingers and waved it under Garrick Kirby's nose. 'I will think on this and give you my decision after I have consulted with my ministers.' He lumbered heavily to his feet, his bodyguards moving to his side. Farouk Juma, who had remained in silent malevolent attendance throughout the procedures, ducked out of the hut.

'Make yourselves comfortable, my friends. I will return. I will have my people bring food and drink.' He paused at the entrance and the hut was immediately darkened. He eyed the envoys speculatively.

'Do you want me to send you a woman, General? She will help pass the hours.'

Even Garside spluttered at this. Garrick Kirby's mouth opened and closed like a goldfish.

Mabato shrugged and squeezed his huge bulk through the entrance like toothpaste out of a tube. Garrick Kirby and Garside regarded each other with bewilderment.

'He's mad,' Garside said eventually.

'That,' Garrick Kirby said, 'is a gross understatement.'

'A certified bloody lunatic!' Garside shook his head in wonderment. 'That poor bastard, Holt.'

Garrick Kirby nodded thoughtfully. 'I didn't like the look of him at all.'

'So, what do we do, sir?'

Garrick Kirby eased his cramped limbs then he removed his sword. 'I suggest, Bob, we make ourselves as comfortable as this hovel will allow. Something tells me that we may have quite a long wait.'

Gregori Alexis Burov's thoughts, as he waited for Mabato, were of a small picturesque wooden dacha sheltering under the pine trees on the shore of the Kuban River a few miles south of his home town of Krasnodar in Eastern Georgia. Even now, standing on the veranda of Mabato's villa overlooking the muddy Jimbu River, Burov had only to close his eyes to smell the heavy fragrance of the pine forest and the scent of woodsmoke.

His brown eyes flickered open and ranged down the slope to the meandering watercourse that disappeared behind a stand of thorn scrub three hundred yards away. Sudden movement. A heron flapped lazily over the river to its nest hidden in the reeds on the far bank, a silver flash of sunlight glancing off the scales of the wriggling fish impaled on its long bill.

Burov was a short wide shouldered man in his fifties. His greying hair was receding at the temples and his broad heavy jowled face was centred by a crooked nose that he had broken as a youth during a boxing tournament in his early days at Kiev University. His eyes, deepset under dark brows, gazed out at the world with a benign disposition. He looked like everyone's favourite uncle. He was dressed in a white cotton shirt and cream slacks.

Mabato walked on to the veranda, accompanied by his bodyguards and the shrew-like Farouk Juma. The President had changed into an olive green tunic and trousers.

'I take it the meeting with the British envoys has taken place?' Burov inquired.

164

Mabato towered above the Russian yet in some ways it was the man from Georgia who radiated authority.

Mabato said: 'Did I not tell you that the British would heed my warning?'

'They had little choice,' Burov replied candidly. 'What did you tell them?'

'To wait.'

'I would like to see the letter, Excellency.' Burov held out his hand. Mabato passed it over.

'As I suspected, platitudes! Are you going to let these empty words influence your decision?' He sneered contemptuously. 'Is there a mention of spares for your armoured cars or a promise that the British press will cease their malicious rumouring? No. They promise you nothing. As I in fact warned you.'

Burov's eyes were now burning with a fierce intensity. 'The British hope to cover their deceit with meaningless rhetoric. Surely you will not allow yourself to be overawed by this diplomatic prose? Excellency, a man of your calibre, your wisdom, deserves much more!'

Burov amazed himself sometimes with the verbal diarrhoea he was forced to emit.

Mabato reflected for a moment. 'What should I do?'

Burov held up a hand. 'Excellency, this is not for me to say. The decision must be yours alone.' He paused for effect. 'But think on this. Did not my government promise you a loan three months ago in order that new factories and houses could be built? And now that loan has been finalized with, of course, a personal consideration for yourself as a gesture of our respect for your stature as a great statesman and warrior.'

Burov cringed inwardly at this. He went on. 'And the recent supply of MiG fighters has proved invaluable in the formation of your air force. Once your pilots are trained, you will have the most experienced operational squadrons in East Africa.' (Might as well teach monkeys to fly!) 'And even now, your new battle tanks are being off loaded from a Soviet freighter at Mombasa prior to being transported by road to Kendura.'

Mabato's eyes lit up. 'That is good. I need those tanks. Soon I will have enough tanks to invade Tanzania and South Africa and destroy my enemies. Tell me, when will they arrive?'

'By tomorrow evening, providing the Kenyan Government give them a clear passage as we were promised.'

Mabato's eyes grew into slits. 'The Kenyan President knows better than to stand in my way. My wrath would be terrible to see.'

'You have no cause for alarm,' Burov pointed out. 'My own government have placed certain pressures on President Nai. There will be no trouble. Also some of our best technicians will be accompanying the vehicles and the Kenyans know better than to harass Soviet citizens. The tanks will arrive, never fear. We do not break our promises.'

'You'll have to play it by ear at first, Gregori,' Nikolai Kolk had advised him on the day he had been summoned to the grey stone building on Dzerzhinsky Square, known as The Centre. A new headquarters complex was located on the outskirts of the city but somehow it didn't have the same atmosphere. It looked more like a big hotel. Most of the hierarchy maintained some presence here in The Centre.

Burov showed his pass and made his way down the light green painted corridor to the stairs that would take him up to the offices on the third floor, his footsteps loud on the uncarpeted parquet.

He had been shown into a high ceilinged room. The office was uncluttered. The furniture consisted of a wide desk, four chairs, a bank of filing cabinets and a large squat safe crouching in a corner. A portrait of Felix Dzerzhinsky, founder of the Cheka, hung on one wall. It matched the one that hung in the Chairman's ornate office further along the passage.

Kolk was a prim, handsome man with thick, wavy black hair. He headed Department Nine of the First Chief Directorate of the KGB. He was responsible for the KGB's activities throughout the English speaking nations of Africa.

Kolk gazed between the steel bars on the window into the courtyard below, hands clasped behind his back. He was dressed in a very expensively tailored grey suit, white shirt and maroon and blue striped tie. His shoes were highly polished black Italian moccasins.

'This Solomon Mabato is a highly unpredictable individual,' Kolk said.

'Unpredictable? He's a bloody maniac!' exclaimed Burov. 'He makes Uncle Joseph look like Olga Korbut!'

'I'll grant you he has an alarming tendency to over react,' Kolk admitted thoughtfully. He turned from the window and walked to the desk. Sitting down, he cupped his well formed hands, placed elbows on the jotter and rested his chin on his knuckles.

'So, why get further involved?' Burov asked.

Kolk smiled patiently. 'Expediency, my dear Gregori. A foothold in East Africa would certainly be beneficial to our overseas policy. Already we hold the Horn of Africa, Mozambique, Somalia and Angola. Greater influence in Lugamba with its central position and borders with Tanzania and Kenya would suit us very well indeed.'

'We don't want another Afghanistan,' Burov said. 'Look

what happened there. We aren't exactly high in the popularity stakes.'

'Have no fear of that. Why, with Mabato sending students to Patrice Lumumba University, we've a finger in the pie already. Don't forget that after he lost favour with the British and the Israelis he did jump at our initial and, if I may say so, rather modest offer of economic and military aid. Mabato has been teetering long enough. I think the time has come to remind him just where his loyalties lie. Now is the time to move. A more generous development loan from us at this moment would see him in our pockets for good.'

'What the hell is he going to develop?' Burov looked incredulously at his superior. 'His industries have collapsed and his crops have withered to dust.'

'Frankly, Gregori, I don't care if he puts the stuff in his Swiss bank account, so long as he is in our debt. That is all that is important at this stage.'

Burov looked sceptical.

'Gregori, we have great faith in you. The Chairman asked for you personally. You did valuable groundwork in Somalia and Angola. Your experience will be invaluable in paving the way for us in Lugamba. Mabato has very few allies. Use that experience to gain his confidence. Believe me, Gregori, he is ripe for plucking.'

'I'm flattered, Comrade Kolk,' Burov acknowledged the compliment. 'Please relay my respects to the Chairman. It seems that the decision has been made for me. When do I leave?'

'In ten days' time a Libyan delegation is visiting Lugamba. You will accompany the delegation and you will be introduced to Mabato at the same time. It will be up to you to do the rest. I will rely on your judgement.'

★ ★ ★

168

Burov dragged his thoughts back to the present. His briefing with Kolk had taken place six months ago. Six months of kowtowing to an overweight, half-witted sadist. However, the ploy had paid dividends in the shape of the MiG fighters on the runway, the balance of Mabato's numbered account at the Credit Suisse in Geneva and the six T-54 battle tanks that were being off loaded from the *Ivan Stetchkin* at Mombasa. Mabato was well and truly in the bag. It wouldn't be long before Burov was back in Krasnodar, leaving Mabato in the tender care of the Soviet attachés who would be sent in ostensibly to promote diplomatic relations between Kendura and Moscow while at the same time ensuring that Mabato honoured his side of the loan agreement. This would be achieved by handing the Russians the building that had once housed the West German embassy for use as a consulate and security base from where they could monitor non-Soviet activity in East and Central Africa.

From there it would only be a matter of time before the first detachment of Soviet ground forces arrived, as military advisers of course.

Jack Case lolled back in his leather chair and rested his feet on his desk. He was heavy set with an expensively acquired tan. His brown hair was well groomed and he sported a John Newcombe style moustache. He was smartly dressed in a cream Cardin suit and gold bracelets adorned each wrist. The overall effect was somewhat ostentatious but nevertheless he presented a picture of a suave, well-to-do businessman. He was all these. He was also very dangerous.

The office was all chrome and glass and low backed sofas. A well stocked drinks cabinet sat against one wall next to a bank of impressive stereo equipment and video screens. When activated, the screens projected various areas of Case's club: restaurant, casino, discotheque and, on occasions, the guest rooms.

'Right, darling,' Case said. 'Let's see what you've got.'

The girl standing in front of the desk was a blonde and strikingly attractive. She regarded Case with cool blue eyes. 'Here?'

'Sure. Why not, babe?' Case smiled. His teeth were very white and even. 'We'll have some music.' He indicated the stereo. 'Help you to relax maybe?'

The girl shrugged. 'Okay. If you like.'

Case reached on to the desk and picked up the remote control unit. He pressed a button and the cassette deck clicked into action. The slow, heavy, rhythmic beat of a Donna Summer record invaded the room. The singer sounded as though she was in the deep throes of ecstasy and rapidly approaching a climax.

'How's that?' Case asked.

The blonde smiled and nodded. 'Oh, that's good.' Her voice had a husky quality that Case found exciting.

The girl placed her shoulder bag on the sofa behind her and stood with hands on hips, legs slightly akimbo, as she listened to the music. She wore a red calf length dress, slit on one side to mid thigh. As she posed, the slit widened to reveal creamy skin sheathed in black nylon. Case felt his pulse quicken.

The girl's eyes were half closed, her mouth open, agile tongue caressing moist pink lips as she caught the beat. Then she began to strip.

She was good, very good. Despite having auditioned scores of girls and therefore being able usually to remain detached from the energetic gyrations, Case found himself only too aware of this particular girl's blatant aura of sexuality.

170

She eased out of the dress as though shedding a second skin and, clad in flimsy black lace bra, minute panties, stockings and suspenders, she turned her back to present Case with a view of rounded hips and taut buttocks, panties tight over the curve of her cheeks. She bent forward and knelt on the thick carpet, rested on her elbows and rotated and dipped her pelvis. Reaching one hand back through her legs, she caught the waist of the tiny panties between finger and thumb and teased them down over her firm rear, at the same time allowing her fingers to caress her cleft.

Case was acutely conscious of his uneven breathing and he felt himself growing hard as Donna Summer moaned on the stereo and the girl, breasts now free of the constricting bra, stroked her inner thighs and brought herself to fever pitch in time to the singer. A thin sheen of perspiration shone over the girl's undulating body as her moans matched the incessant beat from the speakers.

The shrill beep of the telephone jerked Case out of his erotic trance. At the third beep he used the remote control to turn down the music. The blonde, now sprawled on her back with knees bent, seemed unaware of the interruption, her breath coming in quick gasps as she stroked and manipulated her bushy sex. Completely drowning in her own fantasy, she arched her splendid back abruptly and a shuddering groan heralded her self induced climax as Case lifted the receiver.

Case, hard eyes still roaming over the glistening, naked contours, stiffened as he listened. His face clouded and he said sharply: 'No! Get rid of them!' He slammed the receiver down.

The blonde was breathing more evenly now though her eyes were still closed. Her perfect breasts, crested with dark brown, erect nipples, rose and fell. Her hand traced

171

one beautiful orb like a lover and she opened her eyes slowly. As if awaking from a deep sleep, she smiled languidly at her audience. 'Well, do I pass?'

'With flying colours, love,' Case said with feeling. He swung his feet off the desk and moved towards her.

The door opened. Keel walked in with Harry Roan and an irate Ferris.

Case swung. 'What the fuck!'

'I'm Keel. This is Roan and you, dear, had better remove your delectable body pronto.'

The girl had half risen at the unexpected entrance. She made no attempt to conceal herself but, taking one look at Keel's ice blue eyes, she evidently thought better about answering back. Casting a quick, nervous glance at Case standing there with his mouth open and a look of fury on his face, she scrambled for her discarded dress. Breasts jiggling, she shook it over her head, the movement accentuating her sweet curves and flat stomach. Bundling her flimsy underthings into her bag, she scampered for the door.

Roan whistled in admiration as the blonde disappeared. 'Very nice! I sure hope we managed to interrupt something, Mister Case.' He grinned disarmingly.

'What the hell is this?' snarled Case. He backed against the desk. 'This is a private club. Ferris, I thought I told you to get rid of them?'

'He did try,' Keel said. 'But he wasn't too successful. Were you, son?'

Ferris looked very uncomfortable.

Then it dawned on Case. 'You,' he said. 'You're the one who had that dust-up with Ferris and John John. Lassiter's friend.'

'Bang on,' Keel said. He closed the door. 'And don't go near that drawer, Case. It could prove fatal.'

Case pulled back his hand as if he'd been stung. 'So you've come to scare me off,' he said.

'Wrong,' Keel replied. 'I've come to pay you off.'

Ferris began a subtle move away from the two mercenaries, his arm lifting towards his jacket.

'Don't even think about it,' Harry Roan said. 'Just keep perfectly still and you won't get hurt.'

Ferris dropped his arm and Roan smiled.

'Pay me off?' Case chuckled suddenly. 'Hear that, Ferris? It's enough to restore one's faith in human nature.'

Ferris didn't look too impressed.

'I believe the amount outstanding on Lassiter's account is six thousand dollars,' Keel said.

'Plus the interest of course,' Case said.

'Don't push your luck. You'll get six thousand and like it.'

Case watched in silence as Keel threw a wad of dollar bills on to the desk top.

'The debt is paid in full, Case,' said Keel.

'Well, pick it up, Case,' Harry Roan advised. 'It won't bite you for Christ's sake!'

As Case extended a hand, Keel cut in. 'One last thing. If either you or any of your goons make any approach to Kate Lassiter, I will come looking for you. Do I make myself clear?'

'As crystal,' Case replied. His eyes glittered angrily.

'Good. So long as we understand each other. How about you, Harpo?'

Ferris nodded dumbly.

'Right, Mister Case. Thank you for your time. No. Don't fret. We can see ourselves out.' Keel opened the door and he and Roan backed out, leaving Case and Ferris staring after them.'

'Bastards!' Ferris hissed. 'Fucking bastards!'

173

Case regarded his subordinate stonily. He was aware also of a low noise coming from the stereo speakers. Donna was still at it. With a curse of annoyance he flicked the cassette off. 'Not exactly effective are we, Ferris? I mean, they just walked in didn't they? Where the hell were you? Damn it, Ferris, I pay you to protect my arse and my privacy yet they waltzed in like it was bloody Open Day or something! You know, Ferris, having met Mister Keel, I reckon you were let off lightly last night.'

'He was lucky, that's all. I could have taken him.'

'Crap,' Case said. 'He could have killed you. That is one very hard man. He reeks of violence. He could have taken you and John John with one hand tied behind his back. The same would apply to his companion, unless I miss my guess.'

Ferris clenched his fists in frustration. 'So, that's it then? You're going to let them get away with it?'

Case pondered the thought. He had been shaken severely by this turn of events. His defences had been breached and he didn't like that. In fact he wasn't going to stand for it.

'Good Lord! Did I say that, Ferris? Surely you're not serious? I've my reputation to consider. No. I have in mind a means of getting even with our friends, Keel and Roan. Not to mention Kate Lassiter.'

Ferris perked up considerably at this.

'Get hold of John John and get back to me. And another thing. I didn't catch the name of that last girl, the energetic one. I want it and her telephone number. Well, what the hell are you waiting for, Ferris? Your fucking pension?'

At noon, Mabato reappeared. The charade was over for he was dressed in tunic and trousers. Garrick Kirby and Garside, after three hours of confinement in the sweltering

174

hut, had thrown protocol to the winds. They had taken off their jackets, loosened ties and rolled sleeves up to their elbows. They both had splitting headaches.

'Ah, General Kirby, I hope you have been comfortable in my absence. I am sorry for the delay but as you can imagine, I have been talking with my conscience. I have had many things to think about.'

'I understand,' Garrick Kirby replied, dabbing his throbbing forehead with his handkerchief. 'What answer can I take back to my government, Mister President?'

'You will tell the Queen that I am happy to have received her letter. You will tell your Prime Minister that I will execute the Englishman, David Holt, in four days' time.'

Warren-Chase stared aghast at the two distraught envoys. 'You are joking?'

'Don't be bloody silly!' Garside snapped.

Warren-Chase flushed, then he mumbled sheepishly: 'You're right of course. That was a stupid remark to make. Oh . . . damn it to hell! That idiot!' He rested his head in his hands.

After the glowering Mabato had relayed his decision, Garrick Kirby and Garside had wasted no time in returning to the helicopter and flying back to Kendura. They reported the news to Warren-Chase upon their arrival.

'But didn't the President listen to anything you had to say?' asked Warren-Chase.

Garrick Kirby shook his grey head. 'He just wasn't interested.'

'Kept burbling on about spare parts for his bloody armoured cars and malicious reports in the press,' cut in Garside. 'Refused to even consider a reprieve unless the Foreign Secretary put in a personal appearance.'

'And that's out of the question,' Warren-Chase said.

'As you rightly say,' agreed Garrick Kirby.

James Henderson, hovering by the desk, said: 'We'd better get the cable off, sir. London will be expecting word.'

'There's nothing you two can think of that would get us out of this mess?' Warren-Chase looked hopefully towards the general and his aide.

'I think it's gone too far for that,' Garrick Kirby said. 'This can only be resolved at a higher level. It's way out of our league now. If some solution is to be found, it has to be found soon. Within four days to be exact.'

'God! I feel so bloody impotent,' Warren-Chase sighed. 'What are your plans now? You'll be wanting to return to London as soon as possible I suppose?'

'As soon as you can arrange a flight for us.'

'Henderson?' Warren-Chase addressed his aide.

'First thing tomorrow morning, sir. Sabena again. We can get you back through Nairobi and Brussels.'

'Very well,' Warren-Chase said. 'We'll make the arrangements. James, let's get the signal off. I have a feeling that, to quote the vernacular, the shit is about to hit the fan.'

'Holy Christ!' Lennox erupted. 'That's all we bloody need! I felt damned sure their visit would have done the trick.'

'Evidently it didn't,' Wood said.

'You know, David, your powers of observation can be quite staggering at times,' Lennox said testily. 'Anyway, that puts the ball well and truly in our court. You've told Dalkeith?'

Wood nodded. 'Look, there's still time for me to fly – '

'No!' Lennox's tone was firm. 'You will not go to Kendura under duress. How many times do I have to tell you?'

'So?'

'So, it doesn't leave us much choice now, does it?'

'You mean our last resort?'

Lennox shrugged. 'We've run out of time. We've no alternative. Phone Dalkeith. Tell him it's on. He's to send them in.'

They met by the Albert Memorial. Dalkeith was holding a briefcase.

'So, you want them to go in,' Cameron said.

'That's right. Unleash them. We want Holt out.'

'I guessed as much.' Cameron had purchased an evening edition of the *Standard*. By now the envoys' mission of mercy was common knowledge and there hadn't been any delay in the latest news reaching London from Lugamba. The front page carried the disclosure that the pleas of the British envoys had failed. They would be returning home in the morning.

'How soon can you get word to the team?' Dalkeith asked.

'As soon as I get back to the office. I can relay a telex.' Cameron glanced over Dalkeith's shoulder. There was no sign of Frank.

'Excellent,' Dalkeith responded.

Cameron said: 'Once I contact them, they'll go in. Probably tonight.' Where the hell was Frank?

'Fine.' Dalkeith turned away casually and gazed out across Kensington Gardens.

It was a pleasant afternoon. A few couples were strolling arm in arm and office workers were beginning to make their way home. Down Lancaster Walk some youngsters were playing tag. A road sweeper was pushing his yellow cart down the path. The scampering children were using it as a shield.

Dalkeith held out the briefcase. 'The first instalment. In cash as you requested. Sixty five thousand.'

Cameron took the case. 'That's it then. They're committed.'

The sound of laughing children carried across the path. The road sweeper was conscientiously retrieving Mars wrappers and orange peel from the grass around the benches, spearing the offending litter with a long pronged stick. He was dropping the rubbish into his cart, head bowed in concentration.

Dalkeith pursed his lips. 'Let's hope nothing goes wrong.'

'They're the best,' Cameron said. 'If they can't do it, nobody can.'

From the yellow cart, Frank Ketch, in blue overalls, lifted the Pentax and aimed the 80-200mm f4 zoom lens towards the memorial. He took half a dozen exposures before concealing the camera in the top layer of litter and continued his slow, leisurely trundle down the path.

Dalkeith said: 'We won't be meeting again until Holt is secure. You will then be paid the balance of the fee.'

'As you wish. They will deposit Holt with the High Commissioner in Nairobi. He'll fly home from there.'

Cameron watched Frank fade into the distance. All he'd wanted was one clear snap of Hobson. He hoped to God that Ketch had managed that. Anyway, he'd find out soon enough.

After he'd sent the telex to Keel.

8

Shelepin, standing high on the bridge of the freighter, the *Ivan Stetchkin*, watched silently as his First Officer supervised the transfer of the last battle tank on to the back of the big transporter parked on the sweltering Mombasa dockside.

The derrick swung the thirty six ton load up and out of the vast forward hold like a toy and held it over the side of the ship. The T-54 was then winched down slowly until the tracks landed squarely on the back of the MAZ transporter. The tank was secured and the retaining pins on the cradle were released, allowing the derrick to be swung inboard for the last time.

A heavy khaki tarpaulin shrouded the T-54, edges anchored to the sides of the transporter. All that could be seen of the tank was the bottom section of track and the lower curve of the wheels. Six tanks had been lifted off the ship on to the MAZ support vehicles and their presence on the quay had caused a great deal of comment among the dock workers. The latter had not been permitted to assist with the unloading, the union having been squared by donations from the Soviet freighter's agents. Half a dozen Russian technicians, as well as the First Officer, had supervised the work and these were the men who would accompany the convoy to its ultimate destination: Kendura.

Shelepin, unshaven with his cap askew on his head, studied the hectic activity on the dockside and waited for his subordinate to report. His First Officer, Felix

179

Yazelskin, appeared in the hatchway. 'All unloaded, Captain,' he said. 'No problems.'

Shelepin turned and nodded. 'Very good. Secure the hatches and prepare the vessel for departure and don't forget the crew muster either. I don't want to find we are a dozen men short after we cast off.'

The agent and the Lead Technician were awaiting Shelepin's arrival at the top of the gangway. The agent was a thin, cadaverous Syrian called Habash. The technician was heavy set and bull necked and named Leonid Vakov.

Vakov carried the world weary stamp of a veteran; a hard man marked by the rigours that military discipline demands. A man used to obeying the whims of his superiors without question. Sergeant Vakov's present demeanour, however, indicated that his current assignment was a chore he could have done without. Less than a month ago he had been cooped up in a fly ridden, dust blown compound on the outskirts of Kabul, training Afghan troops in the use of BM-21 rocket launchers and BMD fire support vehicles.

After six months' gruelling duty in that hell-hole, interspersed with hair raising convoy duty along the Kotanni Pass and intermittent and often fruitless raids against the Mujehadeen strongholds in the Panjsher Valley, Vakov was looking forward to ten days' well earned leave, lounging on the beach in the Black Sea resort of Sochi.

Until his leave was cancelled.

With a vengeance, as it happened. A Lead Technician was needed to head a small team of military advisors on a mission in the East African state of Lugamba. Vakov hadn't even heard of the place let alone Solomon Mabato and he wasn't relishing the task of training the man's troops in the workings of the T-54s any more than he had enjoyed his tour of duty in Kabul. Small wonder that his disposition was far from benign as he stood above the Mombasa dockside and viewed his massive charges with resentment.

'So, we are finished,' Shelepin confirmed. 'I trust everything is in order?'

Habash nodded fervently, his Adam's apple bobbing violently as he spoke. 'I have briefed Vakov on the route and paperwork involved and he has the manifest and transit permits. The convoy will arrive in Kendura tomorrow.'

'What about the drivers?' Shelepin asked.

'Libyans,' Vakov answered sourly. 'Provided by Mabato.'

Shelepin addressed the Syrian. 'You will relay a signal to the effect that the shipment has been landed and the cargo is en route.'

'It will be done immediately,' the agent said.

'All that remains then,' Shelepin said, 'is for me to wish you a safe journey, Comrade Vakov.'

'And I wish you a safe voyage, Captain,' Vakov replied.

They shook hands and Shelepin retraced his steps to the bridge. Vakov followed Habash down the gangway to the quay. The Syrian took his leave and Vakov walked down the convoy to the lead transporter. Two men were already in the cab; the swarthy Libyan driver and Vakov's fellow technician. Vakov climbed into the cab and slammed the door.

'Okay, let's go! We haven't time to waste and, Valeri Andreyevich,' he addressed the young man seated next to him, 'keep your eyes on these Libyan bastards. I trust them about as much as I would trust a Bulgarian beet farmer!'

* * *

181

CHARTER CONFIRMED CMA FINANCE AS-
SURED CMA GOOD LUCK STP CAMERON

'At last,' Schiller said. 'The waiting is over.'

Keel said: 'You and Harry contact Mendoza and see he
has the equipment. I'll send a confirmation to Cameron
and a cable to Joseph. Then I'll call Lassiter. We go in
tonight.'

Keel felt the tightening deep in his stomach, as if a hand
had grabbed his intestines and twisted. This was the spur
he had waited for. The combination of excitement and
apprehension was like a jolt of electricity and he felt at once
rejuvenated as the adrenalin flowed. He knew that Sekka,
on receipt of his message, would feel exactly the same.

Joseph Sekka had spent his second day in Kendura walking
the streets, getting the feel of the city.

As he walked he found it difficult to believe that
Lugamba had once been known as the Pearl of Africa.
Even along the Kendura Road – the main street of the
capital – the stores were little more than bleak shells.
Indeed, some of them were burnt out blocks filled with
rubble and excrement. About one shop in five had glass
still in the frames protecting a pitiful selection of goods;
perhaps a few pairs of cheap plastic shoes, some tins of
boot polish or canned produce. A few barefoot vendors
were attempting to sell their wares on the dusty pave-
ments. One man's meagre display consisted of a dozen
long playing gramophone records, a selection of straw
trilbys, a box of one and a half volt Vidor batteries and two
dozen tins of bicycle puncture repair outfits.

One street consisted almost entirely of shops fronted by
iron bars and metal shutters. These, Sekka knew, were the
buildings that had once been owned and run by the
expelled Asian community. Mabato had handed the busi-

nesses over to the officers in his army but once the latter had removed the contents from the stores into their homes the buildings had remained locked and barred. In some shops the barriers had been breached by looters. Sekka found the whole scene very depressing.

Philimon had told Sekka that there was a petrol shortage but there seemed to be quite a number of cars and vans on the road. For all he knew they could easily have been driven or owned by the men of DOSS or SASU.

He retraced the route he had taken with Philimon Mkekwe. This took him once again past the hospital, university and the newly built conference centre. He wondered once again at the mentality of a president who, faced with economic disaster and a starving populace, could choose to spend millions on a glass and concrete edifice that was an insult to the desperate inhabitants of the pathetic shanty town that squatted in its shade.

And the squalor that Joseph Sekka saw on his walkabout was matched only by the despair and listlessness on the faces of the people. Mabato's rule had taken its toll.

Beyond the conference centre and in front of the police barracks a large area of concrete parade ground had been cordoned off. The sound of hammer and saw rose above the noise of the traffic and Sekka paused to investigate. The workmen were building some sort of grandstand. Scaffolding littered the ground and in one corner of the square several lorries were parked side by side, backs piled high with folding chairs.

To one side of the grandstand a rectangular raised dais was being erected and Sekka understood immediately what was happening. To celebrate the opening of the OAU conference, Mabato would, inevitably, have planned some sort of ceremony to enhance his standing in the eyes of his fellow delegates. This activity was surely in

183

preparation for such an event. No doubt a parade, probably of a military nature. A grandstand for the delegates and a dais to enable Mabato to take the salute.

And Sekka knew the part David Holt would play in the proceedings. If Mabato could make the British Government submit to his demands, he could face the members of the OAU with the certainty of being elected Chairman.

But there again, if the British did not back down, what would Mabato do to save face? Sekka had the suspicion that the consequences of that action would be grave indeed.

A thoughtful Joseph Sekka returned to the hotel.

At the desk he checked with the receptionist.

'Any messages?'

ATTN SEKKA CMA THIS YR AUTH TO PROCEED WITH ARTICLE CMA PLAN SCOOP SOONEST STP EDITOR

The clerk looked attentive. 'Will there be a reply?'

'No reply. I'll take my key.'

He reached his room and gathered his things together. So, the contract was on. The next stage would be to join Keel and the others at the mission station. Thirty miles away through the bush and he had no transport. He'd have to steal a vehicle. The hotel car park would be the obvious place to find one. It had been a long time since he'd hot wired anything. He hoped he still had the knack.

Sekka changed into a pair of grey cord jeans and a black turtle necked sweater. He put the rest of his clothes into the holdall with his other belongings and checked the room and bathroom to see if he had forgotten anything. As a last precaution he slipped the 'do not disturb' sign over the doorknob, then he opened the window.

The room was on the first floor at the rear of the hotel. It wasn't much of a drop. Sekka watched as his holdall hit the

the ground below then, after a swift glance around to make sure there was no one to see him, he climbed out of the window and lowered himself down the wall until he hung by his fingers from the sill. Then he let go. He hit the earth and crouched as his legs bent to absorb the shock of landing. He remained frozen for several seconds, senses alert to the sounds of the night and the chance of discovery. Somewhere in the clump of bushes at the base of the wall a cicada chirruped noisily, the call repeated around the grounds like the sound of castanets. Night birds called and were answered by the steady croaking of tree frogs. The chorus was carried on the warm breeeze.

He retrieved his holdall and stuck close to the wall as he padded towards the car park.

There were only half a dozen vehicles. A couple of Toyotas, a Peugeot estate, two rust speckled, nondescript hatchbacks and a VW camper. Not very promising but at least there was nobody around to disturb him. He was about to step across to the first car when he heard the sound of a motor and saw the glow of headlights as the vehicle swept into the car park. Sekka melted against the wall.

It was a dark coloured, four door Range Rover and Sekka knew instinctively that he wouldn't have a better choice. It looked new and in good condition and he had the sneaking suspicion that it might be a DOSS vehicle. That likelihood and the fact that he was going to steal it gave Sekka a feeling of intense pleasure. He watched as the Range Rover was parked, somewhat erratically.

The driver turned off the lights, opened the door and fell out.

Realization stirred hope in Sekka's mind. The man was drunk.

So was his passenger. The girl leaned languidly out of

the passenger door, mumbling incoherently. A giggle broke from her lips. With a grunt of annoyance the driver moved to assist, bouncing awkwardly off the bonnet. The girl clasped her arms around the man's neck and together they meandered unsteadily towards the hotel entrance. Twice the girl stumbled and almost fell, only to be hauled upright by her equally inebriated partner.

Somebody up there likes me, thought Sekka as he watched them go. They hadn't even locked the doors. Sekka sprinted from hiding.

It took him only seconds to find the leads and start the engine. So, he thought as he drove the Range Rover out of the car park, who needs Hertz?

Driving between the dark buildings along the deserted streets was like driving through deep canyons and there was that sense of unease as though he was being watched at every turn of the wheel. He would feel safer once he was out of the city. In the Range Rover he would cover the thirty miles in good time if he wasn't stopped. He tried not to think about what might happen if he was flagged down by a patrol though if this was a DOSS vehicle he would probably be left alone. He would just have to take his chances. He had to reach the mission by midnight to assist Keel's arrival. And there was also the matter of the priest.

Father Michael Devlin.

Sixty five years old and as tough as old boots. A boxer in his younger days and still a bit of a bruiser and, if Keel and Sekka were any judges of character, about the only person in Lugamba who wouldn't be terrorized by Mabato and his goons. How could you intimidate someone who'd seen the hell of the Congo or Kenya during the Mau Mau campaign or Biafra?

Devlin ran the mission station at Masambabule with the assistance of six nuns, all qualified nurses. They provided a medical service for the outlying villages. Sekka presumed nothing too advanced; broken arms and legs, stomach ailments and probably minor dental care. Anything more serious would necessitate a transfer to the city hospital.

Sekka smiled to himself as he tried to imagine the look on the old man's face when he arrived out of the night, especially when he revealed to Devlin the reason for his visit. Over the years Keel had kept track of the priest's whereabouts but it had been a long time since they had last met. In spite of the motive, Sekka was quite looking forward to the reunion.

The Zulu crossed the Kenyan/Lugamban border that same night. He was driving a black Mazda jeep which he had daubed with mud so that it blended into the surrounding terrain. Using an old game trail, he had avoided the border patrols from both countries. The trail had once been used by ivory poachers during the heyday of their raids into the Lugamban game parks. Since Mabato's reign the parks had fallen into sad neglect. The staff had long since departed, leaving the herds unprotected. The result being that the elephant population had dwindled from over ten thousand to a few hundred, living mostly in isolated family groups and therefore difficult for the poaching teams to track down. The poachers turned their attention to crocodile skins instead and confined their activities to the shallow tributaries of the Lugopa River and its estuary at the north west corner of Lake Victoria.

Under the blanket of night Qetuka hoped to cover the distance to Kendura and arrive in the city by dawn. Initially, the going would be difficult and, due to the nature of the country, slow. But he would be off the main highway and therefore out of sight of Mabato's patrols, barring accidents.

187

Driving too fast, along a dirt track that dipped and curved like a roller coaster, Qetuka had only himself to blame. Even with headlights on he hadn't judged the bend correctly. When the jeep hit the shale, the wheels slid as though on ice. Qetuka spun the steering wheel in a frenzied effort to turn the rocking vehicle into the direction of the skid. For a second he thought he'd made it, then in the swathe of the lights he saw the boulder dead ahead. The Mazda whipped broadside across the track and cannoned into the rock. Like a skater rebounding from the rink barrier the jeep careered away, hubs spinning like tops, and slewed over the edge of the track like a rolling oil drum.

The defile was only fifteen feet deep but to Qetuka, bouncing in his seat as he fought to control the vehicle, the uneven slope seemed endless. The end came abruptly with a resounding crash as the bonnet connected with the opposite slope and the front axle snapped like a rotten twig. Qetuka was thrown forward. His head slammed against the dashboard and he was aware of a violent roaring sound in his brain. It felt as though he was drowning and he was dimly conscious of the hisses of steam erupting from the punctured radiator before he drifted into blissful oblivion.

If Corporal Joshua Besigye had felt the need to relieve himself five minutes earlier, his future might have been lengthened considerably. As it was Besigye's bladder was close to bursting as he told his companion, Private Natolo Oketta, to pull over to allow him to attend to the call of nature. The state of the road – cratered and undulating – had not helped matters and it was with some alacrity that the corporal jumped from the vehicle and unbuttoned his fly. With a groan of pleasure he sprayed the vegetation.

Back in the Land Rover, Private Oketta twiddled his thumbs and hoped the corporal wouldn't be too long. He wanted to get back to barracks and a beer and, later, the warm pendulous breasts of his girl, Mary Wafula. The fact that Mary was everyone else's girl did not worry Oketta unduly. Mary was a very generous girl, as the rest of the barracks would testify, and enjoying her sweet embrace, no matter if it was rather more than second hand, had to be a better proposition than performing these useless searches for Lugambans fleeing the warm embrace of Solomon Mabato.

Oketta and Besigye had patrolled this quadrant at least a dozen times over the past few months and so far: nothing. They had been heading back to base when the corporal had felt the need to piss all over the countryside.

The man of the moment was now feeling a great deal more comfortable. He buttoned himself up and prepared to rejoin Oketta.

Qetuka rose out of the darkness like a cobra and from a distance of three feet shot Corporal Joshua Besigye in the head. The bullet entered Besigye's right cheek and blew out the side of his face, shattering his jawbone and sending bits of flesh and bone flicking through the night air The corporal's body staggered and folded like a rag doll. It lay like a broken marionette in the dirt.

Before Oketta had time to blink he found himself looking down the barrel of the Zulu's automatic. The apparition that confronted the bewildered private was like a scene from a nightmare. A wild man with blood seeping from a cut in his forehead. As he clambered out of the Land Rover he caught sight of his companion's corpse and moaned with fear and revulsion. His eyes flickered nervously to the man with the gun.

Qetuka wondered what the strange clicking sound was

189

until it dawned on him that what he was hearing was the sound of the private's teeth chattering. He aimed the gun at Oketta's belly.

'Take your clothes off,' he ordered.

Oketta's eyes grew large with alarm.

'NOW!' barked Qetuka. The gun in his hand did not waver.

As if performing some strange tribal dance, Oketta hopped and skipped like a monkey as he divested himself of his uniform. Clad in ragged underwear, he stood shivering with terror by the side of the Land Rover. His hands were crossed over his concave chest like a young girl hiding her adolescence.

The Zulu nodded. 'Good. Now, turn around and kneel down.'

Oketta hesitated.

'DO IT!' screamed Qetuka.

The private turned and dropped with the agility of a five year old. Qetuka sighted the automatic on the back of the kneeling man's skull and squeezed the trigger. His victim fell forward on to his face and lay still. Qetuka felt for the pulse. The man was dead.

The Zulu retrieved the private's uniform and changed into it, throwing his own clothes into the back of the Land Rover. He ran into the darkness and collected his equipment from the hiding place in the scrub. Jumping into the driving seat, Qetuka jammed the Land Rover into gear and let out the clutch. Then he headed west.

From the shelter of the rocks and undergrowth and the tiny holes and crevices in the ground around the crumpled bodies of Oketta and Besigye the ants and scorpions began to emerge.

* * *

The guns were German made Heckler and Koch MP5s, twenty six inches long and weighing six pounds. They could be fitted with either fifteen or thirty round magazines.

Keel was pleased with the weapon. He hadn't expected to be that lucky and had thought Mendoza would go for the American Ingram.

'A good choice, Paul,' he commented to Schiller, whose eyes had lit up when he saw the guns.

Schiller was well acquainted with the submachine gun. They had been standard issue with all GSG-9 units and had been used in the rescue at Mogadishu when he went into the 737 with Wegener and the two SAS men, Morrison and Davis. The guns had a low muzzle velocity and were very accurate. The SAS duo had been so impressed with their performance that they recommended the weapon to their colleagues in Hereford.

The weapons and packs were lying on a bench in the hangar. The Chieftain was outside on the apron, submitting patiently to Kate Lassiter's final checks.

Mendoza had also supplied four thirteen shot Browning pistols with silencers, double edged sheath knives with six inch blades and four razor sharp pangas in broad scabbards. He had also provided a quantity of plastic explosive, detonators, timers, spare mags even grenades.

And shotguns. Twelve-Bore Creener Remington pump action, with the barrel cut back to the end of the hand grip. A fearsome weapon, perfected by the SAS for close quarter battle.

'Holy shit!' Roan looked aghast. 'We've enough fire power to start World War Three!'

Schiller pointed out: 'We can't take all these, Thomas. It will weigh us down.'

'Personal choice,' Keel advised. 'Remington or the H and K. What we don't need Mendoza can take back. He's got us camouflage suits as well. We can change into them here and leave our own stuff. Joseph is meeting us at the mission. We'll take his gear with us. Don't forget to leave all ID behind. Kate can stash it here. You know the drill.'

They changed quickly into the camouflage suits and Tuf boots and divided the equipment into four packs. They had chosen the Heckler and Koch for themselves and Sekka in preference to the Remington, purely for the sustained fire power. Keel, however, as an afterthought, picked up one of the shotguns and slid it down the side of his pack with a supply of shells. He caught Harry Roan's eye. 'I hate letting things go to waste.'

Kate Lassiter returned from the Chieftain.

'Any problems?' asked Keel, knowing there wouldn't be.

'Everything's fine. She's fuelled and ready to go and I've filed a flight plan with the tower.'

'What destination did you give them?'

'The WHO field research station at Karanga. That's about fifteen miles this side of the Kenyan border. I often do courier work for them and we're in luck as I received a message that they need some samples ferrying back to Nairobi for analysis. No one will think it unusual. I'll just make a small detour, that's all. It'll be a straight run west to Masambabule. I'll drop you off and call in at Karanga on my way back here.'

Keel asked about the drop.

Kate Lassiter said: 'The Lugamban border surveillance teams concentrate on preventing people getting out not in. Air patrols are non existent. Most of Mabato's air force is grounded anyway. He's running out of spare parts and his MiG pilots are still relatively inexperienced. They won't fly at night. Plus I'll be going in low and I'll be in and out before they notice anything on what little radar they have got. It'll be a piece of cake.'

192

'In that case,' Keel said, 'I think we're ready.'

They hefted the packs and weapons and followed Lassiter to the aircraft. Keel sat with Lassiter while Schiller and Roan made themselves comfortable in the cabin. Lassiter spoke to the tower through her head mike, requested clearance and took them down the apron. Minutes later the Chieftain was racing along the tarmac. Kate Lassiter pulled back on the control yoke and the aircraft weaved into the air.

The prints were a lot better than Cameron had expected. Frank had done a good job, notwithstanding the devilish disguise bit. It had cost him a tenner to borrow the cart and overalls for twenty minutes. For a bet, he'd said. And Cameron had been right. All he'd done was point the bloody thing and hey presto. Instant Lichfield.

Cameron had the prints developed in double quick time by a discreet friend who ran a small studio off Frith Street though he'd had to be patient and wait until two redheads in suspenders and a bare arsed photographer with a Pentax had completed their own shooting schedule on the king size bed next to the dark room.

'The things you do for art,' Cameron said. He ended up with a dozen eight by ten glossies. Dalkeith was easily recognizable.

By the time Cameron got back to his flat he was feeling peckish and it was getting late. He took a piece of fillet steak out of the fridge and ice from the freezer and poured himself two fingers of Smirnoff. Before he had taken a sip the telephone was ringing.

Frank. Slightly breathless, croaking and sounding worried. He was in a call box. Cameron could hear traffic.

'I've been trying your gaff for ages, Mister Cameron. I've got something you should see.'

193

'I've been out and it's late. Can't it wait?'

'No.' The answer was swift and decisive.

'Frank?'

'Look, I'd better come round.' Ketch's tone dropped to a hoarse whisper. 'It's about that photo session.'

As soon as the words were out Cameron felt the familiar icy fingers trace their way across his shoulders. 'You'd better get over here.'

Before he put the receiver down he knew that Frank had already vacated the kiosk at a rapid rate of knots.

Ketch arrived twenty minutes later. He looked surprisingly pale. Cameron let him in and waited for an explanation.

'Sorry, Mister Cameron, but this couldn't wait. Really it couldn't.' Frank unzipped his windcheater. 'I was in Topknot this afternoon.'

Cameron looked blank. 'Is that good or bad?'

'Good for them, bad for me. I was getting my hair cut.' He ran his fingers through his hair in an agitated gesture. 'Cost a bloody arm and a leg, what with shampoo and all.'

Cameron surveyed the result. 'Very nice,' he said patiently.

'I'm getting there,' Ketch said. 'Don't rush me. It was while I was waiting to be done. I was reading the magazines.'

'Is this going to take long, Frank?' Cameron hoped Ketch wasn't going to tell the old one about the *Titanic* going down but one look at the minder's face told him Frank wasn't in the mood for old jokes.

'Like I said, I was reading the magazines. They've got all sorts. *Weekend, Reveille, Men Only* if you're lucky . . .'

'High class establishment then?'

Frank ignored the jibe. From inside his windcheater he took a rolled magazine. 'They also had this.' He passed it over.

It was a three month old copy of the West German magazine, *Stern*. On the front a girl in a bikini was pouting at the camera.

'Thought it was a girlie mag,' Ketch said.

'Only it isn't.'

'Page twenty five,' Frank said. 'Take a look.'

The man in the photograph was certainly Gerald Hobson. Only according to the magazine his name wasn't Hobson. It was George Dalkeith. Cameron's command of German was good. He read the text.

According to *Stern*, George Alan Dalkeith was the current Director of Operations, SIS. Cameron's palms were clammy. His forehead throbbed and his eye socket, covered by the patch, was itching abominably.

It was all there. Details of his education at Cambridge, where he had taken a First in History, and his war record. He had served in the Middle East and with the partisans in Greece and Yugoslavia, rising to the rank of Lieutenant Colonel in the Intelligence Corps. After the war he had been swallowed up by the Foreign Office and delegated unspecified duties. Whatever the hell that meant, Cameron thought.

Following tours abroad in Washington and Rome he had moved back to the UK and the corridors of Century House under the cover of the Department of the Environment, in the early seventies. He had taken on the mantle of Director in 1975. The magazine even listed his clubs as the Athenaeum and the Royal Commonwealth Society. Above all, he was credited with a quick brain and a remorseless dedication.

Cameron stared at the photograph. In it Dalkeith was

195

about to enter a limousine. He was being seen away by a short, bespectacled man named as Karl Heinz Shroeder, head of the West German Intelligence Service, the BND, following a Joint Intelligence Chiefs' meeting in Bonn.

Sweet Jesus.

'If I'd known we were dealing with the bogeymen, Mister Cameron . . .' Ketch looked distinctly worried. As well he might. 'Soon as I saw the photo I got one of the guys in the salon to translate,' he said. 'He's a Kraut. Comes from Frankfurt. Been over here two –'

'Stow it, Frank. I'm trying to think.' Cameron's tone was harsh. 'You didn't tell him why you were interested? About the snaps you took?'

'Oh, sure. And after I'd told him I went and stood at the end of Haymarket and bawled my friggin' head off, didn't I? Leave it out, Mister Cameron!'

Cameron said nothing.

'What happens now?' Ketch asked.

Cameron threw the magazine down. 'You bugger off, Frank. You go home and speak to no one about this. You don't even think aloud, old son. Quiet as the grave, Frankie boy. Or maybe that's where you'll end up.'

The minder paled.

Cameron's good eye seemed to burn with a fierce intensity as he laid a hand on Ketch's arm. 'You haven't seen me either, Frank. Got that? You are a man with a white stick and an Alsatian as far as I'm concerned.'

'You don't have to tell me!' Ketch was already moving.

Cameron saw the leg man out of the flat and closed the door.

It didn't make sense, he thought. The British Secret Service recruiting mercenaries? With the Angolan fiasco still fresh in the mind, the idea was preposterous. The

196

smallest leak that such a venture was under way would damage the credibility of the government beyond salvage.

What if there was a leak though?

Who else knew that Cameron had handled the contract? Just how vulnerable was he if the lid was lifted?

And the answer to that question he didn't like one little bit. And he'd lost his appetite completely.

Sergeant Abraham Adoko was a worried man. His two-man border patrol was long overdue. Corporal Besigye and Private Oketta should have returned to the field base two hours ago and it had been four hours since their last radio call, announcing a routine patrol. If they had run into any trouble their standing orders were precise. They were to call in reinforcements immediately. There had been no call. Perhaps, thought Adoko, they had met with an accident or the radio was on the blink.

Or worse . . . maybe.

Adoko knew that if the men didn't show up he would have to answer to his Company Commander, who just happened to be a second cousin of Solomon Mabato. He didn't relish that confrontation one little bit for it would not be the fate of his men that would be the talking point. It would be the loss of one military vehicle – the Land Rover.

Sergeant Adoko decided on his course of action. He summoned Corporal Moyo. The corporal was to take one trooper and back track along the route that the returning patrol would take. If they found anything, they were to call in. At once.

9

The mission building at Masambabule was shaped like a U. The base of the letter housed a small office and reception room. The left wing consisted of the staff's living quarters and the right wing held the dispensary, surgery and a small, twelve-bed ward. To the right of the low building, a tiny whitewashed chapel stood under the branches of a sycamore tree.

The airstrip was a mile long stretch of bare earth that ran behind the mission from east to west. The mission and the strip lay at the base of a thorn-scrub crested escarpment that sloped northwards towards a shallow defile that had once held a meandering tributary of the Mvula river.

Father Michael Devlin glared down at his quivering patient with undisguised anger. From the rear of the mission could be heard the low hum of the generator and the light above the examination table flickered briefly as the priest bent forward and said: 'It's your own damned fault, Elias. How many times have I told you to lay off the bottle, you loafer! Jesus! I don't know why I waste my breath! For Christ's sake, Sister, hold him still! He's all over the place! And stop blubbing, man, or so help me, I'll anaesthetize you with my boot, so I will!'

Sister Constance turned her eyes heavenward in exasperation and clamped her hands over Elias's bony shoulders as the latter rolled his eyes dramatically.

The priest held the cotton wool pad over the neck of the bottle and after soaking it in the antiseptic, scrubbed the patient's forearm, lips clamped in concentration. Elias squirmed.

The gash ran from the inside of the elbow to within an inch of the wrist. It was an ugly cut, made worse by the puckered flesh and strips of flayed skin that oozed blood like a piece of rare steak.

Elias watched with dreadful fascination as Father Devlin threw the used swab into the bin under the table and picked up the hypodermic. To the frightened man the instrument looked as long as an assegai. However, despite his angry tone earlier, the priest administered the local anaesthetic with great gentleness.

'There,' Devlin said soothingly. 'It won't be long now. We'll soon have you sewn up. Isn't that right, Sister?'

Elias did not look like a man convinced, although his arm was turning numb and the feeling was not unpleasant. Sister Constance, sensing the change in his condition, eased her hold. The sight of Devlin attempting to thread gut through the eye of the needle, however, proved too much for Elias to bear. He promptly lost consciousness.

The priest snorted. 'Fainted my eye!' he muttered in answer to Sister Constance's observation. 'Drunken stupor more like!'

The neatness of stitch left a lot to be desired but purpose was served. Elias's arm wouldn't win applause at a BMA convention. Devlin and his staff performed no more than basic medicine. With the facilities at their disposal they were equipped to do little else.

Sister Constance and the other five nuns were qualified nurses. In the villages surrounding the mission they were the next best thing to a team of Harley Street surgeons.

Devlin studied his handiwork. 'Not pretty, Elias, but sufficient I think. You can thank me when you wake up. I'll leave you to finish off, Sister. I'd leave him then to sleep it off. I'm going to put my feet up.' He ran a gnarled hand through his untidy silver thatch. 'It's been a long day.'

'Very well, Father.' The elderly nun looked down at Elias. 'You know, they're just like children.' She sighed. 'I wonder how they ever got on without us.'

Devlin frowned. 'You know,' he said, 'for a nun you do talk a deal of rubbish! All this righteousness isn't good for you. I sometimes feel that I'm working with Julie Andrews. It isn't all doh, ray, me and drops of golden sun. You've been here long enough to know that. These people are motivated by the same vices we are, only to a lesser degree because their horizons are more limited. But it's all there; avarice, lust, envy, greed, I don't have to go through the whole list. The fact that Elias had the ill sense to put his arm through a window while attempting to break into the dispensary goes someway towards proving my point. Particularly as he was under the influence of alcohol at the time. If you can call that concoction they drink alcohol. It'd never catch on on Ballyferriter, I'm thinking.'

He smiled suddenly, eyes twinkling. 'Nevertheless, Sister, you can't help liking them, can you?'

With that he closed the door behind him, leaving Sister Constance open mouthed and perplexed. She shook her head. 'Father Devlin,' she said softly, 'you are a constant source of amazement to me.'

He was certainly unorthodox.

Sixty eight years old with a face like a relief map of the Devil's Causeway. Blue eyes as bright as buttons and a head of silver hair that looked as though it had been trimmed with a pair of blunt pruning shears. In a film he would have been portrayed by Spencer Tracy with an Irish brogue.

It had been four years ago that Sister Constance and the

other nuns had arrived in Lugamba. Their brief: to assist Father Michael Devlin in establishing the mission at the foot of the Masambabule escarpment.

It had been a new challenge for them all. Sister Constance's years of nursing service at the hospital run by the nuns of the Order of the Sacred Heart on the outskirts of Brussels had hardly prepared her for the rigours of life in the African bush. The five novices who had been chosen to accompany her had, equally, been somewhat out of their depth. However, with a perseverance born of their vocation, they had come to grips with their new, hostile environment as well as their new mentor.

Father Devlin was a surprise to them all and initially, it had to be said by the middle aged Sister Constance, a source of embarrassment. No timid parish priest this but a man deeply committed to the welfare of his flock. A walking enigma was Michael Devlin with the craggy face and stocky frame of a fairground pugilist and the scarred hands of a lumberjack.

So, he had the unnerving tendency to take the Lord's name in vain and perhaps he did like the occasional drop of whisky but was that so bad? Sister Constance, her five colleagues and, presumably, the Lord Himself, had come to an agreement. They turned the other cheek.

At first, Devlin told them little about himself save for a brief account of his boyhood in a small village on the Dingle Peninsula in the windswept storm tossed south west corner of Ireland.

It was much later that he told them about Changi and the Japanese and Korean interrogators and the pain. But that had been nothing compared to the Mau Mau rebellion and the dreadful atrocities he had seen in the Congo before the liberation of Isangi by Mike Hoare's mercenary Commando. Then it had been Nigeria and the horrors of Biafra followed by Lugamba and the emergence of the man they called the Liberator.

And yet, despite it all, he had kept his faith. The reason was simple. He had survived.

'Father Devlin.'

The priest had almost reached his office when he was addressed. The speaker was one of the other nuns, the youngest member of his nursing staff, Sister Elicia. Pretty and wide eyed, she seemed to treat the priest with awe whenever she spoke to him. She whispered now in hushed, almost reverent tones.

Devlin smiled. 'I thought you would have been asleep, my dear. It's very late.'

'We have visitors, Father.'

Devlin's eyebrows rose fractionally. 'At this time? You don't say? Now, who could this be, I wonder?'

'I saw headlights through my window,' she explained.

'How interesting. Well, let's go and see who it is. Maybe it's Saint Teresa herself come to check up on us.'

Sister Elicia had long ago ceased to be concerned by Father Devlin's irreverence though he really was the most unusual man of God she had ever known and she often chuckled inwardly at the thought of what her old Mother Superior would say if she ever came face to face with the irascible old Irishman.

The vehicle was a Range Rover. There was one occupant; a tall, well built negro. The man approached. He walked softly, Devlin noticed. Like a cat prowling and for a brief moment the priest was reminded of someone. There was something disturbingly familiar about him. Devlin stared.

'Dear God! Joseph? Joseph Sekka? I don't believe it. I thought my old eyes were playing tricks. What the hell are you doing here? Is Thomas with you? My boy, how long has it been? Years! Incredible!'

The two men embraced. Watching from the doorway, Sister Elicia found the sight of the tall negro and the silver haired priest holding each other close strangely moving. She couldn't be sure but was there the trace of a tear in the old man's eye?

Sekka spoke quietly and Devlin broke away and turned. He smiled awkwardly and ran a hand through his hair. 'My dear Sister Elicia, please forgive my rudeness. It is just that Joseph is a friend I have not seen for some time.'

'It's quite all right, Father. I understand.' She smiled nervously at Sekka.

Devlin rubbed his hands together happily. 'Well, don't stand out there, Joseph! Come on inside! Sister, perhaps you could make some tea?' A quick sly look at Sekka. 'Or what about something a little stronger. I'm sure I've a drop of the hard stuff and you can forget that rot about having it only for medicinal purposes too!'

Sekka said: 'Father, that can wait. I've something very important to tell you. My visit isn't entirely social. I need your help.' He looked at his watch. 'We don't have much time.'

The priest blinked. 'I don't understand, Joseph.'

Sekka laid an arm on Devlin's shoulders. 'Thomas is coming here by plane, tonight. We need the airstrip lit.'

'What?'

'I want a string of lights on either side of the runway. We have about thirty minutes.'

The priest stared at him. 'What the devil is going on, Joseph?'

'We haven't time for that now. I'll explain later. Right now, we need lamps, torches, anything you have, and we can use the lights of the Range Rover. I see you've got a Land Cruiser. We'll use that as well. And we'll need help. Where is everybody?'

'Where do you think? It's nearly midnight!'

'Wake them up.'

The old man's eyebrows disappeared into his hairline.

'Please, Father. It's important.'

About to remonstrate, Devlin saw the look in Sekka's eyes and turned quickly. 'Right, Sister, forget the tea. Wake everyone. You'll find Sister Constance in the surgery with Elias. Tell her to join us.' He growled at her amazement. 'Well, don't just stand there with your mouth open like a goldfish, girl! Hurry!'

Sekka squeezed Devlin's arm. 'Thank you, Father. Now, when everyone is ready, they're to grab all the lights you have.'

'We have empty paint tins in the store and oil for the generator, we can rig makeshift lamps with rag wicks.'

Sekka smiled. 'Good. Let's get to it.'

The nuns arrived, tousled with sleep, excepting Sister Elicia and Sister Constance. The latter viewed the priest with bewilderment and Sekka with suspicion.

'Joseph Sekka is a friend,' Devlin told them. 'You are to do exactly as he tells you.'

Under Sekka's direction they drove the two vehicles out to the strip and spaced the make-do lights along the ground. Then, armed with flickering, oil-soaked brands, he told them to stand by and keep quiet.

In silence they waited. The night robes of the women, illuminated by the flames of the torches, gleamed whitely like ghostly shrouds. Then, inevitably, it was Sekka who heard it first. They were coming in fast, looking for a sign.

Sekka yelled: 'Lights! GO! GO! GO!'

One by one the strip lights came on, followed by the wider beams of the Range Rover and the Toyota Land

Cruiser. The figures of the nuns looked like wraiths as they ran between the beacons.

'There!' Kate Lassiter was peering down through the windscreen when Keel tapped her shoulder and pointed.

'Going down,' Kate said. 'Hold tight. This could be bumpy.'

The aircraft dipped on one wing and the string of lights grew brighter. The Chieftain swooped below the level of the escarpment and bounced on a cross current. The wheels hit the ground and Kate throttled back. The tone of the turbo charged Lycomings dropped and the run along the strip became an uneven taxi. A yard or two beyond the last pair of lights the aircraft turned in its own length. Caught like a moth in the headlight beams of the Range Rover, the nose bobbed as the undercarriage trundled over the scrub.

Sekka gunned the motor of the Range Rover and drove out to the Chieftain. The aircraft came to a halt. The side door lifted and the steps were lowered. Harry Roan appeared in the doorway.

'Hey, Joe! How's it going?'

'Fine, Harry. Good flight?'

'Hell! The lady's a great pilot! It was real smooth.' He disappeared into the cabin and emerged with pack and machine pistol. He passed them to Sekka who stowed them in the Range Rover. Paul Schiller appeared behind the American similarly ladened.

At the side of the airstrip, the mission staff watched the arrival with fascination. The shadowy figures of Roan and Schiller passing packs to Sekka. They were dressed in camouflage suits.

A third man stepped from the Chieftain. Tall and well built, dressed like the others, his hair was cut short and by the way he was smiling he was pleased to see Sekka. Standing next to Sister Constance, the priest stiffened abruptly.

More gear was taken from the aircraft and placed in the Range Rover. A fourth person appeared and Sister Constance exclaimed: 'Why it's a woman!'

The priest observed quietly: 'The formidable Kate Lassiter.'

'You know her, Father?' Sister Constance asked in surprise.

'Oh, yes.' Devlin did not elaborate.

The men were climbing into the Range Rover. Except Keel.

'Thanks for the lift, Kate,' he said.

Lassiter nodded. 'Anytime, Thomas.' She watched the mercenary's face closely. 'I'll be back in twenty four hours. You be here.'

'We plan to be.' He paused. 'If we aren't here by midnight, Kate, you head back to Nairobi.'

'Thomas – '

'I mean it, Kate. Get out fast.'

She reached out and touched his cheek with her palm. 'You had better be here, Keel, or you'll have me to answer to.'

'Yes, ma'am.'

Her hand formed a fist which she tapped against his chest. A spark deep in her green eyes caught Keel's senses. He held her clenched hand to his lips and kissed it softly. 'Have a safe trip,' he said.

'Take care, Thomas. I'll be coming for you.' She stepped back into the Chieftain. The steps retracted and the door was secured. Keel walked to the Range Rover and Sekka drove off the strip and parked. The props turned with a lurch, the Chieftain began its run. It rolled over the ground, gathering speed, and lifted into the darkness. Immediately, Sekka ordered the lights along the field to be doused.

Like a large moth, a figure detached itself from the shadows and ran through the headlight beams. 'Have you no words of greeting, Thomas? You warmongering heathen!'

'The wrath of God personified,' Keel said, climbing out of the Range Rover. 'How are you, Father? How goeth the teachings of the Lord?'

'The day that I convert you will be the day my work is finished. I will be fulfilled.'

'Dream on, Father,' Keel smiled.

'Ah, but you're a terrible man!' The priest's face softened and his bright eyes searched Keel's hard features. His hands lifted to the mercenary's shoulders. Devlin was almost on tiptoe. 'Are you well, Thomas?'

'I'm well, Father.'

Roan and Schiller stepped out of the Range Rover. Schiller was already lighting a cheroot, Harry Roan smiled easily.

'Who are these men?' queried Devlin.

'The one with the moustache and high forehead is Harry Roan and the good looking one trying to smoke himself into an early grave calls himself Paul Schiller. They are friends of mine. Gentlemen, meet Father Michael Devlin. God's answer to Rocky Marciano.'

Devlin nodded to each in turn. 'Any friends of Thomas Keel are welcome here.'

Movement over the priest's shoulder at the edge of the light. Women in night attire looking at the visitors as though they had arrived from another planet.

Keel returned the perusal, a slight smile playing on his lips as he regarded their study of him. 'Introductions, Father?'

The nuns looked quite worried. 'My nursing staff, Thomas.'

'Sisters.' Keel acknowledged them. 'I suggest, Father, we get back to the mission.'

Sister Constance ushered the nuns back into the building. 'That includes you, Sister Elicia.' She glanced at the priest and thought, He doesn't know what this is about either. She supposed they would all find out soon enough.

'Mother of God!' The priest was aghast. 'You cannot be serious, Thomas!'

The four mercenaries and Michael Devlin were in the office, the nuns having retired to their quarters after reassurances from the old man that there was nothing for them to worry about. They were in no danger.

The packs and weapons were stacked in a corner of the room.

'We've accepted a contract to snatch David Holt from prison,' Keel said. 'We're going ahead with it.'

'But he's being held in Maboru for God's sake! You'll never get him out!'

'We're going to try, Father. We're going to try real hard.'

'But I don't understand. He'll be released surely? The British Government will –'

'Not negotiate with Mabato, Father.' The grey haired mercenary's voice was stern. 'To do so would set a precedent for every two bit, fanatical dictator to follow.'

'He's right, Father,' Harry Roan continued. 'The British won't give in to Mabato's demands and the President sure as hell won't release Holt. Heck, you know this country, you know Mabato. He'll execute the guy just for the fun of it, probably in a matter of days unless we can get him out first. He might not even have that long.'

Devlin shook his head in confusion. 'But who on earth is paying you? Who is behind this?'

'We were hired through a broker, a man we trust. He has guaranteed our fee. We suspect he's acting on behalf of a cartel; colonial diehards.'

'I came in as an advance party,' Sekka explained. 'As you might imagine, I'm a trifle less conspicuous than the others.'

Devlin looked at each of them in turn. 'You're mad,' he said finally, shaking his head.

'He might have a point,' Harry Roan muttered wryly, and stole a glance at Schiller.

The priest was silent for a moment or two. He looked at the equipment they had brought with them. 'When are you proposing to attempt this foolish gesture?'

'In about nineteen hours,' said Keel. 'We'll bring him back here and Kate Lassiter will airlift us out.'

'It's nice to be consulted,' the priest bristled. 'Thomas, I'm running a medical mission here, not a transit halt for brigands. Don't think for one minute that our friendship gives you the right to place my staff at risk.'

Keel advised reluctantly: 'I had little choice. This strip is ideally situated for our needs. We had precious little time to prepare. An airlift was the only practical solution, having you here was, I'll admit, a bonus I couldn't ignore. Father, we need your help.'

'You mean you are taking in your marker?'

'Don't insult our friendship, Father.' Keel's eyes blazed.

Devlin blanched. 'I'm sorry, Thomas. That remark was uncalled for. What do you want from me?'

'We need a place to stay until we make our move.'

'We have a small isolation ward. It is empty at the moment so you can use that. You will not be disturbed. I will advise the sisters.'

'Thank you.'

The door opened suddenly without warning. Sister Elicia, flushed and breathless, in a long white cotton gown buttoned to the neck. Her hair was loose. Her gaze lingered on Paul Schiller for two seconds before she addressed the priest.

'Father, there are soldiers!'

'Christ!' Roan moved like a rocket to the machine pistols and a Browning appeared in Schiller's hand as if by magic.

The priest sprang to his feet. 'No violence here, Thomas! For the love of God!'

'Grab the gear!' Keel snarled. 'Move! Joseph, where did you park the Range Rover? If they spot that . . .'

'In the store, out of sight.'

The young nun stood by the door, doe eyed, fearful. She caught Schiller's eye again as he swept pack and weapon off the floor. Incredibly, he smiled at her and for some inexplicable reason she no longer felt afraid.

Devlin pushed her out of the room. 'Tell them I'm coming. Go! Thomas, you and the others follow me!'

They left the office at a run, moving into the corridor. The priest led the way through the building. A door was flung open and in the gloom they saw half a dozen beds shrouded in mosquito netting. The room carried the taint of disinfectant.

'Into the beds. Pull the nets around you. I'll try and get rid of our visitors.' Father Devlin left them, slamming the door. They heard him running back down the passage.

They slung the packs under the beds and crawled between the sheets. The mosquito nets hung around the beds like veils.

The corporal's name was Moyo. His companion was a tubby, unsavoury individual whose name Devlin didn't catch. Both soldiers fingered the triggers of their assault

210

rifles. The corporal explained that they were looking for a missing Land Rover and its two occupants; a border surveillance patrol that had failed to maintain radio contact with its base.

'You think they may be here?' Father Devlin asked, eyeing the guns speculatively.

'Perhaps,' Moyo grunted. His answer carried the veneer of insolence.

Devlin said curtly: 'This mission was established under the auspices of the Lugamban Government. Neither I nor my staff have any knowledge of the men you are seeking. I suggest that you pursue your enquiries, Corporal.'

Behind the priest's shoulder Sister Elicia felt the stirrings of alarm once more as she caught the corporal's look. The skin at the base of her neck prickled uncomfortably.

'We will search,' Moyo said.

They pushed past her into the office. The sour smell of the fat private was almost overpowering and Sister Elicia wrinkled her nose instinctively. The priest's eyes flashed her a warning that was clear. On no account antagonize them.

The other nuns had gathered in the corridor outside their rooms. They huddled, bewildered and frightened, and stared at the soldiers. Corporal Moyo and his odorous companion paid the rooms a cursory examination. As they emerged from the last room Moyo looked towards the door at the end of the passage. He held his Kalashnikov across his chest and stalked down the corridor.

'I wouldn't go in there, Corporal.' Devlin's hand rested on the door handle. His expression was beseeching.

Moyo ignored the remark. He gripped the priest's arm and took the hand away.

'I beg of you.' The old man's face was pale.

Without a word, Moyo raised the Kalashnikov, turned

the knob and pushed the door open. He strode into the room.

In the second bed Keel lay on his back and watched the door swing open. In the light from the corridor three figures were silhouetted immediately and through the muslin film he saw the stocky shape of Devlin and two blacks in army fatigues. Concealed by the single cotton sheet Keel cradled the Remington, his finger curling around the trigger. He knew the other mercenaries would be tensed like springs.

The taller of the two troopers traversed the room with the barrel of his weapon, his eyes taking in the double row of beds and their barely discernible occupants. Moyo moved to the first bed. Sekka's eyes were closed and he appeared to be asleep.

A few feet away Keel was acutely aware that a river of perspiration was coursing between his shoulder blades.

Corporal Moyo, the snout of his Kalashnikov pointing at the silent figure in the bed, gripped the crumpled corner of the mosquito net and raised it an inch.

Keel started to uncoil, the Remington becoming an extension of his arm as he prepared to draw back the sheet and let rip.

Suddenly the priest stepped forward and muttered hurriedly in the corporal's ear. Abruptly the man swore and dropped the net as though it had been charged with electricity. He recoiled from the bed as if he had been shot, brushed past the priest and melted into the corridor, the second trooper flanking. Father Devlin followed them outside and closed the door.

Tension drained out of Keel like a torrent. His grip on the shotgun relaxed and from the bed across the room Paul Schiller whispered an obscenity and closed his eyes as relief flowed through his body.

'Sweet Jesus, Thomas!' Harry Roan lifted his net. 'I thought we'd have to take them out.'

Keel swept back the sheet and swung his legs to the floor.

'You and me both.' He clasped the Remington across his knees. 'I wonder what Father Devlin said to make him back off. He looked as if he'd come face to face with Old Nick.'

From Sekka's direction came the unmistakable sound of a chuckle.

Keel prodded the bed with the squat barrel of the shotgun. 'What the hell are you laughing at?'

Sekka stirred and emerged from the net like a moth from a cocoon, uncocking the Browning in his fist. He was grinning widely.

Paul Schiller held the MP5 nonchalantly. 'What's the joke?'

Sekka laughed. 'He told them we were lepers.'

The silence was broken eventually by Harry Roan's long exhalation. Keel shook his head in admiration for Devlin's quick thinking.

The door swung open. Sekka whipped into a low crouch, the heavy Browning held in both hands. Keel and the Remington were as one in a smooth synchronized ballet. Roan and Schiller were spinning apart, machine pistols lifting in unison.

Father Devlin cocked an eyebrow and said quietly: 'You will be relieved to hear they have gone.' He pointed to their firearms. 'They will not be required. I suggest you stow them in a safe place and return to your beds. I think we've all had quite enough excitement for one night. You will not be disturbed.'

'That was a brilliant ruse, Father,' Schiller smiled.

'I'll second that,' said Roan. 'What made you think up that story?'

The priest looked nonplussed. 'I don't see why it should

213

sound unusual. This is an isolation unit after all. The last occupants of those beds had lassa fever.'

He had already left the room and closed the door before they could think of a reply.

10

Qetuka's progress into and through Kendura was un-eventful. No one thought twice about a man in army fatigues driving a military vehicle and he had kept to the side roads to avoid the possibility of having to explain himself to a genuine patrol.

His first intention was to conceal the Land Rover.

The shops were shabby, gutted shells. They resembled a row of rotting teeth too far decayed to repair. The narrow alley ran down one side of the block and opened on to a litter strewn parade of lock up garages. Qetuka drove the Land Rover through a minefield of broken bottles, moun-tains of rusting tin cans and walls of splintered packing cases. In the gloom the garage entrance gaped like the mouth of a cavern. The door was the up-and-over type, suspended on creaking brackets and broken springs.

He reversed in, retrieved his bag and after some effort and noise, managed to pull down the door to hide the Land Rover. He shouldered the bag and walked down the passage, picking his way through the rubble and refuse, always keeping to the shadows.

The woman looked terrified. No doubt she thought his tapping on her door to be the prelude to a visit by SASU. She regarded Qetuka with undisguised apprehension through the gap above the security chain, gaze flickering quickly over the uniform.

'I am Qetuka,' he said.

At the mention of his name she gasped aloud and the door was opened. The Zulu stepped inside the apartment.

The woman locked the door and fastened the chain. Qetuka watched her. She was very tall and slim hipped, unlike the majority of Lugamban women. The cotton kaftan she wore did little to hide her figure, the thin material moulding itself to her firm breasts and shapely legs; dancer's legs. Her eyes were large and her lips full. Her hair was short like a man's and it served to emphasize her graceful neck. Her ebony skin was flawless and she wore no makeup.

Elizabeth Wakholi had been one of the lead dancers with the State Dance Troupe. The dancers often entertained foreign dignitaries at state functions and Elizabeth, as one of the stars of the troupe, had also featured in travelogue films produced by the Lugamban Tourist Board. In this role she had come under the eye of Solomon Mabato.

Mabato's exploits with women were legion for he regarded his sexual prowess as an extension of his power and authority. Many women even made themselves available in order to increase their standing in the community, and it was said that the muling offspring of Solomon Mabato crawled and dribbled their way through every facet of Lugamban society.

Mabato had made his intentions towards the dancer plain from the start.

She recalled the first occasion with loathing. It had followed a display by the troupe at a banquet held to honour the arrival of the Libyan delegation. The dancers, men clad only in breech clouts and the women in G strings, their bodies shiny with oil, had gyrated and writhed before the hundred or so guests in the huge ballroom at the President's residence.

Throughout the routines Elizabeth had been aware of the keen gaze of Mabato as he had followed her every move

216

with unmistakable lust. At first she had felt flattered that the Liberator should pay her such a compliment but then she caught him making an obscene gesture in her direction, to the amusement of his aides, and she felt the first twinges of fear course through her body.

As the glistening dancers made their exit to applause from the guests she had glanced towards Mabato's table and seen him whisper to one of his companions and nod in her direction. Back in the room that served as a dressing area she knew instinctively that she had been singled out for special attention and would receive a summons. The most distressing fact was that she would be unable to refuse.

The director of the troupe had approached her with concern on his face. He had told her softly that he was there to present His Excellency's warm congratulations and to tell her also that the President wished to express his appreciation of her dancing in person.

Fully aware of the stares of the other troupe members, she nodded dully. The expressions of the other dancers varied from envy to sympathy. Conscious of this she clutched a robe around herself and followed the director from the room.

Close to, the President looked even more ferocious with small, pig-like eyes set in a vast round head that sat like a football on a mammoth trunk. He smiled as she entered the ante room, the triple scars of the Makesi standing out on his cheeks like a tattoo. The cowering director had made hurried introductions before leaving her to her fate.

Conscious of Mabato's frank admiring gaze she drew the robe closely to her body and waited for him to speak. Beyond the closed doors she could hear laughter from the dinner guests and the light tinkle of glasses.

Mabato said: 'The dancing was excellent. I am very pleased.'

217

Elizabeth remained silent. She did not know if a reply was expected.

'You are a very beautiful woman,' Mabato continued. He grinned and tapped his vast buttocks. 'Not fat here like the others. I like that. You are sleek like an animal.'

He moved towards her, his chest medals clinking in unison as he approached. They were spread across his dress uniform in tiers. Standing close, her eyes were on a level with his shoulders. She became aware of his smell. It was heavy, like musk. Not pleasant. She was uncomfortably conscious of her nakedness beneath the robe.

'You are afraid of me,' he said abruptly.

When she didn't answer he said: 'That is not a bad thing, I think.' Without warning he touched her arm. It was like an electric shock and she flinched.

'Your body is like fire to my touch.' A nerve jumped on his mutilated cheek. 'Take off your robe.'

When she hesitated he said: 'I want to look at you. Take it off.' His voice rose. 'Now!'

With trembling fingers she undid the sash and let the thin garment slip down her shoulders to the floor. Still anointed with oil, her body shone like black marble.

As her magnificent form became exposed Mabato let out a heavy sigh of pleasure, his eyes raking her from head to toe. His gaze flickered over her proud, thrusting breasts and lingered on the tiny G string covering her loins.

As his huge hand reached for her breast she backed away.

'Stand still!' he ordered.

Her head jerked up as his fingers brushed her nipples. They were like buds, taut with anticipation and the brief caress made her gasp. Using both hands Mabato stroked the shining flesh, a look of intense concentration on his face.

218

Then his hands moved lower to her waist and buttocks, thick fingers sliding under the thin ties of the G string.

Without warning, he ripped the flimsy triangle away. leaving her totally naked. A tiny scrap of material was caught between her thighs. He removed it from the apex of her long legs with a delicate touch, taking the opportunity to probe her cleft with rigid fingers.

Her initial reaction was to press her thighs together.

Mabato slapped her face with his open palm. Her head whipped away with the force of the blow, tears welling in her eyes.

'Do not reject me!' Mabato hissed. 'You whore! I have seen the way you dance, using your body to excite men.' His hands had left her thighs and he was fumbling at his belt. Then she was being pushed back towards a writing desk that sat in the corner of the room.

Mabato held her with one hand, the other holding his trousers as he manoeuvred the woman before him. They reached the desk and Mabato twisted her around until she had her back towards him. His grip was like iron. A scream rose in her heaving throat but no sound came except a low whimper. With one hand pushing into the small of her back, Mabato released his trousers and undergarments in a heap around his ankles.

Her own hands were free. She was scrabbling at the desk top, trying to get leverage to tear herself away from his terrible embrace. A bottle of ink fell to the floor and rolled away and her long nails raked the blotter as she bucked but she couldn't move her legs. With both hands he grasped her trembling thighs and forced them apart brutally. She struggled but his strength was too much for her and his hands were like two huge clamps burning their way into her skin. She felt herself being lifted backwards then something was touching the back of her leg and Mabato was grunting like a bear. Then came the first, clumsy attempt at penetration. She bit her lip, the sweet tasting blood running inside her mouth as she jerked her head from side to side. Mabato began to thrust himself at her. The sensation was as if a bar of steel was forcing its way into her body. Mabato was heaving himself back and forth, groaning with pleasure.

He had left her afterwards, fastening his trousers almost absently as he gazed at her bruised body crumpled by the desk.

'I think I will use you again,' he said. 'You have much to learn but you excite me.'

He picked up the discarded robe and tossed it at her. 'Get dressed.'

He adjusted his jacket and tie and walked towards the door. As he reached it he turned. His expression was one of detachment.

'When I feel the need, I will send for you.'

He opened the door and the sound of merriment rose a fraction and then died as he let himself out.

There had been many occasions since that first meeting and all of them just as degrading. Mabato's appetite was insatiable and his scope for variation seemingly endless. His gross demands reduced his victims to almost bestial acolytes.

Elizabeth Wakholi had learned to accept her role with a resignation that disgusted her. She had thought of fleeing more than once but the realization of what Mabato would do to her family prevented her. The last girl who had rejected his advances had turned up in one of the refrigeration units in the morgue at Magula Hospital, her legs and arms having been cut off and placed in a sack next to the dismembered torso. Her mother, father and two sisters had disappeared from her village, never to be seen again.

Elizabeth Wakholi had two teenage brothers and an

invalid mother so she submitted to Mabato's demands without question. Two or three times a month, less if she was lucky. Mabato had a ready supply of women. He could pick and choose.

But that didn't stop her plotting.

Because of her place in Mabato's affections – if it could be called that – she had been a prime target for Hamilton Kemba's agents. She had been recruited a month after Mabato had taken her to his bed and anywhere else he could think of when the mood took him. Mabato had no propensity for pillow talk but Elizabeth nurtured the hope that some day her sacrifice would pay dividends. Her long suffering patience had been rewarded at last.

Qetuka was here.

'Are you hungry?' she asked him. 'I can prepare you something.'

A welcome thought. He nodded.

She withdrew to the kitchen area. Qetuka reached for his bag and moved to the couch. The rifle was in three sections. It was a Czechoslovakian 7-mm Sahka with a thirty-power horsehair scope, the butt hollowed to hold half a dozen crossed dum–dum bullets capable of blowing a man apart like a ripe melon at three hundred yards. It was a formidable gun. His second firearm was more conventional; a Colt automatic with silencer. For short range kills.

The Zulu's last weapon was the most curious and yet gruesome in its simplicity. It was a garotte. The thin cheese wire was concealed in a leather wrist bracelet with the toggles an integral feature of the design. Qetuka could release the weapon in a second, using one of the toggles as a weight to flick the wire around the victim's throat. It was a simple yet cunning device and in the Zulu's expert hands it was lethal.

She was watching him from the doorway, eyes following

221

every movement as he tested the bolt action of the rifle and automatic.

He looked up.

She asked him if he wanted coffee. Apart from eggs and butter and the soap in the bathroom, it was the only other luxury she possessed. Since the Asians had been expelled the production of coffee had dropped drastically.

'Strong and black.'

She had used some of the precious butter to cook the eggs. Qetuka ate them with relish. She poured a drop of condensed milk from a can into her own coffee and studied him over the rim of her cup.

She had been instantly conscious of his grace as he moved into the apartment. His body flowed. He was lithe, honed like a machine. His aura had taken over and she was now the interloper.

Qetuka was aware of her perusal and knew she was afraid of what he represented.

He pushed the plate aside. 'That was very good.'

She shrugged. 'A small payment for what you are here to do. When I was told you were coming to kill Solomon Mabato I wept with joy.'

He looked at her calmly, noting her beauty. 'You seem to think I am some sort of messiah. I am not. I am a man sent to do a job.'

'Man, messiah, avenging angel,' she said. 'I will pray for your success.'

Qetuka said: 'I will need your help.'

'Ask. I will do whatever you require. I want that butcher dead.' Her vehemence was startling in its intensity, as though her entire body was racked with emotion.

So, this was one of Mabato's bedmates, he thought.

As though she had read his mind she stood and turned and unfastened the kaftan.

From the hollow between her shoulder blades to the curve of her buttocks the vicious weals that criss-crossed her skin were like some macabre lattice work. Some of the wounds had healed and formed thin scabs but others, recently inflicted, ran in pink and tender tendrils across her back.

'You see now,' she said.

'He did this to you?' the Zulu asked softly.

'He mates like an animal,' she hissed. 'He enjoys giving pain, to hear his women scream with agony as he takes them. It is the only way he can achieve a climax. He is incapable of love. If I had the means I would kill him myself.' She covered herself. 'When I am taken to him they search me. It is impossible to conceal a weapon . . . anywhere.'

Qetuka looked thoughtful. 'You are taken to him?'

'A driver collects me and drives me to the Command Post.'

'The same driver every time?'

'No. I have had the same man more than once but never at regular intervals.'

'When you go to the Command Post, do you always use the same room?'

She nodded, curious. 'Yes. His other women may be taken elsewhere but I do not know about them.'

'I see.' He frowned. 'And when are you to visit him again?'

She shivered. 'The time comes around so quickly. It will be this afternoon when the driver will deliver me to Mabato.'

Leonid Vakov nudged his companion awake. 'Stir yourself, Valeri Andreyevich. We have arrived and not before time either.'

223

Litvinof yawned and mumbled: 'I could have slept for a week.'

'I don't know how you slept at all,' Vakov said. 'Not over those roads! And with these bloody drivers!'

Valeri Litvinof sat up and peered through the windscreen. Ahead of them, the lights of the city glowed like fireflies. In the wing mirrors he could see the bright headlights of the other transporters in the convoy. The vehicles were strung out along the highway like a goods train.

'We've made good time,' he commented, looking at his Sekonda.

'We'd have made even better time if the Kenyans hadn't detained us at Nairobi. We lost four hours there!'

'Wait a minute!' Litvinof said suddenly. He pointed at the road ahead. 'What's happening?'

A mile up the highway someone was waving a light to and fro and the two men could make out the dim, squat shapes that were military trucks. The swarthy Libyan driver was also peering ahead. It looked like a road block.

'That's all we need!' Vakov muttered. 'Take it easy on the clutch, you imbecile!'

The driver was shifting down through the gears. Vakov and his mate were staring at the sight ahead. Half a dozen soldiers were strung across the road, blocking the advance of the convoy. Vakov was cursing steadily. Litvinof was tense and expectant.

By now, with the huge MAZ transporter heading towards him like a steam locomotive, the corporal was swinging the signal lamp like a man possessed. He debated whether or not to ditch the lamp and throw himself aside. Behind, his men were beginning to shuffle their feet as the Soviet transporters lumbered out of the darkness with a thundering roar.

In the event the first MAZ shuddered to a halt inches from

the quivering corporal with a searing hiss of air as the brakes locked. Vakov swung open the door of the cab. Below him, on the tarmac, half a dozen blacks in army uniforms stared at the huge vehicles and their concealed cargo.

'Who the hell is in charge here?' Vakov glared at the cluster of men. The words, spoken in English, slammed into them.

He was unprepared for the reply.

A stocky figure detached itself from the shadow of a troop carrier and stepped into the patch of light cast by the corporal's lantern.

'Ah,' the stranger said. 'Comrade Vakov, unless I miss my guess? I trust you had a good journey?' He smiled broadly and reached up, obviously intent on shaking Vakov's hand.

Vakov stared back. The man had spoken in Russian.

'My name is Burov. I am military and economic adviser to the President. Welcome to Lugamba.'

The bodies lay where they had fallen. Besigye on his side with half his head blown away and Oketta face down and almost naked.

And Oketta's scalp was moving.

Ants. A colony of them scurrying across his neck and into his hair. They were foraging in his skull and weaving trails through his curls like Indian trackers. Something else moved on the corpse's leg. A scorpion, sting raised, sidled down Oketta's thigh and disappeared between the cleft of the dead man's buttocks.

Corporal Moyo clicked the flashlight off and stared thoughtfully into the darkness. At least the larger scavengers hadn't found the bodies yet but it was only a matter of time before a wandering jackal or fox caught the scent of death and came to investigate.

Moyo recognized gunshot wounds when he saw them. He'd seen the aftermath of a SASU assassination squad often enough. What intrigued him was that he should find such a scene out here, miles from anywhere.

The corporal's companion was crouching over the remains of Besigye. The tubby private turned the body over. Tiny insect feet scampered away. The blood had congealed and dirt, stones and twigs adhered to the ghastly crater in the dead man's skull. Bone gleamed whitely.

There was no sign of the patrol's Land Rover.

Moyo looked for tracks with the aid of the flashlight. The ones he found indicated that the Land Rover had been driven west, towards the capital.

Unusual. If the patrol had been killed by Lugambans intent on fleeing for the border the tracks would surely have headed back the other way. And the killings had been professional. The hole in the back of Oketta's head signified as much. And why strip the body?

Moyo called to his oppo and between them they widened the area of search.

And found the Mazda in the gully.

The wreck carried no identification. The registration plates had been removed. Ideas began to form.

An anonymous vehicle, disabled and abandoned. A border patrol murdered, their Land Rover missing. Logical conclusion: a straight swap. But there was more to it than that; there had to be. Moyo considered the possibilities and none of them made sense. He was out of his depth and knew it. There was only one course of action.

Contact Base.

Keel watched the huge Crowned eagle soar overhead like a glider, effortlessly sweeping through the sky as it latched on to thermals. It was a stranger out here and more at home in the dense forests than the flat plains. The natives called it the 'leopard of the air'.

It was mid morning and the temperature was high. The crest of the escarpment shimmered above the airstrip. One hundred yards behind his shoulder the white mission buildings shifted in the heat haze like a desert mirage. In the confines of a wire mesh run six scrawny hens pecked dispiritedly at anything that crawled and in a wicker pen a pair of goats bleated like wailing children as they watched the approach of Sister Elicia with a sack of leftovers from the kitchen.

'Well, Thomas, should I offer a penny for them?'

Father Devlin stood a yard away, head on one side like an inquisitive blackbird as he regarded the thoughtful mercenary with his bright eyes.

'That's a trifle generous, old man,' Keel said. He continued to gaze out over the scrub, his blue eyes narrowed against the sun's glare.

'You are worried about this contract, Thomas? Second thoughts perhaps?'

Keel shook his head. 'We've had tougher assignments than this. I was wondering why I feel the need to undertake the contract at all. All my senses tell me that I should have stayed in Holland to enjoy my retirement. I think it's a sickness, a virus. A blood lust perhaps, I can't explain it. I only know it is like a drug. It takes a hold of you and doesn't let go.'

He sighed. 'Maybe it's a subconscious desire to prove that I still have the ability or maybe the panache to even carry out another contract.' He shrugged. 'Maybe I'm talking too much.'

'The trouble with you, Thomas,' Devlin said, 'is that you have something that is unique in your profession.'

'What's that?'

'A conscience,' Father Devlin said abruptly.

In the shade of a small, stunted acacia a puff adder stirred, its doze temporarily disturbed by the slow passage of a dung beetle a hand's span in front of its broad, arrow shaped head. In the goat pen Sister Elicia was calling the goats to her with promises of sweet, succulent peelings.

'Why don't you go back to Amsterdam, Thomas. Take Kate Lassiter with you.'

'You think I need domesticity, Father?'

'You need roots, Thomas. Someone to go home to. A link with sanity.'

'House in the suburbs? Car in the garage? I can't see it, somehow.'

'Well, use your bloody imagination then! By God, you're a stubborn man, Thomas Keel!'

To Keel's amazement the priest turned and stumped off in the direction of the chapel.

Behind him, Joseph Sekka stood with arms folded. 'I was going to ask if you'd like company,' he said. 'But now I'm not so sure.'

Keel hadn't heard him arrive. Sekka moved like a breath of wind; in silence.

'Not if you're going to bend my ear too,' Keel replied, his mouth creasing into a smile.

'I'll leave the sermons for those more qualified.'

'I'm glad to hear it, but I think I've upset the good father.'

'It's not that he doesn't care, Thomas,' Sekka said.

Keel nodded. 'I know.' He gazed towards the chapel.

Sekka squatted. 'So, what's the plan, Thomas? How do we get Holt out?'

Keel glanced into the sky, screwing his eyes against the

glare. After several seconds he lowered his head and turned. He answered softly.

'By the dark of the moon.'

Harry Roan was sitting in the first row of the low wooden pews. His eyes were closed. He sensed a presence. The priest.

'I'm sorry, Mister Roan. I didn't mean to disturb your prayers.' Michael Devlin looked faintly embarrassed as though caught with his hands in the biscuit jar.

'No problem, Father. I wasn't praying. Just biding my time.'

'And what better place in which to do so, my son. Do you mind if I join you?'

'Take a pew, Father.' Roan grinned apologetically. 'Sorry, I guess it is an old joke. Now, you look to me like a man with something on his mind.'

Roan moved over to make room on the bench and the priest sat down. A comfortable silence fell between them.

It was cool in the chapel. The sun's rays filtered obliquely through the sheltering leaves of the big sycamore, down through the chinks and cracks in the roof, forming narrow shafts of light from floor to rafters, in which tiny specks of dust hung almost motionless as though suspended in time and space.

'You're worried about Thomas aren't you, Father?' Roan said gently.

'My concern is for you all, Mister Roan. You have taken on an almost impossible task.'

'Don't worry, we can look after ourselves, Father, we're professional soldiers.'

Roan caught the expression on Michael Devlin's face. It was one of resignation tinged with infinite sadness.

'Okay, Father,' he said. 'So, we're mercenaries, soldiers of fortune, dogs of war, call us what you will. We're members of the second oldest profession in the world. We enjoy it and we're good at it. Dammit, it's all we know!'

'I'm not passing judgement,' Devlin said.

Roan's expression softened. 'I know. It's just that I can't take all this holier than thou attitude of people to whom the word mercenary means a group of thugs who kill people for money.'

The priest blanched.

'Sorry,' Roan said. 'I suppose that wasn't the most subtle of phrases given the circumstances.'

'Mister Roan, you have a directness that is disconcerting to say the least.'

'That's as maybe. Oh, I'll not deny there are men who take the promise of a bounty for no more reason than a blood lust but a lot of guys fight for a principle, a belief. Doesn't matter if it's anti communist, anti fascist or whatever. It's not always for the money, I can tell you. When I was with the Selous Scouts tracking guerillas in Mozambique I sure as heck wasn't in it for the bread because, considering the risks, the pay was lousy. We don't just provide a gun, we provide experience and discipline. We've all had exceptional training. You know Thomas. He was SAS before he turned freelance and I guess I don't have to tell you how good that makes him. Paul was in the Bundeswehr before he joined the GSG-9 anti terrorist squad. You remember the Lufthansa hijack to Mogadishu? Paul was a member of the rescue team. Me? I spent three years in Nam with the Special Forces. That's where I met Thomas. God, we've shared a few contracts since then.' He chuckled, remembering.

'And Joseph?' the old man asked.

'Now Joseph is a mite different,' Roan conceded. 'Until Biafra he'd had no combat experience. Then he met Thomas. Joseph is a natural. It's in his blood.'

The priest looked away. He appeared to shiver as if a chill wind had passed through him.

'Let me tell you, Father,' Roan said. 'Whatever feelings you may have, don't try to change Thomas, or Joseph or any of us for that matter. You'd be wasting your time. Believe me.'

Roan frowned. 'Mind you, my instinct tells me that you might just have tried already. Am I right?'

'You are also very perceptive, Mister Roan.'

'It really wasn't too difficult,' Roan replied.

Devlin's eyes clouded.

'You've known them both a long time; longer than Paul and I. You want to tell me about it?'

The priest seemed to hold his breath for a second or two as he collected his thoughts.

Another time, another place.

Biafra.

The rebels were pulling back before the onslaught of the Federal forces. Gowon's 1st Federal Division was pushing south, driving Ojukwu's men into the path of the advance guard of Adenkunle's 3rd Commando Division in a pincer movement that was squeezing the rebels like toothpaste out of a tube. Ojukwu's men had a clear run to the river and they were looting and murdering as they went.

Then someone mentioned the mission station at Brandt's Crossing. It lay directly in the rebels' line of retreat and there wasn't much time left to warn the staff. Ojukwu's men were ravaging the country like a swarm of locusts and they weren't averse to killing innocent men and women who stood in their way. Not that one old priest and a dozen nuns presented much of a threat.

231

No threat at all, rather like the four Italian priests and six nuns who had composed the staff of a small mission hospital a few miles west of Bende. The priests had been stripped naked, their rectums pierced with sharpened stakes, their genitals severed. The nuns, Nigerian and Belgian, had been tied to the perimeter fence and raped. Their patients, all from the outlying villages, had been killed in their beds. Over thirty people murdered or mutilated.

Colonel Adenkunle had asked for volunteers and Keel, Sekka and a dozen Federal troopers headed for Brandt's Crossing in two Bedford trucks to rescue the staff and whoever else might be there. They had driven during the night, through bush and over terrain that would have defied a Centurion tank, arriving at the river crossing at dawn, ahead of the rebel forces.

The priest turned out to be old, Irish, defiant and adamant. He wasn't going to leave. Father Michael Devlin had heard that Ojukwu was an honourable man. Their small infirmary held one patient – a twelve month old girl with a broken leg – and it was obvious that the occupants would not be harmed. Keel pointed out that whereas Ojukwu might have all the saving graces, his followers hadn't. They were still arguing when the rebel advance party crested the ridge above the mission and peppered the building with small arms fire, killing two nuns.

Windows exploded and Keel's men returned fire. The trucks had been parked at the rear. With the Federal troopers covering them, Keel and Sekka ushered the remaining terrified nuns through the building and out of the back door. Father Devlin ran to the infirmary and returned clutching a wide eyed infant, her thin leg encased in plaster from thigh to ankle. They were bundling the women into the first truck as the rebel wave broke from the trees, yelling and shooting as they ran towards the mission. Five fell in the attack, tumbling like skittles as the Federal troopers raked the line.

As the rebels faltered, half of Keel's force withdrew from their positions and the Bedford, with the frightened nuns on board, lurched down the bank and began to ford the shallows. It hadn't reached halfway before the mortars began to rain down. The shrieking salvo smashed into the mission, wiping out half the defenders at a stroke. The building began to burn fiercely.

The truck exploded in midstream. A fearful detonation that blew the vehicle apart, sending a muddy tidal wave crashing against the shore. Ruptured bodies erupted from it like offal.

Father Devlin viewed the devastation with horror. The child in his arms was screaming in fear. Gathering his wits he ran, stumbling, for the surviving truck. Keel and Sekka and the rest of the Federals threw themselves after him. With debris from the shattered mission falling about them, they scrambled aboard and drove the Bedford down to the ford.

Almost across and the wheels were spinning in the mud and the rebels had reached the mission. Keel and the others were firing over the tailboard as Ojukwu's men ran on to the bank. A trooper on Keel's right jerked aside, his face a red morass. The wheels caught and they were free and surging through the water. On the ridge the main rebel phalanx appeared across the skyline but by now the truck had gained the opposite bank and was thundering towards the treeline. Then they were free.

They recrossed the river ten miles upstream before turning back on a heading that would lead them to the Federal lines. It was almost noon when they hit the highway but at least they were able to pick up speed.

Then they hit the mine.

The explosion lifted the truck like a toy, shredding the tyres and splintering the front axle like matchwood. The driver died at the wheel, torn apart as the floor of the cab burst asunder. With a scream of tortured metal the heavy Bedford slammed back on to the tarmac and slewed across the road.

For those in the back it was a helter skelter ride until the truck came to a grating halt. Father Devlin, still holding the girl and therefore unable to support himself, bounced against the tailboard with a bone jarring thump. He lay, winded and bruised, the child wailing hysterically. He was dimly aware that Keel was yelling at his men to vacate the vehicle and then someone took the girl from him and he was being helped from the back of the truck.

He heard Keel bellowing: 'Cover! Cover!' and the thump of bullets into the Bedford. Sekka and the others were firing their weapons into the brush on the opposite side of the track and Keel was at his shoulder, the whimpering infant in his arms, urging him off the road and into shelter, keeping the bulk of the stranded truck between themselves and the attackers.

There was a shallow ditch at the edge of the road and this bordered a cane field. With the rattle of automatic fire bombarding his senses, Father Devlin paid heed to Keel's instruction to keep his head down. He didn't keep down far enough. He felt the punch as the bullet hit his right shoulder, swinging him around and then he lost his footing and slid down into the ditch. He tried to stand, the movement aggravating the wound.

Keel was at his back. 'Get up, Father. You can't die here. It'll be inconvenient.'

Father Devlin forced a smile on to his lips and struggled to his feet. 'If you think I'm worth the trouble, my son.'

Keel gave the priest's shoulder a cursory examination. 'The slug went right through, Father. You'll live . . . if you keep moving. Joseph and the others will keep them pinned down until we get clear.'

The child was silent now, exhausted and staring at the priest with puppy dog eyes. The old man wondered if she had gone into shock but, as if in answer, the little girl tightened her grip around Keel's neck and buried her face in the mercenary's shoulder.

They stumbled over the furrowed ground, away from the scene of the ambush though the shooting could still be heard beyond the curtain of cane stems. Keel led the way, his arms about the girl, turning frequently to check that the priest was behind him.

They had travelled about half a mile through the cane crop and the old man was flagging. It was blisteringly hot and Devlin could feel the energy draining out of his body like sap from a tree. Keel granted him a second to catch his breath before they moved off again. A hundred yards further on they broke from the cane belt into waist high scrub. Then the ground started to dip and Keel led the way down a scree slope into a muddy defile. It was easier going and Devlin guessed that they were close to one of the meandering tributaries. The undergrowth was getting dense and it had begun to get cooler out of the direct glare of the sun. A narrow track led into the trees.

The priest had no idea when Sekka rejoined them. He had three troopers with him – all that remained out of the original rescue squad – and they had held off the ambush party for an hour before the latter had withdrawn, leaving four dead.

The old man had collapsed at the side of the path. By now his throbbing shoulder was severely inflamed and he was feeling the effects of dehydration. He was finding it difficult to focus and his tired legs had refused to support him. He came to as Sekka tipped the water canteen to his swollen lips. The lukewarm liquid trickled down his chin and through the haze of pain he acknowledged Sekka's Samaritan gesture with a cracked grin. A few feet away Keel was dabbing the child's face with a damp cloth.

'The priest is feverish, Thomas. He needs medical attention. The girl also,' Sekka said.

'I know it, Joseph.'

With the troopers acting as point and flankers they set off again. To Devlin, hunched piggy back on Sekka's shoulders, the journey – what he could remember of it – was a nightmare. Four hours later they emerged from the forest under a moonlit sky and walked into the arms of one of Adenkunle's night patrols. From there it was a jeep ride back to the base.

Harry Roan's face said it all. 'My God!' he breathed when Devlin had finished.

'He was certainly looking over our shoulders that night,' the priest said. 'They took it in turns to carry me and the girl. Over fifteen miles through the bush. How can anyone ever repay men like that?' He shook his grey head in wonderment.

'And the girl?'

'She survived,' Devlin replied. 'As I did.'

'Paul and I knew none of this,' Roan said. 'Now I understand what they mean to you.'

'I don't want to see them dead, Mister Roan – Harry.'

Roan gripped the old man's wrist. 'Paul and I will look after them. We'll watch their backs.'

'And will they watch yours, Harry?'

'You can count on it. I told you, we're a team. You know what they say, Father; all for one and one for all.'

Despite his reassurances, Roan saw that the priest wasn't smiling.

Maybe that was an omen.

Paul Schiller was watching Sister Elicia feed the goats. He had seen the brief altercation between Keel and Father Devlin but hadn't moved to interfere. He knew Keel well enough for that. Besides, Joseph was with Thomas now and Sekka was closest to Keel out of the three of them. They were like brothers, he thought. Probably closer than kin if one did but know, having shared contracts together from the shores of the Caribbean to the deserts of Chad.

Sister Elicia had the feeling she was being observed. She turned. It was the fair one with the nice smile and the calm brown eyes. He was leaning against the fence, looking on with amusement as the goats butted her in their search for food.

'I'd say their table manners were definitely lacking.' He opened the gate and walked into the pen. He closed the gate behind him and the goats approached, expecting titbits. Schiller stroked their soft necks, patting the kids, talking softly.

Sister Elicia handed him the bucket. 'Would you like to feed them?'

The goats moved in, bleating loudly, jostling for morsels. Sister Elicia laughed gaily at their antics as Schiller dispensed the contents of the pail.

The girl looked very young in her white working habit and grey head scarf. Her face was a picture of innocence, her complexion as fresh as morning. Blue eyes sparkled with enjoyment as she looked on.

'When we were very young,' Schiller said, 'my sister and I used to spend our summer holidays on my uncle's

237

farm in Bavaria. Our special chore was to feed the animals. We would feed the pigs and goats and the chickens and collect eggs just as the sun came up over the mountains, when the ground held the last trace of dew. We never wanted to go home.'

Sister Elicia stared at Schiller for as he spoke his voice faltered. For a second only but it was time enough for her to notice the catch in his voice and the hurt in his eyes. It was as if a shadow, dark and fleeting and evil, had passed over him.

'What is it?' she whispered, sensing in him sorrow, a pain that had crawled out of some deep recess.

'Just a memory,' Schiller said. 'That's all.' He looked down at her, at the concern on her face. A stray whisp of hair had escaped the scarf and was curling down one cheek. Schiller realized again just how much she reminded him of Anna-Lise. He'd caught the resemblance that first night when he'd arrived with Keel. Now, standing here with her, he was even more conscious of the striking similarity.

Anna-Lise. His sister; slim, graceful, lovely, warm, alive. Until Augsburg.

It had begun in the spring of 1972 with a bomb attack at the headquarters of the US 5th Army Corps in Frankfurt, as retaliation against American involvement in Vietnam. It was the advent of a series of urban guerilla actions that became known as the Devil's harvest. The reapers were Andreas Baader and Ulrike Meinhof. Their terrorist campaign escalated rapidly with more bombings across the country and among their targets was the police headquarters in Augsburg.

Anna-Lise Schiller was a secretary in the records division. Eighteen years old, four years younger than her brother, not long out of school. With everything to live for, she died in one senseless act of savagery as the device exploded, shattering walls and windows and what had been, up until that awesome atrocity, a conviction that such wanton barbarism could not possibly occur in an ordered, law abiding society.

It was a belief that for many was to be well and truly demolished three months later in an arena shared by an audience of millions; the Olympic village, Munich.

Schiller received the news of his sister's death while on a military exercise in the Oberpfalzer Wald along the Czechoslovakian border. He would never forget the terrible looks on his parents' haggard faces as they stood at the side of the grave and saw the coffin being lowered. If Paul Schiller harboured thoughts of revenge they were of little consequence for both Baader and Meinhof were caught within weeks of each other not long after the funeral of his sister.

The murder of the Israeli athletes by the Black September unit, however, provided Schiller with an opportunity for indirect reprisal. Special anti terrorist squads were set up to combat the threat by both left and right wing factions who advocated reform through violence. Among these was GSG-9. Schiller was a weapons expert in the Bundeswehr and as such was attached to the new unit as an instructor. At his own insistence and through the personal recommendation of Wegener himself Schiller made the transfer permanent.

Paul Schiller exacted retribution for his sister's murder when he stormed the Lufthansa jet on the runway at Mogadishu. It was a long time coming but it gave him immense satisfaction. Anna-Lise had at last been avenged.

Sister Elicia, of course, knew none of this. She was aware only that a change had come over the fair haired one with the nice smile. What she perceived frightened her.

She retrieved the pail and moved on to her other tasks, leaving Schiller on his own at the side of the goat pen. Schiller watched her run off with a sombre expression on his tanned face. He reached for a cheroot, lit up, and sat smoking it with his back against the fence.

Keel had called them together in the isolation ward.

'Any problems?' he asked them.

'We're as ready as we'll ever be, Thomas,' Harry Roan said. He held a block of C4 plastic explosive in his hand. It looked like a cube of putty and had the same malleable consistency.

'Paul?'

Schiller shook his head. 'No problems, Thomas.' He was fitting shells into the magazine of the Browning. A fresh cheroot was stuck between his lips.

Keel caught Sekka's eye and the latter winked. They both understood Schiller's mood. A workman is only as good as the tools he uses. Weapons were the tools of Schiller's deadly trade.

'I've spoken with Father Devlin,' Keel said. 'He's brought me up to date with the conditions at Maboru. I didn't think we'd be that lucky but he's been inside this place and knows the layout. He was there when they took Holt in.'

'He saw him?' Roan asked.

'Only briefly. Seems that the DOSS boys lifted a couple of black priests for questioning. Devlin got wind and demanded their release. Didn't do any good mind you but he did manage to see Holt. He had to drop the guards a little something to gain access though.'

'Jesus!' Roan said. 'What the hell did he bribe them with?'

'In Lugamba, Harry, you could probably bribe anyone

240

with anything,' Sekka put in. 'I would think it would have been drugs from his dispensary.'

'A priest peddling drugs!' Roan looked at Sekka with disbelief written all over his face.

'A few morphine tablets and a bottle of aspirin is hardly the French Connection, Harry.'

'Christ!' was Roan's only comment.

'What condition was Holt in?' Schiller took a drag on the cheroot. 'Is he mobile? Can he walk?'

Keel merely shrugged. 'That we'll have to find out. He was barely conscious when Devlin saw him. He doubts if the poor devil even knew he was there.'

'They've roughed him up then?' Roan's voice was hard.

'Devlin didn't think so. He figured Holt was just exhausted as well as scared to death.'

'I'm not surprised,' Sekka said. 'He thinks he's going to die.'

'He still might,' said Roan. 'Unless we get to him first.'

'Well, that's what we're here for, Harry. Any questions? Paul? Joseph?'

He got no response.

Keel stood up. 'That's it then,' he said easily. 'It's on. I suggest we all get some rest. We go in at dusk.'

11

David Wood's day had started brightly, rather like the morning weather forecast. There was a clear blue sky and a freshening breeze. The car had collected him at his flat at an early hour but, as they swept on to the Embankment, Wood ordered his driver to stop and climbed out. He walked slowly, gaze fixed on the grey waters of the Thames, his own footsteps echoed by the measured tread of his personal detective a pace or two behind. The Daimler kerb crawled on the opposite side of the road.

Wood strolled to the parapet and watched a heavily laden string of barges plough its way down river, Tilbury bound. There was a sense of tranquillity about the scene that prompted him to retain the view for several minutes. It was with a sigh of reluctance that he recrossed the road and entered the car again. Engine purring, the Daimler filtered into the stream of traffic and headed towards Westminster.

The telephone call came like a bombshell.

A moment of terrible disbelief.

Wood, senses reeling, reached an unsteady hand towards his intercom. 'I want the PM. I don't care where he is or what he's doing. Get him . . . NOW!'

He couldn't believe it. He sat staring into space until the intercom squawked, jolting him into action.

'The Prime Minister on line two, sir.'

He was already grabbing for the receiver.

'I'm putting the scrambler on,' Wood said.

Lennox's voice was gruff. 'Make it quick, David, I've a meeting with the West German anbassador and . . .'

'We've got a problem,' Wood cut in. 'A big problem, concerning Holt.'

There was an ominous silence at Lennox's end. Finally, the PM said: 'What sort of problem?'

'I've just had a cable from Nairobi. It appears that the President of Kenya has intervened on our behalf. He has secured the release of David Holt.'

Deathly silence.

Wood thought he had been cut off. Only the red light on the scrambler indicated the line was still active.

'Oh, Christ!' Lennox said eventually. 'What the hell is going on?'

'Apparently Mabato was handed an ultimatum by President Nai for and on behalf of the other members of the OAU. The gist being that if Mabato wanted the position of Chairman for the next twelve months he was to release Holt. It was also mentioned that unless Mabato agreed to this, Kenya would place an embargo on all goods due to transit Kenya for Lugamba. This would affect the passage of military vehicles being unloaded at Mombasa. There has already been some minor confrontation over a convoy of transporters that has recently arrived in Kendura.'

'And Mabato agreed to all this?' Lennox sounded sceptical.

'He wants that Chairmanship. He's gone to a lot of trouble over the conference including the construction of the new centre in Kendura. The last thing he wants is for the OAU to disown him. I must say they've come up with a heck of a lever.'

'And it puts us right in the shit,' Lennox rasped. He went on slowly: 'I don't suppose there is the remotest possibility of calling off the rescue attempt?'

'God knows,' Wood replied unhappily. 'It may be too late.'

243

'Fucking hell!'

'I'll get hold of George Dalkeith. Maybe he can come up with something.'

'I bloody well hope so.' The Prime Minister's voice dropped several octaves. 'This mustn't get out, David. Any of this. I can't emphasize that enough. You understand?'

You bastard, Wood thought. 'Of course, Prime Minister.'

'Keep me informed,' Lennox said. 'Every step of the way.'

The receiver went dead. Wood clicked off the scrambler and touched the intercom again. 'Joan, get me George Dalkeith. Again, I don't care where he is.'

It took a minute. Dalkeith sounded tired or bored. Either way, this would wake him up quicker than a twenty one gun salute.

'My office,' Wood said. 'Soonest.'

'Recall them!' Dalkeith's voice was like ice splintering. 'Judas Priest! What the hell is this, Wood?'

Wood told him.

'Oh, Jesus!' Dalkeith said.

'What about the broker, this contact of yours? Can he do anything?'

'It's too damned late.'

'Find out. Get hold of him.'

Dalkeith gritted his teeth and moved to the door. 'I'll get back to you.'

'With the speed of light,' Wood prompted. 'If this leaks out, George, our heads will roll.'

'Not only our heads,' Dalkeith said grimly. 'It'll make Hitler's night of the long knives look like a bar mitzvah.'

* * *

'Of course I can't abort!' Cameron blew up. 'They're already in Lugamba! For all I know, they're running the snatch right now! They're out of contact. They might as well be on the dark side of the moon.'

But Cameron was speaking to himself. Dalkeith had hung up. The recruiter slammed the receiver down. What had gone wrong? To contact him at this stage, it had to be something massive.

Then he thought about something else.

'If you have a suggestion, George, now's the time to make it.' There was more than a trace of despair in Wood's voice. He looked drained.

Dalkeith looked pensive. He said: 'I would have thought the solution was obvious.' His tone was calm.

Why did the bastard always look so bloody self assured? Wood thought.

Dalkeith seemed to be waiting for something; a spark of intuition from Wood.

Then it came.

Obvious and drastic.

'We warn Mabato,' Wood said.

Dalkeith nodded. 'It's the only thing we can do,' he said. 'We've got to tell him they are going in. We can redeem the situation.'

'They're dead men,' Wood said heavily.

'We knew it was virtually a suicide mission when we set it up.'

'There's no need to sound so bloody smug. We both know what Mabato will do to them. It doesn't bear thinking about.'

'Nor do the consequences if we don't warn him. It'll be a blood bath with no quarter given. President Nai has opened the door. Let's not slam it in his face.'

245

'We could be too late,' Wood pointed out. 'Maybe they've made the snatch already.'

Dalkeith shook his head. 'I doubt that. Lugamba is – let me see – three hours ahead of us which means it's still daylight. They surely wouldn't go in until dark and beside we'd have heard from Warren-Chase by now.'

'Which means – ' Wood began.

' – that we don't have a second to lose.'

'I'll inform the PM and shoot a cable off to Lugamba,' Wood said. He shook his head unhappily. 'You know, I never thought it would come to this: warning Mabato about a plot against him. My God, if it wasn't so bloody tragic, it'd be funny.'

'Count your blessings that we got the news in time,' Dalkeith said. 'At least there's no way that Mabato will connect us with the rescue bid; not now. Even he wouldn't believe that we would sacrifice our own men. We'll be in the clear. All in all, it's probably the best thing that could have happened. This way there'll be no loose ends.'

Wood eyed Dalkeith thoughtfully. 'Tell me, George, I'd really like to know. If it had been a couple of your Sandbaggers out there, would you still warn Mabato?'

Dalkeith gave a sly smile. 'What do you think, Foreign Secretary?'

'I think,' Wood said darkly, 'that you are one ruthless bastard.'

'Why, coming from you, I take that as a compliment,' was Dalkeith's parting shot as he left the room.

A heady trace of aftershave lingered in the air after his departure. Paco Rabanne. Wood wrinkled his nose. 'Supercilious sod!' he swore under his breath.

There wasn't much time left. A matter of hours, maybe even minutes before everything fell apart. As Wood prepared himself to send the warning to Mabato he was now very much aware of one irrefutable fact.

In Lugamba, David Holt's role in the affair had taken on a new and deadly connotation.

David Holt wasn't a hostage any longer.

He was bait.

Qetuka had been sleeping, conserving energy. He came awake instantly at the touch of the woman's hand on his shoulder. His arm moved swiftly, steel fingers catching the slim wrist. Elizabeth Wakholi gasped at the speed of the man. The Zulu found himself gazing into frightened brown eyes.

'It is time,' she said.

She answered the door at the first rap. The soldier standing on the threshold – Mabato's messenger boy – eyed her speculatively. She was dressed in a tight, turquoise silk sheath that moulded itself to her full body. The corporal's eyes travelled from thigh to cleavage, his stare arrested by the low neckline and firm breasts that thrust proud and provocatively against the sheer material. She might just as well have been naked. Elizabeth smoothed her hands over her body and half turned. The movement was openly suggestive and the soldier's breath escaped in a low moan of admiration. Instinctively he stepped after her, a cunning smile on his face.

Something moved at the extreme corner of his field of vision.

Or someone.

He was fleetingly aware of a small, pebble-like object curving past his face and a thin, reed-like whistle of sound as the wire cut through the air.

The first touch was like the caress of a tear and then his throat was on fire. His hands shot up to his neck, fingers

247

clawing at the garotte that had encircled his larynx. His right forefinger hooked behind the wire.

Qetuka now had a toggle in each hand and his knee was braced against the corporal's spine, arching the man's back like a bow. A dark bubble burst across the soldier's neck as the wire severed the trapped finger, the attempted scream becoming a rasping gargle as the garotte sawed through his windpipe with the ease of a knife blade cutting through melted butter. Blood welled out of the mutilated throat as the victim spasmed violently. With a final, searing jerk Qetuka broke the soldier's neck and allowed the body to sink to the floor. He released the tension in the wire and ripped it loose. He wiped it clean and secured it at his wrist.

Throughout the kill the woman had remained frozen, struck motionless with the speed and ferocity of the strike. Qetuka dragged the corpse across the floor into the tiny bathroom.

He snapped: 'Don't just stand there! Collect your things! Hurry!' He walked back into the room and picked up his holdall. 'Pack a bag,' he continued. 'You won't be coming back.'

She was confused. 'Not coming back?'

'Use your head! Once Mabato is dead, I'll be heading back across the border. I presume you don't want to remain here?'

'You mean I go with you?'

'Unless you can think of an alternative? What is there to come back to? Besides, there's a dead man in your bathroom. You would have great difficulty explaining that away.'

'You . . . you mean I can stay with you?'

'Don't get the wrong idea, woman. Once across the border you will be on your own. All I am doing is giving you a chance.'

248

She stared at him for a moment then, silently, she walked into the bedroom and began to throw a few items into a plastic shopping bag. Qetuka waited for her.

She looked around the apartment seeing the threadbare rugs, chipped plaster, cheap furniture and saw it for what it was: a tiny squalid bolt hole. She gazed at the Zulu, her eyes mirroring apprehension. Her chin lifted and her face showed a new emotion.

She smiled hesitantly. 'I'm ready.'

They walked out of the apartment and as the door closed behind her, Elizabeth Wakholi knew that from now on there could be no turning back.

Solomon Mabato was like a child with a box of new toys. He had been to view the Russian tanks with Burov and he was ecstatic. He had greeted the transporter crews and technicians with affection so overpowering it had positively turned Leonid Vakov's stomach. Burov had watched the latter suffer the president's bear-like embrace with amusement.

'My friends, my dear friends!' Mabato was bursting with camaraderie. 'They are magnificent! How my enemies will tremble! I will soon embark on my prime object; the overthrow of the white imperialists in South Africa! With your help, my dear Burov, I will drive them into the sea! What do you say?'

Burov shuddered inwardly. The man was mad. Nikolai Kolk, safe behind his desk in The Centre, had much to answer for.

'Let us not attempt to run before we can walk, Excellency,' Burov said hurriedly. 'Better to assess the situation before making any sudden moves. Perhaps it would be possible to er . . . mull over the idea with the other members during the coming conference?'

249

Burov had a brief, horrendous vision of Mabato sweeping south across the veldt like a mechanized Attila the Hun.

'I can afford to wait,' Mabato said magnanimously. 'Until you send me more guns and tanks. Then the South Africans will see that I mean business. They may very well surrender.' He speculated on that idea for some moments.

Vakov and those technicians who understood English eavesdropped on the exchange with wonderment. Vakov caught Burov's eye and the latter grabbed at the distraction with relief.

'My men and I would like to eat, Comrade Burov,' said Vakov. 'After which the President might like a demonstration of fire power.'

'An excellent idea,' Burov agreed. He put the suggestion to Mabato.

To his amazement, the President declined. Despite his evident pleasure and his enthusiastic response to the arrival of the tanks, he had another, more important matter on his mind.

An appointment with a woman.

Qetuka turned the Peugeot off the road and approached the locked gates of the Command Post. Elizabeth Wakholi occupied the rear seat. The Zulu's weapons were concealed in the holdall stuffed in the well before the front passenger seat.

A squad of troops squatted at the side of the road. A jeep and troop carrier were parked nearby. All the soldiers were armed with automatic weapons. Qetuka wound down the window and awaited the approach of the sentry.

'What is your business?' The trooper stared hard at the Zulu before his attention was diverted to the passenger and her neckline.

'A visitor for His Excellency,' Qetuka said. He caught the man's eye and winked.

'You are not one of the usual drivers.'

'My first time. Lucky huh?' Qetuka grinned.

'Let me see your identity papers.' The sentry snapped his fingers impatiently.

'Of course.' Behind Qetuka the woman froze. She felt sure that the guard would sense her panic. Qetuka had no papers. What was he going to do?

She leaned forward over the front seats, giving the sentry the full benefit of the cleft between her breasts. She reached out and touched the outstretched hand.

'Surely you know me, Corporal?' She pouted coquettishly. 'You aren't going to ask me for my papers?'

She stroked his hand before withdrawing her fingers slowly. She lifted her hand and traced the neckline of the dress pausing in the deep shadowed valley that opened invitingly before the man's gaze.

Qetuka had one hand inside his jacket, as though reaching for identification. 'You are delaying us,' he said. 'We are late as it is. His Excellency does not like to be kept waiting. You wouldn't like us to tell him that you held us up?'

The sentry withdrew his hand rapidly. 'We have to be careful. One of our border patrols was ambushed last night and a jeep was stolen. We have orders – '

'But this is not a jeep,' Qetuka pointed out. 'I doubt that your instructions include the harassment of the President's friends . . . intimate friends.'

Elizabeth smiled at the flustered sentry, pink tongue running around her full lips.

Abruptly the trooper stepped away from the car and signalled to the man on the gate. As the wrought iron barrier swung aside Qetuka drove the Peugeot forward into the grounds. Behind him the woman shivered violently. The Zulu caught the movement in the mirror.

'You did well,' he said.

The drive led up from the gates through a dusty brown lawn and swept in a horseshoe curve in front of the house. Two other vehicles were parked outside on the gravel: a dark blue Volvo and a SASU Datsun. More guards flanked the entrance. Heavily armed men in battle fatigues: Mabato's Praetorian Guard.

Qetuka parked the car and turned in his seat. No one had made a move towards them as they had obviously been cleared by the men at the main gate.

'Get out,' he ordered.

The woman opened the rear door and Qetuka reached for his choice of weapon; the Colt. He tucked the gun inside his tunic and vacated the car. Together the woman and the assassin walked towards the house.

The Zulu studied the sentries. They were of a different calibre to those on the main gate. No lacklustre loafers these but hard men, fighters, seasoned troops, their stern faces bearing the Makesi tribal scars. They watched Qetuka and the woman approach through unblinking eyes. The Zulu returned their stares brazenly, the Colt burning a hole in his belly under the ill fitting tunic. He expected the challenge at any moment.

But they made it through the gauntlet and into the lobby with its high white ceiling and revolving fan blades. And more guards. Mabato wasn't taking any chances. Getting out wouldn't be easy.

At the bottom of the sweep of stairs stood a desk manned by a corpulent Black in the uniform of a captain. Behind him, sinister in dark glasses with a machine pistol over one shoulder, a DOSS officer stood alert. The aide looked up expressionlessly as the woman walked to the desk.

'His Excellency is expecting me,' she said.

'Wait.' The fat captain eyed Qetuka. 'This is the driver?'

She nodded.

A telephone was at his elbow. He picked up the receiver. 'The woman is here. Inform him.' He paused then replied: 'Yes, of course, immediately.' A brief nod towards Qetuka. 'Take her up.'

The Zulu took her elbow and guided her to the stairs. He could feel the tension gripping her.

'Wait!' The captain's voice halted them in their tracks and Qetuka froze, his hand leaving the woman and moving to his belly. He looked over his shoulder. The aide was standing, his expression severe.

'She has not been searched. Bring her here.'

The Zulu looked on as the man ran his hands over her body. The action was neither gentle nor subtle. Broad fingers kneaded and cupped the ripe breasts, stroked the rounded hips and taut buttocks. The captain grinned as he thrust his palm between her thighs, enjoying her final indignity. All the time she suffered the pawing in silence. Qetuka didn't move a muscle.

Satisfied on all counts, the captain jerked his head. 'Don't keep His Excellency waiting!'

'Animal!' she hissed as he led her away. He could feel her shaking.

'That was the last time,' Qetuka said. 'Remember that.'

They reached the first floor and Mabato's apartments; his offices and private chambers. Qetuka knew he was close, very close.

She paused outside a door. 'This is an ante room to the President's living quarters. You must escort me inside and then wait to escort me back after Mabato has finished.' She spoke matter-of-factly and laid a hand on

253

his arm. 'After I enter his room wait five minutes. By that time he will be ready.'

Qetuka nodded. 'Let's go,' he said.

He opened the door.

The guards on the main gate gawped in astonishment as the Mercedes slewed off the highway and skidded to a halt, tyres squealing. The front passenger door flew open and the occupant screamed at the sentry to open the gates.

The soldier sprang to attention as he recognized the identity of the man in the car and gabbled an order at his companion by the gate. The car door slammed and the gates swung open. The Mercedes surged forward, dust trailing in its wake, and sped up the drive.

The sentry breathed a sigh of relief and rolled his eyes at the gate man. Some people you just didn't want to get on the wrong side of. Major Farouk Juma, the head of DOSS, was definitely one of them. Mabato's head of State Security instilled cold fear into the hearts and minds of the Lugamban population. No one who valued life ever questioned the Nubian's actions or impeded his authority. It was hinted that in his presence even Mabato guarded his back. So, what was the hurry? He had arrived like Nemesis.

The Merc stopped below the house and Juma sprinted up the steps into the lobby. 'The President, where is he?'

The fat captain, startled by the hectic arrival, stumbled to his feet. 'In his quarters, Major. He – '

'Alert him! I must see him at once!'

'He is engaged, Major, and not to be disturbed!' The aide was highly agitated. He was scared stiff of Juma but the thought of interrupting the President's pleasure terrified him even more.

'Imbecile!' Juma screeched. 'Follow me!'

'Major, His Excellency has a woman with him!' implored the hapless aide. The man was visibly cringing.

Juma paused. He looked ferocious, like a weasel turning on a rabbit. 'Captain, we have just received word that an attempt is to be made to free the Englishman, probably within a few hours. Do you wish to be held responsible for the delay in this news reaching the President?'

A vehement shake of the head.

'Cretin!' Juma spat. 'We must inform His Excellency at once. We have no time to lose! These men may already be in the city!'

Juma ran for the stairs.

Qetuka stole a glance at his watch. Five minutes she had said. Time was up.

But he wasn't alone.

They stood either side of the doors that led into Mabato's inner sanctum. Grim faced, Libyan mercenaries – private bodyguards – in olive green safari jackets and slacks. They each held squat Israeli machine pistols: Uzis.

Qetuka crossed to the window and looked out over the large grounds. He could feel their hooded eyes on him. How good were they?

He turned casually, the silenced Colt in his hand. He brought the gun up fast in a two handed grip, sighted and shot the nearest guard in the head. The bullet took the Libyan between the eyes, shattering the skull, and blew brain matter and crimson bone fragments against the flocked wall paper.

The second guard's reactions were commendably quicker. He at least managed to aim his Uzi. A burst from the machine pistol scythed past the already moving Zulu's right shoulder and the window exploded in a thousand pieces. Qetuka's second and third bullets slammed into the guard's chest with the force of a hammer. The man

255

cannoned backwards against the door and slid down the woodwork, the Uzi dangling from lifeless fingers. Even before the sagging corpse had touched the floor, Qetuka sprang for the entrance to Mabato's apartment and flung himself through the doors.

Solomon Mabato knelt on the bed, his hands grasping Elizabeth Wakholi's hips as he thrust himself between her buttocks. She was leaning forward, supporting herself on her elbows, submitting to the violation without a sound as Mabato grunted and pumped his way to a noisy climax. The tears began to flow as they always did during this act of degradation, her body racked with loathing for the grossness of the man who used her and abused her as though she was some kind of dumb animal.

Satisfied, Mabato eased himself from her body. He was breathing heavily, his eyes glazed with pleasure. He was about to reach forward to turn her around to face him when the sound of the guard's machine pistol shattered his concentration.

With surprising agility for a man of his vast bulk, Mabato scrambled to his feet, flesh quivering with the effort, his skin shiny with perspiration. His huge frame wobbled as he reached for his robe. As he belted the sash around his girth the doors crashed open and he found himself face to face with a crouching black holding a silenced automatic pistol.

Qetuka swung the Colt around, his aim taking in both the sight of the woman sprawled naked on her stomach and Mabato moving sideways to find cover. The Zulu, following his dramatic entrance, was slightly off balance when he fired. The slug tore into Mabato's upper arm. It passed through muscle and left a ragged exit wound before tumbling into the drapes behind the bed. Mabato spun away and a high pitched shriek of rage pierced his lips as he half fell and half threw himself to the floor.

The Zulu steadied himself and followed the heaving body with the barrel of the Colt. He aligned the silencer on Mabato's chest and squeezed the trigger.

The blast from the Uzi raked into the room and hit Qetuka in the thigh. Pain and shock exploded through his body and as he fell he knew that his second shot at Mabato had missed the target.

Farouk Juma, the machine pistol in his thin hands, ran into the room and prepared to blow Qetuka into little pieces.

'NO!' bellowed Mabato. 'Do not kill him!' He was clutching his wounded arm. Blood was seeping between his podgy fingers. 'I want him alive!'

The Zulu was lying on his side, one hand clamped on his thigh, the other clawing for the Colt that lay only inches away. Through pain misted eyes he watched Mabato lumber to his feet. Juma was panting as though he had run a great distance. The fat aide had been joined by the DOSS agent from the lobby and was blinking owlishly at the carnage. More people were running into the room; some waving automatic rifles like war clubs. No one seemed to notice the woman on the bed, sheet held against her body, staring at Qetuka's twitching form with horror and the mind numbing realization that the assassination attempt had failed.

Juma picked up the Colt and lashed out at the aide. 'You allowed this scum to reach His Excellency with this!'

The captain's face was etched with terror. He stared first at Juma and then at Mabato who was glaring at him with venom.

'He . . . he came with the woman, Excellency. Naturally we searched her thoroughly. Excellency, I swear – '

Mabato's voice cracked like a whip. 'Silence! I will deal

with you later.' He walked around to Qetuka and gazed down impassively.

'You thought you could kill the Liberator? I am a lion. I am invincible. I am Mabato! My friend, you are a dead man. You will experience pain such as you have never known or imagined. Then you will answer some questions. I want to know all about you.' He took the gun from Juma and placed the end of the silencer against the Zulu's right eye. 'You will tell me everything, believe me.' He swung towards the woman.

Walking to the bed, Mabato ripped the sheet away and slapped her face viciously with his open palm. Her head whipped back and hit the pillows. She lay there, legs splayed in abandon. Mabato pushed the smooth cylinder of the silencer between her open thighs. Elizabeth felt the cold blue steel pressing against her vagina and screamed, arching her back in a spasm of terror as the sound erupted from her throat.

That scream was the last sound Qetuka heard before the pain in his leg proved too much to bear and he passed beyond the edge of conscious thought into a deep black well of darkness.

Burov's raised eyebrows emphasized his scepticism. 'The British? What makes you think the British sent this man? Surely if they wanted to assassinate you they would hardly warn you of a plot to free Holt.' He felt like adding that the British, if they had engineered the assassination, would probably have succeeded.

Mabato frowned, forced to accept the logic.

They were in the President's office in the Command Post. Burov had his back to the big bay window and Mabato was seated at his desk, his arm now dressed and in a sling. His broad brow was furrowed in anger, a sign that

Mabato was at his most dangerous. Burov knew he would have to tread carefully.

'I suspect, Excellency,' he said, 'that the person or persons behind this attempt on your life are rather closer to home. Ask yourself who is most likely to gain from your death.' He paused expectantly.

Mabato bared his teeth. 'Kemba!' he growled. 'That dogspawn planned to assassinate me and take over.'

Burov asked if the would-be assassin had been questioned.

'He passed out before we could begin. He has been taken below with the whore. They will be dealt with.'

'You will interrogate him?'

'Of course. It will be very painful.'

'I would like to be present, Excellency. If this is part of a planned coup I may be able to advise you of further security measures.'

Mabato nodded slowly.

Burov didn't show it but he was worried. If this failed assassination attempt was a prelude to invasion by Kenyan or Tanzanian sympathizers of Hamilton Kemba, his own position and, consequently, the Soviet foothold in Lugamba, was tenuous to say the least. He would have to report back to Kolk at Moscow Centre and wait for instructions. He was struck with another thought.

'What are your intentions, Excellency, with regards to the warning that an attempt will be made to free Holt. It is not beyond the bounds of possibility that the two incidents are connected.'

Mabato, much to Burov's surprise, smiled hugely. 'Do not worry, my friend. That matter will be taken care of.'

'You have made arrangements for Holt to be moved of course?'

Mabato chuckled. The sound was sinister. 'Comrade

259

Burov, I have taken steps to ensure that these dogs of war will live to regret the day they chose to oppose Solomon Mabato.' He got to his feet. 'Now, let us pay a visit to this assassin. I think our discussion with this man will be very enjoyable.'

Burov, by the tone of Mabato's voice, knew that the so called discussion would be anything but enjoyable, particularly for the would-be killer. With some apprehension he followed Mabato from the room.

The pain revived him. Through a grey mist he began to focus. Not fully aware of his surroundings, he was conscious only of the agony in his left leg. It was dark where he was. Some light came from a single bulb hanging by a thin woven flex above his head but it wasn't much more than a dim glow. He tried to move himself, to raise his hands. He couldn't.

His arms and legs were secured to the table by metal clamps at wrists and ankles. He turned his head. He appeared to be in some kind of cellar. He couldn't make out much; brick walls and ceiling and what looked like a work bench along one wall on which hung hammers, screwdrivers, chisels, saws, spanners and other handyman paraphernalia. In one gloomy corner steps ran up into shadow. Presumably a door to the rest of the building.

He wondered how long he had been out. There was no way of telling.

A noise in the shadows by the steps alerted him; voices and footsteps approaching. He tried to turn his head to see. Mabato walked down into the cellar followed by Burov and the emaciated figure of Farouk Juma. They approached the table and examined the prone body. Behind them appeared two armed DOSS guards.

Mabato studied the Zulu for several seconds, his small

eyes flickering from head to toe. He held a thin malacca cane in his hand. He was still wearing the sling.

'Who sent you?' he said.

Qetuka remained mute.

Mabato raised the cane and whipped it down on the wounded leg.

Qetuka's scream lanced through the cellar and bounced off the walls. His body heaved as the excruciating agony knifed through his thigh. His voice dropped to a bubbling moan and tiny beads of sweat oozed from his brow.

'The name!' Mabato yelled. He lifted the stick again.

Qetuka's head rocked from side to side.

Mabato's arm dropped and the man on the table shrieked. Burov winced. Blood welled from the wound, soaking the Zulu's fatigues.

'He has courage,' observed Burov.

Mabato shrugged. He raised the cane for the third time and Juma said: 'Why not show him the woman?'

Mabato lowered his arm. He nodded. 'Release him.'

Juma snapped his fingers and the DOSS men unlocked the clamps and lifted Qetuka off the table. Inevitably they were not gentle and his leg flamed. They hauled him into an upright position and dragged him across the uneven floor towards a low archway in one wall. Burov wondered what was in store.

The second room had a similar layout except that in place of the work bench along the wall there stood a waist high white cabinet about eight feet in length. In the centre of the room, also lit by a single bulb in the ceiling, stood another table. Something lay on the table covered by a red blanket. Burov screwed up his nose. A strange smell, sickly and cloying, pervaded the cellar. He couldn't think what it was.

Qetuka hung between the two DOSS heavies and looked drunk.

Mabato walked to the table and raised a corner of the blanket. Burov peered closer then he drew in breath. It wasn't a red blanket at all. It was a white sheet, soaked in blood. Pools of it lay under the table, black in the dim light. Burov felt his gorge rise as Mabato drew the sheet away from the thing on the table.

At first sight it looked like a side of beef, freshly butchered like meat on a slab. Burov swallowed bile as he looked down on the mutilated torso. His mind could hardly cope with the ghastly sight. The woman's limbs had been severed at shoulder and thigh and switched. Her right arm and leg lay along her left side and vice versa. Burov felt certain that he was going to throw up. Nothing he could possibly have imagined had prepared him for this. Then he noticed something else. There was no head.

Qetuka, supported by the two goons, heaved suddenly and vomited noisily. The stench, mingled with the awful odour of the remains on the table, was overpowering.

Mabato put down his cane and strode over to the cabinet. He grasped a handle on top and Burov, at that moment, realized what it was: a chest freezer.

The lid now rested against the wall. Mabato reached inside. He straightened. In his hand he held a polythene bag tied at the neck. There was something in it, round and dark. It was difficult to make out as the polythene was frosting over but Burov knew what it was. Her severed head.

Mabato held the bag out at arm's length and laughed. Burov thought it was the most terrible sound he had ever heard. He looked at the prisoner. Qetuka was staring at the grisly trophy. With casual indifference Mabato tossed the head into the open freezer.

'Now,' he said, smiling. 'See how I deal with my enemies.'

Burov was wondering what other delicacies were stocked in the freezer. It was too horrible to contemplate. As was the ultimate fate of the wretch Mabato was gloating over.

The prisoner was sagging in the grip of the DOSS agents. His shirt was stained with vomit and his breath was coming in short, sharp gasps. Blood from his leg was trickling down his leg and forming pools on the floor. Mabato had retrieved his cane and with it he lifted Qetuka's chin. The touch was gentle.

Mabato said casually: 'Major Juma and I are going to ask you some questions. Pay very close attention. Answer quickly and truthfully.' He nodded to the guards. 'Bring him.'

They took him back to the table and shackled him once again.

'Now,' Mabato said. 'We will begin.'

Qetuka stared at the roof.

'Who hired you?'

Nothing. Not a flicker. Burov held his breath.

Mabato sighed and nodded slowly. Juma walked over to the work bench. He scanned the tool racks and made his selection, returning to the table with a chisel and hammer.

'Who hired you,' Mabato asked again.

Qetuka remained silent. His eyes were almost closed.

Solomon Mabato raised his eyebrows. Juma placed the blade of the chisel against the knuckle of the little finger of the prisoner's left hand. Then he struck down with the hammer.

The sound that burst from Qetuka's lips wasn't human. It battered the senses as the blade severed the joint. The finger lay on the table top. Blood bubbled from the stump, soaking the wood. Juma placed the tool against the next finger and raised the hammer.

263

'The name!' Mabato said.

The name was hardly more than a gargle, escaping from tight lips pursed in agony. 'Kemba.'

'Aahhh!' Satisfaction from Mabato. 'That snivelling whelp! And what value did he put on my life? How much were you to be paid?'

'One . . . one hundred . . . thousand doll . . . ars.'

Mabato grunted. 'Not very flattering, eh, Burov?' He smiled and Burov's heavily jowled features remained grim.

'How many in your group?' Mabato addressed the man on the table.

Burov moved closer.

The President leaned over the prisoner, his eyes black with rage. The prisoner seemed not to have understood. His face was creased with pain and bore no sign of comprehension.

'I will ask again. How many of you are there? We know that you are part of a plot to overthrow the legitimate government of Lugamba and we know of the plan to free the Englishman, Holt.' His voice had risen in tone.

In his pain Qetuka had bitten through his lip. A smear of blood appeared at the corner of his mouth as he gasped: 'I . . . am alone.'

Mabato jerked his head and another scream rent the air as a second finger was severed. Despite the shackles at ankle and wrist, the prisoner's body bowed in a spasm of agony.

'You are the spearhead to an invasion force! Admit it! Who is supporting Kemba? Tanzania? Kenya? The American CIA? The British? Or the Jews? Is it the Jews?'

Burov couldn't believe that the man could still talk. Any normal human would have lapsed into a state of shock, especially with the leg wound never mind the mutilation which followed. The prisoner had incredible reserves of strength and courage. Even Mabato and Juma were looking puzzled. They hadn't expected this sort of resistance.

'Perhaps I may question him, Excellency?' Burov queried.

Mabato shrugged noncommittally and Juma placed the edge of the chisel over another finger.

Burov said quietly: 'Tell us how you crossed the border. How did you enter the city?'

'Last night . . . My vehicle crashed . . . I stole . . .'

'The patrol Land Rover!' Juma hissed, raising the hammer.

'Wait!' Burov commanded. He was suddenly conscious of a pungent smell and looking down the prone body he saw the damp patch at the prisoner's crotch as the man's bladder emptied steadily. Mabato appeared not to have noticed.

Burov's gruff voice was cajoling. 'You say you know nothing of a plot to free the Englishman? You expect us to believe you? The plot to kill His Excellency was surely a prelude to an invasion, if not then at least a diversion for the escape attempt?'

'I know nothing of this.'

'His Excellency does not believe you.'

'I am telling the truth.'

'My friend,' Burov urged, 'you will save yourself a great deal of pain. They will not stop at two fingers. Tell us, is Kemba planning to invade? That is why he sent you.'

'He chose me because I am the best. I am Qetuka!' The voice was growing weaker now but even the suffering couldn't disguise the pride in the voice.

Burov nodded. 'I have heard of you. I heard you were good.'

Incredibly Qetuka's mouth twisted into a grin. 'I was

265

'. . . not good enough.' He coughed and his features contorted as the pain gripped him.

'You are a brave man, Qetuka. I may save you still if you give me the information.'

'I cannot tell that which I do not know.'

'You make things very difficult, my friend.'

'For you or me?'

'You are the one on the rack,' Burov said.

Qetuka blinked.

'I don't think he knows,' Burov said.

'He is lying!' Juma's voice was shrill.

'No, I think not, Excellency. I agree that his pain threshold is remarkably high but whatever else he is, the man is not a fool and I think he would talk to save himself.'

Juma said: 'Perhaps if we cut off something else?'

Burov yelled: 'You are an animal! That man has more guts in his remaining little finger than you have in your entire pox-ridden body!'

Juma's eyes were like glowing coals.

'Enough!' Mabato cried. 'We have wasted enough time.' He addressed Juma. 'Deal with the prisoner!' He turned to go and paused. 'And save me the head.'

They had reached the bottom step when a croak came from behind them. Mabato stopped in his tracks. Qetuka had his head on one side. It looked like a shiny black mask.

Mabato approached the table. 'Well?'

From cracked lips, framed with blood and vomit, Qetuka said: 'There was a man with Kemba.'

'Yes! Go on!'

'A European, grey haired. Kemba said he was a soldier of fortune. A mercenary.'

'His name!' Mabato snapped.

'I do not know. I only saw him as he was leaving.'

'Nationality!' Burov asked sharply.

'A white man. European.'

'Or American?' Burov mused.

'You think the Americans would lead an invasion?' Mabato asked the Russian.

'I think it unlikely, Excellency. He could just as well have been British or French. It was purely conjecture on my part.' Burov drew closer to Qetuka. 'Can you recall anything else?'

Qetuka sighed noisily. It sounded like a death rattle. No words came. He wasn't going to last much longer. Burov said so.

Mabato shrugged. He was thinking about something else. The plot to free David Holt.

'What news, David?' Lennox was speaking to the Foreign Secretary through the scrambler.

'We've informed Mabato that our security service has uncovered a plot to free Holt. In the light of the Kenyans' initiative we felt it our duty to inform His Excellency of the plot in order to avoid undermining the negotiations for the legitimate release of David Holt.'

'Oh, very diplomatic. One might even say pious. What sort of acknowledgement did we get?'

'None yet,' Wood replied. 'Just an ominous silence.'

'I see. Well, our next move should get a more positive response.'

'You want me to repeat the cable?' Wood sounded sceptical.

'I've been in touch with the RAF,' Lennox said. 'I called Leyton-Grant half an hour ago. It's all laid on with Transport Command.'

'What is?' Wood was floundering.

'A VC-10 at Northolt. It's standing by to take you to Lugamba. You'll refuel at Cyprus. I . . .'

'Just a bloody minute!' Wood cut in. 'I thought we'd all decided that I wasn't going!'

'I've changed my mind, David. I think, on reflection, that it would be a wise move on our part. After all, we didn't back down. The donkey work was done by President Nai. All you have to do is fly in and collect Holt from the clutches of Mabato and bring him home. Shake hands, smile at the press and Bob's your uncle! Hell, we might even pick up a few votes along the way. The Party that cares!'

'What happened to all that Britain-will-never-give-in-to-this-sort-of-terrorism crap? This is a decided inconsistency, if you ask me!'

'President Nai would view it as a firm measure of the cooperation between Kenya and Great Britain,' Lennox said.

'Stuff President Nai!' Wood expostulated. 'What we are talking about here is a climb-down. A compromise in which we are going to look like right idiots!'

'Look, let's be rational, David . . .'

'Rational be damned! You're capitulating!'

'If I remember correctly,' Lennox pointed out, 'you were all for flying out to Lugamba when this mess started.'

'Like you, I am entitled to change my mind.'

'Oh, touché, David. Nevertheless . . . you'll go.'

'Do I have a choice?'

Silence from Lennox.

'I suppose that answers my question. When do I leave?'

'Let me put it this way, David. If I were you, I'd ring Dorothy and tell her you won't be home for dinner.'

Dusk.

'All stowed, Thomas,' Harry Roan said.

Keel acknowledged the information. He looked at Schiller and Sekka. 'All set?'

'As we'll ever be,' Sekka replied.

Schiller lit a cheroot and inhaled. Taking it from his mouth, he smiled. 'Just say the word, Major.'

They were grouped outside the mission with the priest. Sister Elicia stood by the door, her eyes on Paul Schiller who appeared to be unaware of her attention.

Keel addressed Father Devlin, his hand on the priest's shoulder. 'You know what to do?'

'Don't worry, Thomas. I understand.'

'Kate Lassiter will come in around midnight. Light the strip and guide her down.'

'You'll come straight back to the mission?' The priest sounded concerned.

'Not directly. We don't want to lead Mabato's men here. We'll engage them in a few diversionary tactics.'

Schiller caught Sister Elicia's eye then. She looked away; too quickly. The priest noticed. He regarded Schiller quizzically but any thoughts that might have harboured in his mind remained unvoiced as, at Keel's command, the four mercenaries climbed into the Range Rover. Schiller drove. He reversed the vehicle in front of the building and steered in on to the track. The Range Rover jolted over the ruts and was outlined briefly at the top of the ridge before it sank from view beyond the darkness. None of the occupants looked back.

The old man and the girl watched them go in silence before turning and walking into the mission.

12

Kate Lassiter stretched her long legs in the confines of the sleeping bag and wondered briefly what time it was. The clock in her mind told her it was close to the time she had set herself to wake up but something other than her subconscious had roused her. A noise.

She was lying on the cot in the office adjoining the workshop in the hangar. The Chieftain, refuelled that afternoon, stood ready on the apron outside, facing the taxiway. She raised her arm and squinted at her Rolex. It was half an hour earlier than the time set on her mental alarm.

The sound again. Nothing much more than a soft footfall somewhere in the darkened hangar. She pulled the zip down and eased herself out of the bag. She was naked. Shadows dappled her svelte body as she reached for the overall that hung over the back of the chair. In the hangar a metal object clattered to the ground. The sound was followed by a muffled curse.

She slipped her feet into a pair of pumps and stalked to the door. Looking around for a weapon, she picked up a wrench that lay on the desk. Holding it firmly, she opened the office door.

The main hangar doors stood open and a shaft of moonlight intruded. From what she could make out the building was empty. No one was lurking behind kerosene drums or hiding under the work bench but something or someone had woken her. It might have been a stray dog –

they sometimes got through the perimeter fence – but dogs don't curse in the dark.

There! A shadow, a vague shape flitting through the gap in the doors. Like a spectre it was there for only a split second before disappearing into the gloom at the edge of the moonlight.

Towards the Chieftain!

Christ! Still holding the wrench she ran for the doors and the Chieftain exploded.

The tremendous blast would have sent her sprawling if the doors hadn't been in the way, protecting her from the shock wave. As it was she flung up her arm, instinctively shielding her face from the searing heat as the fuel tank detonated, turning the aircraft into a raging fireball and showering the building with blazing kerosene and shrapnel. The starboard propeller catapulted over the wing and spun into the huge door with a fiery cascade of sparks. An angry, obscene catherine wheel.

Then, oblivious to the heat generated by the explosion, she ran out of the hangar and watched the Chieftain expire like a Viking corpse on the way to Valhalla. Pools of flaming aviation fuel flickered on the tarmac and she felt the crunch of glass underfoot as she skirted the funeral pyre, her eyes brimming with angry tears at the devastation.

She stood there helpless for several minutes before the shouts and engines and sirens jolted her out of the trance. A hand touched her shoulder and she jerked around. It was Stan Mason, one of the Intercorp mechanics, his craggy face carved in horror as he stared at the dancing flames that were consuming the shattered fuselage.

'Kate! I heard the explosion. What the hell happened?' His concern was evident. 'Are you okay?'

'I'm all right,' she replied hollowly.

271

Mason surveyed the carnage. 'Jesus wept!' His voice was tinged with relief as well as amazement for he was only too aware of the danger if the fire had spread. The two Intercorp Lear Jets were parked around the corner of the hangar along with half a dozen other aircraft. If that lot had caught as well the tarmac would have looked like a World War Two airfield after an enemy strafing run.

Kate Lassiter wondered what explosive Case's men had used. Whatever it was had done the job; quickly, efficiently, spectacularly. Had it been Ferris or John John she had heard skulking in the hangar? Ferris probably. He had the technical know-how. John John was nothing more than a dumb enforcer. Ferris had the brains and the qualifications.

The fire crew had doused the flames with foam. Wisps of the stuff drifted in the air like sea spume.

Mason was handing her something; a hip flask. 'Have a swig, Kate. It'll hit the spot.'

She declined. She needed a clear head.

'A hell of a thing to happen,' Mason muttered. He tilted the slim flask, his neck muscles jerking as he swallowed.

A slim figure detached itself from the fire tender, now idle at the side of the apron, and walked towards her.

'Oh well,' Mason said. 'Here come the questions.'

The Fire and Safety Officer was called Fisk. He nodded briefly at Mason, raising a superior eyebrow at the flask. He looked grim.

'That is the remains of your aircraft, Mrs Lassiter?'

Kate nodded silently.

'How did it happen?'

'It blew up,' Mason said.

'Thank you,' Fisk said tightly. 'I was asking Mrs Lassiter.'

272

'This sounds like the prelude to an interrogation,' Kate said.

Fisk allowed himself a thin smile. 'Not so. I'm just trying to ascertain the facts.'

'Of course,' Kate agreed wryly, 'but it is as Mr Mason said.'

'You mean it blew up? Just like that?' Patent incredulity. 'Without warning?'

'Are you for real, Fisk?' Mason cut in. 'Of course we had warning! We all got our deck chairs lined up and then we got some beer in and then we sat back and . . . BOOM! Don't tell me you really are that stupid? I thought it was an act you put on! Was it without warning! Jesus!'

Fisk's face hardened. 'Look, Mason, I could do without the sparkling wit. I'm trying to do my job for God's sake!' He looked appealingly at Kate Lassiter.

She said: 'Cool it, Stan. Things are bad enough. Let me handle this. Okay?'

Mason caught her meaning. He nodded. 'All right, Kate.' He ignored Fisk. 'I'll see you later.' He walked away.

'I'm sorry,' she said to Fisk.

He shrugged. 'I get used to it. To be honest, I could see his point. Most of the questions I have to ask must seem bloody silly but you know how it is.'

Looking at the pathetic, twisted pieces of metal that had been the Chieftain Kate Lassiter found it hard to summon the resolve as she said: 'Yes, I know how it is.'

'Can you tell me anything at all?'

'It all happened so suddenly.' Despite the warmth of the night she hugged herself as though warding off the cold. 'I'm still trying to take it all in. I was in the office at the back of the hangar. I've a camp bed. I was dozing, trying to sleep but it was too hot I guess. I got up to go to the loo. Opened the office door and bang! This terrific noise, as

273

though the world had come to an end. By the time I reached the main doors she was a ball of flame. There was damn all I could do.'

Fisk looked thoughtful. 'You didn't hear or see anything unusual? I mean before the explosion.'

'I'm afraid not. I didn't hear a thing.'

He pursed his lips. 'Mrs Lassiter, this is rather odd to say the least. What if I asked you if you could think of anyone who might want to destroy your aircraft? Any names or people spring to mind?'

'Good God! No!' She hoped she had sounded genuinely shocked and outraged.

He paused, choosing the words. 'I presume the aircraft was insured?'

She flared. 'I'm not sure that I care for your line of questioning. Naturally it's insured. If you are inferring that I intended to benefit from the policy then perhaps Stan Mason wasn't far off the mark in his opinion of you. Dammit, Fisk, you know me. You shouldn't have had to ask. That Chieftain was my living!'

She saw that he had the grace to look abashed.

He shrugged apologetically. 'Just thought I'd ask.'

At that moment she looked at her watch and her stomach lurched. In less than three hours Thomas Keel expected her to drop out of the night sky on to the landing strip at Masambabule; and the aircraft he and the team were counting on was now a misshapen lump of molten metal hidden beneath a skein of white foam tendrils; the victim of a sadistic vendetta instigated by Jack Case and his henchmen. Without the Chieftain Keel's chances of getting David Holt out of Lugamba were the wrong side of slim.

'Damn you, Case!' Kate Lassiter hissed. 'If it takes forever I'll get even!'

'Sorry?' Fisk said. 'I didn't catch that.'

'Nothing,' she said. 'I suppose I can expect a visit from the heavy brigade with more questions?'

'You can bet on it,' replied Fisk. 'You'll probably have a Piper rep padding around as well as the insurance investigators and the rest. It'll look like a convention of Bow Street Runners I shouldn't wonder.' He smiled; a weak attempt at levity.

'In that case,' she said, 'I'm going to need all the sleep I can get.'

Fisk looked sombre. He said: 'For what it's worth, Mrs Lassiter, I am deeply sorry. For someone like yourself, where the aircraft is a means of livelihood, the tragedy is doubly upsetting. If there is anything I can do you know where to reach me.' He held out his hand. 'I expect I'll see you tomorrow. I suggest you get some rest in the meantime.'

Kate Lassiter forced a smile. 'Thank you for your concern. Good night, Mr Fisk.'

She watched him walk back to the tender, skirting past the debris on the apron.

Now what?

Well, she needed an aircraft and there was only one place she could acquire one in the precious little time she had left.

Back in the office she collected her flight bag and charts. And ran.

Stan Mason's surprise and pleasure at seeing Kate Lassiter was exceeded only by his sense of disbelief at her urgent request.

'You want what?' He swung his legs off the desk in his cramped office.

'The Commander.'

'That's what I thought you said. You're not serious?'

'Never more so, Stan.'

'What the hell do you want it for? And at this hour?'

'A mission of mercy.'

'So, what's wrong with the Red Cross?'

'You're closer and I haven't the time and don't look like that! Dammit, Stan! I've more hours under my belt than you've had hot dinners so don't treat me like a junior flyer! I can fly rings around anyone else on this field and you know it! I need that aircraft, Stan. I need it now. Lives depend on it. I wouldn't ask otherwise.'

Mason stood up. 'My God!' he breathed. 'You really mean it!'

'You had better believe it.'

The mechanic stroked his unshaven chin thoughtfully. 'So, what's it about? Look, you want to borrow Intercorp's runaround. I think I'm entitled to know why. Okay, so it's not for a joy ride. I gathered that but this isn't like borrowing a bloody library book! That's an expensive piece of hardware, Kate.'

'Which your boss uses to take his nubile secretary down to the game lodge at Tsavo or to Malindi for a dirty weekend. Well, right this minute my need is greater than his!' Her vehemence was startling. Mason was clearly nonplussed.

Kate Lassiter's green eyes flashed. 'Stan, it's important! Please! I need the Commander tanked up and ready to go in thirty minutes. You can name your own price.'

He was silent for several seconds. He sighed eventually. 'I never could resist a plea from a beautiful woman and for your information she's already fuelled. The boss likes me to be on call for immediate departure. I guess he's never too sure when his secretary's going to get the urge.' He grinned, his face creasing like an old mat.

Her face brightened and she hugged him gratefully. 'I owe you for this, Stan. I'll not forget.'

'How long will you need her?'

Another glance at the watch and the minutes ticking away. 'I'll have her back before dawn.' Sotto voce she added: 'God willing.'

'One thing, Kate,' Mason said. 'If the shit hits the fan you're on your own. You took it when my back was turned. That's the only price I ask apart from you being damned sure that you bring her back in one piece. I . . .'

He was talking to himself. Kate Lassiter was sprinting towards the tarmac.

'Bloody women!' Mason muttered. Reluctantly he broke into a lope and followed her darting figure towards the small, single engined, four seater monoplane that was parked alongside the sleek Lear Jets.

In Maboru they were stacking the dead, in preparation for collection by the disposal squads. David Holt was watching them from his cell window.

The guards were removing the corpses from the death cells. They looked like mutilated rag dolls with lolling heads and loose matchstick limbs – puppets without strings. In the stark glare of the arc lights along the walls the scene was grotesque and the heap of human debris grew. Rivers of dried blood ran across the naked backs and buttocks, shining like fresh talon marks on the dull flesh. Holt had stopped counting after the first score. As the pile in the corner of the compound rose steadily he turned away from the window with the sour taste of bile in his throat.

In the next cell the guards were dragging something across the floor and Holt could hear them muttering and grunting with the effort. He crouched on the filthy mattress, tears of frustration trickling down his gaunt cheeks.

It was the same procedure every evening at this time. Half

an hour or so after dusk the gory refuse would be taken to the cage in the compound. When the truck arrived the bodies were thrown aboard. Heavily laden, the truck would then leave and proceed to the observation platform above the Kiggala Falls where the rotting corpses were tossed into the thundering black water. Sometimes the truck would have to make two trips, depending on whether the interrogation teams and the executioners had been particularly enthusiastic during the day. Sometimes the bodies were not whole when they were removed. The stench of the dead filtered into every nook and cranny of the prison.

Footsteps halted outside the door. Keys grated and rattled in the lock and the heavy door swung open with a crash. Holt felt the flood of fear course through his body as the two guards thrust themselves forward. The thin waif-like figure of Farouk Juma stepped into the cell, a smile on his lips. He jabbed at Holt with his swagger stick and the guards sprang. Holt shrank back against the wall.

'Get away from me!' he shrieked and scrambled ape-like along the mattress, seeking the dark corner of the cell, dirty, dishevelled, terrified by the ferocious gleam in Juma's eyes.

Behind Juma, through the open doorway, Holt's frightened eyes saw two more guards carry some formless thing down the passage. There seemed to be a great deal of blood in evidence.

He was grabbed by his arms and hauled off the mattress, whimpering like a small dog. His gaze settled fleetingly on the tunic of one of the guards. It was streaked with some yellowish gristle-like substance and scarlet splashes dotted the man's chest. The sleeves were matted with a dark brown stain and the smell of the man made him retch.

Through the bile, he whispered hoarsely: 'Where are you taking me?'

Juma said: 'You are being prepared, Mister Holt, for your final journey.'

Holt began to struggle. 'No! You can't! For God's sake! PLEASE!' He kicked out at the guards but it was a futile motion.

They dragged him screaming from the cell and his last recollection as he passed out was the sight that greeted him in the passage. The stone floor was slippery with black, viscous matter. The guards he had observed earlier were bundling an object into a burlap sack. It wasn't until the sack toppled over and disgorged the bloody stump of a human arm that Holt's befuddled brain grasped the reality of the situation. He uttered one piercing ululation of terror and slumped abruptly into the arms of his gaolers. Silently they carried his limp, unprotesting body down the passage towards the disposal point.

Kendura sprawled under a rapidly darkening sky. The slums and corrugated ghettos were painted in shadow though here and there pinpricks of light from cheap kerosene lamps twinkled weakly through chinks in ragged walls. The centre of the city fared little better. Most of the large buildings remained unlit.

Some streets were illuminated, like the wide Kendura Avenue that bisected the city and ran alongside the high walls of Mabato's Command Post, behind which the President's bodyguards watched and listened.

The side streets were like empty canals, running forlornly past rubble-strewn, vermin-infested alleyways and gutted stores. A twilight pall of desolation hung over the capital like a grey burial shroud.

The truck swung around the corner and moved slowly

down the centre of the street like a giant roach on a foraging mission, headlights probing weakly like dying torch beams. The truck had two occupants: driver and front seat passenger. They were blacks; brutal, unsmiling men in floral patterned, short sleeved shirts. The DOSS disposal squad en route to Maboru to collect the dead.

They both saw the figure by the roadside at the same time. Caught in the wavering beams of the lights, the man beckoned to the truck. Even in the gloom they could see he was dressed like themselves, in shirt and slacks; a member of Mabato's security force. He waved again before turning to attend to a dark bundle at his feet; a body dressed in army fatigues, huddled as if unconscious or in pain. As the man waved the headlight beams reflected on the barrel of the machine pistol he was holding.

The truck slowed and veered towards the kerb. It halted. The doors opened and the driver and his companion stepped down, drawing automatic pistols from shoulder holsters as they approached the beckoning figure.

'What is happening here?' The driver peered uncertainly. His voice was rough and uneducated. He regarded the body on the ground without compassion.

The man who had beckoned answered. 'A looter. I caught him running out of a store. The bastard tried to kill me so I dealt with him. I was going to leave the body in the rubble when I saw your truck. You can take the pig to the falls with the rest from Maboru.'

The driver spat into the darkness. His companion said: 'Well, one more won't make any difference.'

The man holding the machine pistol knelt over the body and tugged at something out of sight. His hand emerged holding a panga. The vicious weapon was nearly two feet long with a broad, flat blade. 'This is what he attacked me with. He won't be needing it anymore. Here, give me a hand to get the body into the truck.'

They reholstered their guns and moved to assist. The driver stepped over the body and turned it over. His jaw dropped in surprise.

The looter was white!

Keel's arm moved with the speed of a striking mamba. His hand grabbed the driver's collar and pulled him off balance and on to his knees.

The second DOSS man was quicker to react. He grabbed for his hand gun and moved half a pace backwards.

Sekka swung the panga.

The blade curved through the air and sliced into the cruel face, splitting the broad features into a bloody ravine, cleaving nose and cheeks into a morass of tissue and fragments of bone. The scream of pain died on the man's lips as his face was ripped in one micro-second of bewildering, searing agony. A bright, crimson spray caressed the air as Sekka followed through with the blow, sweeping the blade forward as he pulled it free.

Keel's right hand smashed like an axe against the driver's neck. There came the sickening crack of breaking bone. He thrust the body aside and got to his feet.

Two figures ran stealthily from the shadows.

'Christ, Joseph!' Harry Roan gasped. 'That was too damned close!' He stared at the ruined, gaping face. 'Hell! You sure didn't pull any punches!' He glanced at Keel. 'You okay, Thomas?'

Keel nodded. 'Get them out of sight. You know what to do.'

As he spoke he felt a tap on his shoulder and then his neck. He lifted his face and the third drop struck his face. For a second he remained motionless, absorbing the knowledge of what was happening and realizing that it might prove an invaluable aid to their endeavours.

It had begun to rain.

In the time it took them to dump the bodies behind a pile of rubble in the lee of a gutted building, they were soaked to the skin and the raindrops were bouncing off the road like bullets. Sekka and Keel, faces streaming, climbed into the big Bedford. Schiller and Roan ran through the deluge towards the Range Rover they had concealed nearby. The noise on the roof of the cab was like one continuous rattle of gunfire. Keel peered out through the windscreen. Without the headlights he couldn't see thirty feet beyond the bonnet.

The mercenary had no qualms about killing the two DOSS thugs. They had been active members of a unit that dealt in fear and death on an unprecedented scale under the direct and frequent orders of Solomon Mabato. If Keel did have any reservations they lay in the certain knowledge that from the moment Joseph Sekka had swung the panga they were committed irrevocably to their prime objective: the rescue of David Holt from Maboru. From now on there could be no turning back. The die had been cast.

The signal from Head of Station in Nairobi, Giles Slattery, reached Dalkeith late in the afternoon. It was little more than an echo of a rumour but something, as Dalkeith's friends in Grosvenor Square might have put it, was definitely going down. Slattery had received a report, unconfirmed, that Solomon Mabato had been the victim of an assassination attempt. No details as yet. The Lugambans had, not surprisingly, thrown a blanket over the incident; although it appeared that Mabato was still alive and, if his past record was anything to go by, probably exacting vengeance.

There was no further word about Holt.

And all this less than two hours after Wood had departed Northolt. He'd likely be indulging in a G and T at thirty thousand feet by now, Dalkeith supposed, in ignorance that was, if not blissful, at least expedient. However, Wood was due to layover in Cyprus so he'd get the news upon his touchdown in Nicosia.

But then what?

Dalkeith's recommendation would be to proceed as planned and continue on to Kendura. After all, whatever the situation in Lugamba, even if Mabato was head hunting, Whitehall was in the clear.

So, why was George Dalkeith beset by a niggling degree of unease? Perhaps it was the fear that events were beginning to overlap each other; gaining momentum like a juggernaut out of control or like a tiny spark that ignites tinder dry brush, that before long is fanned by the wind and whipped into a raging wild fire, destroying all in its path.

Perhaps it was already too late for all of them.

On the promontory overlooking the dark, rain lashed northern reaches of Lake Victoria, Maboru squatted in the night like an ogre; wet, grey walls rising out of the headland, menacing in its isolated silence.

The death truck rumbled out of the curtain of rain and approached the main gates. Immediately the lights above the entrance arch sprang into life, lancing through the downpour, holding the rambling vehicle in their beams as it moved forward and slowed to a halt, engine chugging throatily.

An eye level trap in the left hand gate slid open to reveal suspicious eyes set in a black face. Joseph Sekka looked back through the jerking wipers with what he hoped was a

283

bored and vacant expression, one hand resting idly on the steering wheel, the other gripping the stock of the Heckler and Koch that lay across his knees.

The bulbous bonnet was bathed in white light as the guards on the wall directed the beams over the truck. Instinctively Sekka's hand moved to the gun under the shadow of the dashboard. It was unlikely, however, that the guards could see anything clearly through the rain.

The trap shut abruptly. There was a pause of several seconds before the gates split apart with a groan of protest to form a gaping maw. Sekka let his pent up breath escape in a long sigh of relief. He let out the clutch and eased the truck forward through the mud. As he did so the probing slivers of light jumped the wall to follow the progress of the Bedford into the compound.

Less than one hundred yards away, behind a wall of dripping foliage at the edge of the track, Harry Roan crouched and watched cautiously as the truck was swallowed up by the prison gates.

Hidden there, with the rain trickling down the back of his neck, clad in tiger stripes that rendered him virtually invisible against the terrain, Roan might have believed himself back in the jungles of Cambodia or Vietnam. It could have been a recon mission, a search and destroy operation or a night ambush.

Anything but a repeat of the other rescue mission. The one that had ended so ignominiously. The raid on Son Tay.

US military analysts had identified Son Tay, twenty or so miles west of Hanoi, as a prisoner of war camp. Roan and other Special Forces volunteers had been heli-lifted into the camp under the command of Colonel 'Bull' Simons to rescue American troops. Upon landing in the compound, however, the rescue force discovered that all the prisoners had been moved weeks before. The camp was long abandoned. So much for Intelligence.

Not again, Roan thought grimly, as he watched the Bedford disappear. That was all they friggin' needed. He gritted his teeth, erased the thought from his mind and got to his feet. Gripping his pack, he began to weave his way through the undergrowth towards the prison wall.

13

Sekka was immediately aware of the smell. Not the sweet, cleansing fragrance of a tropical storm but the sickly odour of human decay. Within the walls it permeated every pore. The cloying, persistent stench of putrefaction hung in the darkness like a cloud. He wrinkled his nose automatically.

The gates opened on to a courtyard with the guard post built into the left hand wall, just inside the entrance. Ahead was another, lower archway, beyond which lay the main compound, divided into two quadrangles by a central run of cells. Sekka knew the layout of the prison from the plans the team had studied in Amsterdam and from the updated information supplied by Father Devlin. He knew the bodies would be stacked inside a small wire enclosure in the quadrangle on the right as he turned through the inner archway. The bulky figure of a prison guard strode out of the guard post. He was draped in a waterproofed cape and his face was hidden under the peak of a forage cap pulled low over his forehead. He carried a Kalashnikov rifle and he looked wet and very miserable.

He barked an order and the search lights swivelled their beams away to cover the outer walls and inner quadrangles. Spot lights strung along the walls of the yard gave some clarity to the scene as the guard approached the truck. Sekka's finger curled around the trigger of the machine pistol.

'You are alone?' The guard's brutal face stared up at the cab window with suspicion. 'Where is your companion?'

Sekka grinned. 'With his woman!' He made an obscene

gesture. 'Where else would anyone with any brains be on a night like this? And you should see his woman!' Sekka rolled his eyes. 'Big and juicy, with tits like melons and thighs that would break your back and squeeze you dry!'

Joseph Sekka chuckled. 'I grow hard just thinking about him rutting like a bull. I bet she screams while he's screwing her too! It's a good job this rain is cooling me down, man, or I would have you face up against the wall over there!'

To Sekka's intense relief the guard took a step backwards, no doubt prompted by Sekka's lascivious grin.

He eased out the clutch.

'Wait!'

Sekka froze. The guard was unslinging his rifle. Sekka's fingers stroked along the barrel of the machine pistol on his knee. The guard moved towards the rear of the truck. Rain sluiced through the open window of the cab as Sekka followed the man's progress in the side mirror. He watched, pulse hammering, as the guard disappeared around the rear of the Bedford. He knew the man was going to raise the canvas flap.

The guard reappeared. Sekka relaxed.

The soldier snapped: 'What are you waiting for? Move! Those pigs are beginning to smell.' He jerked the Kalashnikov and moved back.

Sekka breathed in deeply, tension ebbing. As the guard retreated he floored the gas pedal and drove through into the compound.

The headlights were probing dimly, the weak beams seeming to bounce back from the wall of rain. The once dusty ground was now a sea of mud. As Sekka turned the corner he felt the wheels skid in the quagmire. He corrected the spin and jockeyed the truck towards the darkened enclosure in the vee of the walls.

287

Sekka switched off the engine and viewed the scene through the open cab window. Oblivious to the rain, his eyes were drawn inescapably to the horrible vision in the shelter of the prison walls. The bodies, piled in grotesque abandon, shone wetly in the shadows as the torrent poured down over bare, upturned buttocks and twisted limbs. Half a dozen burlap sacks lay sodden at the base of the pile.

Sekka's sense of outrage was intense. Nothing he had experienced during the Biafran campaign or since could have equalled the gut wrenching sight that met his gaze.

A porch ran around the edge of the compound. Huddled underneath its roof two guards regarded the truck through the rain. They made no move as Sekka opened the cab door and jumped down. He was drenched in seconds. The thin shirt and slacks, still damp from their previous dousing, stuck to his body like a second skin.

Beneath the Bedford, Thomas Keel and Paul Schiller released themselves from the harness they had slung underneath the chassis and dropped silently to the ground. They were dressed in their camouflage suits and both wore black cotton ski masks to conceal their European features, in particular their hair.

They carried a machine pistol each as well as Brownings in shoulder holsters and commando knives. Keel had the Remington strapped across his back. In waist packs they carried spare magazines and, in Keel's case, grenades and extra shells for the shotgun. By all the rules they were travelling light.

Sekka waded through the mud to the rear of the truck and lowered the tailboard. He pulled the canopy aside and secured it. 'Two guards,' he said calmly. 'Under the porch to your left and no sign of any others. The rain is keeping them inside.'

'We hear you, Joseph.' Keel's voice came from the underside.

Sekka entered the enclosure.

Sightless streaming eyes followed his approach. He saw fingers curled in claw-like paralysis and tongues swollen and protruding from mouths gaping in rictus. He drew breath, fighting the urge to retch as the sight and smell hit him like a hammer. He walked back to the truck and through gagging lips he yelled through the rain: 'Hey! You two give me a hand! Move it! Major Juma's orders!' He guessed the name would have the desired effect.

With undisguised annoyance they ran into the open, cursing the weather and Sekka's ancestry. They huddled against the side of the truck, muttering bleakly.

Keel and Schiller struck.

Their feet were pulled from under them and they could do nothing to avoid being jerked off balance. They landed with a thumping squelch and Sekka finished off the job with massive, crushing blows from the butt of one of the guards' dropped rifles.

Keel and Schiller rose from concealment.

The guards on the wall were concentrating the lights over the enclosure and in the rain and the darkness Keel and Paul Schiller remained undetected in the shadow of the big Bedford.

'Dump the guards in the back, Joseph, and start humping the rest of them on board. You'll have to try and manage them on your own while Paul and I grab Holt. Once we bring him out, God willing, we'll slip him and ourselves over the tailboard. You can close up and take us back through the gates.'

Sekka nodded and Keel touched his arm briefly. 'It has

to be done, Joseph. The guards in the towers will grow suspicious otherwise.'

'Then you had better get a move on,' Sekka said. Quickly he turned away.

Keel and Schiller exchanged glances and then they were melting through the flood like ghosts. Sekka moved slowly to the first body and tugged at a stiff arm. The glistening rain on his face merged and ran with the tears that were trickling down his cheeks.

It was dry under the porch though the rain was battering down onto the corrugated roof and torrents of water were cascading down over the edge of the guttering. They were now well hidden from the other guards.

The door opened into a dimly lit passage that ran the length of the building. The cell doors were spaced along the walls. There were no guards. No doubt the men they had taken out in the compound had taken it in turns to patrol the corridor. Keel counted off the number of doors. Holt's cell was the third on the left. Father Devlin had confirmed this during the briefing with Keel at the mission. The mercenary tapped his blond companion on the shoulder and they padded towards the cell door. They were conscious of the sickly smell that seemed to ooze from the walls and floor and more than once the soles of their boots met tacky resistance in the slimy patches on the stones beneath their feet.

They reached the cell.

There was a trap in the door at eye level. Keel slid it open and peered into the tiny room. Schiller guarded his back. It seemed incredible that they had made it this far without being discovered. Their nerves were stretched to breaking point.

It took a second or two for Keel's eyes to make out details. By the light from the barred window he could tell that the cell was about nine feet square and a mattress lay against one wall. What looked like a bucket stood in one corner. Obviously a crude latrine.

The body on the mattress was covered by a thin blanket and Keel could see that the figure was turned towards the wall, knees bent; the attitude of a man huddled for warmth. Holt was evidently asleep despite the sound of the rain outside.

'He's there, Paul. Let's get the hell out of here. Our luck can't last for ever.'

The door was secured by a large bolt. Schiller pulled it back and they froze as metal grated.

'Christ!' Keel whispered. 'That's all we bloody need!'

No one came and the passage remained silent. Keel let out his breath. 'Okay, Paul. Bring him out while I cover you. And take it easy. He won't be in too good a shape.'

Schiller ran into the cell.

'Mister Holt!' Schiller called softly as he crouched down and touched the hunched shoulder. The blanket slid away and the body moved and in those final seconds Schiller knew they had made a terrible mistake.

Qetuka's throat had been cut and he had bled a great deal judging from the saturated state of the mattress beneath his mutilated body. His arms and legs had been broken in such a way for his corpse to be placed in a sleeping posture. His upper chest was matted with gore and in the ruin that had been his neck the stump of bone that was the top of his spinal column gleamed white.

All this Paul Schiller grasped in the seconds before the grenade that had been rigged beneath the Zulu's chest exploded as the body was removed.

Schiller died instantly. Within the confines of the tiny cell the force of the blast was catastrophic. The mercenary's body disintegrated into a creamy web of ragged flesh

291

and a gruel of bone fragments that splattered every wall, leaving runnels of pink gristle and other grey nameless substances on the pockmarked brick work.

Keel, guarding the passage, had been protected by the cell wall and saved from the gory cascade by the open door behind which he was crouching, though his ears rang like the bells of Notre Dame. He sprang to the entrance of the cell and through the swirling dust of the explosion he saw the tattered remnants of the mattress and the other, more hideous traces of human debris. And all his brain could register was the dreadful realization that a trap had been sprung and he was reacting automatically, cocking the machine pistol and wheeling to face the attack he knew would follow.

Two doors at the end of the passage crashed open and a trio of guards emerged at a run. They were in the open before the presence of a survivor hit them. By then it was too late.

Keel squeezed off a burst with the Heckler and Koch and watched with grim satisfaction as the force of the low velocity slugs ripped the guards apart, sending them twisting and bouncing like grotesque tumblers. Already he was retreating down the passage. Two more guards broke from the cells and fired a volley at the camouflaged mercenary. Keel dropped as the bullets scythed over his head and tore chunks from the masonry. He fired in return, bringing them down in a heavy flurry of broken limbs. As he reached the door to the compound he had the grenade in his hand. He lobbed it underarm along the length of the passage and was out of the door and under the porch as it detonated. A piercing scream rose above the sound of the explosion, telling him that another guard was maimed or dead.

The compound, still shrouded in driving rain, was now

an open killing ground. Cries and yells of alarm sounded through the wall of water and in answer the lights on top of the walls punched their beams into the quadrangle.

Sekka, alerted by the shooting and commotion, sprang up into the cab. The engine roared and he floored the clutch. He thrust his own gun through the window and fired upwards. Glass exploded and one of the lights blew out. Across the compound indistinct shapes were fanning out under the downpour. There was no sign of Keel.

'THOMAS!' Sekka screamed into the flood. Under his feet the engine of the truck was revving like a grand prix contestant.

A black figure erupted from the wet darkness and Sekka heard Keel yelling: 'GO! GO! GO!'

Mud spurted at Keel's feet as someone fired down from above. Keel raised his weapon and loosed off another burst. There was a long wail from the wall and a body toppled off the parapet. It had been a lucky hit and the result of a pure reflex action.

Sekka released the clutch and floored the gas pedal at the same time. The Bedford almost reared. Sekka was aware of the wheels slipping in the mud as the windscreen exploded and a bullet slammed through the back of the passenger seat, expending itself in the pile of bodies in the rear.

As the tyres gripped, Keel flung himself forward and grabbed the loose end of the webbing strap that secured the canvas canopy to the metal framework. He felt it burning his hand, rasping through his grip like sandpaper as the truck lurched around. His body twisted and bucked as he was dragged across the mud and for a brief second he experienced blistering agony as his thigh swung against the spinning rear tyre. Incredibly he was still grasping the Heckler and Koch in his other hand. He hurled the machine pistol into the back of the truck and made a grab for the edge of the tailboard. A phalanx of guards ran from under the porch and as Keel hauled himself aboard a fusillade of shots shredded the canopy and ricocheted off the back of the lorry. He rose above the tailboard and threw a grenade into the rain. The missile exploded among the front runners, lifting them off the ground in a bright fireball, like ferocious marionettes.

Ahead of the truck two men ran into the open, firing from the hip. Sekka spun the wheel and felt the bullets pass through the cab. There followed a sickening crunch and a wailing screech as the bumper broke the nearest man's back, catapulting him against the wall with the force of a jack hammer. The other guard jumped aside as the Bedford careered through the archway and into the entrance yard.

Harry Roan knelt, wet and uncomfortable, under dripping leaves at the edge of the tree line and heard the grenades explode and the commotion of shots and screams. The rattle of gunfire was flattened by the heavy swathe of rain but it was his signal. He withdrew the small, box-like transmitter from his pack and pressed the switch.

The charges he had placed with such precision on the main gates under the covering thunder of the deluge after the truck had entered the prison, detonated immediately. The explosions lifted the gates off their hinges and smashed them into matchwood as the Bedford roared out of the inner compound.

That had always been the weak point in their plan: the getting out.

Two ways in. By force or by stealth. Likewise the escape. And they knew that the odds against an undetected exit were colossal. So, Keel had planned on a random

294

factor. Harry Roan with enough plastique to blow the doors and maybe cause a diversion and maybe give them the edge; a chink through which they could squeeze if the mission fell apart.

As it had done, with a roar that had blown Paul Schiller into oblivion and warned Harry Roan that the world might just end sometime in the next few seconds.

Joseph Sekka was driving by instinct. He could hear the devastation wreaked by Keel from the back of the truck and knew they didn't stand a hope in hell of coming through this one.

Guards were tumbling from the guard house, fumbling with their rifles, yelling alarm and watching in horrid fascination as the huge truck veered towards them like a locomotive.

When the gates blew apart with a deafening, earth shaking thunderclap of sound they were caught in the shockwave and, as though scythed by grape-shot, were sent twirling and stumbling like ninepins. A jagged splinter, as sharp as a javelin, struck one guard between his shoulder blades, punching its way out of his chest, propelling him forward and pinning him in the mud, where he lay squealing and squirming like a beetle on a pin, legs and arms jerking like broken matchsticks.

As the guards reeled, Sekka thumped the accelerator and the truck stormed forward. The heavy vehicle barrelled towards the demolished entrance to the prison.

The bullet took Sekka high on the right shoulder, thumping its way into sinew and muscle. Sekka was pushed back with the force. He yelled as the steering wheel spun from his grasp then he was jolted forward and in the same instant regained his grip, clenching his teeth with the effort. The rain was driving relentlessly into the open gap that had been the windscreen.

Sekka knew that the real pain would come later with after shock. For the moment he could bear it. Besides, if he couldn't get them through the front gates the pain in his shoulder would be the very least of his problems.

Keel tore off the ski mask and threw it behind him. He no longer felt as though he was suffocating. The mask had become clogged with mud as he had been dragged along. It had flown into his eyes and nostrils and penetrated to the back of his throat. Thankfully he spat out mucus and felt air on his face once again. He fought for balance in the heaving Bedford, the Heckler and Koch discarded and the Remington at his shoulder.

The touch of a hand on the side of his face as a flopping limb came adrift from the pile of dead bodies at his back. He shook it away in disgust. The brief touch had been almost beseeching.

As they boomed through the yard more soldiers ran from cover like ants from the woodwork. The Remington bucked and rubble blew from the wall like chaff in the wind. He curved a grenade into the melee. It exploded viciously. The guards cowered then came on. The canvas by his face was flapping like a vulture's wing. Keel ducked low, feeling the breeze of a slug pass an inch from his throat.

Then they bounced once more and Keel saw the mangled, broken corpse emerge from beneath the wheels, blood and mud mingling with the dark mush that, seconds before, had been a living, breathing entity.

And they went under the arch at a battering lurch, blundering like a charging rhino. The Remington roared again and a second arc light went out. Then, incredibly, they were clear.

Harry Roan watched incredulously as the truck cannoned out of the prison and he ran out from the trees to intercept. Sekka saw him and slowed sufficiently to allow the American to grab at Keel's outstretched hand. Roan was hauled aboard, legs kicking as he dangled momentarily, half-in half-out of the swaying vehicle. He lay, breathing heavily, trying to ignore the almost overpowering stench of the human waste only inches away.

'Jesus H. Christ! Thomas, what the fuck happened in there? By the sound of things I thought you'd started World War Three! I didn't think you were going to get out!' Roan stared at Keel.

'If you hadn't blown the gates, Harry, we wouldn't have got out. Your timing was impeccable! Mind you, another two or three seconds and we'd have gone up with the gates!' Keel slammed a fist against the tailboard. 'What a fucking disaster!'

Roan glanced around the inside of the truck. 'Where's Paul?'

'Back there. What's left of him.' Keel's voice was curt. 'It was a trap, Harry. They were waiting for us. No wonder it was so easy. They knew we were going in. They'd rigged a grenade in the cell. Paul went in to get Holt and triggered it. He was blown to pieces.'

'Shit!' Roan digested the information. His mouth was dry. 'What about Holt? They wasted him too?'

'God knows. I can't believe they'd kill him like that. My guess is that the bugger on the mattress was probably an inmate once, like these poor bastards.'

'Sonofabitch! So, where's Holt?'

The Bedford skidded through a pothole and Keel winced as his elbow collided with the floor. Sekka was driving fast and somewhat erratically. The prison had disappeared around the bend beyond the mist of rain.

'Somewhere where we can't get to him, that's for sure. We were set up, Harry, like ducks in a fairground shooting gallery. We walked right into it. We were just lucky that Mabato's thugs are incompetent and inexperienced in combat. We had more fire power and expertise than they could cope with in the time span. If they had been Libyan or Cuban it might have been a different matter. Joseph got us out. He was driving this heap like a maniac. I felt as if I was on a roller coaster. I think my stomach is back there somewhere.'

'What the hell do we do now?' Roan was peering out of the truck for signs of pursuit.

'Get the heck out of Lugamba. We're well and truly blown. We head for home. It's all we can do. There's no way we can help Holt now. The Lugambans'll have everything sewn up as tight as a duck's arse. We grab the Range Rover and hightail it to the mission. Kate can fly us out.'

'So, that's it?' Roan's voice betrayed his disgust. 'Just run for it, tails between our legs. That was a good man we left back in that cesspit. And for what? Christ! I'll have someone's balls for this! Whoever blew this mission to Mabato had better watch out!' Roan's eyes narrowed. 'You think Cameron . . . ?'

'I think . . .'

The explosion sounded enormous. Keel's words were lost. The truck swerved and hammered over the scree and thorn scrub as the ground erupted in a spume of orange flame, sending mud flying against the canopy like hail.

Roan and Keel were flung against the side of the Bedford, their bodies bruised and battered. The truck seemed to be heading down a slope then it came to a bone jarring halt, bonnet resting in a stunted bush growing from the side of a narrow gully some twenty yards from the track. The pile of bodies had shifted towards the back of the cab. The two mercenaries extricated themselves from the tangle of mis-shapen, shrinking limbs. They could hear Sekka yelling, screaming at them to get out and take cover.

A crump away to the right and the darkness split into a fireball only yards away as they clambered over the back of the stricken truck.

The rain had stopped. The forest was glinting and gleaming as each leaf shimmered with raindrops held in its embrace. The air was heavy and humid. Sekka blundered into them. He was panting hard. There was a dark stain that wasn't water high on his right shoulder.

'Scorpion!' he warned. 'On the road. Come on! Move it! If I hadn't spotted it and turned we'd be hamburger meat.'

'Your shoulder?' Keel said.

'Beginning to hurt like hell, but the bullet went through. As long as I keep moving it won't stiffen up. If we make the mission Devlin can take a look. Let's go.'

There was the throb of an engine on the track and abruptly the thin white beam of a search light lanced through the darkness like an arrow, glancing off the trees before pinpointing the truck. Voices yelling with feverish excitement as Mabato's troops caught sight of their quarry.

'Fuck!' Harry Roan spat.

They turned and ran, keeping the truck between their jinking backs and the Scorpion light tank. A burst of automatic fire cut through the bushes, raking the truck along its length. The soldiers were too enthusiastic and were shooting wildly.

The mercenaries were seventy yards away when the Bedford exploded. Burning debris pattered down between the branches like flecks of molten lava.

'Fuel tank,' said Keel.

Sekka's thoughts were on the mauled bodies they had carried from the prison. Now they had suffered another indignity. Blown into a thousand gobbets and crisped by Mabato's killer squad.

'Get your ass into gear, Joseph.' Harry Roan tapped his shoulder. 'Those poor devils are beyond help, son. We've our own skins to worry about.'

Behind them, figures could be seen running and leaping around the flaming vehicle like savages around a sacrificial pyre. Leaving the grisly scene, the mercenaries began to run through the forest.

Keel knew they had to get back to the Range Rover. Without it they would never make it to the mission in time. He had looked at his watch. They didn't have much time left.

They had travelled about a mile and a half from the point they had jumped from the truck. Now they turned towards the spot where they had concealed the Range Rover. In the time they had been running there had been no sign of pursuit. That didn't mean there wasn't any. No doubt Mabato had jungle trackers. If they got the scent it would be virtually impossible to shake them off. So far luck was still with them.

They hit the road fifteen minutes later, emerging from the trees cautiously, scanning left to right, senses alert for the sudden cry, the brittle cocking of weapons or the crack of a twig underfoot.

'Too damned good to be true,' Sekka whispered.

Keel was already running out of cover. The others followed, low and fast.

The Range Rover appeared undisturbed under its covering of foliage. Within seconds they were aboard, Keel behind the wheel, and reversing out of the bush. They had one hour to reach the mission and the rendezvous with Kate Lassiter.

Solomon Mabato was almost hysterical with rage. His vast frame shook as he screamed down the telephone. The sting of his venom was aimed at a nervous Farouk Juma who was holding the receiver at a respectable distance from his ear. He was in the guard house at Maboru, trying to cut out the noise of the surrounding chaos as the soldiers ran to and fro like termites.

'Escaped! Imbecile! How could they possibly escape?' Mabato bellowed.

Juma cringed at the sound of his master's voice. Better to remain silent and let the President vent his wrath uninterrupted. In his rage there was no telling what he would do or threaten. If Juma said the wrong thing he could well find himself joining the unfortunate inmates of Maboru on a permanent basis. An enraged Mabato was capable of anything, as had been proved by the way he had dealt with the assassin. Juma's throat constricted with the memory.

Mabato's tone had dropped several octaves. 'You have displeased me, Major. You have failed in your duty. I do not see how an entire guard company could have been outwitted by a handful of foreign terrorists.'

Juma felt it would be unwise at this juncture to mention that there had only been, as far as he could judge, three men. Three! They had left enough carnage in their wake for a raiding party four times that number!

'I am holding the commandant for questioning,' Juma said. 'Perhaps he can explain why his men were so inadequate.'

Mabato saw through the ruse. 'I hold you both responsible for this. Do not underestimate me, Major Juma.

301

Disappoint me again and I will crush you like a rotten grape. Now, the armoured patrol. Have they reported in yet?'

'They caught up with the truck, Excellency. It has been destroyed.'

'And the terrorists?'

'It is believed they escaped into the bush. The patrol has reported that they are in pursuit. The terrorists cannot get far. They will soon be in open country with nowhere to run.'

'Nevertheless, the incident at Maboru proves that these men are not lacking in determination and expertise. They are clever and desperate. Believe me, Juma, I want them badly. Take them alive if possible. If you are successful in this I intend to make an example of them. Following public execution their heads will grace the walls of my Command Post.'

'If we cannot take them alive, Excellency?'

'Kill them and bring me their heads.'

'It shall be done.'

'Juma.' The voice was now like brushed velvet.

The major felt his innards grind. 'Excellency?'

'If, by some misfortune, they should slip through your net, I warn you that my vengeance will be swift and absolute. If you fail to bring me their heads I will dispatch my warriors to you. They will deliver to me your head as forfeit.'

It took the stricken Juma several seconds to realize he was listening to an empty line. Having delivered his ultimate threat, Mabato had hung up.

Farouk Juma had no doubt whatsoever that he was in serious trouble. Unless he could apprehend the raiders. The Scorpion patrol had, so far, failed. Perhaps the road blocks he had established earlier would have better luck.

302

He hoped so. The short hairs on the back of his scrawny neck were already beginning to tingle uncomfortably.

They came upon the road block two miles out of the city. They were travelling fast, hammering along, headlights ablaze, sacrificing stealth for speed in a hell for leather dash to make the rendezvous point.

Hitting the bend too fast, the Range Rover came off the curve like a Formula One Ferrari and Keel was pumping the brakes and aiming the squared bonnet towards the scree at the side of the road, turning them away from the obstruction two hundred yards away. Illuminated by a cordon of kerosene lamps, the poles, balanced across a zig-zag of oil drums, bisected the highway. Weapons glinted in the half light over the shoulders of the dark clad figures grouped in the shadow of a big Soviet BTR Armoured Personnel Carrier parked behind the barrier.

'Shiiiiitt!' Keel wrestled with the spinning wheel as they swerved across the macadam, Harry Roan and Sekka cocking machine pistols and trying to brace themselves against the erratic motion.

The men clustered at the road block were yelling and breaking apart, some running into the road and firing their Kalashnikov rifles. The rear window of the Range Rover exploded into an opaque cobweb. Bullets slammed into the chassis, slewing the vehicle aside.

'Jesus!' Roan extended his body through the opening and loosed off a burst at the soldiers. In the chaotic interior of the Range Rover the noise was deafening. An answering hail smashed the rear lights and punched holes in the side panels as Keel took them over the edge of the highway. Incredibly none of them had been hit and Roan voiced their surprise.

'Fucking typical! Godawful lousy shots!'

The soldiers stampeded to the BTR to give chase. The

massive personnel carrier clattered into life and the NCO herded his men to their places, at the same time calling to his radio technician.

'Alert Major Juma! Tell him we are in pursuit of the raiders! Hurry, you dolt!'

The BTR rumbled out of the night, troops huddled in the rear, priming their weapons and chattering loudly amongst themselves. The exhaust coughed and the vehicle picked up speed.

The Range Rover was bobbing through the scrub, low branches lashing against the windscreen like whips as Keel fought for control. Roan saw the gully ahead in the jumping lights.

'Left! Left!' he screamed.

Keel scraped them past, the tyres scrabbling for a grip on a surface still sticky from the storm. The front nearside wheel struck a stray rock, jolting them out of their seats with a gut wrenching lurch. Sekka gritted his teeth as pain knifed in his shoulder. He threw a glance out of the rear window. 'They're still behind us!'

The BTR was bulldozing its way across the terrain, its upper chassis a bank of lights as its commander tried to follow the fleeing Range Rover. The Personnel Carrier didn't have the manoeuvrability of its quarry but what it lacked in agility it made up for with brute force. It was crashing along, mowing everything in its path like a snow plough. But it hadn't a hope of keeping up. The commander knew that.

The Range Rover churned up a slope as Keel took them into four-wheel drive. They veered between thorn trees like a slalom skier. They crested the rise and Keel stamped on the pedal to gain speed on the flat. 'How're we doing?' he yelled.

'They're dropping behind, Thomas!' Harry Roan said

gleefully. He knew the Range Rover had over twice the speed of the Soviet vehicle, even on the rough. 'That was close! How the hell did they manage to get a road block up so damned fast?'

'The same way they set the snare in Maboru,' Sekka replied. 'We've been suckered all the way. The quicker we are out of here the better. Can we make it, Thomas?'

'Let's find out,' Keel said. 'They'll be watching the roads now, that's for sure. We'll have to cut to the mission overland. It'll be like an obstacle course. I hope the springs can take it.'

'Not to mention my ass!' Harry Roan muttered with feeling.

The BTR appeared like a battle tank over the rim and shuddered to a halt, engine rumbling like a furnace. The quarry had disappeared into the night, swallowed by the veldt. Cursing heavily, the commander reached for the radio.

14

Burov ran a stubby finger along the thin red line on the map that represented the highway. 'They left Maboru and turned north,' he said, tapping the map. 'We know they left the road here, at the road block, heading north east. According to your troop commander, Mister President.'

Mabato muttered darkly: 'He will be punished for letting them slip through his hands.' Piggy eyes glinted as he spoke.

'But not until after you have apprehended the terrorists,' Burov suggested. 'You need every man to run them down.' He stared at the map. 'I wonder where they are running to?' he mused.

The Kenyan border lay in that direction but it was a long drive. Burov felt a grudging admiration for the raiding party and he had the sneaking suspicion that if these men were as resourceful as he thought they would know that Mabato would have the border buttoned up so tightly a lizard wouldn't slip through. So, they had to be making for an alternative destination.

Lake Victoria lay to the south. Burov ruled that out. If the men were to escape by boat they would have gone in the opposite direction. Besides, a boat was too slow unless it was a high speed launch. Burov didn't think so. So, what was left? North? That way was the desert and the dry dusty plains that spread beyond the Sudanese foothills. Not practical. No, consider the picture. There had to be an explanation and some sixth sense told him the answer was staring him in the face. If only he could see it.

There were a few isolated hamlets scattered between Kendura and the border. A few spaced along the railway line; no more than way stations or watering holes. He pored over the ordnance survey sheet. What was that? A farm? No, something else. He peered closer. The dot on the map had a name.

Masambabule.

Two tiny symbols by the name. A cross and, unmistakably, the letter A in a circle, designating a mission station and an air-strip. Burov felt his pulse quicken. Why did the name sound familiar? He searched his memory.

Of course.

A link. The priest. The old, grey haired man who visited the prison. He ran the mission. Coincidence? Possibly, Burov thought to himself but the airstrip; that was the deciding factor. For what better way was there for spiriting Holt out of the country? He relayed his suspicions to Mabato.

'Devlin!' Mabato hissed angrily. His eyes were like shards of coal. 'That man has tried my patience for too long. He will answer to me!' Mabato reached for the telephone. His voice vibrated with evil. 'Get me Major Juma!'

Juma's rat like face split into a malevolent grin as he replaced the handset. He ran out of the guardhouse and shrieked orders at his men.

'Alert the Scorpion patrol! They are to proceed immediately to the mission station at Masambabule! I want two mobile units with me now!' He ran to the first jeep and clambered aboard, joined by four heavily armed soldiers. The vehicle was already leaping out of the prison as four more troopers split to the remaining jeep. The two vehicles, each with a machine gun sited above the cab, fell into line and headed for the highway.

'We must have broken them, Thomas.' Harry Roan let out a sigh of relief. 'That BTR'll never catch us in a month of Sundays.'

They were rocketing over the bumpy terrain, brushing past clumps of undergrowth at an alarming rate. They dived down gullies and raced along dried river beds, Keel's unerring sense of direction keeping them on course across the moonlit wilderness.

They had been travelling for some time and made good progress when the engine coughed suddenly. There was an immediate loss of revs. Keel pumped the accelerator as they began to slow down. They managed another hundred yards before coasting to a spluttering halt.

'Anybody see a Texaco sign?' Roan asked.

'We had plenty in the tank,' Keel said. He got out and walked to the rear of the Range Rover, knowing what he would find. He grunted with understanding. 'The tank's holed. Must have happened at the road block. I guess we were lucky to have got this far.' He looked up and studied their surroundings. They were stranded under a stand of spindly acacias. Ahead of them the ground rose from a winding, rock strewn, dry river valley to a savannah cloaked ridge that stretched across the horizon.

'How far?' Roan got out of the Range Rover, followed by Sekka who was cradling his injured side.

'One mile maybe. No more than two,' Keel said. 'This lady has had it. We'll have to trek. How are you, Joseph?' He gazed at Sekka with concern.

'I'll make it, Bwana.'

'Attaboy,' said Roan.

They gathered weapons and packs and, taking their

bearings from the encircling heights, moved across the lower uneven slope of the valley and began to climb the ridge.

The Rockwell Commander dropped over the edge of the escarpment, wing dipping and swooping as it lined up its approach. The wheels touched and the aircraft hopped and skipped along the ground between the flare lines before slowing to taxi and turn so that it faced back down the landing strip.

Even before the prop had stopped spinning Kate Lassiter knew something was wrong. An awareness coupled with the way the priest was hurrying towards the plane, anguish etched on his face, told her as much. She jumped to the ground, sweeping raven hair from her cheek. She studied the old man's seamed features. 'They haven't made it have they, Father?'

She knew what his answer would be.

Devlin looked tired. 'Not yet.'

'Damn!' She bit her lip.

Lights were on in the mission. In the dark they looked welcoming.

'There is still time . . . and hope,' the priest said. Then puzzlement flitted over his face as he stared at the Commander, dappled in flickering shadows over Kate Lassiter's shoulder. 'The aircraft, it is different, surely?'

She nodded. 'I had a bit of trouble.'

'Trouble?' Devlin said.

'Some son of a bitch blew up my aeroplane . . .'

'Mother of God!' the priest's jaw dropped.

'. . . into iddy biddy pieces, Father. I had to bust my butt to borrow this rich man's runabout and I've pedalled all the bloody way at zero feet.' She smiled ruefully.

'You'd have thought that Thomas would at least have had the decency to get here on time.'

He noticed that her fists were clenched knuckle white, while her voice betrayed her apprehension at the team's absence.

'Sister Elicia is watching the road,' Devlin told her. He frowned. 'I don't pretend to be an expert, my dear, but even these old eyes of mine can see that that little bird behind you can't possibly carry six people.'

She sighed. 'I know but it was the best I could do at short notice. I can take Holt and two of the team. Whoever's left will have to make their own way to the border.' She looked at her watch. 'It's after midnight. They should have been here by now, God dammit!'

'They'll make it, Kate,' the priest said. 'They'll be here. Don't worry.' He took her arm. 'We'll wait in the mission.'

The old man was just as worried, she saw, despite his brave attempt to reassure her. Thomas Keel was resourceful and, when backed into a corner, extremely dangerous. But he was still only mortal. He had set his own deadline and his instructions to Kate Lassiter had been precise. If the team hadn't made the rendezvous by the agreed time she was to leave.

'Come on, Thomas,' she whispered into the darkness. 'Where the hell are you?'

It was already fifteen minutes past the hour.

That was when the figure of Sister Elicia appeared, running quickly. She was excited, laughing with relief. 'They're here, Father! They have made it!'

'Thank God!' Kate Lassiter cried.

They ran back towards the mission and had reached the road as the first jeep swung into sight over the brow of the hill, its headlights trapping them like startled rabbits. It was swiftly joined by a second, in line behind. They bounced down the track in quick succession.

Sister Elicia, seeing the glow of the fast approaching lights had, sadly, assumed too much. The bewildered expression on her pretty face said it all.

Kate's first instinct was to make a run for the Commander but, as the jeeps screeched to a halt, disgorging heavily armed soldiers, she knew, with sickening finality, that she wouldn't have made two yards.

Juma's search of the mission revealed nothing, to his obvious annoyance. Father Devlin, bristling with rage, watched as, under the Major's instructions, Sister Constance and the other four nuns were herded out of their rooms to join the others. The elderly nun had managed to retrieve her robe and was nervously tying the sash around her waist. The rest wore only their night dresses and stood together in the moonlight, fear showing clearly on their faces. The soldiers stood around them in a sullen semi-circle.

'Did you find what you were looking for, Major?' Father Devlin did little to hide the contempt in his voice.

Farouk Juma, flanked by his cohorts, swaggered forward. Kate felt the flutterings of alarm in her belly as she watched the diminutive Nubian's approach. He exuded evil like ectoplasm.

'My men tell me there is an aircraft on the airstrip,' he said. 'Where is the pilot?'

Kate stepped out and Juma raised his eyebrows. 'A woman?'

'Don't look so surprised, Major,' she countered. 'Female emancipation is all the rage these days.'

If he understood the jibe, Juma chose to ignore it. He said, matter-of-factly. 'You are here to pick up the terrorists who escaped from Maboru. Where are they?'

She looked at him blankly. 'Terrorists, Major? I'm afraid you're way off centre. I'm on my way to Nairobi. My aircraft developed engine trouble and I was forced to land here. I was very lucky.' Her heart was hammering wildly. So Keel was alive!

Juma smiled thinly. 'I know your purpose here. Please do not try to make me look a fool.'

'Oh, I wasn't trying, Major. Believe me.'

The weasel eyes flashed. 'What is your name?'

'Katherine Lassiter.'

A warning look flashed from Devlin. Don't do anything to arouse them.

'Lass-it-er,' Juma said. The pronunciation dripped with menace. 'Your comrades failed in their mission. Their freedom is temporary. As is yours.'

His words made her heart sink. The Lugambans still had Holt and Keel and his team were heading into a trap. And there was nothing she could do about it.

'You miserable little shit!' Kate Lassiter seethed.

Juma's malacca cane flicked through the air. She swung her head aside to avoid the blow. The tip of the cane lashed her cheek, sending ribbons of pain through her jaw and splitting the skin. She tasted the warm trickle of blood on her lip. Juma, incensed, raised his cane for another strike.

'NO!' The defiant bellow erupted from the priest. He rushed forward and, before anyone could stop him, smashed Juma across the skull with his gnarled fist. Juma's boots took off and he flew backwards. He hit the ground rump first and the look of shock on his face was matched only by the awestruck expressions on the faces of his men.

'You bastard!' Devlin shouted. 'You cowardly, malodorous runt! Get up! I'll break your scrawny neck!'

Farouk Juma got to his feet very slowly and shakily. His cap lay several feet away in the dust. He screamed at one of the wide eyed soldiers who retrieved it and handed it to his twitching superior. For what seemed like minutes the major and the priest glared at each other, faces only inches apart, Devlin breathing heavily, Juma trembling with rage. In those heart stopping moments Devlin knew he was very close to death.

'You will regret that, Holy Man!' Juma hissed. The Nubian's threat was chilling in its ferocity and Kate Lassiter, nursing her throbbing jaw, knew they had all just run out of time.

The pain in his belly had become unbearable. What had started as a dull ache in his gut had gradually developed into raging stomach cramps and a desperate urge to loosen his bowels. He had held out for as long as possible but the limit of his endurance had been reached and overtaken. Hugging his churning, heaving paunch, he staggered, wheezing with discomfort, into the trees. He laid his Kalashnikov against a log. His fingers scrabbled at his belt and he tugged his pants over his plump buttocks. With a groan of relief, he squatted.

He was aware of the presence the second the hand clamped under his chin, whipping his head back to expose his windpipe. Even as his hands lifted to defend himself the knife swept round and severed the carotid artery and vocal chords. A dark, viscous fountain gushed from his torn throat and a gobbling rattle bubbled in a crimson torrent from mutilated organs. His legs, fettered by the pants gathered at his ankles, kicked ineffectively in the undergrowth. The body spasmed uncontrollably and the already strained sphincter muscles relaxed. The body collapsed in an untidy sprawl in its own waste.

It had not been a clean kill. Far from it. Harry Roan achieved no satisfaction from the act as he wiped the blade of the knife on his sleeve. It had been necessary in order to achieve an objective.

Schooled in the harsh, bloody reality of the Special Forces infiltration units, Harry Roan had an impressive number of swift, silent kills to his credit. To his credit? Had it become like a game now with the score counted in the tally of the dead he had left behind him? Had the cost of a life become so cheap?

He'd known men in Nam who kept score. The men who had developed a taste for killing; the ones who wore their hair in braids or Mohican cuts and hung scalps at their belts. The ear collectors who wore the withered trophies around their throats in grotesque necklaces.

He sheathed the knife and picked up the dead trooper's panga.

He hadn't expected two men. He had crouched in the forest and watched the airstrip. Two guards in fatigues and forage caps. AK 47s over their shoulders, pangas in their belts and the furtive glow of a cigarette. He would be forced to make a move soon. They didn't have much time left. But he had to deal with both of them silently. How? Then the reprieve as one of them – the plump one – trotted towards him, clutching his belly and passing enough wind to waken the dead.

One down, one to go. The second soldier would be more difficult. Roan would have to cross open ground to make the kill. Twenty five yards, give or take.

Roan picked up the Kalashnikov and forage cap. He pulled the cap low over his forehead and, shouldering the automatic rifle, he walked from the trees. The second soldier was temporarily hidden by the fuselage. Roan made the first fifteen yards undetected. About ten paces to go when the trooper stepped into the open. Immediately Roan ducked his head and altered his walk. He hunched his

314

shoulders and assumed a heavy waddle, at the same time seeming to fumble with his belt as though fastening his pants. He was holding the panga in his right hand. The guard laughed bawdily, imitating the act of defecation, poking fun at his companion's discomfort. The grin was wiped off his face as Harry Roan, now only two yards away, looked up and caught his eye. For a second the man was transfixed. Then he unslung his rifle and opened his mouth to yell.

Roan covered the remaining few feet like a striking cobra, his arm curving back. The panga slashed down across the man's face, parting the cheekbone like tissue paper and splitting the jaw into a bloody ruin. The trooper went down like a felled tree, a fearsome gargle dying on his mangled lips as he hit the earth. Roan tugged the panga free and with a second blow finished the job. He ran back into the bushes and collected his own gear.

Sekka was lying face down in the scrub, a dark shadow on the ground. He was naked. The brightly patterned shirt he had worn during the infiltration of Maboru would have prevented his unseen approach; the trousers would have snagged on the rocks and undergrowth. His target crouched ten feet away, Kalashnikov resting in the fork between two stout branches of a mimosa, as he covered the road. In the subdued light the Makesi shifted restlessly, easing his body into a more comfortable position. Using the movement to mask his progress, Sekka wormed forward. He was without weapons for the noise and metallic glint would have betrayed him to a sharp eyed and cautious sentry. This man, however, was neither of those.

Sekka rose out of the night. The trooper, with dreadful awareness, turned his head and died. The heel of Sekka's left hand crunched into the flared nostrils, forcing bone and cartilage up and back into the brain in a move so fast the Makesi died on his feet as the lethal blow ruptured blood vessels and severed nerve endings. Almost nonchalantly the corpse leaned back against the bole of the tree and slumped aside. Quickly Sekka removed the cap and fatigues and put them on. He went back to his gear and then ran towards the mission building. As he ran, a steady pulse at his shoulder told him his wound had opened up again.

Farouk Juma knew they were out there, somewhere close. He could sense it. He hoped only that his pickets would spot them on the way in and give enough warning. Outside on the veranda a board creaked. Juma stiffened. His men caught the reaction. They were restless and fidgeted impatiently. The priest and the women were under guard in the dispensary. Two soldiers watched over them. The rest of Juma's men, not counting those outside, were deployed at various points within the mission, poised behind the windows and doors. Juma peered between the slats in the door screen. Outside the night seemed strangely quiet, eerie in its silence. It was as if the mission and all those within were poised on the edge of some great abyss.

There was a sudden movement at the edge of the tree line. A figure darted into a patch of moonlight and Juma's heart beat quickened. The soldier was keeping low as he ran towards the front of the mission, glancing over his shoulder at something or someone behind him. Juma felt a surge of relief. The sentry had spotted the terrorists. He hissed a warning to his men.

The building moved.

Juma felt the boards ripple under his feet a micro-second before the wall imploded. Two of his squad had been crouching by the wall as Keel detonated his one remaining explosive charge. The two Makesi were torn apart as the side of the building burst inwards with a blistering roar, their bodies shredded instantly.

A third trooper wheeled away with a piercing shriek, his eyes gouged by a score of needle sharp splinters, as Joseph Sekka hurled himself through the front entrance screen and raked the corridor with a hammering burst from his Heckler and Koch.

As the doors flew open under Sekka's onslaught Farouk Juma had but a second to realize the shadowy figure he had seen flitting towards the mission had not been one of his own men. He threw himself aside in a frantic effort to avoid the murderous hail from Sekka's machine pistol. The corridor was filled with swirling smoke and debris and the frightened major lost his sense of direction. That made him all the more terrified as bullets slammed into the wall above his head.

Sekka twisted to his right and squeezed off another burst as he spotted a target. The trooper literally ran into the spread of bullets. The low velocity slugs impacted like shrapnel, fragmenting the man's torso and shattering his spine. The corpse was pitched aside like a sad rag doll spraying blood and guts along the floor.

Juma, having miraculously survived the first attack, rolled and jerked to his knees. As he lifted his pistol and aimed it at Sekka's exposed back an awesome apparition thrust itself through the shattered wall. Juma's brain registered the danger even as Keel fired the Remington from waist height. The heavy shells lifted Juma two feet in the air, removed the left side of his head and shoulders and sent his mutilated, gyrating body careering backwards in ungainly flight.

Harry Roan had figured on no more than two seconds' grace as he heard the explosion on the other side of the

317

building. He was waiting by the dispensary door. As he felt the shock wave he moved fast, smashing his boot against the lock. The door crashed back against the wall and Roan went in low.

He yelled: 'Get down, dammit!' He was shooting from the hip and was desperately aware of Kate Lassiter throwing herself across the stout body of Sister Constance as his initial shots scythed into the first trooper's legs, cutting the man down before he could retaliate. The second soldier was already spinning, open mouthed in fear and alarm, Kalashnikov cocked in his hands. Roan dropped, firing as he went down. A line of craters appeared in the wall, the ragged pattern culminating in a final burst over the soldier's chest, ripping flesh into a bright scarlet blossom. The Makesi slid down the wall, his body smearing the woodwork.

The air was heavy with the smell of cordite as Roan gained his feet fluidly. 'Everybody outside! Now! Move your asses, for Christ's sake!' His attention was on the door, expecting reprisal as he gestured wildly at the bewildered group. Two of the nuns were weeping hysterically.

He yelled: 'Get them out of here, Kate! Do it! Out! Out!' He didn't know if Keel and Sekka had managed to neutralize the rest. He had to get the priest and the others out of the building smartish.

But he shouldn't have turned his back.

He knew it instinctively, recorded the fact in his brain even as he started to react, for the Makesi he had taken off at the knees had somehow come to life, raising himself by a supreme effort of will power. No more than a fleeting squeeze on the trigger and Roan felt the sledgehammer impact between his shoulder blades, punching him forward where he hung momentarily as though suspended like a puppet on a string before falling what seemed to be a long, long way down. He saw the floor rising to greet him. It was tilting at the same time; a most curious sensation altogether. The Heckler and Koch slipped from his fingers. He tried to hold on to it but the weapon had a mind of its own. He heard someone shouting his name. It came from far away. Kate Lassiter was running back through the open door, a stricken look on her beautiful face. She was lifting his discarded machine pistol and aiming it, her mouth open in a snarl of anger. Then she was firing and the gun was bucking in her hands and spewing bullets across the room.

Through the haze Roan found he was facing the Makesi who had propped himself against the wall. The Kalashnikov lay at an odd angle over his shattered legs. Kate Lassiter's shots had cut him in half. His stomach was a gruesome crater and his eyes carried an opaque glaze.

Roan was aware that Kate Lassiter was bending over him and there was somebody else at her shoulder; an old man with white hair and a face like a walnut. The priest was holding out his arms as though in supplication and Harry Roan immediately felt at ease. He was going to be all right. The priest must have known it too though by his expression you would hardly have thought so. Roan tried to work out that mystery but he couldn't. For some reason he was finding it very hard to concentrate and, strangely, everything around him was kind of fuzzy at the edges. Come to think of it, he couldn't feel his legs anymore either; they'd gone to sleep. Kate Lassiter was whispering something but he was having difficulty hearing her. He tried to lift himself but he was so weary that it was a real effort. Better to rest for a while. He smiled tiredly. When he sagged against Kate Lassiter's breast the smile was still in place.

He was still smiling when Keel and Sekka burst in through the door.

Keel had dug the grave in the shelter of a jacaranda tree. Roan's body lay wrapped in a cotton sheet. Keel had stripped the American's corpse to remove identification. He had contemplated burning Roan's remains to erase any possibility of exhumation but he couldn't bring himself to perform the act. A man had a right to be interred with dignity if nothing else.

Which was more than he intended for Juma and the remains of his squad. The bodies lay where they had fallen; splayed and strewn in the shambles that had been the mission building. Michael Devlin, stumbling along the ruined corridor, had viewed the chaos with horror. His face was pale. He looked about a hundred years old.

'You have brought death and destruction to this place, Thomas.' Devlin was trembling.

'It was not of my choosing, Father.' Keel had spoken sadly. 'The moment we came over the hill and saw the arrival of Juma and his thugs the decision was made for us.'

'But this, Thomas! This . . . carnage! I cannot condone this action!'

'I'm not asking you to condone nor am I seeking absolution, dammit! How long do you think you'd have held out under their interrogation?'

'They wouldn't dare . . . !'

'Wouldn't dare! They wouldn't have hesitated! Somehow Mabato knew we'd come here. How he found out I don't know, but as soon as the connection was made your position here became forfeit. If we hadn't intervened, God knows what would have happened to you. Do you honestly think they'd have given up the wait and gone home? You can't be that naive!'

320

'But this was butchery, Thomas!'

'It was necessary,' Keel said harshly. 'Us or them. That's what it came down to. It's that simple.'

The priest flinched and Keel regretted instantly the manner of his reply. He regretted also the fact that he had involved the priest and his staff in the first place. By his own admission he had used them. As a means to an end.

And for what, he thought bitterly. They hadn't even got Holt out. He was still held somewhere. Mabato must be laughing himself silly. Paul Schiller and Harry Roan dead. Two good men who hadn't deserved to die in this bloody country just so that he could prove to himself that he had what it takes to carry out one more contract. One last sodding job that had turned into an epic disaster.

'What are your plans now?' Devlin asked.

Keel shrugged. A resigned gesture. 'We don't have a great deal of choice. We get out of Lugamba. Post haste.'

'And David Holt? He is still a hostage.'

'That fact gives me no pleasure but I'm being practical. It would serve no purpose for Joseph and I to remain. The contract is blown.'

'So, all this bloodshed was unnecessary.'

'I'm not arguing with you. Just get your things together. I want you all ready to leave in fifteen minutes.'

The priest blinked. 'Leave? You cannot be serious?'

'Deadly serious. Come the dawn and this place will be swarming with government troops. You don't want to be around. Joseph and I will escort you to the border in the Toyota or you can go with Kate. Either way split yourselves up into two groups. We'll meet Kate and her party in Karanga.'

Joseph Sekka winced as Sister Elicia applied the dressing and bandage to his shoulder. She had helped him remove the top of his fatigues and had swabbed and cleaned the wound expertly, her initial shock and concern swiftly overtaken by professional skill as she determined the severity of the damage. They were in the small surgery and Sekka watched her trim figure with admiration as she busied to her task.

He wondered what emotions were going through her mind for he had been conscious of the stricken look on her face when she realized that Paul Schiller wasn't with them. He knew there had been some sort of bond between her and Schiller for he had seen the looks they had exchanged but beyond that awareness he had refused to speculate. The girl herself had offered no explanation and he hadn't considered broaching the subject. Her sorrow had been apparent to all.

They placed rocks on the earth above the grave as protection against scavengers digging for Roan's body. Hyenas and jackals had scant respect for the dead. Kate Lassiter, Father Devlin and the nuns were in attendance. Clouds drifted across the face of the moon as they stood with heads bowed by the sad pile of stones. It was, by painful necessity, a brief and poignant homage.

Mabato would send more men. It was time to move out. Excepting . . .

Keel exploded in anger. 'Good God Almighty! I don't believe what I'm hearing! What the hell d'you mean you won't leave?'

Father Devlin faced the mercenary with his chin up, his gaze calm but full of determination. 'Simply that, Thomas. The sisters and I will remain at the mission.'

'For heaven's sake, Father . . . !'

'Thomas, my son, we are needed here. This decision was not made out of some whimsical desire for martyr-dom. Without the facilities at this mission – meagre though they may be – the villages would receive no help, no medical aid, no welfare of any sort. How can I explain it to you, Thomas? We are all they have. Can't you see that?'

'All I can see,' Keel said bluntly, 'is a stubborn old fool. This is insane! Hell's teeth! Tell him, Joseph. See if you can ram some sense into his thick Irish skull!'

'You know what Mabato will do to you, Father,' Sekka said.

'He won't harm us, Joseph. He knows he has nothing to fear. We are no threat to him.'

'Seems like we've had this conversation before,' Keel said in exasperation. 'Remember Brandt's Crossing? You didn't think you were in danger there either. Your memory must be fading along with your brain. Mabato will have your guts, literally. He'll be looking for revenge. Take it from me, you don't want to be around. And what about the women? You think their fate will cost him any loss of sleep? Are you willing to have that on your conscience?'

'The decision to stay was unanimous, Thomas,' Father Devlin said.

The priest was obviously adamant. Keel, knowing from past experience the old man's obstinacy, was stumped. 'I hope to God you know what you're doing,' he said finally. 'Come on, Joseph. We're wasting our breath.'

Devlin walked with them to the aircraft. The sisters had illuminated the strip. Kate Lassiter was already on board.

'Go with God, my friends,' Michael Devlin said.

'I think he'll be more use to you here, Father,' Keel replied. He nodded briefly to the six nuns grouped at the edge of the flare path then he climbed into the cabin. Behind him, Sekka gazed at the priest with concern.

'Take care, Joseph,' Michael Devlin said warmly.

'You too, Father.'

The door closed and the priest stepped away. The engine coughed and broke into a steady throb. As he joined the nuns the trim Commander raced down the strip and disappeared into the dark sky. Devlin and his staff walked the length of the field and extinguished the lights.

There was much work to be done. Their first duty lay in removing the dead from the mission and preparing them for burial. With a grim countenance Michael Devlin began to issue orders. They had carried all the bodies outside when the sound of a heavy engine reached their ears and the Scorpion rumbled over the brow of the hill.

David Holt wore a clean white starched shirt and a pair of newly pressed brown slacks. They were a trifle large. He looked thin and more than a little bewildered at the attention he was receiving.

He was in the Command Post.

He had been taken by car from Maboru to the offices of the Department of State Security. He had felt sure he was being driven to his death in the DOSS cellars so he was sobbing uncontrollably as they drove through the main gates and bundled him out of the Peugeot. He was frogmarched into the gaunt building and hustled down dank stairways. The smell of death was all around. They had thrown him into a stinking cell and left him to dwell on his uncertain future.

They had come for him with the dawn, ignoring his questions and his incessant pleading. Eventually he lapsed into silence. Then another car ride and he had stared in confusion as he was taken to the President's residence. He was even more confused when his escort took him to a huge bedroom with an adjoining bathroom. Fresh clothes were laid out on the bed and he was told to bathe and dress. His filthy, matted prison garb was taken away.

They had brought him breakfast; hot rolls, honey and real coffee. He couldn't believe it and was instantly suspicious. What terrible game was Mabato up to?

Mabato's aide took him down the long, high-ceilinged corridor and escorted him into the large council chamber.

Solomon Mabato was smiling. 'Good morning, Mister Holt! I hope you enjoyed your bathe and breakfast.'

Holt nodded. He was totally nonplussed. He was also staring at the other man in the room. He knew him. He'd seen him before though he couldn't recall where exactly. He racked his brain and tried to remember.

The stranger, sensing his discomfort and trepidation, walked forward, hand extended, a welcoming smile on his face. 'Hello, Mister Holt. I'm David Wood. I've come to take you home.'

15

'Well, I can't say that I'm sorry it's all over,' Lennox admitted. He was addressing Dalkeith who had been summoned to Downing Street early that morning. 'In fact I'm chuffed to buggery!'

They were in the conference room and early rays of sunlight were streaming through the windows overlooking the rose garden. Dalkeith examined the creases in his dark grey trousers. Immaculate as ever in his Dover Street suit. 'Yes,' he said. 'You must be.'

Dalkeith could see the headlines in his mind. Lennox would come out of it smelling like a bunch of Harry Wheatcroft roses, basking in the glory, taking the credit for securing the release of David Holt.

'They're flying Holt out to Nairobi sometime today,' Lennox said. 'I sincerely hope the stupid sod realizes how lucky he is. I must say that all parties appear satisfied at the outcome. Mabato's invitation to the Foreign Secretary to attend the opening ceremony of the OAU Conference is evidence of that. I thought it prudent that Wood should accept. It would have been churlish to refuse and President Nai might have been offended after all he's done for us.'

'Quite,' Dalkeith said. 'And what about the team that went in to get Holt out?'

'Routed,' Lennox replied. 'We got word to Mabato just in time. He was able to take preventive action.'

'They're dead?'

'I believe two of the team were killed. The others

managed to escape. I've no doubt they are well out of the country by this time. Now, how about a coffee, George?'

'Poor bastards!' Dalkeith muttered half to himself.

Lennox glanced quickly at the security chief, a hard look on his face. 'Spare me the sympathy, Dalkeith. They knew the risks involved. They weren't boy scouts! Bearing in mind the carnage they left behind, particularly at that mission station, they got no more than they bloody well deserved. Hell, we guessed there might be people killed in the snatch. Some of Mabato's bully boys for instance but an old priest and six nuns we didn't bargain for. God Almighty, Dalkeith! What sort of hoodlums were they? The report we got was that they used the priest and his staff as hostages when they found their escape route blocked.'

Dalkeith remained silent as Lennox continued his tirade. 'I thought that Wood told us these men were reliable professionals? They sound like an offshoot of the Wild Bunch!'

'It was a damned fool idea in the first place,' Dalkeith said. 'Absolutely irresponsible . . .'

'Don't lecture me, Dalkeith! If you remember it was Wood's brainchild.'

'My God! The buck stops anywhere but here!'

'And you had better believe it!' Lennox growled. 'Nothing but nothing will ever link this office to the recruitment of mercenaries. We are snow white on this one, Dalkeith. Bloody Persil bright! Do you read me?'

'Unequivocally, Prime Minister.'

'Excellent, George. Just so long as we understand each other.' Lennox smiled silkily. 'There will be no leaks, no smears of any kind. I'm relying on you, George, and the facilities of your department. I will, of course, leave whatever action is required to your own discretion.'

And don't think I don't know what that means, Lennox, you bastard! Dalkeith thought to himself.

'Right, George. If there's nothing else?' Lennox looked pointedly at his watch. 'I know you're a busy man and I have a meeting with the Home Secretary in twenty minutes . . .'

The girl's eyes were half closed as though in pain, her neck muscles taut, head thrown back as she moaned through tight lips. She shuddered and her breathing quickened and emerged in ragged gasps.

A thin sheen of perspiration covered Jack Case's heaving body. The girl's long tanned legs were drawn up over his back, her ankles locked. Case was grunting, his face buried against the girl's neck. He was pumping hard now, his pelvic bones grinding against hers as she pushed and gyrated her hips to meet his deep thrusts. Case felt sharp fingernails rake his spine, moving down his flanks towards the cleft between his buttocks. He lifted his head, taking intense pleasure at the flushed honey brown skin and coral lips, full and swollen with desire as she whimpered throatily. Her back arched and her fingers had begun to tease and probe. Case was driving towards his climax. The girl began to tremble and the tempo of her thrusting increased.

'Yes . . . yes! Ooohhh . . . God! . . . Yeesss!'

The telephone rang.

'Jesuuuz!' Case was past the point of no return. He bucked violently, matching the girl's shattering exhalation with his own. The trilling at the side of his bed was as persistent as a cicada chorus. They were both breathing hard, the exertion showing on their perspiring faces. Case collapsed across her thighs.

'Fucking hell!' He reached out and dragged the telephone through the dishevelled sheets. 'This had better be good!' he spat into the mouthpiece.

He sat up quickly, his tousled companion gasping as his knee caught her elbow.

'What?' His features that only seconds before had been drawn with excitement were now composed in a rigid mask of disbelief and anger. He cupped his hand over the mouthpiece and snapped: 'Get dressed!'

The girl pouted, feigning annoyance. She stroked a still prominent dark nipple with a long scarlet fingernail and flicked a pink tongue over half open lips.

'I said get dressed!' The tone in his voice jerked her into complying. He was listening intently, teeth clamped together.

'I don't give a damn!' he barked. 'Get hold of Ferris and tell him to meet me there. Move it!' He slammed down the receiver and jumped off the bed.

'Jack?' The girl was sliding brief black panties over taut buttocks. 'What's happening, lover?'

Case grabbed his slacks. His voice, when he replied, was hoarse with rage. 'Some fucking bastard has torched the club!'

By the time Jack Case got there it was all over and the destruction of the night club was total. The once plush interior with its bars, dining room and gaming tables was a picture of complete devastation. Not a single piece of furniture remained intact and the floors, walls and ceilings resembled the dark insides of a grim and gloomy cavern. Not a vestige of the expensive decor was left.

'It was a very professional job, Mister Case,' the attendant fire officer admitted. 'Separate charges detonated simultaneously in all the rooms. Probably coupled to incendiary devices if the initial evidence is any indication.

Whoever was responsible knew exactly what they were doing right down to the degree of damage they could inflict without risk to the adjoining premises.'

The Negro officer shook his head almost wistfully and it sounded to Case as if the man's voice held more than a hint of admiration.

'I don't suppose anybody saw anything?' Case asked.

The fire officer shrugged. 'You'd have to ask the police about that. They're talking with your manager over there.' He pointed to a small group of men standing next to the fire appliances.

Benny Tainsh watched Case's grim faced approach over the broad shoulders of the police sergeant with a mixture of relief and apprehension. Case looked fit and ready to commit murder.

'What the hell happened, Tainsh? I mean just what the bloody hell is going on?'

Tainsh wasn't much help. He'd been about to let himself into the club to get the place ready for the evening's activities when someone had knocked him cold. He hadn't heard a thing and had woken up behind a row of trash cans in a nearby alley, bound hand and foot, aching like nothing else with six inches of masking tape over his mouth. He had heard the explosions as he came to and had summoned assistance by kicking over the trash cans to attract attention.

So, where were Ferris and his attendant thug John John? Case fumed.

And of course the police wanted to know if he had any enemies. As if they didn't know that for a man in his line of business enemies were virtually an occupational hazard. But out of those, how many harboured that large a grudge? Answer: quite a few. Case held a number of prominent markers but blowing up his club would hardly cancel the debt. Where matters of debt were concerned Jack Case had a very long memory.

After the police and fire services had left, Case picked his way gingerly through the charcoaled wreckage. Ashes crunched underfoot and water dripped from the doused and blackened beams above his head. His features were twisted into a cruel grimace. His first task would be to find those responsible and deal with them. A man in his position couldn't afford to take this open act of provocation lying down. Then he stopped dead in his tracks. Because he knew.

This was a warning. This was retaliation.

For Lassiter's Chieftain.

A distinct chill crept down his spine as he recalled the promise made by Lassiter's grey haired friend when the latter had paid off the pilot's debt. Perhaps it had been taking matters too far; sending Ferris to destroy the aircraft. Maybe razing the club was just the beginning.

Case decided that it was time to marshal his forces. He needed Ferris.

Only Ferris wasn't going to be any help at all. Neither was John John.

When Case returned to his apartment he sensed something was wrong as soon as he opened the door and switched on the light. He knew he wasn't alone. It couldn't be the girl. She had left with him earlier. In a huff. He'd dropped her off on his way to the club.

Case closed the door quietly behind him and walked cautiously down the hall, his footsteps cushioned by the deep carpet. He paused by the mirrored stand and carefully opened the shallow drawer. The loaded .357 Magnum lay next to a box of shells. Case picked it up and continued along the passage. The door to the bedroom was ajar. The bedclothes were still in disarray. Looking at them Case felt his crotch tingle as the sight brought back memories. She had been very energetic and very inventive. He dismissed the thoughts from his mind.

The door to the lounge was closed. Case rested his left hand on the knob and took a deep breath. Then he pushed back the door and went in fast and low, the Magnum tight in his right hand.

Ferris was sitting in a wing-backed cane chair. John John was to his left on the low sofa. Neither of them moved as Case lowered the gun and straightened. 'You stupid bastard, Ferris! I could have shot you! How the hell did you get in?'

Ferris wasn't listening.

The hole in his forehead, an inch above the bridge of his nose, was neat and round and there wasn't a great deal of blood. The crater in the back of his skull was a different matter. Case could have put his fist in it. Jagged bone fragments and brain matter smeared the back of the chair and part of the wall behind. John John had been dispatched in a similar fashion. His blood was staining the cushions on the sofa. Case stared, appalled. Nothing could have prepared him for this. The scene bore all the hallmarks of a professional hit. He thought about Lassiter and her friends. They had hit back with a vengeance.

There was something else. A slim envelope lay on the coffee table. It contained one airline ticket for the next morning's British Airways flight to Johannesburg. The name on the coupon was Case. J.

The doorbell rang.

Case whirled. His knee caught the edge of the chair and he recoiled, horrified, as Ferris's corpse slid sideways. The blond curls were matted with congealed blood and tissue. Ferris's eyes were still open. They gazed sightlessly at a point beyond Case's left shoulder. Case stifled the sudden urge to vomit. The bell rang again. A longer, insistent buzz this time. Case wavered, unsure. Then he composed his features and backed out of the room, closing the door as he did so.

Two men. Black. In ill fitting suits. Strangers. Their expressions polite but cautious. One held out a brown leather wallet. A warrant card was displayed. Police.

Case felt his bowels churn. 'Yes?'

Maybe it concerned the fire at the club. Maybe they had a lead. Maybe.

'Mister Case? CID. We've received reports of a disturbance from some of the other residents.'

'Disturbance?' God! He was sweating. He could feel beads of perspiration on his brow. Why were they staring at him like that?

'Gunshots, Mister Case,' the taller of the two said. His companion's eyes roamed down the hallway.

'Gunshots?' The word almost sticking in his dry throat. Why, in God's name, was he repeating everything they said?

Why were they staring at him? Only they weren't staring at him rather than at something in his hand. Sweet Jesus! He was holding the Magnum!

They moved very quickly then, disarming him and propelling him back into the apartment and up against the wall. He was frisked expertly. The policeman was smelling the muzzle of the gun. He opened the chamber and Case knew then just how thorough Lassiter's friends had been. He knew even before they took his arms and led him down the hall. He knew.

The Magnum had been fired twice.

Cameron was more than a little perturbed. Almost two days had elapsed since the media had first proclaimed

Holt's release and subsequent passage to Kenya and the recruiter had received no word from Keel or members of his team.

The release had been front page news. Banner headlines and photographs showing a subdued David Holt in attendance as David Wood shook hands with a beaming Solomon Mabato. A formal acceptance of terms for the release which, naturally, pandered to the hovering pressmen. Iain Cameron found the pictures too patronizing and somewhat stage managed. As he read the text he was all too clearly aware that the rescue attempt had been sold down the river. But by whom?

Mabato's security forces had disclosed limited details of the abortive raid on Maboru. The identities of the would-be rescuers or their paymaster had not been revealed but the raid may well have been undertaken with the blessing of ex-President Kemba and his aides skulking in Kenyan exile. Mabato's security advisers were still investigating.

Items within the report had caught Cameron's attention. The correspondent had quoted a source close to Mabato as stating that Lugamba had been warned of the rescue attempt by the British Government. The other snippets had been to the effect that two of the raiding party had been killed during the escape and shoot-out at the mission. This as well as the slaughter of the priest and six nuns. Further details would follow the investigations.

The fact that the British may have alerted the Lugambans weighed heavily on Cameron's mind, particularly in the light of his discovery of Hobson's identity. The implications were too devastating. Not only had the British sanctioned the recruitment of mercenaries but, following President Nai's initiative, they had been forced to abort the operation in the only way possible. Alert Mabato. Betray the very men they had sent in.

Cameron knew full well that if, as he suspected, the British Government had been the shadowy paymaster his own position was precarious to say the least. There was also the matter of the alleged massacre at Masambabule. Cameron knew Keel well enough to know that the mercenary would never have condoned or been involved with the killing of the priest and the mission staff. He had no idea how the holy man was linked with the rescue but Hobson, or rather Dalkeith, didn't know Keel and if he believed the reports from Lugamba he'd think that Cameron had sent in murderers not professional soldiers. Which meant that the government would be even more determined to ensure that details of the Holt contract did not become public knowledge and that could involve neutralizing all loose ends.

Cameron knew he was one of those loose ends.

16

In Kendura preparations for the ceremony that would precede the OAU summit meeting were almost complete. The Yugoslav contractors, ENERGO-PROJECT, had worked around the clock to finish the conference centre and hotel complex in time. Mabato had directed that no effort be spared in getting the job done. The final cost had been some three hundred per cent over budget but Mabato was pleased with the result and unconcerned with the expense.

Bunting fluttered gaily from every lamp standard and in the plaza in front of the conference centre the flags of the attendant states rippled gently in the warm evening breeze. In the main square workmen were putting the finishing touches to the saluting base and delegates' rostrum. The highlight of the opening ceremony was to be the parade; a review of Mabato's armed forces, with the President himself taking the salute. This gave Mabato a splendid opportunity to show off his new acquisitions – the six Soviet T–54 tanks – and impress the delegates.

Following the negotiations for the release of Holt Mabato, in an unexpected burst of cordiality, offered David Wood and President Nai the unprecedented honour of standing beside him on the saluting base. Mabato also extended the invitation to his Soviet advisor, Gregori Burov.

Thus all parties, although inherently wary of each other, were looking forward to the celebrations on the morrow.

★ ★ ★

The Commander flew in low, heading west, skimming across the veldt like a bird. It dipped into the ravine and dropped like a swooping hawk before pulling up to float in gently over the dusty valley floor. It taxied and turned, single engine keening as it rolled to a standstill under the full moon. Five minutes elapsed before it took off. As it rose and banked over the ridge two figures crouched together and watched it depart. Like a tiny bat the aircraft crossed the face of the moon and its former passengers collected their packs and turned towards the head of the valley and the track that would take them into the city and the rendezvous point.

The delegates were beginning to leave the hotel. Mabato's fleet of gleaming Mercedes were lined up in a convoy ready to transport them to the main square. The temperature was high and Kendura was shimmering in the mid morning haze. The new conference centre, with its magnificent glass façade, shone like a giant mirror as sunlight flashed off the glittering tower.

Crowds were gathering along the route to be taken by the limousines. A ring of soldiers cordoned the main square and eyed the crowd with suspicion. Sunlight gleamed on the barrels of their Kalashnikov rifles.

The Presidential dais stood to one side of the delegates' rostrum and press stand. It supported seats for Mabato and his guests and a stand of microphones. A bright red canopy served as protection from the sun. The delegates would be banked in three tiers of tightly packed seats under a sky blue awning. The press would have to fend for themselves. There were no representatives from the Western media. Men were moving along the rows of empty seats; security teams making sweeps.

Within the crowd agents of SASU and DOSS stalked in

337

their flowered shirts, machine pistols in their hands, dark sun glasses reflecting the fear in the eyes of those who moved aside to make way for them.

Somewhere in the distance a band began to tune instruments; a sure sign that festivities were about to commence and, as if on cue, the first of the limousines slid smoothly into view and the crowd around the square began to press forward.

Seated in the back of the Mercedes, David Wood had to admit to himself that he would be glad when the whole charade had faded into memory and he was back home, away from the pollution represented by Mabato and his cronies. This despite the fact that his visit had presented him with an excellent opportunity to meet with some of the OAU delegates. His relations with the Kenyan President were very cordial, bolstered inevitably by President Nai's initiative over the Holt affair.

Holt was now in Nairobi, shaken but safe, thanks to the intervention of President Nai and, in no small measure, to prompt action by HMG.

And not only had the escape plot been foiled but so too had an assassination attempt.

Wood had been briefed on this development by Warren-Chase who had filled the gaps in the rather sketchy report the Foreign Secretary had received during his brief stopover in Cyprus. And, incredible though it appeared, the assassination had been thwarted literally at the last second due to the critical timing of the cable sent by Wood warning Mabato about the rescue bid. There was speculation too that both plots had been related. Wisely, Wood ventured no opinion.

The raid on Maboru had, by all accounts, been a debacle. Holt had been spirited away from the prison before the rescue team struck and a trap had been laid.

According to the Lugamban security forces, one of the raiders had been killed in the prison. The remainder had been pursued through the bush and cornered in the mission at Masambabule.

Facts surrounding the death of the Catholic priest and the nuns were cast in shadow. Mabato insisted they had been murdered by the fleeing mercenaries and no one seemed able or inclined to contradict him.

Except Warren-Chase, who did have other ideas and voiced them to Wood.

Wood was horrified. 'You're telling me that Mabato had them killed! In God's name, why?'

'I would have thought that was obvious,' Warren-Chase had replied testily. 'They sheltered the rescue team, provided them with a haven. The raiders used the airstrip at the mission don't forget. It's my guess that there weren't fifteen or twenty men as Mabato would have us believe but more likely half a dozen at the most. But they tore Mabato's men apart and Mabato wouldn't stand for that. Notwithstanding the fact that they didn't succeed in getting Holt out of the country, Mabato would want blood. He'd be satisfied with anybody's.'

'Dear God! He was an old man!'

'In Mabato's eyes he was a conspirator.'

'And the nuns his accomplices I suppose?'

Warren-Chase had looked directly at David Wood, his eyes as sharp as flints. 'I'd say they were scapegoats. Wouldn't you?'

The Mercedes slid towards the square. Wood looked back at the conversation with sickening despair. Mabato may well have passed sentence on Michael Devlin and the others but the responsibility for their deaths rested elsewhere.

Wood felt tainted.

The British Foreign Secretary considered Burov. The Russian seemed particularly close to Mabato, even to the extent of occupying the President's right hand at the banquet in the Command Post the previous evening. They had been introduced to each other – Burov by name only, no rank or title – and the event had not been especially illuminating. Wood made himself a promise to check the man's credentials with George Dalkeith as soon as he returned to London.

Everyone and his uncle knew that Mabato had Soviet advisors. Burov couldn't be anything else but it wouldn't hurt to delve a bit deeper. In any event, Mabato evidently valued the man's judgement. Burov would certainly require watching. Then it transpired that the stout Russian would be joining the British Foreign Secretary and President Nai on the saluting dais. Strange bed-fellows indeed.

Leonid Vakov walked past the line of troops and entered the compound. The six T-54s were parked side by side, muzzles aligned like some awesome firing squad. The crews stood alongside their vehicles. The T-54s carried four-man crews consisting of commander, driver, gunner and loader. Vakov and his technicians had drilled the Africans mercilessly in the operation of the tanks but Vakov wasn't overly impressed with the rate of progress. At least Mabato's soldiers knew how to start, stop and steer the thirty six ton monsters. Who knows? Within a month they might even be able to hit what they were aiming at. Until such time, however, each crew would be composed of three Lugamban troopers from Mabato's Suicide Battalion and one Soviet technician to act as tank commander.

Vakov reviewed his men and their charges with a jaundiced eye though the teams looked alert and the tanks had been cleaned, their turrets already displaying the Corps insignia: the head of a jackal.

The rest of the troops in the parade were beginning to fall into order, running into file under the barked instructions of their NCOs. The band was in position at the head of the column. Vakov and his men would be moving out shortly.

Undoubtedly the Soviet battle tanks were to be Mabato's pièce de résistance for they would lead the British supplied Scorpions. Vakov had been briefed on the significance of this by Burov. The invitation to attend the opening ceremony made to David Wood had not been Mabato's idea. It had been Burov's. The Russian had jumped at the chance to show the British Foreign Secretary just where Mabato's loyalties lay. After all, the incarceration of David Holt and the resulting furore had been a direct result of the lack of British Governmental consideration. To wit: failure to provide spares for military equipment sold by Britain to Lugamba. It would be a blatant act of confrontation and Burov intended to savour the moment to the full.

The outriders, Mabato's motorcycle escort, appeared on the horizon to warn of the arrival of the cavalcade. The soldiers around the square shuffled to attention and Mabato's agents moved through the throng like panthers.

Mabato was in the lead car. As it drew into the kerb an aide vacated the front passenger seat and opened the rear door. Mabato didn't move until his bodyguards were in place. There were four of them; Nubians in olive green safari jackets. Their shifting eyes scanned the crowd as the President alighted.

President Solomon Mabato looked magnificent. His vast bulk was encased in the dress uniform of a Field Marshal, complete with paratrooper wings and campaign medals, including a self-awarded DSO and VC. Only one thing marred the overall effect. His uniform was sky blue. Hermann Goering blue to be precise. He even had an embossed baton. His left arm was no longer in a sling.

Mabato was smiling brightly, enjoying the effect his arrival had on the crowd. As he moved away from the Mercedes his bodyguards shifted to protect his flanks and rear. Mabato paused to greet his guests in the other cars. Both Wood and Burov appeared taken aback at the gaudy apparition that faced them. President Nai, on the other hand, seemed unfazed and smiled benignly. Wood adjusted his tie and fell into step with the Kenyan Head of State. Together with Burov they trailed Mabato and his cohorts. Among them was the gaunt figure of Hassan Boma who, since the death of Farouk Juma, had been placed in charge of the Department of State Security. Boma was also the head of SASU. After Mabato he was now the most feared man in Lugamba. Looking at him, Wood felt a cold shiver run down his spine.

Mabato and his guests of honour broke through the cordon of troops and strolled towards the saluting dais. The gathering of OAU delegates broke into applause and Mabato acknowledged the ovation with a happy wave of his baton.

They mounted the dais to cheers from the crowd. To Wood it seemed as though the greeting was being orchestrated, as though the people were being prompted by unseen agents. Many faces looked drawn and nervous. The uncomfortable feeling had not left him by the time he had taken his seat on the saluting base. He was seated to one side and a little behind Mabato and Hassan Boma. President Nai sat beside him. Burov was again on Mabato's right. The Liberator's bodyguards stood at the back of the dais like black androids.

★ ★ ★

342

Vakov's tanks and the British Scorpions were about to join the parade. The tank crews were on board and awaiting his command. The Scorpion crews were about to follow suit. Vakov waved his arm and with an earth crumbling roar the big diesel engines exploded into life, pumping dense clouds of exhaust into the air.

Vakov walked quickly to the lead tank and climbed aboard. He glanced back along the line and took his place in the turret, only his upper torso visible. He rapped instructions to his Lugamban driver and braced himself against the side of the hatch as the ungainly machine lurched into motion. His driver, peering through the observation slit, rammed the tank into gear and steered them out of the compound. As the remaining T–54s began to swing ponderously into line behind Vakov the Scorpion crews moved to their places.

'Corporal!'

The officer was standing next to a white Peugeot parked unobtrusively alongside the last Scorpion in the line. It carried the unmistakable taint of a SASU vehicle. The corporal and his driver paused. The other teams were boarding their tanks. The soldier blinked nervously.

The officer glared at him. 'Are you deaf? I want you both. Move!'

They approached the car. The officer was holding the front and rear passenger doors open. When they reached the Peugeot they were sheltered in the lee of the Scorpion, hidden from view. The corporal automatically raised his hand in a salute. The tall officer returned the gesture stiffly, as though in pain, features shaded by the peak of his forage cap. He indicated the interior of the Peugeot.

'Take a look, Corporal. I want an explanation.'

The soldier frowned. 'Sir?' He hadn't a clue what his

superior was driving at. He glanced sideways at his crewman, mystified, and moved to the rear door.

An eruption of sound announced that the other crews had started their engines and masked the exclamation of surprise as the corporal peered into the car. He was aware of something moving towards him very fast, a glint of steel rising and flashing into his startled view. An iron band around his throat, cutting off his air supply, pulled him into the back of the car and the shock and the pain welled through his belly as the blade rammed under his ribcage. The knife twisted and his body heaved. The hand that held his neck was squeezing like a vice, crushing his larynx. His eyes rolled in their sockets, showing white muscle.

The second crewman had time only to see his companion slide from view before Sekka drew the silenced Browning from behind his back and shot the trooper in the heart. The man fell backwards against the Peugeot. Like lightning Sekka pulled the corpse upright and thrust it down across the front seats.

Thomas Keel wiped the blade of the knife on the corporal's tunic and pulled the dead man's forage cap low over his own forehead. His face was blackened with camouflage cream. Even from a short distance he was as dark as Sekka.

'Go, Joseph!' Keel tugged two rugs from the window shelf and threw them over the bodies. Grabbing his pack, he closed the car doors and followed Sekka. They climbed into the Scorpion.

It was getting hotter under the canopy. Wood could feel the sweat trickling under his arms and down the small of his back. He looked enviously at the cane fan the Kenyan President was wafting in front of his face. Even Burov didn't seem affected by the humidity. The Russian was lounging comfortably in his seat, clad in a cream suit and a wide brimmed fedora, enjoying the spectacle.

Mabato was also enjoying himself. As the band swirled past in their tartan, to the gurgling wail of the pipes, the President stood at the front of the rostrum to take the salute. His huge body seemed to fill the podium.

The Liberator's battalions followed the swaying musicians, dressed in olive green fatigues and soft jungle hats. They clomped by the saluting dais, backs ramrod straight, arms swinging as they turned eyes right towards Mabato. The crowds were applauding automatically as though they were part of the drill.

The BTR reconnaissance and troop carriers ground over the tarmac in the wake of the infantry, rattling and cranking past the delegates' grandstand like lethargic armadillos. They were followed by a phalanx of Ferret Scout Cars and Alvis Saracens. Then there was a buzz of interest as the T–54s came into view, rolling in single file.

Wood's face betrayed no emotion as he watched the Soviet armour trundle past. He caught Burov's eye and was infuriated to see the Russian smile and incline his head. He looked back at the parade. On the trail of the T–54s, the Scorpions approached.

Joseph Sekka estimated they were about two hundred yards from the saluting base. Ahead of them the other Scorpions ranged in line and beyond them he could see the line of Soviet battle tanks. The Scorpions were ten yards apart and moving a little under ten miles an hour. Sekka, from his vantage point in the turret, could see the distinctive figure of Mabato, a corpulent blue land-mark under the red awning.

One hundred yards and closing. Sekka glanced behind

him. In formation were light half tracks towing field guns. No immediate threat.

Fifty yards. Wordlessly, Sekka dropped into the hull of the tank and closed the hatch.

Burov squinted at David Wood from the shade of his fedora. The British minister's face was without expression as he watched the tanks roll by but Burov guessed at concealed anger. Then the Russian's attention was diverted.

The Scorpion was level with the saluting base when Keel hauled the tank around to face the target. The manoeuvre was swift and totally unexpected. Mabato's jaw dropped open in astonishment, his brain barely registering the danger as the Scorpion pivoted.

Then he realized.

Too late.

Keel screamed the order and Sekka fired. The vehicle recoiled and a tongue of flame belched from the muzzle. Sekka had used an HE round, a canister which operated like a shotgun cartridge for use against infantry at close quarters. At a range of barely fifty feet, the effect was devastating.

Wood had risen instinctively from his seat as he saw the Scorpion begin to traverse. President Nai, slow to react but sensing something untoward, stopped his fan in mid wave. Burov seemed to move in slow motion. He had glimpsed Sekka's head and shoulders disappearing into the Scorpion's hull and when the tank started to slew around, a hint of what was about to happen flashed into his brain like some dreadful hallucination.

He managed to bawl: 'EXCELLENCY . . . !' but his words of warning were lost in the mind numbing explosion as the saluting base blew apart and Mabato disintegrated into crimson fragments. The blast shattered

Burov's eardrums and he was lifted over the back of the dais in a whirling vortex of pain. Miraculously, his body retained life.

Wood felt himself falling into a chasm, dimly aware of the broken body of President Nai being tossed backwards by the force of the explosion, right leg severed at the knee, a long jagged splinter sticking out of his chest like an arrow. Hassan Boma's headless trunk cartwheeled like a ghastly decapitated puppet, blood cascading.

Wood's ears were ringing. He was trying to raise himself when Sekka pumped a second shell into the podium. Wood's corpse tumbled into the air like a grotesque rag doll, upper torso torn asunder by screaming chunks of shrapnel. Mabato's bodyguards were carved into gruel, their shrieks merging with the dying echo of the Scorpion's gun.

The crowd broke into a pulsating wave of panic as the first shock wave rippled across the square. Keel knew they were into reaction time by now. The shock of the assault would be fading and the troops would counter attack. He released the smoke canisters from the dischargers on the Scorpion's turret. As the tank jolted forward the first fusillade rattled against the hull.

Vakov heard the explosion and the screams and swung around. Over the line of tanks he saw the rain of debris and the commotion among the spectators. Delegates in the stand were hurling themselves flat, scrambling for cover with ungainly haste. The second detonation jerked Vakov into action. Somewhere in the chaos behind him was Gregori Burov. What the hell was going on?

'Reverse, you idiot! Reverse!' Vakov thundered orders at the top of his voice. He could see the smoke, ejaculated from the Scorpion's turret, begin to drift and swirl about the vehicle and the troopers that had cordoned the main square were running around like ants. He could hear the rattle of small arms fire. The other Scorpions were stalled in a line between his own group of tanks and the matchwood remains of the saluting base.

The T–54 began to reverse with irritating slowness. The turret rotated one hundred and eighty degrees. Vakov watched as the renegade Scorpion jerked into motion.

Keel accelerated and the Scorpion rolled forward, increasing speed. He had to get them out of the square and away from the bottleneck. The smoke was helping. Like a London pea souper, it was curling and billowing in and out of the armoured column in grey tendrils. When the first shell had been fired, the crowd behind the saluting base had broken apart like a bursting bubble. Keel headed for the nearest gap and the route that would take them away from the carnage.

Their main worry was the proximity of the other armoured vehicles. One shot well placed from one of the Soviet battle tanks or the British Scorpions would incapacitate them in a second. They would have to make a run for it. At a pinch the Scorpion could achieve nearly ninety kilometres an hour.

By the time Vakov's driver had the T–54 turned about the Scorpion and half the line of armour had disappeared beyond the smoke screen. Vakov could still hear shooting. It rose above the sound of the stampeding crowds. He slammed his fist against the metal rim of the turret in exasperation. Composing himself, he spoke crisply into his radio mike.

'All unit commanders form up on me! Battle stations! On my command, move out!' The T–54 began to grind its way back down the line towards the point where the Scorpion had unleashed its attack. The remaining Scorpions were attempting to move out of the way but the inexperience of their crews was only too evident. There was little coordination in their efforts.

Sekka had turned his attention to operating the Scorpion's 7.62mm machine gun. He was firing at any troopers that broke from the curtain of smoke. The Scorpion was churning past the remains of the saluting dais. A soldier materialized before them, dropped to one knee and took aim with his AK–47. Sekka squeezed the trigger and the crouching figure was sliced in half by the withering hail. Keel took the Scorpion over the body, the tank slowing not a bit as it smashed into the riddled corpse. They had reached the edge of the square. Bouncing into the clear road, the Scorpion picked up speed.

Vakov's tank burned its way over the tarmac. It had reached the dais and already the smoke was clearing. Vakov could see the back of the fleeing Scorpion but he couldn't order his gunner to open fire as the angle was too acute. The corner of the delegates' rostrum was obstructing his field of fire and there were too many people milling in his sights. He would have to pursue.

Within the debris, hidden by the smoke and mangled platform and chairs, a bruised and bloody figure was stirring. A hand, raw and bleeding, reached out and clawed painfully for support. A battered apparition rose unsteadily to its feet.

Gregori Burov swayed precariously and tried to focus through the dusty haze. His once cream suit was in tatters, torn and stained with the gory remains of those who had died with Mabato. His face was a mask of flayed skin, blood and grime. Crimson trickles ran from both ears. He couldn't hear the noise around him but his head was ringing like a peal of bells. He couldn't find his feet. He was off balance, reeling like a drunk. He opened his mouth but no sound came save a rasping croak. He tripped over a half buried obstacle and dropped to his knees. He was caught in this bizarre genuflection when Vakov's battle tank broke out of the smoke screen like a tug from a fog bank. Burov looked up in time to see the colossus bearing down on him and he raised his hands and tried to scramble out of the way, his attempt to scream dying in his throat as the heavy track crushed against his quivering body. His hands pushed ineffectually against the terrible weight that bore down with such force on his chest. His ribs cracked and popped as he disappeared beneath the tank. The tracks ground over his remains as Vakov turned in pursuit of his prey. The tank commander didn't even see Burov die. By the time the T–54 had travelled its own length, Burov was no more than a bloody smear on the concrete.

The troops were firing rapidly now, the bullets ricocheting loudly off the body of the Scorpion. They angled left and thundered over the tarmac. Sekka's vision was limited. He opened the hatch and eased his head out of the turret. He was holding his machine pistol and was temporarily out of sight of their pursuers. Then the first jeep slid into sight, tyres screeching as the driver spun the wheel and put his foot down.

As the accelerating jeep broke from cover, Sekka opened up with the machine pistol. The windscreen of the jeep blew apart, ripping into the faces of the soldiers like a rain of fléchettes. The driver shrieked in agony and threw up his hands to protect his face. The jeep veered out of control, plunged over the kerb and barrelled across the pavement. It hit the plate glass window like an express train. The shop front collapsed, showering the occupants of the jeep with lethal shards as it plummeted into the building where it crashed with bone jarring finality against the rear wall of the store.

The Scorpion was moving fast again. Keel knew that time was running out – they had been incredibly lucky to have made it this far – and they were still two blocks from the pickup point.

Vakov's tank turned the corner in time for the Russian to follow the progress of the Scorpion as it raced up the street. He rapped orders to his gunner. 'Traverse left!'

In the cramped turret, the gunner was almost sitting in Vakov's lap. The movement was jerky and Vakov gritted his teeth in frustration at the lack of expertise. The muzzle swung and Vakov relayed directions to his gunner again. He yelled the order to fire. The tank recoiled and the stench of cordite filled the hull.

Vakov knew they had fired too soon. The procedure had been hurried and unprofessional and it would take time to reload for the gun had to be fully elevated to give the loader room to extract the spent casing and insert a new shell and then the gun had to be resighted. He was astounded, therefore, to see the shell burst beneath the rear tracks of the Scorpion, the explosion lifting the back of the tank off the ground and punching it around with an ear rending scrape of metal. The left track was a mess, the rear wheels having been blown away. The back end of the hull was a concertina of buckled armour plate.

Vakov thumped the T–54's turret with glee. 'Again! Again! Fire, you dolts! Destroy them!'

Sekka felt the ground erupt beneath the tracks and he was all but thrown out of the tank. He could see the Soviet tank commander a hundred yards away, bellowing into his headset. They were lining up for another shot. He was aware that Keel was extricating himself from the front driving seat, hurrying to vacate the crippled vehicle. Sekka looked back. Already soldiers were running into the street from behind the shelter of the T–54. Bullets were hitting the sides and rear of the Scorpion and the wall of the building a yard or so from their position. He clambered awkwardly from the turret, keeping the bulk of the Scorpion between his body and the advancing troops.

Somewhere inside the tank Keel had forsaken cap and goggles. As his head and shoulders emerged, Sekka unleashed a blistering hail of covering fire from his machine pistol. He took two grenades from his waist pack, primed them and lobbed them at the soldiers. The front men ran into the explosions, their bodies lifting in a cascade of debris and flame. As the dust cleared, Sekka and Keel staggered away from the Scorpion. A few feet away a narrow alley ran between two high buildings. They reached the sheltering walls as Vakov's second shot slammed into the Scorpion and detonated the fuel tank. The Scorpion disappeared in a vivid balloon of flame. Arcs of fire curved into the air as the fountains of petrol ignited. Savage lumps of shrapnel sliced outwards, hammering into the surrounding walls, scattering mortar like hail stones.

The mercenaries were pitched onto their knees by the shock wave. Regaining their feet in a second, they sprinted down the alley. Behind them Vakov's tank trundled forward slowly and Mabato's troops began their pursuit. Vakov began to relay orders to his other mobile commanders. Their quarry was now on foot and with his squads spread out he could begin to tighten the noose. Vakov's stomach spasmed with anticipation for he had experienced a second of disbelief when the two men had crawled from the wreckage of the Scorpion. That moment of sheer incredulity when, through the drifting smoke from the grenade explosions, he had seen Keel's grey hair and realized that, despite the dark makeup, one of the assassins had undoubtedly been a white man, possibly a European.

That knowledge and the implications it represented made it imperative that the two fugitives were captured with the utmost haste. With a quickening pulse, Leonid Vakov began to close the net.

Keel and Sekka broke from the far end of the alley, breathing hard. Sekka glanced around. The troops were entering the passage now, dim shapes zig-zagging from cover to cover. The first soldier was fifty yards away and running fast. Sekka fired from the hip. The soldier spun, his shoulder blown away by the heavy slugs. Before the tumbling body hit the ground Sekka tossed another grenade. In the confined recess the effect was total. Without waiting to see the result Sekka turned and ran after Keel. They hadn't made ten yards before the first of Vakov's mobile units turned the street corner ahead of them.

Keel wheeled left, his body jinking and weaving as he tried to present a difficult target. Sekka was hard on his heels as they ducked around the side of the nearest building.

They pulled up short. There were more troops cutting off their line of retreat. Another Scorpion and a squad of soldiers were moving towards them. Vakov's men had moved quickly. His trap was closing rapidly.

'Shit!' Keel looked for an opening, a way out. At the side of the building a wrought iron fire escape led upwards. It was the only chance they were going to get.

'Go! Go!' Keel yelled. He pushed Sekka ahead of him and together they pounded up the steps. At the first level they crouched and fired at the soldiers running towards them. They were moving again as fire was returned. Bullets ricocheted off the metal stanchions and whined away.

The building was an empty office block, ten storeys high. At the top of the fire escape a small square platform led onto a wide flat roof, an asphalt plateau broken only by a squat blockhouse that probably housed the elevator mechanism or ventilation units. Even as they ran out the first troops were climbing the fire escape below them, their boots ringing on the stairs.

They sprinted towards the blockhouse. Gaining its shelter they waited. The leading soldier jumped onto the roof. Keel took him out with one sharp burst. The trooper dropped his weapon and fell back over the edge of the building as though pulled by an invisible string. His companions seemed in no hurry to share his fate and remained out of sight below the rim of the parapet.

Keel glanced grimly at Sekka. 'How much ammunition are you holding, Joseph?'

'Three mags for the H and K, hand gun and one grenade.'

Keel sighed. His body sagged as he crouched and peered round the wall. There was still no movement from the troops on the fire escape. They seemed to be waiting for something.

'Reckon this could well be the end of the line, Joseph.'

'Something tells me you could just be right,' Sekka replied. 'What have you got?'

'Hand gun and two magazines.'

'Wonderful.'

Keel said calmly: 'You know I didn't think we'd make it, not in a month full of Sundays.' He smiled, half to himself. 'Still, we took that fat bastard with us. That's some consolation.'

'Not for Michael Devlin and the rest though,' Sekka said. He looked beyond the edge of the roof, out over the city. The sun was high and a haze hung over the roof tops. The asphalt surface was almost too hot to touch with the bare hand. At the moment the two mercenaries were in shadow but as the day lengthened the sun would shift to the other side of the blockhouse. But by then they would probably be dead.

It could only be a matter of moments before Mabato's men rushed them. Sheer weight of numbers would tell in the end but they would take some of the soldiers with them. With pleasure.

Attack.

A figure sprang into view and died as Sekka used his machine pistol. The body crumpled and lay where it had fallen, a pool of blood widening across the roof.

'They're going to use grenades,' Keel advised. 'I can sense it. Then they'll hit us in a group. Better get ready, old son.'

But Sekka wasn't listening to him. He was hearing something else. He spoke one word: 'Chopper!'

The Bell Jet Ranger was skimming over the city, a yellow and black dragonfly approaching fast, its propeller arc a spinning, gleaming disc as the sun bounced off the blades, the WHUP WHUP WHUP of the rotors heralding its arrival. It was weaving towards their position, coming in low, barely clearing the tops of the buildings. Keel jumped to his feet. Still no movement from the troops. Christ! They must be ready to hit them by now! Surely to God! He stared at the helicopter. The rear doors had been removed for easy access and exit. Gunship rigged.

He yelled and waved his arm, heart pounding now. 'Come on! Come on!'

Vakov had left the T–54 and was running up the fire escape, the thrill of the chase coursing through his veins like a drug. He hadn't felt this elated since the thrust against Masud's guerilla stronghold in the foothills north of Kabul.

By this time all mobile units had converged on the

building and soldiers were beginning to work their way up to the roof floor by floor. There was nowhere the fugitives could hide. An excited NCO informed Vakov that the assassins were cornered. Troops were massing on the last flight of the fire escape prior to launching an assault on the roof. Above the rim, however, the broad stretch of asphalt in front of the blockhouse was an open killing ground. Two men had gone over the top and died. No one had a desire to be the third.

But Vakov's blood was up and he was growing impatient with the NCO's reluctance to send his men in. They'd be up there all day. Unless . . .

Vakov decided to take matters into his own hands. He nudged the platoon commander who was only too willing to defer responsibility. A minute later Vakov was kneeling below the parapet. Beside him half a dozen heavily armed troopers awaited instructions. On his command they would lob in grenades and in the ensuing blitz they would attack the blockhouse. Vakov glanced at expectant faces and raised his hand as a signal.

Then he heard the approaching clatter of the rotor blades. For a brief second he couldn't identify the sound. Then it dawned on him just what might be happening up there. With a cry of warning he swept his hand down.

Clem Wallace could see the two mercenaries through his wind shield. They were sheltering behind a small bunker type construction. He could also make out the body of the dead trooper and from his side window, in the streets below, tanks, jeeps and armoured cars were milling like bees around a honey pot.

'Jesus!' he breathed. He moved the yoke and the helicopter dropped fifty feet. Wallace was in a dilemma. There was nowhere he could put the chopper down on the roof except close to the corpse and that would place him between the mercenaries and their grim pursuers. An insane proposition. Wallace studied the movements of the soldiers below and considered the possibilities.

The helicopter was three hundred feet away and whipping down like an angry hornet. Keel watched it fly in while Sekka guarded the roof. Their predicament was obvious. Wallace couldn't land. The options were limited and they hadn't any time left. The pilot hauled on the yoke and the aircraft pulled up sharply and tracked sideways towards the parapet where it hovered noisily, port skid almost touching the edge of the roof on the opposite side of the building to the fire escape and Vakov's assault team. Clem Wallace tore his headphones off and bellowed through the open side at Keel and his companion. 'Come on, Major! Move your friggin' arse!'

But they were already running, ducking low into the down draught from the rotors and sprinting towards the edge of the roof. They were five yards out from the cover of the blockhouse when the first grenades rolled across the asphalt and the lead troopers rose into sight and attacked.

The mercenaries were shielded by the blockhouse. Even so the shock waves buffeted them as Sekka threw himself into the helicopter.

The bullet hit Keel in the thigh as he leapt for the Jet Ranger. Wallace was already anticipating his arrival and the chopper was beginning to lift and turn away as the mercenary launched himself forward. As the slug struck him and his leg gave way Keel knew he had mistimed it. His hand clawed at the sill of the door and his fingers raked along the fuselage. Sekka stared in horror as Keel's body dropped from view. But the mercenary wasn't finished. With catlike reflexes his hand shot out and

357

hooked around the skid. The soldiers had reached the blockhouse. As Keel's weight was transferred the helicopter yawed violently. With a curse Wallace counteracted the motion.

Sekka was lying across the rear seats. He extended his machine pistol through the open doorway and raked the blockhouse. From the corner of his eye he saw Keel's right arm curl around the skid and he screamed at Wallace: 'NOW! NOW! For God's sake!' He fired at the running figures on the roof, closing his mind to the body hanging beneath the aircraft. He felt for his pack. His hand closed on his last grenade and as Wallace took them up in a fast corkscrew, turning the machine away from the rim, Keel swaying below like a raggedy doll, he hurled it out of the door.

Vakov was up with the soldiers, pounding through the smoke and chaos, dodging the jagged craters in the asphalt. He could see the helicopter now and felt the wash from the blades and the vibrations through the soles of his feet. Someone was firing at them and the soldiers were yelling loudly and returning shots. At the edge of his field of vision something small and round curved towards him at head height. Then an unseen hand plucked him into the air and he was aware of incredible pain and there was only a bloody stump where his left leg should have been and he was soaring high like a bird in graceful flight, up and over the edge of the building.

The port windshield starred suddenly as a bullet struck. Wallace swore loudly. More slugs were hitting the fuselage and it would only need one shot to put the rotors out of action and send the helicopter spiralling into the streets below. Sekka was still firing, lips curled in a savage grin as he emptied the clip. The machine pistol bucked and chattered in his hands, spitting death. He couldn't see Keel now and was unable to tell if the mercenary was hanging on or had relinquished his desperate hold.

Then they were swooping behind another building and out of the angle of fire. Beneath them Mabato's men were scrambling like rats in an alley. Small arms fire rattled faintly but it was ineffective and the tanks and armoured cars couldn't traverse and raise their guns fast enough.

They were clear.

Keel knew he couldn't hang on much longer. His grip on the strut was slipping and his leg was growing numb. He had also been hit again, on his right side, low under the ribs. He had no idea how badly he was hurt. He had felt the bullet thump into his leg with all the force of a mule kick but he had been unaware of the second wound until he had looked down and seen the blood on his jacket. He sensed a movement above him in the doorway of the chopper. Sekka was there, yelling at him. He couldn't hear the words above the beat of the blades but he presumed that Sekka was urging him to hang on. Stupid, but he didn't think he could.

He realized that Sekka wanted him to reach up. Joseph was leaning out of the door, arm outstretched, beseeching, mouth framing the instruction. Keel had dropped his automatic when he had been hit. He now had both arms wrapped around the skid. He tightened his hold on the metal strut with his right hand and felt immediately the warm slow trickle of blood on his stomach. His shoulder felt as though it was being twisted from its socket as he released his left hand from the skid. The noise from the rotors was becoming hypnotic. A heavy, deadening throb that jarred every nerve as he fought to remain conscious.

Sekka could see that Keel was in real trouble, with eyes almost closed and teeth gritted. He needed assistance fast. Sekka gripped the edge of the doorway and eased himself out of the cabin until his boots rested on the skid an inch from Keel's hand. Wallace was battling to keep the chopper on an even trim. They were still flying over the city but ahead of them were the suburbs and the first traces of bush and open savannah.

Keel felt his hand touched then his wrist was held in a vice. He curled his fingers around Sekka's arm and hung for a brief moment like a trapeze artist. He steeled himself for the final effort and released his hold on the skid. His body grazed the strut as Sekka dragged him up and he was able to grab the sill of the doorway with his free hand. Sekka altered his leverage and pushed Keel into the cabin. The mercenary's body folded across the seats as Sekka pulled himself back into the aircraft. A sharp pain in his shoulder told him that his own wound had opened up but he ignored the distraction as he examined Keel.

'Thomas?' Sekka began to undo Keel's jacket. He was working fast and perspiration was pouring down his face following his exertions a few hectic moments before.

Keel grunted as Sekka pulled the material away from the wound. 'Will I live?'

'You'd better,' Sekka replied. 'After all I've just been through to get you in here.' His probing fingers moved gently around to Keel's back and he gave a low sigh of relief when he felt the edges of the ragged exit wound. 'Straight through, Thomas. May have nicked a rib though. You've lost blood.'

He found the chopper's first aid kit and applied dressings to staunch the bleeding before turning his attention to Keel's leg. He shook his head in wonderment. 'You have the luck of the Irish, my friend. Two holes again. The bullet has transitted and how it missed the femoral I'll never know. I can't tell how bad it is. Muscle damage at the very least. All I can do is clean it up for now.'

Keel nodded acceptance. 'Best get a move on then.' He winced as the chopper bounced on a thermal. The effort of raising their voices above the noise of the engine was intense.

Sekka strapped gauze pads to Keel's thigh with a length of bandage. He handed over two tablets. 'Penicillin. Take them.'

'Sorry I was late, Major!' Clem Wallace yelled above the clatter of the rotors. He twisted in his seat. 'How bad is it?'

'No sweat,' Sekka found the rear head sets. 'How far to go?'

Wallace looked out over the terrain. The land was rising into a spread of low hills, purple crested. They were flying fast, no more than two hundred feet above the ground. 'We'll be over the rendezvous point in fifteen minutes.'

'What about Mabato's fighters? His MiG squadron can still catch us.'

'Mabato's air force couldn't scramble this side of Christmas,' Wallace said emphatically. 'They're a bunch of fucking imbeciles!'

'Well, that solves that problem,' Keel muttered.

Wallace went on: 'I guessed you wouldn't make the pickup point. I was monitoring the ground units on the radio so I knew they had hit the Scorpion. I thought I'd track in and see if I could pick you up on the run. I didn't think I'd be that lucky, Major. I could hear they had you holed up somewhere, the way they were zeroing in. Christ! There was so much bloody radio traffic it was like the commentary on the Melbourne Cup!'

He grinned suddenly. 'I didn't believe it when I got the brief from Kemba's agent. Thomas Keel, as I live and breathe! I thought he must have got it wrong. I never figured you two for an assassination team.'

Sekka had removed his own tunic. He was examining

361

the wound in his shoulder. It had stopped weeping but the flesh felt tight and tender. 'This was payment of a debt,' he said.

'To Kemba?' Wallace looked puzzled.

Sekka held a dressing to his skin and eased back in the seat. 'No.' He didn't elaborate.

Wallace raised an eyebrow. The Jet Ranger was hugging the wooded contours of a narrow valley. The Australian exclaimed suddenly: 'Jesus! You guys hit the bloody prison! You were the mad buggers who tried to snatch Holt! Streuth!' He shook his head and chuckled gleefully. 'Y'know, Major, I haven't felt this high since I was in Nam, flying gunships and zapping Charlie. I used to think I had come a long way since those days, airlifting you Special Forces squads out of Bien Hoa. Remember, Major?'

'I remember, Clem,' Keel said. He smiled wearily and eased his injured leg into a more comfortable position. Sekka was staring down at the ground that was flashing below them like a brown and green patchwork quilt. There was an occasional glint of muddy pewter as they swept low over meandering creeks.

'How long have you been Kemba's man?' Sekka asked.

'Whoa, I'm strictly freelance,' retorted Wallace. 'Oh, I've passed information to his agents once in a while.' The pilot shrugged. 'It was bloody well inevitable that Kemba had Mabato's card marked. I reckoned that the Liberator's days were numbered. If Kemba ever was to stage a comeback you could bet your bottom dollar that anyone who grafted for Mabato would be in the little black book. I just took out some insurance. Lucky for you I did.'

'We're obliged, Clem,' Keel said.

'Please, Major.' Wallace sounded quite offended. 'Don't embarrass me by presuming that I'm doing this for anything other than the lure of the greenback.' He smiled. 'Well, okay, maybe it is for old times' sake. Now, grab your gear. We're going down. Looks like our taxi's waiting.'

The strip wasn't much more than a sun scorched stretch of beaten earth a mile long by perhaps one hundred yards wide, carved out of the bush like a giant scar. An aircraft was parked at the edge of the treeline and almost hidden; a DC–3 in camouflage markings. As Wallace touched down a figure left the Dak and ran across to the helicopter. Kate Lassiter.

'Dammit, Keel!' Kate cried. 'I was worried sick! Can't you ever be on time?'

Then she saw the blood and bandages. 'Oh, God!'

Wallace had switched off. The rotors flicked around slowly and stopped. The swirls of dust abated.

'He's okay, Kate. He'll make it.' Sekka reassured her as Wallace ran to help him lift Keel out of the helicopter. The grey haired mercenary grimaced suddenly as his thigh brushed the side of the machine. Pain was etched into his face and trickles of perspiration traced pale patterns in the dark makeup that still partially concealed his normally tanned features.

'Hello, Lassiter,' Keel said. 'As you can see, we had a spot of bother.' He regarded her calmly.

His gaze seemed to steady her. Wordlessly she took his hand and lifted it gently to her cheek. She felt her fingers gripped in acknowledgement. A smile flickered at the corner of his mouth. He turned to Wallace.

'Okay, Clem. You know what to do. Joseph, make sure all our stuff is out of the chopper. Quick as you can. We don't know how much time we have. Get to it.'

As he spoke the twin engines of the Dakota clattered into life and the aircraft rolled out from the trees and trundled towards the end of the narrow strip. By the time the DC–3 had lined up for take-off Sekka had retrieved what remained of their weapons. With Lassiter's help he assisted Keel across the clearing.

Wallace watched them go, Keel hobbling, before jumping into the cabin of the Jet Ranger, rummaging and emerging with a can of kerosene. Opening the nozzle he doused the inside of the chopper with the fuel, splashing it liberally over the seats and instruments. He climbed out and sloshed more kerosene over the fuselage. Finally he backed away from the machine with the upturned can in his hands until a thin river of fuel ran across the ground. When the can was empty he hurled it into the cabin of the chopper.

He stood for a second, staring sadly at the Jet Ranger. A look of affection flitted across his face before he gave a resigned shrug. 'This,' he muttered to himself, 'is going to break my heart.'

He bent down and took the Zippo lighter from his pocket. One flick and the fuse was alight. The flame danced and raced along the kerosene trail towards the chopper. Wallace turned away and began to run.

The fire spread over the helicopter like a pestilence, enveloping the bright fuselage with bewildering speed. Wallace was still sprinting for the Dak as the tanks blew up with an impressive boom and the Jet Ranger disappeared under a billow of flame and a mushroom of black smoke.

The others had already reached the Dakota and were on board. The undercarriage jolted and the Dak began to move. The engines increased their pitch as Wallace ran up and hauled himself through the door. He was sweating and panting hard.

'Nice of you bastards to hang around,' he gasped as Sekka closed and secured the door behind him. 'Thought I might have to catch the bloody bus!' He added as an afterthought: 'Or walk home!'

The bay of the Dak had been stripped long ago to accommodate the maximum amount of freight. It was empty apart from its human cargo. Keel sat on the floor, his back propped against the port bulkhead. He looked very tired. Kate Lassiter crouched over him, her face tense and watchful.

'Don't you dare tell me it only hurts when you laugh, Thomas Keel,' Kate muttered severely. 'If you do I'll brain you!' She examined his dressings as she spoke.

'It hurts when I do anything, love,' Keel said. His eyes were half closed.

The Dakota picked up speed as it bounced along the airstrip. The engines were roaring and the air frame seemed on the verge of popping its rivets. Sekka sat down and put his arm around the wounded mercenary's shoulders, bracing them both against the switchback ride as the old aircraft battled to take off. Lassiter supported Keel's other side. Across the bay Clem Wallace gritted his teeth.

'Lift her up, Lafitte! Lift her up!' Kate clenched her fists in taut anticipation, willing the Dakota to rise.

Then, with a lurch, they were airborne and banking. Sekka let out a whoop of relief.

Wallace swore under his breath. 'About bloody time!'

On the strip beneath the retracting wheels the remains of the Jet Ranger continued to burn. Fifteen minutes later they were flying at six thousand feet and heading east on auto pilot.

The curtain concealing the flight deck slid aside and a figure stepped into the bay. He was a lean and tanned man, dressed in a grubby brown leather windcheater, faded Levis and a baseball cap. He sank to his haunches by the weary group and remarked casually: 'I see you've been in the wars again, Major.'

The words, pitched loud above the hypnotic throb of the engines, were spoken in a lazy Texan drawl. A wedge of gum moved against one cheek.

'You know me, John.' Keel managed a weak smile. 'Anything for sympathy.'

John Lafitte nodded in wry amusement. Smartass limey, he thought.

Lafitte had been, until three days ago, on charter work in Zambia. The contract had ended and the Texan, at a loose end, had flown back to Nairobi on the off chance that Mendoza might have a consignment to move. Lafitte wasn't bothered about the legitimacy or contents of the consignment. He had done enough work for Mendoza not to allow minor inconveniences like borders and embargoes to stand in the way of making a fast buck. Ethics, whatever they might be, never even entered into it. His three years with Air America, the CIA financed airline, had spawned that point of view. Hell, he'd flown opium out of the Golden Triangle, dropped guns and ammunition to Laotian anti communist guerillas over the Plain of Jars and smuggled South African Special Forces into Namibia. The greasy, gold toothed Portuguese was small change. Pin money.

As it happened, Mendoza did have need of his services. An airlift.

It was Keel's game plan, Mendoza's contacts, Kemba's money. Keel knew they would require an escape route. Mendoza was the only person he could think of who could arrange one at such late notice.

The freighter was the *Zanzibar Queen*, five thousand tons, registered in Liberia. She was berthed in the Somali port of Mogadishu, awaiting a cargo of what was, osten-

366

sibly, agricultural machine tools. In reality the crates in her hold contained Soviet weaponry. Grenade launchers, Kalashnikovs, SGT–43s and anti-personnel mines. Destination: Maputo, Mozambique and, eventually, the guerilla bases and training camps along the eastern borders.

Rolf Steyn was operating out of Maputo. He would be waiting to fly them south to Durban. From there, with documents supplied by Mendoza's agents, they could take a scheduled flight to Johannesburg and on to London and Amsterdam. With luck.

Mendoza relayed a message to his contact in Mogadishu to brief the freighter's captain. The ship would be taking on passengers. This would entail the *Zanzibar Queen* making an unscheduled stop to pick them up; off the coast at Chisimaio, two hundred and fifty miles south of Mogadishu. Chisimaio had an airfield. Six hundred miles from Kendura.

The Jet Ranger didn't have the range and even if it had the damned machine was too easily recognizable. Lassiter's Chieftain was hors de combat and the Intercorp Commander was out of the question; Kate Lassiter owed Stan Mason that much. In any case they couldn't go back to Kenya. They'd just killed its President and Kemba didn't want to be implicated more than was necessary.

So along came John Lafitte, fresh from his contract in the Copper Belt, with his old lady: one temperamental Dak with more miles on the clock than anyone cared to imagine. Willing to do anything if the price was right.

'How far behind are the opposition?' Lafitte asked.

'Light years by now,' Keel said. 'We left them running around with their arses hanging out.' He grunted with pain and pressed a hand against the pad on his stomach.

'You're sure you're okay, Major? We've got another three hours to go and I ain't risking a direct course across country. I'm making a dog leg. North along the border and then east over the Elemo Hills towards Lake Rudolf. It'll be a straight run then down across the Sardindida Plain to the Somali border and on into Chisimaio. We're less likely to be picked up if I keep that far north.'

The Texan glanced anxiously at Kate Lassiter and Sekka who were still supporting Keel's shoulders. Clem Wallace appeared to have drifted into sleep.

'Just put the hammer down, John,' Kate Lassiter said.

Lafitte got to his feet. 'You got it. I understand Mendoza has a doctor standing by when we land but if it gets too bad that he can't take it there's morphine in the first aid kit. It's in the locker.' He pointed. 'I've also got coffee and grog in a thermos up front. Help yourselves. There are blankets with the first aid kit. It might get kind of cold up here.'

Wallace opened one eye. 'Don't suppose you got a beer?'

'Tusker suit you?'

Wallace's eyes widened. 'Ripper!' he announced joyfully. 'Lead on, Tex!' He raised himself and followed Lafitte up to the flight deck.

'I don't think that'll compensate for burning the chopper.' Sekka chuckled. 'D'you?'

'Kemba's been very generous,' Keel replied. 'Clem'll get over it.' He looked thoughtfully at Kate Lassiter. 'I guess you could probably get yourself another Chieftain too.'

Tears glistened in her green eyes.

'Damn you, Thomas Keel!' He voice shook.

'Now what have I done?'

'My God! You have the nerve to ask? Look, why on earth can't you get yourself a steady job; nine to five with luncheon vouchers? It would save me a great deal of heartache, not to mention sleepless nights and the exorbitant cost of aviation fuel! I can't be expected to go gallivanting all over the bloody veldt at your beck and call indefinitely! I must have flown more mercy missions on your behalf than the Berlin Airlift! Enough's enough!'

'What the hell's she on about, Joseph?' Keel appealed to Sekka. 'If I didn't know better, I'd say the lady's going soft on us.'

'Oh, brother!' Sekka rolled his eyes. 'I can't believe he's that dumb, Kate!'

Keel grinned then winced as pain spasmed through his belly. 'I didn't think you cared, Lassiter.'

'Always the joker,' she said. 'Well, this macho image doesn't fool me one little bit! Let me tell you something. As from now you're stuck with me, Keel. I'm grounding myself. Somebody's got to look after you. I'm not sure this glorified house boy here is doing such a good job!'

'I'd swear,' Sekka said, 'that I've just been insulted.'

Keel didn't respond.

Kate Lassiter was holding the mercenary's hand. The ice blue eyes were closed. The Dakota hit an air pocket. Keel's weight shifted and he sagged against Sekka. The Hausa's hand cupped Keel's head and drew it down to his chest. His touch was gentle. He eased his own exhausted body back against the bulkhead. He remained in that position, barely awake, as the DC–3 droned east towards the border and sanctuary.

17

In his first floor study, Arthur Lennox was very nearly incoherent with rage.

News of the dreadful events in Kendura had ripped through the corridors of Whitehall with the ferocity of a tornado. Lennox had wasted no time in summoning Dalkeith to his side.

'Christ Allbloody Mighty! Of course it's disastrous! I'd even go so far as to say it's fucking incredible! What I want to know is what the hell you intend to do about it!' Lennox's face was suffused with blood. He was spitting out the words.

'Prime Minister, I . . .'

'Jesus wept! What sort of Pandora's box has been opened here? The Foreign Secretary and the President of Kenya murdered by a unit of mercenaries that you recruited! If the report from Warren–Chase is anywhere near accurate the bloody square looked like a Chicago stockyard! I'll have you for this, Dalkeith!'

'We don't know for certain that there is a link,' Dalkeith said carefully. 'The assassination may well have been a quite independent action.'

'Good God, you don't believe that any more than I do. Look, I'll shed no tears for Mabato or, for that matter, his Soviet bedmate. What was his name? Barovski . . . ?'

'Burrov,' Dalkeith corrected. 'Gregori Alexis. He was KGB. One of Nikolai Kolk's boys and Nikolai is First Chief Directorate with connections all the way to the top.'

'Well, whoever, Dalkeith. The fact remains that if our part in this ever gets out it'll make Watergate look like open day with the Brownies!' He shuddered. 'I could become incontinent just thinking about it.'

'I say again, Prime Minister. The two events may not be connected.'

'Hellfire, man! What will it take to convince you?' Lennox thumped his desk in exasperation. An onyx pen holder bounced. 'The facts speak for themselves. We know that a white man, possibly European, maybe even British, was involved in the killings. He was seen after the attack in the square. As far as we can gather only two men took part in the hit, not counting Mabato's personal pilot who aided their escape from Kendura, and we were almost sure that members of the original rescue team had survived. I think it is reasonable to assume, therefore, that this was a revenge attack for the death of their comrades. Come on now, admit it is quite feasible.'

Dalkeith nodded reluctantly. 'So, I'll admit it is a possibility.'

Lennox grunted then asked: 'Do we have any ideas on the whereabouts of the hit squad?'

Dalkeith shook his head. 'They've vanished. They obviously had an escape route mapped out.'

'What about the helicopter then? Someone must have a lead on that, surely?'

Burnt out wreckage was found. No doubt it was destroyed to cover their tracks. The country is vast. It is an enormous area to search.'

'They had help.'

Dalkeith looked thoughtful. 'Kemba?'

'Who else? He had everything to gain from Mabato's death.'

'But not from Nai's or Wood's, although I doubt they

were the main target. Anyway, Kemba will never talk. Christ, what a mess!'

Lennox said: 'The implications are too horrendous to even contemplate. I warned you at the outset that this office is unimpeachable. I reiterate that most strongly. I want us waterproof, Dalkeith. I want this closed up as tight as a virgin's fanny. All traces erased and I mean erased. By every means at your disposal.'

Dalkeith asked quietly: 'Do I take it that includes terminal sanction?'

Lennox's voice carried heavy menace. 'Whatever it takes, Dalkeith. Do it.'

Dalkeith remained silent for several moments before he rose to his feet. 'I'll see to it. Will that be all, Prime Minister?'

Lennox's expression could have been carved out of granite.

'Isn't that enough?' he said.

Noon.

Dalkeith initiated contact, using a call box. The number he dialled was unlisted and closely guarded. He pushed the coin into the slot and waited for the time lapse as the answering machine was activated. A low buzz told him that the tape was ready to receive his message.

'Trip-wire,' he said, slowly and distinctly. Then he hung up.

By six that same evening he was at home in his flat in Eaton Square. Dalkeith was a bachelor and the apartment reflected this status. It was spacious and uncluttered yet still retained a comfortable elegance. The lounge held a long, low sofa and several snug armchairs. A number of signed watercolours hung on the walls. One – Russell

Flint's 'The Fountain' – mirrored the brown and cream colour scheme in the room.

Dalkeith let the telephone ring three times before he picked up the receiver. He said nothing.

'This is Grail.' The voice was soft and well modulated.

'Thank you for returning my call,' replied Dalkeith.

'A pleasure. It's been a long time since I last heard from you. The Bulgarian affair, I believe. I thought you'd forgotten all about me.' The tone was mocking, slightly reproving.

'Not at all,' Dalkeith said. 'It's just that I haven't had a need for your particular talents for a while.'

'But now I'm back in demand. I'm flattered.'

'This is rather short notice, I'm afraid,' Dalkeith went on.

'My fee will reflect that of course.'

'I understand perfectly.'

'Very well. Now, suppose you give me the details.'

Dalkeith did so.

When he had finished, Grail said: 'I don't see this presenting any difficulty.'

'Excellent,' Dalkeith responded. 'I'll await confirmation.'

'I'll be in touch,' Grail said quietly.

The line went dead. Dalkeith replaced the receiver and moved to a tray of drinks. He poured himself a hefty tumbler of Canadian Club and added ice. The smooth taste did little to alleviate the uneasy feeling that was gnawing its way through his stomach.

Lennox had likened it to the opening of Pandora's box. Dalkeith had the terrible premonition that with the introduction of Grail to the plot he might just have unleashed something even more potentially devastating.

* * *

Two days after the event it was still front page news with most of the dailies carrying the opinion that the assassination conspiracy had been hatched by Hamilton Kemba as a bloody prelude to his return to power in Lugamba. Kemba, needless to say, vigorously denied the allegations. As if he would admit anyway to a scheme that had encompassed the slaughter of the British Foreign Secretary and the Kenyan Head of State. The latter having granted Kemba sanctuary from Mabato's thugs following his enforced exile from Lugamba and his subsequent departure from Tanzania.

And of the assassins there had been no word, no trace. It was as if they had vanished into thin air.

Iain Cameron had combed the news columns and listened to media reports for any clue that would tell him that it had been Keel's handiwork. Despite not finding one he remained convinced that the mercenary had been responsible. But why no contact? And what in God's name had happened to have forced Keel into such massive retaliation? Whatever the reasons the ramifications were obvious and Cameron's sole intention was to go to ground as quickly and as effectively as he could. He made preparations. His briefcase held three passports – British, Swiss and Irish – as well as currency and airline tickets. The Aer Lingus flight to Dublin left at one o'clock and he planned to be on it. In Eire he could connect to any flight routing direct to the continent, arriving on a different passport and under a different name than the one he had used leaving Heathrow. He had contacts in Berne and Zurich and an account with the Grande Banque de Geneve. It was a way out.

He collected his things into a small leather holdall, picked up the briefcase and locked the door of the flat behind him. It was a fine morning; warm with a clear blue sky. He walked to the kerb and pitched the luggage into the back seat of the BMW.

The car exploded when he turned the ignition key. Windows in the street shattered as the saloon erupted in a searing ball of flame that sent the bonnet hurtling through the air to crash against the stone pillars flanking the entrance to Cameron's flat. The tyres melted instantaneously. Ribbons of burning petrol spread out over the road and pavement. Iain Cameron metamorphosed into a black, charcoaled husk that disintegrated as the BMW continued to burn furiously.

No one else was injured by the explosion. Somewhere a dog began to bark loudly and as people emerged cautiously into the street, open mouthed in disbelief, the sound of a police siren could be heard approaching from a distance.

'Hardly subtle,' admitted Dalkeith. 'But certainly effective.'

'Satisfaction guaranteed,' Grail said. 'As always. And you did say it was a rush job.'

'I am suitable impressed,' Dalkeith commented.

'I trust you will show your appreciation in the usual way?'

'Your account has already been credited.'

'I thank you. It is a privilege to conduct business with you,' said Grail smoothly. 'Now, I don't suppose you've anything else for me? While you've got me, so to speak.' The words held a trace of humour that Dalkeith found chilling.

'Not at the moment but you never know. I'll keep in touch.'

'Do that,' Grail said silkily. 'You know where to reach me.'

* * *

Solicitors – Commissioners for Oaths

John D. Hillyard. LLB (LOND)
Maurice Tankerton. LLB (LEEDS)
William R. James. LLB (LOND)

17 Cheapside
High Road
Wood Green
London N22 6HH

Tel: 01–888 9372/9373

Our ref. JDH/KW/569

The Editor
The Daily Mail
Carmelite House
London EC4Y 0JA

May 18th

Dear Sir,

Please find enclosed sealed documents relating to the estate of our client Iain Michael Cameron, late of Cameron Security Consultants, 101a Sloane Street. We are forwarding them to you under instructions issued by our client prior to his death on May 16th.

The instructions given to this practice by Mr Cameron were quite precise. In the event of his death the testament was to be despatched to your office without delay. We are required to advise you that identical packages have been delivered to the following: The Times, The Daily Telegraph, The Daily Express, Detective Sergeant Alec Macraig of the Criminal Investigation Department, New Scotland Yard.

I would be grateful if you would kindly acknowledge receipt of the aforementioned either in writing or by telephone. I would also advise you that neither my partners nor myself have any knowledge of the contents of the testament enclosed.

Yours faithfully,

John D. Hillyard

The Legacy.
Before Grail.
They were back in the snack bar. The tables appeared not to have been cleaned since their last visit. The spout of the plastic tomato was clogged with sauce and sugar lay scattered on the formica top in tiny brown lumps.

'Just in case, Frank,' Cameron said as he handed the package to the minder.

'In case of what, Mister Cameron?'

'My demise, Frank. Violent or otherwise.'

'You're kidding, Mister Cameron!' Ketch took one look at Cameron's drawn face and realized he wasn't.

'I want you to rent a safe deposit box,' Cameron said. 'Put this in it. I want it secure. Use any bank. Barclays is as good as any other.'

'Then?'

'You wait, Frank.' Cameron smiled. Crow's feet appeared at the corner of his good eye.

'For what exactly?'

The place was, surprisingly, beginning to fill up. Ketch kept his voice low. The rasp in his throat seemed more pronounced than ever. He eyed the envelope speculatively.

'My death,' Cameron said.

Ketch had missed the radio bulletin. He'd been propping up the bar in the Pilgrim, contemplating a lager and an apology for a pork pie that went a long way to prove that British Rail didn't have the monopoly on welded crusts. He had an hour to spare before his next job; collecting a high rolling Texan stud player from the Tower Hotel and taking him to a house in Hampstead to a game where the stakes would make the wheeling and dealing in Dallas look like a village beetle drive.

A punter strolled into the public bar with a copy of the

Standard under his arm and ordered a light and bitter. He'd laid the paper down to forage for change and there it was on the bar in black and white. By the time the man had paid for his drink his paper and Ketch had disappeared. Rapidly. The doors were still squeaking on their hinges. Ketch had abandoned both the lager and the pork pie. The Cortina was parked around the corner. Ketch sat in it, feeling ill.

'I'll probably go away for a while,' Cameron had said.

He hadn't got very far. About fifteen feet from his front door, all deep, crisp and even.

The photograph, under the headline 'BOMB OUT-RAGE – RETURN OF THE IRA?', showed the remains of Cameron's BMW; a twisted tangle of metal at the side of the road, cordoned by police cones and white ribbon. No one had claimed responsibility. The newspaper was guessing and the police were making no comment. There followed a brief, lurid and somewhat inaccurate assessment of Cameron's activities. It was an incomplete biography.

Ketch made the bank thirty minutes before closing time and signed out the contents of the safe deposit box; one manilla envelope plus instructions. The Texan stud player would have to make his own arrangements. Ketch had an errand to run.

The money was with the instructions. Ketch counted it out. Three hundred pounds to cover his expenses.

Including return air fare to Amsterdam, Club class.

Cameron had felt he owed it to Keel. The mercenary had a right to know who had set him up and why. That's if he and Sekka ever made it back to the bar on the Zeedijk.

The manilla envelope was similar to the others he had lodged with his solicitor, its contents the same. The dossier was typewritten and comprehensive; names, dates, a record of conversations, even the Rover's registration number and a telex slip confirming that the sum of sixty five thousand pounds had been credited to Cameron's account in Geneva. Plus photographs of course; damning evidence.

Everything in fact except the identity of the team.

When he had composed the dossiers he had removed all record of Keel and the others from his files, substituting instead detailed biographies of mythical individuals, complete with fake personal data and qualifications. He had to give Keel a chance; an edge.

With the resources available to him it was conceivable that Dalkeith could instigate a successful trace but that would take time and Cameron fully intended that Dalkeith and his associates were hung out to dry long before they caught up with Thomas Keel.

Hence the legacy with the sting in the tail.

Maybe the press would act on the information and release the sordid details and maybe they would be shackled by a 'D' notice. Cameron would have no way of knowing. But Keel, if he had survived, would have a weapon with which to protect himself and counter attack should it prove necessary.

And there was always Macraig. He had wanted to know what Cameron was into. Now he would find out. And Macraig on a murder trail wouldn't care a damn whose toes he trod on. He'd be like a bloodhound following a spoor and, with his gift for tenacity, the spoor would lead him back to Dalkeith and possibly beyond. They'd have to prise him off the scent with a crowbar.

And Cameron knew that Frank Ketch was the only person he could trust to get the dossier to Keel in Amsterdam. The minder would be his courier.

* * *

By the time the Trident had rolled onto its stand at Schiphol it was early evening. The sky was slate grey and a thin drizzle was drifting over the aprons and runways. Ketch had no luggage to collect from the baggage claims area for he had travelled with only his passport and a shoulder bag containing the manilla envelope. The customs officer spared him little more than a cursory glance as he made his way through the barrier and into the terminal. Despite this, the hands clutching the straps of his bag were itching and clammy and he was suffering from the uncomfortable urge to turn and look behind him. Dispelling the desire to break into a run, he walked quickly through the concourse towards the sign marked Uitgang and looked into the rain for the taxi rank.